VIKRIN
FIRE

VIKRIN
FIRE

S M HINTON

BREWIN BOOKS

BREWIN BOOKS
19 Enfield Ind. Estate,
Redditch,
Worcestershire,
B97 6BY
www.brewinbooks.com

Published by Brewin Books 2024

A CIP catalogue record for this book is
available from the British Library.

ISBN: 978-1-85858-771-4

Printed and bound in Great Britain
by 4edge Ltd.

For Amy

Chapter 1

It was mid-May and it had been raining miserably for days. Corridor stall holders had hurriedly erected awnings over the market from one side to the other in an attempt to create a makeshift roof as the persistent rain had continued day after day. Successful in keeping out the worst of the weather it had, however, had an adverse effect by creating a cauldron of humid stale air culminating in a horrendous stench and subsequent fear of the sickness. The upshot being that it had unfortunately frightened almost all of the market visitors away. The traders desperately resorted to prayers for dry weather, which today it seemed, at last, were finally being answered. The sky was a vibrant blue with not a single cloud in sight. The hot May sun was shining and you could already feel the comforting warmth on your face. The stall holders were busily pulling down the sodden canopies, which allowed the early morning sunshine to flood through the marketplace and the fresh air to permeate upwards into the Corridor. Several market sanitary workers were efficiently swilling out the central drain, driving the foul waste into the ocean. Incense burners were lit to temporarily mask the smell, as well as bales of clean dry straw being scattered over the cobbled street. The traders were very quick to react to changing conditions as keeping their market free from disease was paramount to their existence. A few years earlier a sickness had ripped through the market causing illness and death for many of its occupants, resulting in another petition for demolition from the residents of Trevelyan. The Corridor's survival hung on a very thin thread; any excuse to close it down was a regular threat, particularly from the landowners in the south who had opposed the market from its conception.

The stalls on the quayside at the mouth of the Corridor were already bustling with fishermen unloading their daily catch;

numerous customers were vying for the fresh fish. The pleasant weather seemed to have brought the whole of Trevelyan out into the sunshine, and back to the market, much to the delight of the traders. With a recent shipment of fine fabrics having only just arrived from Vikrin, and with the impending Mercia annual balls in July, they all hoped it would bring more eager buyers from far and wide in order to purchase the latest designs for the ball gowns of the rich young ladies.

The Corridor was built after the civil war, fourteen years earlier, by Eastern prisoners following their devastating defeat at the hands of King Charles and the Crown Knights. It stretched from the Corstir Forest in the north to the Port of Trevelyan in the south. Originally a single wall was built as a border in retribution for the destructive war against the Crown.

Following the death of Charles, his only son Osbert ascended the throne and commissioned a second wall that was to be built parallel to the first, creating a trading route from the eastern lands to the south coast. It became a well overdue lifeline for the people of the East who had suffered greatly after the war and had relied on their own hard work and determination for survival. The seas to the east of Mercia were fierce and impassable. All links to the west were blocked by either the dark impenetrable Corstir Forest or the wall; life in the East was hard but they survived and became stronger and evermore resilient. Although stringently patrolled in the early days, restrictions had eased and traders had begun to set up stalls along the route. Permanent two-storey structures replaced the old wooden stalls over the years, creating not only the multicultural marketplace you see today, but also a permanent home for its many inhabitants.

Sir Arlen Barlett stood on the quayside; he casually breathed in the fresh sea air, watching as the marketplace came to magical life. There was a pleasing warm breeze coming off the ocean as he momentarily closed his eyes, listening to the familiar buzz and chatter all around him.

Arlen was a Crown Knight who had been stationed in Trevelyan for the past three years. He was the second son of Lord Douglas Barlett, whose family estate, Wenlock Hall, lay to the west of Kingslea, the capital of Mercia. A tall man with an ease of manner, wavy blonde hair, piercing blue eyes and ruggedly handsome features. His openness and friendliness had enabled him to gain the trust and respect from the Corridor occupants. Essentially commissioned to oversee law and order, the mutual regard had made his posting an easy one. His friendly demeanour however was by no means a weakness as once good opinion was lost, it was lost forever. Law breakers were dealt with hard and swift; any perpetrators were left under no illusion as to his fearless duty as a Crown Knight.

He was dressed in the traditional Crown livery of a dark navy-blue surcoat decorated with the emblem of the Crown Knights – an embroidered compass with a gold medallion depicting an image of the King at the centre and a precious jewel sewn at the four points representing the four regions of Mercia: North, East, South, and West. A single shoulder cape was draped over his left shoulder and secured under his right arm, leaving it free to wield his arming sword. He also wore a tricorn hat adorned with a red and white ribbon fashioned in the shape of a rose. The jewels adorning his surcoat sparkled in the morning sun, casting rays of light out into the crowds of people milling around the quayside.

Arlen felt a little melancholy this morning as his posting to Trevelyan was coming to an end. He would certainly miss the place he had called home for the last three years. He had recently been recalled to court to serve under his particularly good friend Henry Morton – Lord Morton as he was now known after the sudden death of his father. Arlen and Henry were the same age and had trained together at Chesterford, the prestigious training college for the sons of the Lords of Mercia. They had both opted for the gruelling education required in becoming a Crown Knight, both excelling and becoming remarkably close friends. Henry was also to be Arlen's best man at his up-and-coming wedding to Florence Ainsworth at the end of June. Arlen had met Florence at the Mercia annual balls the previous year; the daughter of Lord Hagan Ainsworth, the match had been well received by both families.

Unfortunately for Arlen he didn't love Florence; she was a beautiful young woman, delicate in appearance with fair hair and striking blue eyes; he had been attracted to her sweet nature, asking for her hand only days after their first meeting. Arlen however believed himself to be in love with another woman, but marriage to the lady in question was not possible due to her low-born status. He had toyed many times over a possible introduction to his family but had never quite found the courage or real commitment. The lady herself had always been opposed to the idea and therefore never encouraged him. His marriage proposal to Florence was a feeble attempt to forget the lady and move on, but the reality of giving her up was not so easy for Arlen and it caused him to ashamedly regret his marriage proposal.

It was still relatively early, but the Corridor was already busy and lively. The smell of freshly baked bread wafted down the marketplace and exotic herbs and spices from lands far away, as well as freshly brewed teas, made Arlen's nostrils twitch with excitement. The flurry of sweeping to banish the foul damp stench seemed to have paid off and the market began to smell sweet once again. Arlen felt at home here. He loved all the unusual sights and smells; coloured fabrics hung off every stall and candles flickered in lanterns creating kaleidoscopes of light – it really was a wonderful workout for the senses. As well as the never-ending list of wares, there didn't seem to be anything you could not buy here, there were people from all corners of Mercia and beyond; the pleasant weather was almost certainly bringing them all back to the market today.

Arlen slowly made his way into the growing crowd of people for the weekly patrol, passing the various stalls and chatting to the traders as he went. Most of the conversations were about the weather, with some talk of the great sickness years ago as well as many congratulations on his impending wedding; news travelled fast here and most traders wished him well.

"Good morning, sir," a young boy shouted cheerfully as he sped past Arlen carrying an armful of hot-off-the-press pamphlets. He was racing to the mouth with all the latest news and gossip from the Corridor. People had actually started queuing for the weekly rag; it was quite the thing, with some traders paying the printer for advertisements and promises of special offers and discounts to entice customers to their stalls.

Arlen was about a quarter of a mile in as he approached his favourite bakery. He was relieved to see that the tables at the side were free and picked up his pace slightly so as not to miss out on the table at the very back.

Casually throwing off his hat, cape and surcoat, and unbuttoning his doublet he quickly claimed his table, which was relatively secluded and away from prying eyes. Arlen needed to rid himself of his restricting uniform, if only for a brief time. This far up into the market the air was still extremely humid and he was stiflingly hot. He had barely sat down when he felt two hands on his shoulders.

"Good morning handsome," came a soft female voice, followed by a quick kiss to his cheek. "What can I do for you today?"

Before the lady could say any more, Arlen twisted around and gripped her by the waist, pulling her down onto his lap and passionately kissing her on the lips.

"Good morning," he replied, smiling broadly and only releasing her temporarily before pulling her back for another kiss.

The lady gently slid her hands under his open doublet, pulling herself closer towards him. "My, my, you are hot," she grinned seductively. "I shall bring you some ale to cool you down ... Anything else?"

"No, just ale ... Oh, maybe one of your delicious pies," Arlen replied, wiping a trace of flour from the lady's cheek. She kissed him again before promptly jumping up from his lap. She straightened and patted down her skirts as she walked away, creating a large cloud of flour that wafted behind her.

"I'm so glad the rain has finally stopped," Arlen shouted over, as she busied herself at the counter.

"Yes, me too. According to Rose it's a sign of terrible things to come. She said the last time it rained like this we had a civil war."

"Why, has Rose been on the wine again?" Arlen asked in a sardonic tone, stretching leisurely back in his chair.

"Rose is always on the wine, you know that," the lady replied, throwing Arlen a sweet smile. "But she does seem rather more melancholy than usual."

"She needs to get out of this bloody Corridor once in a while," Arlen suggested, knowing only too well that would never happen.

"Rose leave the Corridor?" the lady scoffed. "The only way Rose will leave this Corridor is in a wooden box." She promptly returned to the table and placed a freshly baked pie and cold ale down in front of Arlen before seating herself opposite him.

"Christ, I need this," he groaned, swiftly gulping down the ale.

The lady watched him affectionately just for a moment as he enthusiastically tucked into the pie, until finally, she spoke. "Arlen, will you go and see Rose for me?" she asked, a hint of concern in her voice. "I saw her yesterday and she's terribly worked up about something. She says there are men in the Corridor up to no good. She is right mithered about it, I certainly ain't seen her like this before. It took me an absolute age to calm her down. She keeps asking for you."

Arlen didn't answer straight away. Instead he finished off the pie before swallowing down the remains of the ale. He knew Rose was desperately lonely and always making up tales and requesting he call upon her. He didn't mind really; in fact, he sometimes rather enjoyed her many stories of life before the war. Casually leaning back again in his chair he stretched his arms up over his head, exhaling loudly. Then, suddenly tipping forward, he held the lady's face in his large hands and pulled her towards him, planting a lingering kiss to her lips.

"I will go and speak to her," he said, with a huge smile on his face.

Arlen had met Harriet very soon after he had arrived in Trevelyan and it had not been long after that when they began their passionate love affair, making love for the first time on the flour bags at the back of the bakery. Harriet was a widow, only a couple of years older than

Arlen, and her husband had been a fisherman from Trevelyan. He was killed at sea after only a year of marriage. Harriet, with her long curly dark hair and large vibrant green eyes, was small in stature but big in personality with the most beautiful, sweet smile. She was extremely well thought of by the other traders. Originally from the East she had come into the Corridor with her father who had first established the bakery, which was now her permanent home. She had absolutely no intentions of ever going back east. Harriet cared for Arlen very much. Though his departure from Trevelyan was inevitable, they never spoke of it, instead they were just content to savour their last few weeks together. Their relationship had been nothing more than a casual love affair in the early days, but quite recently Harriet suspected Arlen may have fallen in love with her, or perhaps it was just the thought of having to leave her. Either way he had begun to talk of marriage; bringing Harriet to Kingslea and introducing her to his family, but they both knew deep down, it was not possible.

"Thank you," she replied, smiling back at him, considering for just a moment how much she would very much miss him once he had gone.

Arlen then suddenly jumped up, clasped his hands around Harriet's waist, and, pulling her up from her seat, planted a kiss on her lips and gently rubbed his hand up and down her back.

"I will see you later, will I not?" he breathed in between kisses. "Christ, woman, I want you," he groaned, pressing himself against her.

"Yes, I'll finish up early and we can walk back down together, now you had better get going as I have a lot of work to do, and so do you," she teased, buttoning up his doublet.

"I really do want you," Arlen whispered in her ear. He had been hoping for a brief encounter at the back of the bakery, instead he reluctantly replaced his surcoat, cape and hat.

"I know you do but you will have to wait … now go, the faster you get up the faster you be down, and please don't forget Rose," she said, planting another kiss to his lips.

7

"I'll go now," Arlen promised, eventually releasing his hold on Harriet with a deep sigh. Harriet giggled, then kissed him again whispering "later," in his ear as Arlen finally stepped back into the throngs of people milling up and down the Corridor.

Rose was on the opposite side of the Corridor to the bakery and about six stalls up. She was one of the original traders that had established themselves in the early days of the market, selling fortunes and recommending remedies for all manner of ailments. The fortune telling business was slow, so she diversified by charging a penny for half an hour of her company. Business boomed for a while and she was able to purchase a permanent stall. Apparently, so the story goes, she was once an exceptionally beautiful woman, but the lifestyle had taken its toll and she now relied heavily on the goodwill of the other stall holders. She had been offered quite a lot of money over the years for her pitch; although it was not one of the largest, it was right in the heart of the Corridor. Rose of course had refused all offers to sell and now, apart from reading the odd fortune to loyal clientele, it had become, to all intent and purposes, just her home. Folk often used her stall as a reference point, "Meet me at Rose's" was often heard. If young children happened to get lost, the reunion point was always outside Rose's; she was something of a legend in the Corridor.

Arlen stood in front of her stall looking at the elaborately embroidered fabrics that were draped over the doorway. The smell of incense mingling with the opium was overwhelming. Religious symbols of every god there has ever been hung between the multi-coloured fabrics. If you didn't know what lay beyond, I'm sure you wouldn't want to and you'd move along as quickly as possible.

Arlen was just about to announce himself and enter when someone in the stream of people filing past him suddenly caught his eye. "Raven … Raven Westonhall, is that you?" he called out, waving his hand to a gangly well-dressed man in the crowd.

A young man wearing a sumptuous crimson velvet cloak and overly exaggerated ruffled collar stopped dead in his tracks and stared directly at Arlen.

"Arlen, I didn't know you worked the Corridor," the young man said, observing Arlen in his Crown Knight livery. He appeared nervous, glancing over his shoulder and fidgeting around on his feet.

Raven Westonhall, the only son of Lord Bennett Westonhall, was a couple of years younger than Arlen and they had attended Chesterford College together. Raven however showed no interest in training as a Crown Knight; his physical constitution a restriction for the demanding education; illness unfortunately seemed to plague him. A tall man, gangly and effeminate in appearance, with long dark hair immaculately curled, framing his small face. His appearance, along with his desire for all the latest fashions, no matter his state of health, was undoubtedly the reason for earning him the nickname "pretty boy", which he seemed to rather enjoy. It was common knowledge that Raven preferred the company of men, it was somewhat of an open secret.

Raven looked unusually sicklier today, his skin sallow with dark circles around his eyes. He was carrying an overly large leather satchel draped over his left shoulder. As he continued to fidget on his feet, Arlen moved closer.

"Yes, I have been stationed here three years," Arlen replied, eyeing Raven curiously. "What on earth brings you to the Corridor?" he asked, rather surprised by Raven's presence.

Raven didn't answer at first, he twisted his fingers around repeatedly and continued to glance over his shoulder.

Arlen was in no mood to release him from his obvious discomfort, as he was now even more curious to know what he was doing in the Corridor. "Are you unwell?" Arlen asked, watching as Raven shifted from one foot to the other, looking evermore uncomfortable.

Realising Arlen was not going to release him without answers, Raven finally succumbed to interrogation. "I'm here on an errand," he replied, before hesitating for just a moment. "For my father," he continued finally. "I have been ill, yes, a fever but I am quite well now I assure you, are you on your way back down into Trevelyan?"

"No, afraid not," Arlen replied with a shake of his head, "I'm on my way up, only as far as the first checkpoint though, duty calls," he joked.

Raven's face turned evermore pale as a bead of sweat ran down the side of his face, glaring at Arlen as if about to divulge a terrible secret. He quickly lowered his eyes as if fearing Arlen could read his thoughts.

"You don't look at all well Raven."

"No, you are right, I must go."

Arlen was not quite ready to release him yet and deliberately detained him a little longer. "Your errand, can I help you at all?" he asked, catching Raven's eye once again.

"No, no all taken care of thank you. I must go Arlen," Raven insisted, instantly looking away.

"You are coming to my wedding?" Arlen asked, refusing to give in.

"Your wedding?" Raven replied, looking slightly confused by the question. "Oh, yes … yes of course I'm coming, please Arlen, I must go," Raven insisted, turning abruptly on his heels, not allowing himself to be kept any longer in conversation.

Arlen watched curiously as he disappeared out of sight, swallowed up by the hordes of people that had returned to the Corridor. *How strange*, Arlen mused to himself. *Perhaps he was here for the boys and felt embarrassed, most unlike Raven though.*

There were several establishments in the Corridor that catered for Raven's taste, but he had never been coy about his sexual orientation in the past, he was almost boastful about it in fact.

Hovering outside Rose's for just a moment longer trying to fathom Raven's presence, Arlen finally gave up. Shrugging his shoulders, he stepped towards the entrance of Rose's stall then suddenly stopped, turned on his heels and headed up towards the first checkpoint. "I'll speak with Rose on my way down," he muttered to himself aloud.

Arlen made haste as best he could; the Corridor was heaving with so many people that it slowed his progress, much to his annoyance. The good weather was obviously encouraging back the crowds. He noticed quite a few Mercia ladies with their daughters in tow. The gentry were very quick to decry the Corridor but more than happy to spend their money here, particularly if a new ball gown was required.

Arlen momentarily glanced upwards, as the sun was bright and high in the sky he concluded it was fast approaching midday. He had almost reached the first checkpoint when an enormous booming sound, followed by a ferocious shudder, ricocheted around the marketplace, knocking Arlen to the floor. Stunned for just a moment, he shook his head – the deafening noise still ringing in his ears. Unable to comprehend what had just happened, he slowly rose to his feet. His eyes and mouth filled with debris. As he hastily spat out the dirt and cleared his eyes, he could hear people screaming all around him as a cloud of thick black smoke billowed upwards and out from an explosion point further down the Corridor.

"Harriet!" he screamed aloud, instantly heading back down the market into the mayhem, scrabbling past the terrified crowds as they all desperately moved in the opposite direction.

Just at that very moment there was another explosion, this time closer to his position. The force literally lifted him off the ground, throwing him backwards violently – his body thrust sharply against a wall. He hit his head hard as he landed, knocking him temporarily unconscious.

Several minutes later Arlen slowly came to. There was an eerie silence all around him, bloody bodies covered in all manner of debris lay sprawled out on the ground, not one of them moving. The stench of burning smoke filled his nostrils as a sense of choking began to consume him. The whole of the Corridor it seemed was on fire.

Arlen lay motionless on the ground. He felt a sharp searing pain in his left thigh. Tentatively reaching down, he could feel his own warm blood seeping from a wound to his leg. Desperate to stem the flow of blood, and using all his strength, he managed to pull himself into a sitting position. The black smoke burned the back of his throat as he retched, struggling to breathe. A shard of wood had imbedded itself into his side. Bravely bracing himself, he pulled the sizable splinter from his leg, wincing in pain. Blood now began gushing from the wound as he efficiently ripped his shirt out from under is doublet, tying it around his upper leg in an attempt to slow the flow as best he could. Becoming evermore desperate to quit his current position he attempted to rise, but failed, falling back to the ground; blood now trickling down his face from a gash to his forehead. The ghostly silence suddenly broke as terrified screams rang out all around him, the black smoke continuing to fill his lungs as the blood now running down his face blinded his eyes.

Shall I die here today? He thought to himself as his battered body woefully slipped back down onto the ground. A young man lay beside him, his eyes wide and vacant – he was clearly dead, blood still seeping from a fatal wound to his neck. Arlen reached over and gently closed the young man's eyes, he then tightly closed his own eyes, and began to hopelessly pray.

After what seemed like hours lying on the ground, but was in fact only several minutes, Arlen suddenly thought he could hear someone talking to him. Slowly reopening his eyes, wiping away the blood and grime, he peered up at a young man leaning over him.

"Sir, sir, can you hear me?"

A young checkpoint guard had made his way down into the chaos, looking for survivors. With only minor cuts and bruises to his face he had been fortunate enough to have been relieving himself at the back of the checkpoint tower, which had shielded him from the full force of the second explosion.

"Sir, please can you hear me?" he repeated, carefully lifting Arlen's head and gently pouring cool water over his face.

Arlen spluttered although more than thankful for the cleansing sensation, and, opening his eyes wider, he very slowly focused upon the young man stood above him.

"Jack, is that you?" he asked, relief in his raspy voice.

"Yes sir, I have come to get you out of here."

"Help me up Jack," Arlen groaned, his whole body consumed in pain.

"Are you sure sir, should we not wait for a stretcher?" Jack asked hesitantly, although at the same time not wanting to disobey an order.

"No, please Jack, help me up. I need to get out of here now," Arlen pleaded, not sure how much longer he could manage without fresh air.

The fires were still blazing furiously, the smoke showing no sign of receding. Arlen needed clean air and he needed it now. His throat was burning with a sour bitter taste, his breath strained as he felt himself beginning to lose consciousness once again. He grabbed desperately at Jack's arm.

"There is no way down sir, we need to move further up," Jack replied, wrapping his arms tightly around Arlen.

"Yes, yes just help me," Arlen winced, holding on to the checkpoint guard for dear life.

Jack, thankfully a burly youth, positioned his arm underneath Arlen's back, lifting him up to a sitting position, then cupping him under his arms and lifting him to his feet. Arlen steadied himself, a sudden urge to vomit overwhelming him as he stood, Jack, realising his discomfort, offered the water as relief. Arlen swilled the cool liquid around his mouth in an attempt to cleanse his stinging throat before spitting it out. Jack then took Arlen's weight, successfully carrying him to safety beyond the checkpoint tower.

The two men succeeded in moving beyond the tower where the air was fresher. Arlen took several deep breaths in order to clear his lungs, violently vomiting in between coughing up the black soot. Jack carefully laid him down on a cot, several of which had already been set out in neat rows. Arlen was just able to make out the blurred outlines of other people moving around him before feeling fresh cool water on his face. Someone was speaking to him, a female voice, but he could not quite comprehend what she was saying. He felt himself beginning to drift in and out of consciousness once again.

When Arlen finally awoke, his body felt less in pain, although he was still aware of the gash to his head and left thigh. His breathing had returned to normal, despite the fact he still had the awful smell of rancid smoke in his nostrils and his throat felt scratchy and irritated. Looking up from his position still lying on the cot where Jack had left him, he could clearly see the sun was still bright and high in the sky.

It must be midday, he thought to himself. *How long have I been here?* He wondered, feeling slightly disorientated.

A fair-haired young girl no older than nine or ten suddenly appeared at his side.

"Would you like some water sir?" she asked, confidently, holding a cup in one hand and a jug in the other.

Arlen tried to rise unsuccessfully, nausea overwhelming him. "Yes, please," he replied, peering down at his naked body, covered only by a coarse linen sheet. His wound had been skilfully cleaned and dressed.

The young girl passed him a cup of water; he sipped it slowly allowing the cool liquid to trickle down his burnt throat. It felt soothing.

"Who did this?" he asked, looking up at the young girl and pointing to his leg.

"Mrs Woods sir, she be attending to all the injured, do you need her sir are you in pain?" she asked, her blue eyes wide waiting for Arlen to reply.

The young girl looked dreadfully tired, her simple woollen dress torn and soiled. Trails of tears visible on her dirty face.

"Yes, a little, but I'm quite well thank you. I should like to speak to Mrs Woods if she can spare me the time," Arlen asked with a smile.

"I'll fetch her for you sir," the young girl replied, smiling back before rushing away in haste.

Arlen lay very still, staring up at the sky, listening to the sounds all around him. People were speaking in whispers, hushed conversations. There was a strange sense of calm in the makeshift infirmary considering the horrific events that had just occurred. He observed several other cots around him, all containing bodies – some lay flat, others were sitting up, and some were covered with sheets. Unable to see beyond the rows of cots, he continued to stare upwards. The sky was vibrant blue, cloudless with no sign of foul black smoke. The fires it seemed had all now receded. His mind began to wander. He thought of Harriet, her long dark hair and how beautiful it looked in the morning sun. He imagined her lying in their bed with the sun shining through the open window, her ivory skin so soft and her beautiful green eyes looking up at him. His own eyes began to fill with tears, he knew there could be no hope that she had survived the explosions.

His thoughts were abruptly interrupted as an elderly woman appeared at his side; Arlen hastily rubbed his eyes, not wanting her to observe his grief.

"Don't trouble yourself my dear," she said. "There ain't a person here alive that ain't shed a tear in the last couple of days, don't make yourself uncomfortable, not on my account anyhow … you asked to see me?"

"Couple of days!" Arlen gasped in shock. "How long have I been here?"

"Two days since the explosion," she replied, pulling up a stool and sitting down beside him.

The old woman looked worn out and weary. Her hands were red raw and the sleeves of her old woollen gown were pulled up over her elbows. She wore a linen apron tied tightly around her waist, stained with all manner of muck and blood.

"Two days, Christ, has anybody been up from Trevelyan?" Arlen asked, not quite able to believe he had been comatose for all that time.

"No, not yet sir, the fires have only just burnt out. I be hoping that they will make their way through this afternoon, some of the folk here will not survive much longer without proper care. I have done what I can, but I don't have all the right remedies, and we are fast running out of fresh water."

She paused speaking for a moment, pulling at the bandages around Arlen's upper leg.

"I removed some splinters that may have caused it to fester but good, your wound looks clean with no sign of any infection. You shall need to have it redressed soon though, in fresh bandages. Are you able to sit up my dear?" she asked, holding out her arm in order to aid him.

Arlen paused for a moment, worried he might vomit if he were to move.

"It's alright my dear, we shall take it slowly," the old woman reassured him.

Arlen nodded, then bracing himself he managed to pull himself up. His leg felt painful, but he was determined to sit. Thankfully the nausea did not return.

"Careful my dear, slowly, you don't want to reopen your wound," she said, pulling at the bandage to ensure all was well.

"Good," she smiled. "Right, let's try and bring your legs around to the side."

Arlen braced himself again as he manoeuvred himself around, holding on to Mrs Woods' shoulders. She was surprisingly strong, almost lifting him from the cot. As he sat with his feet on the ground the old woman seemed pleased with his progress. After adjusting the sheet to cover his modesty, she fussed around him for a while longer before leaving him alone to sit in peace and possible contemplation.

From his new position Arlen was able to see further down the Corridor. There was nothing but what appeared to be a large black hole. The smell of acrid smoke and the overwhelming smell of burning flesh wafted unpleasantly up the Corridor to his position. It was almost unbearable.

Surely the opening to hell, he thought to himself, as he sat for what seemed like an eternity, waiting and hoping for salvation.

Jack joined him a while later. He returned Arlen's belt containing his sword and dagger, along with his soiled torn surcoat. Arlen ran his finger over the exquisitely embroidered emblem, the precious jewel at the East point was missing. He began to wonder what on earth the consequences of this devastation would have on the whole of Mercia. The day slowly turned from morning to afternoon when suddenly the mood in the makeshift infirmary changed. Voices were heard from within the dark abyss, as, very slowly, a much-welcomed rescue party appeared from the mouth of hell that was once the Corridor marketplace.

Chapter 2

Lord Henry Morton arrived in Trevelyan two days after the Corridor explosions. He was tense as he stood on the quayside facing the dark blue, green ocean listening to the gentle surging waves breaking against the sea wall. He commanded a stupendous presence dressed in his Crown Knight livery; his surcoat, cape and tricorn hat all trimmed with gold braid denoting his master status. Henry was a tall, muscular man with thick dark hair, very dark eyes and brooding good looks. He enjoyed order and control, demanding respect and obedience in line with his high-ranking Crown Knight status. Immensely loathing social gatherings and rarely attending any, particularly at court, he had earned himself an unfair reputation of being rather proud and arrogant. The truth was he found the intricacies and pretence awkward and uncomfortable. He was in fact a reserved, immensely private person, fearlessly loyal to Mercia, the Crown and a handful of his closest friends. Not only Lord Morton after the sudden death of his father a year ago, but also Grand Master of the Crown Knights and one of the richest men in Mercia. He had been appointed Grand Master on the recommendation of his mentor and friend Lord Bennett Westonhall, former Grand Master and devoted friend of his late father. The decision had not been popular at first, particularly amongst certain members of the Privy Council, given Henry's youthful age – he was only twenty-three years old. He had, however, already earned a great deal of respect in his, to date, short tenure.

Henry stood silently on the quayside, allowing himself to momentarily remove his tricorn hat to run his fingers through his thick dark hair, his only tell when he very rarely allowed his emotions to get the better of him. He took in a deep breath, but even the fresh, comforting warm ocean breeze seemed unable to blow away the stench wafting around the quayside from the mouth of the Corridor. Henry then suddenly turned, squinting into the late afternoon sun, and observed someone hastily approaching his position.

Kian Munro eventually sidled smoothly up to Henry's side. Henry and Kian had grown up together at Elmbridge Hall on the Morton Estate. As Henry had been an only child, his father thought his rather serious young son would benefit from a more carefree, free-spirited companion, so he paid for one from the local orphanage. Being more or less the same age, Henry was eight and Kian looked eight, the two boys instantly formed a close bond, which seemed rather bizarre due to their vastly different characteristics and backgrounds. When Henry was sent away to study at Chesterford at the age of fifteen, Kian remained at Elmbridge. Unfortunately, when left to his own devices he ended up getting himself involved with a local smuggling racket that disastrously resulted in the death of a local gendarme. Kian was arrested, falsely accused of murder and sentenced to death. Days before his execution was to take place, a witness thankfully came forward enabling Lord George Morton, Henry's father, to secure his timely release. Lord Morton promptly sent Kian directly to Henry at Chesterford where he spent the next four years under close supervision – washing, cooking, and cleaning as Henry's valet in penance for his stupidity.

Kian was an extremely large powerful looking man, well over six feet tall, with an unashamedly foul mouth and unruly wavy red hair. He was a lovable rogue, a charmer and not only with the ladies. Henry sometimes envied Kian's ability to be at ease in all manner of social settings. Henry of course much preferred the company of his close friends with whom he felt relaxed. Kian was a self-taught accomplished horse and swordsman, learning most of his skills from his time at Chesterford, albeit not officially. Fearlessly loyal to Henry, their relationship was as strong as any blood brothers and they were rarely very far apart from each other.

"Well?" Henry asked anxiously, as Kian reached his side on the quay.

"They've found him, he's alive," Kian replied, with a sigh of relief. "Christ, it fucking stinks foul in that Corridor, nothing but death and decay," he moaned, taking in a deep breath of fresh air.

"Yes, I can smell it from here," Henry replied. "The desolation is horrifying."

Henry's tense posture relaxed slightly at Kian's welcomed news; the moment he had received word of the explosion he had been struggling to maintain his usual calm composure, and had departed Kingslea at once, riding tirelessly through the night. Besides Kian, Arlen Barlett was one of Henry's closest friends.

Kian knew only too well Henry had been struggling. He placed his large hand to Henry's shoulder.

"He's injured," he said, instantly feeling Henry tense up once more.

"He's alright ... he's well," Kian continued, reassuringly. "Just a gash to his head and left leg, he's being well taken care of. Edwin is here, he was at Blackmore with a company of cadets. He has already arranged for Arlen to be taken there."

Edwin, the older brother of Arlen, was also a Crown Knight who was currently stationed in Glen Ivor in the north, however, he had recently arrived at Blackmore Barracks with a company of young cadets four days earlier. Blackmore was merely three miles west of Trevelyan and was the largest Crown barracks on the south coast.

"Edwin has been coordinating the rescue effort and clean up. He brought all the new recruits with him; they didn't look too fucking pleased though! It's an absolute bloodbath down there, some of the younger boys haven't been able to stop vomiting, poor bastards. It has taken them until now to dampen down the fires. Arlen was up at the first checkpoint, fucking dammed lucky if you ask me."

"Yes, indeed ... do they have any idea what on earth could have caused the explosions?" Henry asked, turning to face the mouth of the Corridor, watching as Crown soldiers, cadets and volunteers from the town continued to bring out the bodies, dead and alive. Their sorrowful, grimy faces were covered with makeshift masks in a desperate attempt to block out the awful stench.

"No, not a fucking clue, some of the old fisher women on the quay are saying it's the work of the devil himself and I have to say I'm inclined to believe them."

Henry glanced over at Kian raising a dubious eyebrow.

"Don't you fucking look at me like that," Kian snarled at him. "You tell me what the fuck happened here then, it is absolute carnage. There are body parts strewn everywhere as well as corpses burnt beyond fucking recognition. Edwin's got a handful of his men taking statements, there might be something there, but otherwise fuck knows."

"Where is Edwin now?" Henry asked, turning back around to face the calming ocean. He took a deep breath, finally allowing himself to relax slightly, releasing some of the pent-up tension in his shoulders.

"He's called a meeting at the town hall," Kian replied. "Lord Thomas Gilmore has been summoned. The arrogant old bastard won't like that, apparently he hadn't even shown his fucking face in town until he heard Edwin had arrived to take charge, thank Christ he was here."

"Yes, indeed," Henry agreed.

Edwin was certainly an extremely efficient, practical man. Possibly the best person to have around in a crisis; his leadership skills were renowned.

"We should go to the town hall," Henry suggested, carefully studying the waves as they continued to collide with the sea wall.

This time it was Kian's turn to raise a dubious eyebrow. "The town hall … you sure about that?"

Henry said nothing, just turned and motioned for Kian to lead the way.

"Right then," Kian replied in surprise.

Henry had an extremely worrying sense of feeling about what had just occurred in Trevelyan. It was common knowledge that the continued existence of the Corridor was contentious, particularly in the south. Petitions for its closure were regularly heard at court, as far back as its conception, but blowing the place up and in such a devastating way, this was something quite different. This was not just some deep-rooted grudge against the Corridor, this was far more sinister and Henry certainly had every intention of finding out what.

The two men promptly left the quayside, mounting their horses and riding swiftly towards the town hall in the centre of Trevelyan. The sight of a Master of the Crown Knights riding through the narrow streets, even after recent events, still caused its residents to stop what they were doing and stare. Kian wore a broad smile, nodding to the onlookers as they rode past. He was certainly enjoying lapping up all the attention. Henry however kept his eyes forward, his face expressionless, all this unwanted attention was not aiding him in regaining his usual calm composure.

Henry and Kian knew Trevelyan very well; they had visited several times over the last three years whilst Arlen had been stationed here. When not on official duty Henry always took on the guise of a lawyer from Kingslea called Francis Bolton. He enjoyed being Bolton; it allowed him an escape from the restrictions of his rank and status, even managing to enjoy himself without much restraint. Trevelyan offered a unique atmosphere, particularly for the young looking to have a good time. Trevelyan was home to an eclectic mix of people thanks to the Corridor and merchants that visited regularly. Not all of its residents enjoyed the diversity however, citing thuggery, fornication, and loose morals amongst other things, continually blaming the Corridor for allowing the town to evolve in the way it had.

Having almost reached the entrance to the town hall, the two men stopped suddenly as an elderly woman threw herself in front of Henry. He pulled up abruptly, causing his horse to rear up, raising its front legs off the ground. The assembling crowd gasped, frightening the horse further. Henry skilfully brought the beast under control. Kian, believing at first it was a threat, reacted like lightening by dismounting his horse and unsheathing his sword with impeccable speed. The crowd pulled back with another loud gasp. The old woman, trembling on the ground, stared up at Henry, her face red and swollen and her eyes bloodshot, she had clearly been crying. Desperately scrambling to her knees, she quivered nervously in the dirt.

"I beg you sir," she sobbed. "I have lost my daughter and granddaughter," holding her old, work-tired hands up to Henry, clasping them together as if in prayer. "Please, promise us justice, I beseech you sir, promise us some justice."

Henry immediately indicated for Kian to stand down, as he held out his own hand to the old woman.

"Please, stand," he said, taking hold of her hand and aiding the old woman to her feet.

Henry looked up and around him at the assembling crowd. They had all fallen silent, their eyes fixed firmly upon him waiting patiently for him to respond. Even Kian with his sword still firmly in his hand, turned to face Henry.

"I promise you," Henry replied, firstly addressing the old woman personally before turning to face the crowd. "I promise you all," he continued. "I shall not rest until I find the perpetrators responsible for the evil atrocities committed here. You have my word as a Master of the Crown Knights, you shall all have justice."

The elderly woman gripped tightly to Henry's hand, kissing it repeatedly. "Thank you, sir, thank you," she sobbed, repeating herself over and over again, refusing to let go.

Henry glared over at Kian for urgent assistance. He hastily sheathed his sword before wrapping his arms around the old woman's shoulders aiding her to move back into the crowd. Another much younger woman stretched out her arms to receive her, comforting her before leading her away.

Just at that very moment everyone's attention was suddenly diverted elsewhere.

"Lord Morton," came a familiar voice from the entrance of the town hall.

Edwin Barlett stood in the doorway dressed in his full Crown Knight livery, smiling broadly over at the two men.

"Please milord come this way," he continued, giving his deepest bow.

Edwin was very much like his younger brother in looks and stature, but unlike his brother, he was far more conservative in his approach. A traditionalist, probably more like Henry in many ways, who did not allow his emotions to ever get the better of him. Also, like Henry, he was utterly devoted to his duty as a Crown Knight with a fair but fearsome reputation.

Henry dismounted his horse as he and Kian skilfully navigated their way through the growing crowd towards the town hall entrance. The onlookers were all still vying for a glimpse of a Master of the Crown Knights, considered as good as royalty by most. A young, keen stable boy promptly popped up behind Edwin, rushing to take charge of the horses as the men finally ascended the steps, much to Henry's relief.

Once safely inside and out of sight, protocol was briefly put aside.

Edwin wrapped his arms tightly around Henry, embracing him fondly. "Henry, it's so good to see you. I could hardly believe my ears when I heard a Master of the Crown Knights was causing a commotion right outside the town hall, " he beamed, genuinely pleased to see his friend.

Kian gave a disgruntled huff.

"And you, you old bastard," Edwin said with a laugh, embracing Kian.

"Hey, less of the fucking old, I'm bloody well younger than you," Kian moaned, holding Edwin so tightly that he almost knocked him over.

The three men laughed loudly.

"I'm so pleased to see you both," Edwin continued with a broad smile. "Excellent speech by the way Henry."

"And I meant every word," Henry replied, pleased he had decided to come, if only to provide support for Edwin.

"And I shall do everything in my power to assist you. The people of Trevelyan are anxious, they need to see that we are doing something. The body count has reached over one hundred and they are still pulling out the dead, let alone the poor souls whose remains have been completely incinerated. The ferocity of the explosions are utterly unbelievable, I have never seen the like. We still have absolutely no idea what on earth could have caused it," Edwin paused letting out a deep sigh. "And besides the how, who? This has to be more than just a grudge against the Corridor, surely."

"My thoughts exactly," Henry replied. "I believe it may be political."

"You really think so?" Edwin asked, curious to hear Henry's assessment of the situation.

"Yes, I do," Henry replied quite adamantly. "If you ask me this is to do with the succession."

King Osbert had been taken ill quite recently and it was feared by some, particularly on the Privy Council, that he may not recover, raising concerns as to the line of succession to the throne of Mercia. Osbert had never married and he had no heir, legitimate or illegitimate. It was common knowledge that in defiance of his father, Osbert swore never to marry and that the DeBowscale dynasty would die with him. Nobody understood or admitted understanding the reason for his obstinate actions, but over the years it had become evident that Osbert had every intention of keeping his promise. His decision however put Mercia into a precarious position, never more so than in recent weeks. The truth was, there was a distant heir to the throne, Lord Sebastian Howard, who was grandson to Osbert's aunt, Lady Margaret Howard. However, the Howards had supported Lord Ivan Lorimer and the East during the civil war, resulting in King Charles removing them from the line of succession.

The Privy Council were not at all in favour of restoring Sebastian's claim, preferring instead to debate and decide on an order of succession between themselves as a solution to the problem. Relationships between the Lords were becoming frayed. With a resolution far from being agreed, the King, who had fortunately fully recovered from his illness, was to date refusing any proposals put to him. The council regularly pressed the matter, citing the stability and safety of Mercia and the all too real possibility of another civil war if an agreement could not be reached. The Lords were already taking sides. Vying for support, the council increasingly split by faction. Osbert continued to remain silent on the matter.

"The question of who will take the throne of Mercia after the death of Osbert has never been more pressing than at this present time," Henry continued. "There is restlessness throughout the land and this attack on the Corridor will not aid in alleviating these pressures. We must find out who is behind this atrocity, it is imperative."

"Yes, I agree," Edwin replied. "Now come, Henry, Kian, there is much to do," he said indicating for the two men to follow him.

The grand room within the town hall, once described by the King on a recent progress as 'a handsome gallery', boasted high ornate ceilings and numerous striking portraits of royalty and former lords of Trevelyan, which all added to the splendour of the space. An overly flattering portrait of Lord Thomas Gilmore had recently been unveiled and was hanging above the large double door entrance off the lobby. Today the room was full of town dignitaries, Crown soldiers under Edwin's command, and senior gendarmes from the town. Lord Thomas Gilmore was already in attendance holding court over to the right of the room as Henry, Edwin and Kian entered. A hush rippled through the occupants, the Crown soldiers all bowing their heads to Henry, recognising his livery if not the man himself. Gilmore glowered at him with contempt, being one of the Lords on the Privy Council who had objected to Henry's elevation to master. Henry immediately headed over in his direction, nodding his head with his usual blank expression, but perhaps with a small hint of disdain. Thomas Gilmore was a short, plump man with a turned-up nose, unfortunately causing him to resemble a pig. The sleeves of his frilled silk shirt hung down well below his hands, with the buttons of his rich velvet doublet straining under the pressure of his rotund middle. A condescending, arrogant man full of his own importance, being summoned here today, and by a Crown Knight, must have been excruciating for him, but as a member of the Privy Council he at least had to pretend a show of compassion and cooperation. Henry could not help but wonder if Gilmore was in some way rejoicing in the recent events as they enabled him to permanently close the Corridor, an objective he had passionately championed for years.

"Lord Gilmore," Henry said, allowing himself a slight smirk.

"Lord Morton," Gilmore replied, desperate to know why Henry happened to be in Trevelyan at such a time.

Pleasantries over, Edwin expertly took charge of the room, running through all the known events of the last couple of days, detailing the extent of the damage and current death count. Several clerks were furiously scribbling away taking minutes of the meeting. Edwin issued orders with impeccable efficiency to his men and the gendarmes, requesting aid from Gilmore and the other dignitaries present, none of whom objected. Edwin declared he would remain in Trevelyan until all investigations had been exhausted. Henry remained silent throughout the proceedings listening intensely to the accounts of the men who had coordinated the rescue effort. He sensed Gilmore watching him but refused to give him any acknowledgement. Kian worked the room skilfully only to return to Henry's side shrugging his shoulders, without any additional information. There was a real buzz of activity within the room when an interruption at the doorway redirected everyone's attention.

"What is it?" Edwin called out, slightly annoyed by the distraction.

"An order from the King sir, for Lord Gilmore," said an exhausted looking messenger standing in the doorway.

Lord Gilmore pushed himself forward to receive the order with his usual air of self-importance, hastily opening and reading it, he then addressed the room.

"The King has recalled the Privy Council; I am called back to Kingslea," he announced, holding the order aloft. "The King requests a full report post haste," he continued, glaring over at Edwin.

"And he shall have it milord," Edwin replied, without any hesitation.

"Excellent, now if we have finished here, I have my own affairs to put in order before my departure."

Puffing out his chest and sticking his piggy nose in the air, Lord Gilmore then quit the room without another word.

Edwin continued to tie up a few loose ends, issuing instructions, before finally closing the meeting. It was by now early evening and the room had become rather hot and stuffy, the occupants very quickly dispersing, leaving Henry, Edwin, and Kian quite alone.

"Henry, I return to Blackmore tonight, I need to check up on my little brother, amongst other things. I shall start reviewing the witness statements in the morning and my men will continue to make enquiries. Once the debris from the Corridor is cleared, we can perhaps start investigations into what may have caused the explosions. Will you accompany me?"

"No not tonight, Edwin, I have business of my own to attend to in town, I shall join you in the morning, please inform Arlen that I shall attend him tomorrow."

"Yes of course, what about you Kian?"

"Not fucking likely, I'm going to make some enquiries of my own. Besides there are no women at Blackmore."

"Oh, Kian you don't ever change," Edwin said with a laugh, giving Kian a friendly punch to his chest.

With that Edwin bid both men good evening and promptly left the hall.

Henry and Kian slowly made their way outside, the young stable boy was already waiting patiently with their horses.

"Where are you going?" Henry asked Kian, quickly glancing around, thankful the crowds had scattered.

"The Drovers, I have an idea about the cause of the explosion."

"Oh, yes?" Henry replied, rather intrigued.

"Do you remember the Battle of Crowforth? It has always been thought of as the beginning of the end of the civil war. The soldiers who were there reported a massive explosion, the like of which had never been seen before, very much like what has happened here."

"Yes, I do vaguely," Henry laughed. "Good God that must have been the only history lesson you ever attended let alone remembered."

"Yes, well I do," Kian replied, throwing Henry a severe look. "It was the only history I was actually fucking interested in, anyway there is an old boy in town, he was at Crowforth. I thought I might speak with him, see what he remembers. A bit of a long shot I know but what the hell I enjoy his many tales if nothing else and besides the barmaid at the Drovers makes a delicious stew."

Henry roared with laughter.

"That is the first time you have ever used a 'delicious stew' as an excuse to see a woman."

"Fuck you Henry, I don't need to ask what fucking business you have here in town," Kian grunted, swiftly taking the reins from the stable boy and throwing him a sixpence.

"Touché my friend," Henry replied with a laugh, flashing Kian a silly childish grin.

Kian grunted louder, not amused in the slightest.

Henry proceeded to remove his shoulder cape and surcoat, neatly folding them and placing them in his saddle bag along with his tricorn hat. He threw on a long black cloak and pulled a black felt cap low over his face. Henry Morton was now Francis Bolton and he intended on releasing some of his suppressed emotions.

"Bring the horses in the morning, will you?" he asked Kian. "We shall ride out to Blackmore together."

"Will do," Kian shouted over, already leading the horses away in the direction of the Drovers.

Henry made his way on foot to the Fisherman's Inn; only a few streets away from the town hall and situated right on the waterfront.

The Fisherman's comprised of a large bar area and private lounge for residents. The Inn was bursting at the seams when Henry arrived, not a single table free with many of its customers standing in groups chatting and drinking. Everyone seemed to be preoccupied in conversation, unsurprisingly talking about the recent events in the Corridor. The Inn smelt warm and inviting, with the familiar smell of ale and a large pot of stew bubbling away on the fire at the far end of the bar. The ale in Trevelyan was considered amongst the best in the whole of Mercia. A few of the bar occupants were momentarily distracted as Henry entered, so not wanting to draw too much attention to himself he nodded his head in polite acknowledgment and pulled his cap lower over his face. Thankfully, they all returned to their conversations. Henry headed straight for the stairs at the back of the Inn, just as a lady stepped from the bar blocking his path.

"Good evening, sir," she said, smiling broadly.

Henry grinned, nodding his head.

The lady in question was Louise Milton, she and her husband George owned The Fisherman's Inn. George spent most of his time on the continent trading ales and brandy. Henry had become acquainted with Louise less than a year ago when he had been in Trevelyan calling himself Francis Bolton and looking for distraction after the sudden death of his father. He had visited her several times over the last twelve months conveniently when Mr Milton was from home. Louise was an older woman, a lady of high standing and well respected in Trevelyan. Her hair of strawberry blond always worn high on her head and secured under a lace bonnet. An attractive woman, small of stature but more than capable of keeping the customers of the Fisherman's Inn in check if ever the need arose. George Milton was rarely at home which suited her well.

Louise stepped aside allowing Henry to continue up the stairs. He opened the door directly opposite at the top of the small landing stepping inside a generously furnished room with a large four poster bed covered in sumptuous red damask. Candles were already lit, sending a golden glow around the space. The room smelt of lavender, the sash window slightly ajar, allowing Henry to hear the chatter of people on the street below, he pulled the drapes across so as not to be observed. Louise entered the room behind him. Once they were both inside Henry turned, closing the door and gently forcing Louise against it. Then, standing directly in front of her he proceeded to undo his belt carefully placing his sword and dagger on a side table. He threw off his cap and cloak and unbuttoned his doublet. Louise smiled at him, her eyes wide and wanting. Henry pulled her closer, kissing her passionately on the lips at the same time as pulling at the ties of her dress, parting the folds of fabric allowing him to caress her now naked breasts. He began kissing and biting her hardened nipples with a growing sense of urgency. Louise was busy loosening the ties on his breeches, reacting to his touches with moans of pleasure and pain. Henry raised his arms allowing Louise to remove his shirt. He then hastily ruched up her skirts to her waist, cupping his hands around her buttocks, lifting her up as she wrapped her legs tightly around him.

"I can't be gentle," he whispered in her ear, at the same time nipping it with his teeth.

Louise nodded in consent, desperately wanting him.

With that Henry pushed her back against the door thrusting himself inside her hard. Louise gasped at the sudden intrusion. Henry moved relentlessly, pushing himself harder and deeper, letting out deep grunts in rhythm to his movements. This was for him and only him. After several minutes of intense pounding Henry gritted his teeth, letting out a muffled groan into the side of Louise's neck and with one final push he felt the tension drain from his body as he finally reached his climax. Maintaining their position together for just a moment, still joined, Henry kissed Louise, enticing her with his tongue before very slowly withdrawing from inside her. Louise let out a small gasp as Henry felt her body quivering in his hold, letting her legs gently drop to the ground. He kissed her again biting and brushing his tongue along her lips.

"Thank you," he whispered, before releasing his hold and flinging himself back onto the bed.

Louise proceeded to remove his boots and breeches, admiring his toned naked body, soaked in perspiration, lying atop the red damask cover. She sat beside him for a while running the tips of her fingers over his naked chest. Henry closed his eyes finally allowing himself to relax.

"I hoped you would come; I have missed you," Louise cooed, leaning down kissing him gently on the lips.

"I have missed you too," Henry replied, still with his eyes closed, a look of satisfaction running across his face.

"It's lucky you only arrived today, what with all the terrible goings on."

"Yes, very lucky."

"There's been some right important sorts in town today apparently. One of the girls was outside the town hall earlier and a right high up Crown Knight turned up, she said he spoke to the crowd. Quite taken by him she was, handsome she said."

"Was he indeed?" Henry grinned.

"He couldn't have been any more handsome than you," Louise mused, rising from the bed, refastening the front of her dress and straightening her skirts before making her way towards the door.

"I'll bring refreshments," she smiled back at Henry.

"Thank you," he replied, opening his eyes throwing Louise a cheeky grin. "Oh, and don't be too long, I haven't finished with you yet."

"No, nor I with you," Louise grinned back, blowing him a kiss from the doorway.

Henry awoke early the next morning, he looked up at the ceiling, tracing the numerous cracks in the plaster from one side to the other, the events of yesterday preoccupying his thoughts. He shook his head still unable to believe what had actually happened. He stared down at Louise as she slept beside him, gently moving her strawberry blond hair from her face and being incredibly careful not to wake her. He ached to take her again before it was time for him to leave but remained patient allowing her to sleep a little longer.

When finally, she did awake, she looked up at Henry smiling. He leant down planting a lasting kiss to her lips.

"I want you," he breathed, teasing her with his tongue, at the same time pressing his hard erection against her.

Louise didn't reply, instead she smiled seductively, tossing her head back against the pillow and opening her legs wide, allowing Henry to once again position himself between her thighs.

Chapter 3

Kian was already in the private lounge of the Fisherman's Inn as Henry descended the stairs, tucking into a plate of freshly prepared food. Louise had just laid the table with a plentiful supply of bread, cheese and meats along with a jug of refreshing ale. She exited the room upon Henry's arrival. They briefly exchanged glances, Henry gently wafting his hand against hers as they passed in the doorway before Louise closed the door behind her allowing the two men to talk privately.

Kian looked decidedly miserable, sporting a large gash above his right eye along with a painful looking thick lip. The left sleeve of his doublet was ripped at the shoulder along with several missing buttons.

"Good night?" Henry enquired sardonically, observing Kian's bruised face and torn clothes.

He grabbed himself a plate of food and promptly sat down at the table.

Kian only grunted loudly in response, filling his mouth with a tasty piece of bread and cheese before swilling it down with a large glug of ale.

The two men both seemed content to sit in silence for a while, tucking into their breakfast. Louise was busying herself in the bar cleaning up from the night before. The only sound being the clatter of empty jugs and beakers and the low hum of Trevelyan coming to life outside the window.

"The old boy's dead," Kian grumbled finally, leaning back in his chair, stretching his arms up over his head and letting out a loud exaggerated yawn.

"The Corridor?" Henry asked, still enjoying the food. He had quite the appetite this morning.

"No, fucking murdered," Kian grumbled, gulping down another cup of ale.

"Christ, what the hell happened?" Henry asked, observing Kian's melancholy expression.

It was evident Kian had been fond of the old soldier.

"It was the night after the explosion. Polly said he was really fucking agitated, more so than usual, ranting on about Crowforth and …"

"Polly?" Henry interrupted, raising a questioning eyebrow.

"Yes, Polly, the fucking barmaid at The Drovers," Kian snapped, annoyed by the interruption.

"I'm sorry," Henry apologised, running a finger across his lips as confirmation of his future silence.

Kian was obviously in a foul mood, and not just because of the old boy, the injuries to his face a clear indication the night had not gone as well as he had hoped.

"He made quite a fucking scene apparently, ended up in a right old brawl. Polly had to send him packing, the poor old bugger," Kian mused, shaking his head in dismay. "Anyway," he continued. "One thing she does remember, the name Westonhall, she said he kept repeating, 'they need to ask Westonhall'. And as well as that, some well-spoken stranger who she'd never clapped eyes on before with a right old scar across his face was showing more than an interest in the old fool, but according to Polly he left before it all kicked off."

Henry's interest suddenly piqued but he remained silent, allowing Kian to finish.

"Apparently, according to some of the other old boys, Lord Westonhall was Knight Commander at Crowforth, he coordinated the explosion. There was a lot of secrecy around the whole thing, some of 'em reckon the field had been rigged in advance with fire powder. Westonhall then skilfully lured Lorimer's forces into position and as they got closer it was lit. Boom! Fucking genius. It wasn't long after that Lorimer surrendered. I can't make any sense of the secrecy though, I would have thought they'd have wanted to shout the victory from the fucking roof tops, it ended the civil war for God's sake. Funny thing is, it would have taken a small army to plant the fire powder in the first place and not one of the old boys knew of anyone who was engaged in the preparation … strange huh?"

Kian paused, swallowing down another gulp of ale.

"Well?" he said, glaring at Henry, now waiting for a response.

"Lord Westonhall was my mentor for years he never once mentioned a thing to do with Crowforth … and the old boy, murdered you say? Yes, strange indeed," Henry agreed.

"The old boy's throat was cut, clean professional like and his gold service medal, still in his fucking pocket," Kian added. "If you ask me somebody wanted to silence him."

"Those gold service medals are worth quite a lot of money," Henry mused.

"Yes, exactly," Kian nodded, now looking rather pleased with himself.

Henry remained silent, popping another piece of delicious cheese into his mouth whilst mulling over what Kian had just said, his thoughts began to race.

Could there be more to Crowforth? Could what had happened there have been recreated in the Corridor? Did Lord Westonhall, my friend and mentor hold any answers? It was unquestionably a possibility. It was time they went to Blackmore; he was certainly not going to jump to any conclusions not yet at least, not without having all the facts in front of him.

"Finish up," he said finally. "We need to get to Blackmore, read through the witness statements and investigation reports and speak with Arlen. Maybe he saw something, after all it was on his watch … Oh and Kian, tell me what happened here?" he asked, pointing to Kian's bruised face.

"Oh," Kian grumbled, patting his sore head. "Polly's husband came home earlier than expected."

Henry roared with laughter giving Kian a friendly punch to his shoulder just as the door to the lounge gently swung open. The two men turned instantly, Kian already with a tight grip on the hilt of his sword. A large weather-beaten merchant dressed in a long black cloak, the hem caked in dry mud and a well-worn felt cap perched high on the top of his head, suddenly appeared in the doorway; Mr Milton it seemed had also returned home early. Louise bolted to the lounge door, quickly intercepting her husband and hastily leading him back towards the bar with a promise of a hearty meal.

"Christ, time to go," Henry squirmed, gathering up all his things in haste.

"Fuck me," Kian exclaimed with a broad grin, seeing an opportunity to get back at Henry for laughing at his misfortune. "If only I had been half an hour later. Why, we might have matching fat lips."

"Move you bloody fool," Henry snapped. "And keep your voice down," he hissed, anxious to quit the Inn as quickly as possible.

"Easy lover boy," Kian teased, as Henry desperately struggled to push past him.

Kian annoyingly stood fast, still sporting a huge silly grin on his face.

"Move," Henry growled, loudly. Not at all amused in the slightest, he finally pushed Kian aside and made for the door. The last thing Henry needed was an altercation with Mr Milton.

Once safely outside Henry quickly mounted his horse, allowing himself a fleeting glance over at Louise who was now standing at the entrance. He smiled over to her, affectionately nodding his head. Louise smiled back. She watched with a little sadness as Henry rode from the Inn, wondering to herself if or when she might ever see Francis Bolton again.

The two men stopped briefly once they had passed through the town gates of Trevelyan in order for Henry to change back into his Crown Knight livery.

"You seem much more relaxed this morning," Kian commented, observing his friend smiling as Henry pulled his tricorn hat back into shape. "Louise must have served you well last night?"

"I am and she did," Henry said cheerfully, throwing on his shoulder cape. "I even managed to get a couple of hour's decent sleep," he grinned. "I do hope Edwin will keep my arrival at the barracks this morning a discreet affair."

"Not fucking likely," Kian laughed. "You know Edwin, he always plays everything by the rules."

Henry sighed deeply, knowing only too well Kian was right. So, accepting the inevitable he remounted his horse and pulled on the reins as the two men continued their short journey towards Blackmore.

It was still relatively early as they approached the barracks, Kian joyfully smirked to himself at the sound of a loud fanfare announcing their arrival. Soldiers and cadets already stood to attention in the parade yard. Henry's hope of arriving quietly and without ceremony as expected had been in vain. He did however fully appreciate how important the traditions were to the men, particularly Edwin and indeed himself. He certainly had no intention of not fulfilling his duties as a master, after all the young cadets all aspired to becoming Crown Knights themselves one day. Henry always remembered fondly how he and Arlen had talked of nothing else when they were in training. How he had been in awe and utterly inspired by Lord Westonhall when he first addressed the naive juvenile boys at Chesterford.

Kian promptly pulled on the reins of his horse, swiftly riding on ahead, away from all the formalities. He was certainly not going to hang around, besides, he was still hungry so decided to head straight for the mess before all the young lads had a chance to devour the food, much like a hungry swarm of locusts.

Henry took his duties and responsibilities extremely seriously, taking the time to inspect the barracks, addressing the soldiers and cadets. Unlike social occasions, Henry was more than confident with the intricacies of Crown Knights rules of etiquette. He spoke with passion and authority, sincerely thanking them all for their efforts in Trevelyan and speaking with several of the young men personally. He hoped that in the same way Lord Westonhall's words had resonated with him, his own words had inspired and aided to lift morale in some way, as it was abundantly clear some of the very young boys had been affected by the bloody carnage they had witnessed in the Corridor.

He called upon them all for their continued support, thanking them for their dedication and professionalism, not just on behalf of himself, but the King and the whole of Mercia. His words undoubtedly seemed to connect with the men, creating a renewed enthusiasm and buzz within the barracks. Once dismissed they scattered with a revived sense of urgency and purpose.

"Thank you, Henry," Edwin said, most appreciatively. "It is a real privilege for some of the young boys to hear you speak so passionately, you are a real role model."

"Really?" Henry replied, rather surprised by Edwin's words of praise.

"Why so surprised? You are the youngest ever master, well deserved I might add, and your sense of duty and dedication is revered."

"I had absolutely no idea, Edwin, thank you," Henry replied modestly, genuinely astonished.

Almost all of Henry's time was now spent at court in the company of courtiers and Lords of the Privy Council. He continually felt the need to prove himself, particularly after certain members had objected to his elevation to master status. Edwin's words were more than gratifying, reaffirming his sense of purpose, although they did cause him a slight pang of guilt momentarily recalling his shameless night of passion with Louise. He quickly shook the image from his head, after all that was Francis Bolton and not Henry Morton.

"Come Henry, I shall take you to Arlen. He is beside himself, he will not settle. He is quite the worst patient we have ever had in the infirmary, pacing up and down with no purpose," Edwin said, holding out his hand in order to lead the way.

Henry sighed. "That doesn't surprise me, he has never been able to sit still for very long, almost as maddening as Kian."

Edwin shot Henry a look of disbelief.

"No, you are quite right, Edwin," Henry said with a laugh. "Nobody is that infuriating." The two men then laughed aloud.

Just as they reached the door to the infirmary, Henry stopped, turning to face Edwin.

"Tell me Edwin, what news of Harriet?"

"She is dead I'm afraid, she would not have stood a chance as the first explosion seems to have come from the bakery. She would almost certainly have been killed instantly, the only consolation I suppose. I did request for some of the men to recover her body, I thought perhaps it might aid Arlen if he were able to bury her, but there was no trace of her at all, absolutely nothing."

"Does Arlen know?"

"Yes, he insisted they halted at the site of the bakery as they brought him down. I know my brother cared for this woman very much. I did suspect at one point ... well, we all did in fact, that he might even ask father permission to marry her and then he went and proposed to Florence, so we presumed it was all over, it seems it was not."

"No," Henry confirmed. "He tried desperately to give Harriet up several times. I am convinced that is why he proposed to Florence, in a lame attempt to move on, but he kept going back to Harriet. He then of course ashamedly regretted his wedding proposal; God knows what on earth he was thinking. He refuses to speak of the wedding even to me. You know your brother Edwin, he is the master of putting things off and burying his head in the sand. It absolutely infuriates me I have to say. It does seem however, in this instance, the decision has been made for him."

"So do you think he will marry Florence now?" Edwin asked, keen to hear Henry's thoughts.

"I have absolutely no idea." Henry replied. "What is his current state of mind?"

"Very angry, agitated, fuelled with a real desire for revenge. He is grieving Henry, you will not allow him to do anything stupid, will you? Father is extremely worried."

"No, of course not, don't worry Edwin. Let us discover the facts. You heard me in Trevelyan, I promised justice not revenge."

"Thank you," Edwin replied with a nod of appreciation, placing his hand to Henry's shoulder.

Arlen was up and dressed in a simple linen shirt worn loose over his black breeches. His hair appeared unkempt and his face sported a thick stubble. The gash to his forehead looked well on the way to healing nicely although there were still traces of blue-black bruises around his puffy eyes. He was busy striding up and down the infirmary looking immensely irritated as Henry and his brother entered the room. He let out a deep sigh of relief upon observing Henry before bowing his head – a show of respect for the benefit of the other men present. Edwin efficiently ushered them all from the room.

"I shall leave you both to talk in private," he said, firmly closing the door behind him.

Once alone the two friends embraced. Henry concluded almost instantly that Arlen was exceedingly tense. After releasing their hold on each other, Henry sat down on a chair beside the bed, as Arlen continued to stride helplessly up and down the infirmary.

"Arlen, please will you not sit down?" Henry implored, observing his friend with great sadness at his painful distress.

"I cannot," Arlen moaned, curling his fists tightly to his side.

"You know, I feared you were dead," Henry muttered, mournfully. "I quit Kingslea the instant I heard the dreadful news."

"I feared I was dead myself at one point," Arlen replied, still pacing with a strange sense of urgency about him.

"Edwin informs me you were injured?"

"Oh, it's nothing," Arlen growled loudly, waving his arms frantically in the air. "My bloody brother fusses too much, it was just a cut to my thigh, and this," he said, pointing to the gash on his head. "I was in and out of consciousness most of the time, some old woman patched me up, Mrs Woods. She was patching us all up," he continued now in a calmer more reflective tone. "She was wonderful in fact; I didn't have the time to thank her properly. When the rescue party appeared, we were all whisked away; it all happened so quickly at the end. I should very much like to find her and thank her." he mused, sniffing into a handkerchief.

Arlen had stopped pacing. He collapsed down onto the bed opposite Henry, lowering his head into his hands, his whole body slumped forward exhausted and defeated.

"Harriet's dead," he breathed barely above a whisper. Raising his head slightly to look directly at Henry, his sorrowful eyes filled with tears.

"I know," Henry replied, his friends anguish upsetting to witness. "I'm so sorry Arlen; I know how much you cared for her."

"Who the fuck did this Henry?" Arlen snapped, his mood suddenly switching back from sorrow to anger as he punched the bed with his fists wildly several times. Arlen was clearly struggling to come to terms with what had happened.

"We have no idea Arlen," Henry replied softly, in the hope of tempering his misery.

Henry stood up and placed his hand to Arlen's shoulder, squeezing gently. He certainly had no intention of burdening Arlen with any theories, not in his current state of mind as he knew only too well he would latch on to any suggestion in a desperate need for answers.

"Your brother has been taking statements from witnesses and we are going to start reading them through today, in the hope they might at least give us some answers … you can help, if you feel up to it?"

"Statements!" Arlen shouted furiously. "Read through fucking statements, for fuck's sake Henry, I want to fucking kill someone!"

"Arlen, you must calm down, take control of yourself. I have promised justice, not revenge. This is far too serious; it has to be handled correctly." Henry commanded, his tone now considered and sharp.

Arlen shot up from the bed, his face red with anger pressed up merely inches from Henry's, his fists firmly clenched.

"Serious, I know it's fucking serious, I was there Henry! I saw all the dead bloody bodies; I lay amongst them on the ground for God's sake. People's limbs strewn about, burnt beyond recognition. There was nothing fucking left of Harriet … nothing … yes Henry, this is fucking serious."

"Then help me," Henry replied sharply, standing his ground. "Help me give these people the justice they deserve. I know you are hurting Arlen, but I need you to pull yourself together."

"Pull myself together, you fucking bastard!" Arlen screamed, raising his fist and promptly planting a punishing blow to the side of Henry's jaw.

Henry's breath whistled through his clenched teeth as he staggered backwards, wincing in pain, and just managing to steady himself in time to dodge a second swipe as Arlen furiously lashed out at him again. Henry reacted quickly, wrapping his arms around Arlen, pinning his arms down to his side and forcefully restraining him in a tight embrace.

"Enough!" he shouted, "Enough, Arlen."

Henry thankfully managed to maintain his tight hold as Arlen roughly struggled against him. Finally, and much to Henry's relief, Arlen gave way – his body slowly relaxing. Henry tentatively released his hold, allowing Arlen to slump dejected back down onto the bed.

"Feel better?" Henry asked, stepping backwards and rubbing his sore chin.

"Yes … I'm sorry Henry," Arlen muttered, cupping his face to his hands. "You're right, I'm so sorry, please forgive me."

Henry replaced his hand to his friend's shoulder. "It's alright Arlen, I understand."

"Thank you … I'm sorry Henry, I should never have lashed out at you like that. I'm a bloody stupid fool," he groaned, feeling utterly downcast.

"It's alright Arlen, I forgive you … besides there's nothing broken," Henry replied, with a smile, moving his jaw from one side to the other in an over exaggerated manner.

Arlen just about managed to raise a slight smile back as Kian suddenly appeared at the infirmary door, having overheard the raucous exchange. He stared knowingly at the two men.

"What the hell is going on in here?" he grunted, raising his arms in a questioning manner.

"Nothing, just letting off some steam," Henry replied, still with a hand to Arlen's shoulder.

"Didn't sound like fucking nothing," Kian grumbled, glaring at Henry, observing the sore red mark across his chin.

Henry shook his head and pursed his lips, a clear indication for Kian to keep quiet. Kian looked down at Arlen, despondent on the bed, then shifted back up to Henry.

"Harriet?" he asked.

"No," Henry replied, shaking his head.

"Fuck!" Kian muttered, as the room fell silent.

After a minute or two of awkward silence followed by a genuine heartfelt reconciliation, the three men eventually made their way to Edwin who had been waiting patiently in the library.

The library was an impressive room with hundreds of books piled up on shelves and numerous side tables. Intricate carvings made of ebony depicting mythical creatures adorned the mantle and above the fireplace hung a splendid portrait of a young man. The room had a sweet, musky smell – it was clearly a well-stocked library. At the far end of the room stood an enormous mahogany desk, covered in papers that had overflowed onto the floor. Some looked as if they had been there a while judging by the layer of dust.

Edwin sat on the opposite side of the room at a large oak desk with piles of papers artfully arranged around him. Four large armchairs were dotted around the desk; he had clearly been expecting them. A side table held two decanters, one containing red wine, the other brandy, with several ornately decorated glass goblets.

"Ah, there you are," Edwin remarked, as the men entered the room. "I was beginning to wonder if you were going to join me. Is everything alright?" he asked, looking up from the desk, directing his gaze towards Henry.

"Yes, all is well," Henry replied, nodding his head with a smile. "This is rather an impressive room Edwin, who is in the portrait?" he asked, pointing towards the fireplace.

"That Henry, is Septimus Alfred Bushnell, 3rd Duke of Blackmore."

"Blackmore is in the North, is it not?"

"Yes, quite right Henry. Septimus fell in love with a young woman from Trevelyan. The barracks were originally a summer house built almost 330 years ago, a wedding gift for the lady. She promptly left the Duke for a Vikrin Prince and was last seen sailing from Trevelyan to the continent. He never visited the house ever again; it was left to go to rack and ruin until the Crown acquired it and converted it into barracks."

"Bloody women," Kian huffed loudly, already with one of the decanters in his hand. Henry and Edwin laughed aloud, much to Kian's annoyance.

"Right," Edwin said sharply, bringing the room back to order. "I have arranged the statements in chronological order, people that were at the Corridor early and fortunately for them departed," he gestured to the pile on his left. "And then finishing with statements from the people that were actually in the Corridor at the time of the explosion."

"Excellent," Henry exclaimed, impressed with Edwin's efficiency and sense of order.

"I have not yet given a statement," Arlen declared, staring indifferently at his brother's neat piles of paper.

"No, quite right Brother," Edwin replied. "That is why I have arranged," he said, waving his hand at a young clerk hovering near the door, "for William here to take your statement now. William, please direct my Brother to my office."

"Yes sir," the young clerk replied, with a deep bow, waiting patiently for Arlen to join him.

Arlen very slowly sauntered off, closing the door behind him.

Once Edwin was sure his brother was out of ear shot, he turned to face Henry. "How is he?"

"Angry and hurting, but he is strong. He shall overcome this, please don't fret Edwin," Henry replied, reassuringly.

"Good," Edwin nodded. "I must tell you that I have received a letter from Florence Ainsworth. News of the explosion has travelled fast in Mercia. I have already written back setting her mind at rest and reassuring her of my dearest wish that Arlen may agree to visit and perhaps spend time recuperating at Moorgate Hall."

"I'm not sure he will agree to that," Henry mused, quite sure he most certainly would not.

"Oh well, we shall see," Edwin replied, not to be put off. "Right then, shall we make a start?" he continued, pointing towards the papers on the desk.

Henry nodded in agreement; he was more than anxious to get started himself.

Henry and Edwin proceeded to spend time fastidiously reading through the statements, making note of any detail that they deemed was of importance. Kian however quickly lost interest, not even able to finish reading the first statement he had picked up. He very soon began to fidget about, popping in and out of the room and succeeding in infuriating Henry to the point that he finally barked at him angrily to either sit down or make himself useful by arranging refreshments. Kian, more than happy to finally have a practical occupation, promptly stomped from the room, returning a while later with three young cadets in tow, laden with trays of food. Arlen joined them, placing his statement on the large oak desk, the break more than welcomed.

Edwin left the library briefly to attend to other business. Henry began pacing up and down the room, running his fingers repeatedly through his hair, in between swallowing down large glasses of red wine. He was becoming increasingly frustrated at the lack of any real detail. Nothing in the statements gave them any clues at all. The only noteworthy fact was a menacing looking man with a scar across his right cheek who got a mention by several eyewitnesses. Henry remembered what Kian had said about a man with a scar at The Drovers Inn talking with the old soldier, but the eyewitnesses put this man down on the quayside, not actually in the Corridor.

Kian and Arlen tucked into the food enthusiastically. Kian succeeding in raising Arlen's spirits a little, reminiscing of their early days at Chesterford when Henry had first introduced them to each other, Arlen positively declaring his life had never been quite the same since. Edwin returned to the library more than pleased to see his brother laughing, giving Henry a quick nod of appreciation.

Henry continued to pace the room, dipping in and out of the conversations. He stopped briefly to refill his glass with more red wine, casually picking up Arlen's statement from the desk at the same time.

"What on earth?" he declared loudly only moments later, glaring directly at Arlen.

"What?" Arlen exclaimed, taken aback by Henry's sudden outburst.

"It says here you saw Raven Westonhall in the Corridor, only a short time before the explosions?"

"Yes, I did, what of it?"

"Nobody else has made any reference to him," Henry barked, still glaring at Arlen opened mouthed.

"Well perhaps nobody else saw him," Arlen snapped back, slightly annoyed with Henry's tone. "Why, what difference does it make anyway, you cannot possibly think he had anything to do with the explosion surely. I have to admit he was behaving rather strangely but even so."

The three men now all glared at Arlen open mouthed.

"What, what the fuck are you all looking at me like that for?" he growled.

"Just think about what you have just said for God's sake," Henry replied, continuing in a sardonic tone. "He was acting rather strange."

"Fuck you Henry, he is strange, he always has been, you know that as well as I."

Henry ignored Arlen's protestations and hastily reread the statement. "You say here he was running an errand for his father," he continued.

"Yes," Arlen barked, sounding cross at the continued questions. "So what?"

"This is too much of a coincidence," Henry declared, glancing over at Kian. "Kian, please relay to Edwin and Arlen what you told me earlier this morning."

Kian repeated his story of the old soldier at The Drovers Inn, the Battle of Crowforth, the explosion and the mention of the name Westonhall. Edwin and Arlen listened intensely without any interruptions.

"Well, that settles it," Henry announced once Kian had finished speaking. He had finally reached a decision. "I have been contemplating travelling to Baines Abbey all day, we shall leave first thing in the morning," he declared, plonking himself down into one of the easy chairs, pleased at last they had something to go on.

"Baines Abbey?" Arlen asked, baffled.

"Yes, Baines Abbey, the ancestral home of Lord Bennett Westonhall."

"I'm coming with you," Arlen insisted, jumping to his feet eagerly.

"If you are to accompany me Arlen, I shall have no talk of killing and revenge, do you hear me?" Henry commanded, his tone now deadly serious.

"Yes," Arlen mumbled under his breath.

"I mean it Arlen. I shall not have you on some personal vendetta."

"Yes, Henry, I understand."

Henry rarely asserted his authority where his friends were concerned but, on this occasion however, he made it abundantly clear who was in charge.

The four men fell silent for a moment, as a certain air of tension whirled around the room. Edwin was the first to speak. "Henry, Baines Abbey is at least two days ride from here, might I propose you break your journey at Moorgate Hall," he suggested, glancing over in Arlen's direction.

"No ... no way," Arlen objected at once, throwing his arms up in the air in a defiant protest.

"Arlen, Florence has written, she was extremely worried, news of the explosion had reached Moorgate. Surely, the least you can do is call upon her, after all you have hardly written, in what, six months? Let alone seen her. When was the last time, Michaelmas?"

"What business is it of yours Edwin when I write or don't write to Florence?" Arlen snapped, angry at his brother's interference.

"Your brother is right Arlen." Henry added. "The wedding is less than two months away. You are going to have to face it sooner or later. Perhaps seeing Florence again will aid you in deciding once and for all what in God's name you intend to do."

"You two have bloody well planned this haven't you?" Arlen yelled, snarling at his brother and Henry in turn. "Well, you can both go to fucking hell!" he screamed, storming from the room, furiously slamming the door behind him.

Henry turned to Edwin. "Please write to Moorgate Hall," he said, calmly. "Arlen, Kian and I shall call upon them tomorrow evening, and if it pleases them, we beg accommodation for one night only." he concluded, finishing off the last of his wine.

"Yes, of course Henry, I shall write at once," Edwin replied, with a triumphant smile.

Later that evening, whilst alone in his quarters, Henry found himself unable to sleep.

There was a comforting hum of activity whirling around the barracks and the night air was pleasantly warm, but the events of the last few days were weighing heavily on his mind. The explosion, the succession, Bennett Westonhall, Crowforth. His thoughts wavering between being hopeful that Lord Westonhall knew nothing about the events in Trevelyan, as he could not comprehend his friend being involved in such a heinous act. And then hoping to God he did because he needed some answers, Trevelyan needed answers. No, Mercia needed answers.

Chapter 4

Blackmore barracks was a rowdy hive of activity the following morning, the young cadets were all jostling for space in the mess, hungry for breakfast before their early morning roll call. A pleasant warm breeze swirled around the parade yard as Kian brought the horses to the front of the main building saddled and ready to go for their journey north. Having attempted to tame his wild red hair with a comb, he had retrieved his repaired doublet from the tailor and, sporting a full quota of buttons, he was now more than eager to get on the road and make the most of the mild weather. Henry had been up since sunrise with Edwin finalising their reports for the King. The two men finally appeared at the main entrance still deep in conversation.

"We need to get going!" Kian shouted over impatiently, glaring at Henry.

"Yes, I'm ready," Henry shouted back, immediately returning his attention back to Edwin.

Kian muttered something vulgar under his breath before mounting his horse and scanned the yard for Arlen who was nowhere to be seen, annoying him further.

Arlen finally materialised from the direction of the infirmary, he looked decidedly tired and miserable, dressed in his Crown Knight livery, with his surcoat still missing the jewel at the east tip. He had insisted it stay that way as a reminder of the horrific events in the Corridor. His sore leg was throbbing and his head ached, though he had however found time to visit the barber-surgeon to have his hair trimmed and face clean shaven, improving his appearance somewhat. Despite this, he was certainly not in any kind of mood for Kian, who he spied glaring at him with an irritated expression running across his face.

"We're waiting for you, get a fucking move on," Kian grumbled as Arlen slowly sauntered over to his horse.

Arlen shot him an angry look, before glancing over at Henry and his brother.

"Yeah, looks like it," he replied testily.

"What the hell is the matter with you this morning?" Kian barked back.

Arlen ignored him and quickly mounting his horse, he walked it around the parade yard, as far away from Kian as he could manage, who was still glaring at him angrily waiting for a reply.

Henry and Edwin finally concluded their business with a handshake and warm embrace. Edwin then spoke briefly with his brother before bidding the party farewell with hopes of a speedy, safe, and informative journey. The three men then promptly rode out of Blackmore Barracks, heading north.

The road from Trevelyan was busy, with folk heading in both directions to and from the port. It was a good wide road, kept in good repair and more than able to accommodate the heavy traffic with ease. The sight of Crown Knights travelling along the road was not unusual in this part of the country and, with recent events, the men attracted little attention. It didn't take them long at all to reach a crossroads; the road to the west Kingslea, the road to the north Dendum and Moorgate Hall.

East Mercia was flat, arable land, bordered by the Corstir Forest and the Corridor wall. It was still relatively rural, beautiful, and unspoilt with numerous small villages and acres of agricultural land. The major urban area was the town of Dendum situated on the river Brida. Not overly populated, East Mercia had seen all the major battles during the civil war resulting in many of its residents fleeing and it was only in recent years that folk had begun to return. Much of the population earned a living on the land. The landowners made their money from the abundance of produce that came from the area and supplied all the major towns and cities, from Cambrian in the north to Kingslea in the west.

The excellent morning May sun was strong and with it fast approaching midday the travellers were becoming increasingly hot and hungry. Kian had been riding up front for the duration of the journey so far, pushing them on hard. Apart from the occasional stop to relieve themselves, they had made surprisingly good time.

"Winkhill ahead," he loudly shouted back to Henry and Arlen. "We shall stop to rest the horses and eat; I hear the Inn serves decent food."

Henry nodded in agreement, thankful to be able to spend at least a short time out of the saddle. He and Arlen picked up their pace slightly in order to catch up with Kian.

Winkhill was a small village comprising of several stone build dwellings, an Inn, and stables. The Innkeeper had capitalised on the location, a perfect distance from Trevelyan to Dendum and he had established the stables, which for the size of the village were rather impressive. The flow of travellers along the road was not excessive, but certainly provided him with a generous income and the abundance of fresh produce from the area had also obtained him an excellent reputation for tasty food at the Inn.

The three men rode into the village, creating quite a commotion. An extremely well-dressed groom appeared from nowhere, keen to serve his important customers. Dismounting, Kian proceeded to accompany the boy as he was very particular on how the horses should be attended. Henry and Arlen headed straight for the Inn. Within a few yards of the doorway the Innkeeper suddenly sprung from the entrance to greet them.

"Welcome, welcome," he beamed.

A jolly looking character with rosy, red cheeks and a button nose. He was as tall as he was round, with a mop of curly white hair, which whirled wildly around his face as he bobbed up and down with excitement. His elaborately embroidered waistcoat in all the colours of the rainbow made Henry smile as he considered the man to rather resemble a court jester.

"Welcome, welcome," the Innkeeper repeated holding the door wide, allowing the men to enter.

The Inn was of a moderate size, immaculately clean and inviting, with only a handful of other customers already sat at the bar. They all instantly halted their conversations mid flow, unashamedly staring inquisitively at Henry and Arlen. The Innkeeper turned a brighter shade of red and hastily ushered the two men in the direction of a private room to the side of the bar.

"That's better," he breathed, fanning his flushed face with his apron. "What can I get you gentleman?" he asked, continuing to excitedly bob up and down.

"Food and ale please," Henry replied, his smile widening at the man's cheery enthusiasm.

"Excellent, excellent," the Innkeeper beamed, scurrying away much like a rabbit down a hole.

Henry and Arlen very quickly settled down into the only two easy chairs in the room.

Kian followed moments later, he glanced around for another comfortable chair, huffed loudly in disapproval before plonking himself down on a hard wooden bench.

The three men had hardly spoken since leaving Blackmore Barracks. This was not unusual for Henry as he seldom spoke whilst travelling, enjoying the solitude and using the precious time to gather his thoughts and clear his mind. Arlen and Kian however were usually jolly travelling partners chatting, teasing, and mocking each other along the way. Today had been quite different. Arlen was still exceedingly melancholy and even Kian had the good sense not to poke that hornets' nest, preferring to navigate from a safe distance.

Arlen purposely stretched back in his chair wincing as a sharp pain shot through his left thigh.

"Everything alright?" Henry asked, concerned the journey was beginning to take its toll. He was not really sure that Arlen was up to traveling so far with his injured leg.

"Yes," he snapped back indignantly.

Henry shot him a warning look. "I know you must be in pain Arlen, physically as well as mentally, it is not a weakness to admit it. If you need more time, you only need say."

"I'm sorry Henry," Arlen replied, apologetically. "It's just my leg, it's aching that's all. I shall take some refreshment and give it a good stretch before we set off again. I shall be fine I promise."

"Very well," Henry replied. "Kian, how much further to Moorgate?"

"Another few hours at most, this excellent weather is aiding us."

The jolly Innkeeper interrupted the conversation by bursting through the door of the private room, followed closely by a young maid no more than eleven or twelve, laden with plates of food and jugs of ale.

"Fantastic! I'm famished," Kian exclaimed, pulling his bench closer to the table as the food was laid out in front of him.

The three men enthusiastically tucked into the feast of meat rich stew, bread and cheese and followed by stewed fruit with honey. All agreeing that it was rather delicious, they cleared their plates and emptied the jugs in no time at all. Arlen and Kian left the small private room soon after, Arlen in order to exercise his leg, Kian to fetch more ale.

"If he doesn't change that miserable fucking expression on his face soon, I swear to God I shall have to change it for him," Kian grumbled, returning a moment later with the ale.

"Leave him be," Henry insisted, shaking his head at Kian.

"But he's moping around like a fucking thunder cloud, for fuck's sake Henry. What on earth Florence is going to make of him I don't know. It would serve him fucking right if she called the whole thing off."

"He would probably welcome that," Henry added, momentarily closing his eyes and leisurely leaning back in his chair.

"Christ, I do hope they have plenty of fucking liquor at Moorgate, I'm getting pissed tonight," Kian grumbled, now joining Henry in the other easy chair.

Henry's shoulders sank wondering if his decision to break their journey at Moorgate was a huge mistake given the grumpy dispositions of his two travelling companions. His brief moment of contemplation however was suddenly cut short by the sound of angry raised voices just outside the window. Kian sprang to his feet in a flash, bolting towards the door. Henry was not far behind him.

A crowd of Winkhill villagers were gathering in the road with a young boy lying face down in the dirt. A menacing looking man dressed in black stood over him, his foot placed firmly to the boy's back cruelly pinning him to the ground, the tip of his sword pressed callously to his neck. Another unpleasant looking man stood beside him, his arm tightly wrapped around the waist of a young girl who was sobbing uncontrollably; a knife pressed to her throat.

"What the fuck is going on here?" Kian shouted, roughly pushing past the spectators.

"None of your fucking business," the man in black snarled, pressing his foot harder into the boy's back. The boy winced and groaned.

"Shut the fuck up," the man growled, revoltingly spitting at the boy with contempt.

Henry elbowed his way through to Kian's side, both men now having unsheathed their swords.

"But it is my business," he said sharply, moving forward towards the man in black, raising his sword level with the man's throat.

The man in black glared at him furiously. "This little bastard attacked me," he snarled, standing firm, increasing the pressure on the boy's back. The young boy cried out.

"Drop the knife," came a low, fierce voice from behind the other man. Arlen stood directly behind him, the tip of his sword pressed into the back of the man's neck.

"Release the girl," he commanded, gently gliding the edge of his sword around the side of the man's neck, applying a little warning pressure.

The unpleasant man obeyed instantly, dropping his knife and releasing the girl, pushing her forward with a force that caused her to fall to the ground. He raised his arms in the air glaring at his associate, both registering the fact that they had been outmanoeuvred. The man in black reluctantly released his foot from the boy's back, slowly lowering his sword and taking several steps backwards.

"We don't want any trouble," he grunted, looking around him nervously, in case there were other men behind him.

"Drop the sword!" Henry said calmly, now positioning his own at the man's throat.

The man in black obeyed, stepping back a little further. Henry cocked his head upwards. The man in black understood his meaning at once and raised his arms in the air.

The young boy quickly scrambled to his feet, his face smeared with blood and grime, his coarse linen shirt torn open exposing his slender frame.

"He was forcing himself on her milord," he spluttered at Henry, spitting dirt and blood from his mouth and furiously pointing his finger towards the man in black.

"She was asking for it," he grinned back, deliberately mocking the boy.

"Liar!" the boy shouted, lurching forward, his fists raised.

Kian swiftly grabbed him backwards, holding him in a tight embrace. The boy wrestled to break free but even the strongest of men would struggle against Kian's iron hold. The man in black gave a raspy laugh, goading the boy further.

"Let me go," the boy moaned, in a futile attempt to break free from Kian's grip.

"Enough!" Henry yelled firmly.

Everyone suddenly fell silent, you could hear a pin drop.

Arlen slowly moved his position, to face the second man, still keeping the tip of his sword firmly positioned at his neck.

"What is your business here?" Henry demanded, addressing the man in black.

"Just passing through, we don't want any trouble, it's all just a misunderstanding."

"Liar!" the boy shouted again, continuing his hopeless struggle against Kian, who increased his tight hold. "Quiet!" he hissed in the boy's ear. The boy winced.

"Then I suggest you continue on your way," Henry replied, pressing the tip of his sword into the man in black's throat. A tiny bead of blood ran down the length.

Both men began quickly stepping backwards, their arms still raised. Henry and Arlen moved forward, mirroring their steps. A third man then appeared from the stables leading out their horses. He had obviously been observing the altercation from a safe distance. He was tall, older, extremely well dressed; his doublet contained pinking revealing a rich purple silk beneath. His long grey hair tied back in a queue, his face clean shaven with a prominent scar running across his right cheek. He glared furiously at the two men as they approached his position, muttering something under his breath.

Henry stared curiously at the third man, who acknowledged him with a nod of his head. Henry moved a little closer, there was something about this man that piqued his interest. The witness statements, the stranger at The Drovers Inn, a man with a scar – although it was not unusual to see scarred faces in Mercia, particularly on older men. This man was certainly the right age to have fought in the civil war, he had an air of authority about him, and his clothes suggested wealth. *What business could he possibly have with these thugs?* Henry thought to himself.

The three men hastily mounted their horses before riding fast from Winkhill, heading north.

"Henry, what's wrong?" Arlen asked, observing his friend staring in the direction of the riders as they quit the village.

"That man, the one with the scar, have you ever seen him before?"

"No, I don't think so, why?"

"Nothing," Henry replied, continuing to watch until the three men disappeared out of sight. He then turned to face Arlen. "That bit of excitement seems to have put the colour back in your cheeks," he said, observing Arlen's flushed complexion.

"I would feel a whole lot better if I'd been able to run the dirty bastard through," Arlen replied with a disappointed scowl.

Henry laughed, placing his arm to Arlen's shoulder as they casually strolled back in the direction of the Inn.

"We don't have to go to Moorgate Arlen, not if you really don't want to. The weather is good and it has been a long time since we spent a night under the stars, it might do us all good. I'm sure the Innkeeper can supply a handsome hamper," Henry suggested, pulling Arlen closer in a friendly embrace.

"No, Henry, it's alright, I want to go; I should see Florence. Edwin is right, I have neglected her for far too long already … I shall conquer this, Henry."

"I know you will," Henry replied, releasing his arm from Arlen's shoulder, patting his friend affectionately on the back.

Kian was busy lapping up all the attention from the villagers who had eagerly assembled in the road. The Innkeeper was refusing payment for the food, but, after eventually succumbing, he showered the men with words of gratitude. The young boy was fiercely washing the blood and dirt from his face in a trough near the stable, shrugging his shoulders at the young girl as she tried desperately to comfort him, both totally mortified by the whole thing. Arlen patted him on the back as he passed by, giving him praise for his bravery for defending a lady's honour, with a little advice that next time he should check out the opposition first before wading in.

"Tell me," Henry asked the Innkeeper, "do you know why those men were in Winkhill?"

"No idea milord, they only arrived … well, an hour before yourselves in fact."

"The man with the scar, did you see him?"

"Yes milord, he ordered food, spoke very well he did, a bit like yourself, if you don't mind me saying so. No idea what he was doing with those unruly brutes, cannot imagine he was best pleased with them causing such a rumpus."

"No indeed," Henry agreed, thanking the Innkeeper for his hospitality and suggesting that the village might want to keep a keen eye out in case the men decided to return.

The mood of the three travellers was very much improved for the second part of their journey. Arlen and Kian were now chatting and laughing together, leaving Henry to his thoughts, which were unsurprisingly occupied by the man with the scar. Passing only a handful of other travellers along the way, they soon reached a fork in the road, to the left Dendum, to the right Moorgate Hall.

Henry looked over at Arlen. "Well?" he asked, shrugging his shoulders.

Arlen pulled on his reins, continuing along the road to the right.

* * *

Moorgate Hall was in utter turmoil. Two hours earlier they had received correspondence from Sir Edwin Barlett appealing for a night's accommodation on behalf of his brother Arlen, Lord Henry Morton, and Kian Munro, as they travelled on a journey north to Baines Abbey. Given the extremely short notice of the request Lady Elizabeth Ainsworth responded like a Commander-in-Chief calling the whole household to order, much like a military campaign. First, the gardener's son was posted on the roof as a lookout accompanied by a gong, which he was instructed to strike as soon as the riders appeared on the horizon.

Elizabeth Ainsworth was a rather flighty, high-spirited woman in her mid-forties. She had produced four children for Lord Hagan Ainsworth, two sons and two daughters. A beautiful woman in appearance, although she was prone to sulking if she failed to get her own way. Her over sociable and gregarious manner sometimes made her appear somewhat ridiculous, which attracted criticism from a number of the more reserved ladies at court. She would almost certainly not have gone to so much trouble if Arlen had been travelling alone, as much as she adored him and was immensely overjoyed at the prospect of him becoming her own son at the end of June. Lord Henry Morton was quite a different prospect. Henry had never attended any Mercia balls, every season the ladies hoped in vain for an appearance. Rumours of his brooding good looks and enormous fortune were common knowledge, making him quite the most eligible bachelor in Mercia.

"Girls, girls," she bellowed, from the stairs as her two daughters returned from their afternoon turn about the park.

"The elusive Lord Henry Morton shall be arriving here within the hour." she shrieked, flitting about the landing with excitement.

The two women stood in the hallway looking puzzled as servants whirled around them in every direction. Lady Ainsworth hastily descended the stairs, barking orders as she went.

"Oh, my dear," she beamed at Florence, "Arlen is with him, I knew they were friends. I so hoped he would introduce us one day, oh, how exciting!" she exclaimed.

"Why are you so excited Mother, of what importance is his visit to us? I am to marry Arlen and Beatrice is already married, you cannot marry us off again no matter how handsome and rich the man might be," Florence smiled, amused by her mother's over exaggerated frenzy.

"I know that my dear, but how popular shall we be this summer if we can boast Lord Henry Morton as our acquaintance," she beamed, all red faced and flustered.

"He is probably excessively fat and only four feet tall," Beatrice said with a laugh, teasing her mother cruelly. "That is why he never attends any balls."

Florence laughed, joining her sister in the joke.

"Laugh all you like girls, you shall not dampen my spirits," Elizabeth Ainsworth huffed, leaving her two daughters giggling in the hallway.

"I suppose it is rather exciting. I shall certainly be happy to see Arlen again," Florence mused, suddenly feeling a little nervous as the sisters made their way to a small drawing room.

"I don't know why you are rushing into marriage my dear sister, you hardly know this man. What, you have seen him three, four times in the last twelve months? He hardly ever writes. I believe you have received more correspondence from his older brother, perhaps you should marry him instead – it would make you Lady Barlett one day after all."

"Arlen is busy that is all, he writes when he can. And besides, I am not rushing into marriage we have been engaged almost a year," Florence replied, fiercely defending Arlen. She did have to admit to herself however that his lack of attention was disappointing.

"Yes, almost a year. How many times did he refuse to set a date until his father intervened? Marriage is no fairy-tale Flo, I should not have you unhappy," Beatrice sighed, her expression a little melancholy.

"You are not happy Bea? Why you have only been married three months, surely it is not so bad?" Florence asked, sympathetically.

Beatrice's recent marriage to Lord Edward Bentley had been arranged by her twin brother Phillip. Phillip was a Crown Knight stationed in Kingslea, an ambitious man with a tendency for cruelty. Over the last few years, he had been inclined to manipulate Beatrice, insisting she bend to his every will. Her marriage to Bentley was just one of the things he had demanded of her.

"Why do you think I have returned home so soon my dear sister, my husband is too old, too stupid and not to mention his lack of skill and inability in performing his husbandry duties."

"Really Bea, you can not mean it, if this is truly your opinion why on earth did you agree to marry him in the first place?"

"For his position and money of course my dear sister. I know you feel quite differently, you dream of love, but let me tell you, you cannot survive on love alone. Besides, Phillip favoured the match, it was his wish not mine."

Florence was fully aware of the unconventional relationship her brother and sister had with each other, she never questioned it, concluding it was merely the fact that they were twins and the bond between them unique.

"Surely you must have love?" Florence mused, trying to recollect Arlen. It had been quite a while since she had seen him last and even then, it had been fleeting.

"Oh Flo, I suppose Arlen may not have a large purse, but let us hope he has a large cock, and all will be well," Beatrice laughed aloud.

"Enough Bea, you say too much. Come we must change," Florence scolded, blushing at her sister's lewd comment.

"You may don your best gown Sister, but I can assure you I shall not make so much effort," Beatrice teased, following Florence up the stairs.

Florence headed straight to her room. Her maid had already laid out her gown on the bed, on her mother's instructions no doubt. Quickly changing, she stood in front of the mirror. The pale peach satin dress was delicately embroidered around the neckline, with a cincture at the waist and large trumpet shaped sleeves trailing to the floor. She wore her fair hair in simple tresses bound with a band on the top of her head. A short time later Beatrice knocked gently on the door before entering the room, despite her earlier protest she had also changed her dress. She looked beautiful in red velvet trimmed with gold brocade. She wore her raven black hair long and it curled around the edges of a silk headdress of pale pink.

"You look beautiful Flo," Beatrice commented lovingly, admiring her sister and giving her a quick kiss on the cheek.

"Really?" Florence replied, nervously.

"Really, you goose. Arlen is lucky to have you, and don't you ever forget it," Beatrice replied, kissing her sister again as confirmation, just as a ringing sound of a gong echoed in the distance.

"Come Sister, our visitors are here," Beatrice declared joyfully, taking Florence by the hand and furiously swirling her around the room.

"Stop Bea, you are making me all dizzy."

"Dizzy in love," Beatrice laughed, continuing to whirl her sister around in circles.

Henry, Arlen and Kian finally rode up the long drive towards Moorgate Hall. It was late afternoon and they were pleased to have arrived ahead of schedule. Moorgate Hall was a compact, rectangular building with two main floors and was built of grey brick with Glen Ivor stone dressing. On the south façade there were twelve sash windows on each of the ground and first floors. The hall was entered from the south with a stone flagged terrace extending the full width.

On arrival the men were immediately shown into the grand hall, a moderate sized room with panelled walls, lofty ceilings with intricate mouldings and an enormous fireplace that had already been lit, warming the space nicely. It was sparsely furnished with only two large tables and benches arranged as if for a banquet. The one table had been abundantly laden with an immense variety of foods, the men were all rather shocked by the excess – it was clear Edwin's letter had arrived in suitable time. The ladies were waiting patiently in front of the fireplace, ready to receive their guests.

Arlen was the first to speak. "Lady Ainsworth, may I introduce Lord Henry Morton and Kian Munro."

The three men all bowed.

"We are most grateful for your hospitality," he continued, "and on such short notice. I do hope we have not put you to any trouble?"

"You are most welcome Arlen, and I can assure you it is no trouble," Lady Ainsworth replied, beaming from ear to ear. "May I introduce my daughters, Lady Beatrice Bentley and Miss Florence Ainsworth."

The women curtsied; Lady Ainsworth continued, "Lord Morton, how pleased we were to hear you were accompanying Arlen, we have hoped for some time to make your acquaintance."

All three women mused to themselves that the rumours were in fact true, Henry Morton was indeed an undoubtedly handsome man.

"The pleasure is all mine; I can assure you madam," Henry replied, bowing his head again.

"Is this your first time in East Mercia?" she enquired, grinning absurdly.

"It is madam, it is a beautiful part of the country, I shall not be sorry to visit again," Henry smiled, politely.

"Well, my Lord –"

"– Henry, please."

"Well, Henry you will be welcome at Moorgate Hall any time."

"Thank you, madam."

The conversation then came to an awkward halt. Lady Ainsworth was still smiling broadly at Henry, causing him to feel extremely uncomfortable. Beatrice grinned, clearly amused by her mother's contrived formality, before finally breaking the uncomfortable silence.

"Arlen," she said. "How are you? We are so pleased to see you, we heard about the tragedy in Trevelyan. The account was rather vague, but it sounded dreadful."

"I'm well, thank you," Arlen replied, "Yes, it was dreadful indeed."

"Flo, do you remember two summers past when Phillip locked me in the priest hole at Trevelyan House. I was stuck in there for hours … Phillip can be so cruel." Beatrice seemed to drift off for a moment. Henry noticed her melancholy expression, she suddenly looked extremely vulnerable.

What Beatrice had never told anyone was that her brother had locked her in the priest hole to ensure her silence. She had inadvertently walked in on him in bed with another man. His attitude towards his sister markedly changed that day, now only treating her with what can only be described as cruelty and contempt. Beatrice however had never breathed a single word about what she saw that day. Glancing up at Henry watching her, she recovered herself instantly, smiling sweetly.

"Yes, I do remember, I didn't care very much for the place," Florence replied. "Anyway," she continued, turning her attention to Arlen. "We do hope you were not badly hurt?"

"No not badly, thankfully," he replied, with a smile. "Just a sore leg," he said, patting his left thigh.

"Not badly?" Kian scoffed. "So why on earth have you been sulking like a small child all day?"

Arlen shot Kian an angry look.

There was another moment of awkward silence before Beatrice and her mother burst into laughter at Kian's refreshing candour.

"Well Mr Munro, I believe we shall be a jolly party tonight!" Lady Ainsworth announced with a broad smile, linking Kian through the arm. "Let us eat gentleman, I'm sure you must be famished after your long journey, and please, call me Elizabeth."

Florence looked slightly unnerved, well aware of her mother's over gregarious nature. Arlen took her hand, squeezing it gently for reassurance. He also knew that with Kian at the helm, it was going to be a raucous evening.

Kian began entertaining the ladies with his usual aplomb. Arlen spent some time talking with Florence alone. He kept the conversation to general chit-chat, not wanting to be drawn too much on his life in Trevelyan. Henry remained aloof; Kian insisted on plying him with wine in an attempt to loosen him up, but to no avail. Beatrice kept catching his eye but made no attempt to converse with him intimately, instead preferring to flirt from a distance. The effort was not lost on Henry, he thought her stunningly attractive, although there was a certain sadness about her. Considering initial reservations on both sides, the evening was a tremendous success, with lots of eating, drinking and merriment. Florence was persuaded to play the harp, which she did beautifully. Arlen watched her intensely, remembering why he had been drawn to her all those months ago in Kingslea, smiling affectionately and causing her to blush. Even more impressively she played a rebec. Lady Ainsworth insisted on dancing with Kian, with Arlen partnering with Beatrice. Henry, more than happy to observe from a safe distance, was admiring Beatrice's womanly figure.

As the night drew to a close, Lady Ainsworth was the first to retire, but not before brazenly whispering into Kian's ear and placing something in his hand. Florence and Beatrice followed their mother not long after. The three men were now left alone to finish off their drinks.

"Well, I have to say, I was not too keen on spending the night here, but your future in-laws are fucking good company, it has to be said," Kian declared, swigging down the remains of his wine.

"Thank you, Kian … I think," Arlen replied hesitantly, grateful that the evening was finally over. "By the way what was it that Lady Ainsworth whispered to you?" he asked, observing Kian already hot footing it towards the door.

"And she gave you something, what was it?" Henry added.

"Well, my friends, I couldn't possibly say, me being a gentleman and all … I will however bid you both a good evening," he said, flashing a smile over his shoulder and dangling Lady Ainsworth's bedchamber key off his finger.

"For God's sake Kian, you cannot be serious," Arlen vehemently protested, throwing his arms up wildly in the air.

"Oh, I can Arlen … I fucking well can," he chuckled, disappearing from the room without another word.

Arlen slumped down into a chair, burying his head in his hands.

"Absolutely unbelievable. I shall never be able to look at that woman in the same way ever again … Oh, for Christ's sake, what on earth am I doing here?" he grumbled, miserably.

Henry promptly jumped up from his seat.

"Don't worry about it Arlen, he will never tell, and I'm damn sure she will not."

"I know that Henry, I just wish to God I didn't have to know about it that's all," Arlen replied, grimacing as if in pain.

Henry laughed.

"Florence is very nice, she is clearly smitten with you. Will you go to her tonight?" he asked, placing his empty wine glass on the table.

"No, not tonight. I think she would prefer to wait until we are married."

"She would prefer, or you?" Henry asked, staring down at his downcast friend in the chair.

Arlen didn't reply so Henry held out his hand, aiding him to his feet and patting him affectionately on the back.

"Oh well, to bed to sleep then," he announced, as the two men headed for the stairs.

Henry climbed into the large four-poster bed. The freshly laundered sheets smelt of lavender, and they were warm. It seemed Lady Ainsworth had pulled out all the stops for their visit. He settled down onto the soft mattress and was on the verge of drifting off to sleep when suddenly the bedchamber door slowly creaked open. Instinctively feeling for the small dagger that he kept under his pillow, he was thankful for the full moon filling the room with light. Beatrice appeared in the doorway, she didn't speak but instead gently closed the door behind her and very slowly turned the key in the lock. Henry released his grip on the dagger watching her closely as she glided across the room towards the bed. She stood perfectly still for a moment, staring down at him before finally loosening the straps of her delicate lace night gown and allowing it to drop to the floor. Henry admired her naked body. Her long raven black hair hung in curls against her voluptuous breasts; she really was an exceptionally beautiful woman. He was becoming increasingly aroused, as she very slowly slipped between the bedclothes, pressing her cold naked body up against his.

This was not the first time a Lady had made her way to Henry's bed. His very first encounter with a woman was when his mother's cousin, Lady Elena Harkness, came to stay at Elmbridge Hall. Henry was on his first summer break from Chesterford and was barely sixteen years old. The first night had been clumsy and awkward and over far too quickly, but by the end of his two-week holiday he had become quite proficient.

Henry embraced Beatrice, kissing her passionately and caressing her shapely breasts as she ran her cold fingers over his muscular torso – both reacting with little moans of pleasure to each other's touches. Beatrice then moved her hand lower. She stopped at the junction between Henry's legs, gripping hard.

"My, my, a Crown Knight ready for action," she mused, planting a lingering kiss to his lips. "I wonder if their reputation for stamina is also true?"

"Well, let us find out shall we," Henry breathed, gently raising himself up and positioning himself firmly between her thighs.

Chapter 5

The landscape decidedly changed as the men continued their journey further north, towards Baines Abbey. The beautiful flat lands of East Mercia were replaced by harsh towering peaks and valleys of desolate lowlands. Thankfully, the road from Dendum to Cambrian was well travelled and kept in good repair. Almost all of the timber supplied to Mercia originated from the town of Cambrian, which was situated on the edge of the Dean Forest. After the civil war, the people of Mercia refused to use timber from the impenetrable Corstir, citing it as cursed. Cambrian took advantage of the superstitions, which regenerated the old town. In time it earned city status and was now regarded as the second largest in Mercia. Their journey north would not take them as far as Cambrian, but they were able to make use of the good road for at least part of the way.

Having not left Moorgate Hall as early as they had hoped, they had lost valuable time. Kian was annoyed, more furious at himself than anything else. Elizabeth Ainsworth, as it turned out, was an extremely demanding woman. Henry and Arlen didn't help in aiding his foul mood; they mercilessly goaded him along the way, which culminated in a torrent of abusive language from Kian and roars of laughter from Henry and Arlen. If nothing else, it succeeded in cheering Arlen up no end.

In a lame attempt to teach them both a lesson, and also in the hope of making up for lost time, Kian rode on hard. Thankfully the fine weather was holding and was aiding their efforts. It was already late in the afternoon by the time they reached the small village of Drayton. Kian insisted that they kept moving, but Henry flatly refused, demanding that they rest the horses and take refreshment. The sun had dipped low in the west, when, finally, they left the small village, embarking on the last leg of their journey.

It was almost dusk when they rode over the brow of the hill looking down upon Baines Abbey. The rectangular three-storied fortified manor house was an impressive sight. Built of local white limestone, giving it an almost magical appearance against the lush green of the valley, the entrance was to the west and was flanked with four towers. To the east, on the adjacent hill, the Abbey itself – a double house combining separate communities of nuns and monks. Both buildings were set in a unique picturesque-like setting within an ancient deer park.

"All things considered, I do believe we have arrived more or less on schedule," Henry declared, as the three men paused for a moment, looking down upon the house.

A carpet of mist surrounded the large building, rising up from the earth and creating an ethereal beauty.

"What an absolutely splendid sight," Arlen remarked. "Have you visited Baines Abbey before Henry?"

"Yes, a handful of times, with my father. It is rather magnificent, is it not? Let us hope Edwin's letter arrived in good time, I'm famished."

"Me too," Kian mumbled, feeling totally exhausted, having barely had more than two hours sleep.

Henry and Arlen could not help but grin at each other, which thankfully went unnoticed by Kian.

Upon reaching the front of the grand house, two young grooms were already in attendance, waiting patiently to take charge of the horses.

Westonhall stood on the steps to the entrance holding a tray containing glasses of the finest Vikrin brandy. A welcome sight indeed thought Henry as they finally came to a halt. Lord Bennett Westonhall commanded an imposing, powerful looking appearance, even now in his later years. Well over six feet tall with sharp features, his thick hair, once jet-black, was now tinged with grey. Still however sporting his impressively large moustache, which like his thick bushy eyebrows remained jet-black. A learned, generous man, extremely intelligent and fiercely loyal to Mercia and the Crown.

"I observed you from the hilltop, I have been keeping a keen eye out all afternoon," Bennett Westonhall beamed, genuinely pleased to see the weary travellers. "Henry, my boy, how wonderful to see you."

"Sir, I cannot tell you how good it is to see you too," Henry replied, dismounting his horse in haste. "It has been far too long," he said, bounding up the steps of the house and embracing Lord Westonhall fondly, almost sending the tray of brandy hurtling into the air. A very rare show of public affection.

"Not since your father's passing," Westonhall confirmed. "How are you? And Kian, and Arlen too? Capital, capital, come on in all of you, I do believe we have much to talk about." Hurriedly ushering the three men inside the house, he clattered the tray of brandy down on a side table, quickly distributing the glasses.

"Follow me," he insisted, smiling broadly. "I have plenty of food and even more brandy," he said, winking at Kian and casually placing his arm to his shoulder as they headed straight for the study.

The study was a sizable room, well-lit with a circular frame containing several candles which hung low from the centre of the ceiling. A sturdy oak desk stood at the far end in front of a large picture window, highlighting the perfect view of the Abbey. The ancient building was just visible in the darkening night. The wall to the left as you entered, housed a fireplace with two enormous stag antlers hung either side. The remaining walls were filled with bookcases from floor to ceiling, they were literally bursting – with some shelves containing two rows of books. The room smelled of smoke and honeyed beeswax mingled with the sweet musky smell of old paper.

"The fire is lit, it can get rather cold this far north," Westonhall joked to himself, ushering all three men into his study with a certain air of excitement. "I cannot tell you how pleased I am to see you all, life is rather dull for an old soldier here in the north. I didn't think it possible to miss the stench and bustle of Kingslea, but I have to confess I do miss it at times."

"Eat!" he ordered, refilling all the glasses with brandy, pointing to a sideboard brimming with meats, cheeses and fruit. "We cannot talk on empty stomachs," he declared. He was clearly overjoyed by the arrival of his three young visitors.

The food was delicious and more than welcomed and they all tucked in eagerly. Besides a poor excuse for a beef broth eaten in haste at Drayton, they had not had a thing since leaving Moorgate Hall.

Lord Westonhall watched Henry with much pride and affection as they chatted together as only old friends can. He considered Henry like a son in many ways, a lifelong friend to his father and his mentor at Chesterford. He had pushed Henry hard, much harder than the other young men, but he never complained just continually strived under his tutelage to become stronger and evermore disciplined. Henry's advancement to master at such a young age had been a very proud day for Lord Westonhall. His own son Raven was somewhat of a disappointment to him. His many illnesses aside, which was unfortunate, Raven was also weak in personality, extremely gullible and easily deceived. Lord Westonhall found himself continually having to bail his son out of some ludicrous scheme or other as he frequently got himself mixed up with all manner of unscrupulous characters.

"You look tired Henry my boy," Westonhall commented, all too aware of Henry's nature to suppress his emotions. He could clearly see behind Henry's hard exterior; he obviously had a lot on his mind.

"It has been a difficult few days sir," Henry admitted, before letting out a deep sigh and relaxing back casually in his chair.

"I can imagine," Westonhall replied. "I have received sketchy reports from Trevelyan, but I'm afraid by the time news reaches us this far north the details can get a little lost. Edwin's letter said I may be able to help you in some way. Is there something in particular you wish to speak to me about?"

"Yes, sir, we do," Henry replied, pleased that Westonhall was the first to broach the subject.

"The cause of the explosion, perhaps?" Westonhall continued, knowingly.

The three men suddenly had his full attention.

"Yes, sir, " Henry replied, now sitting upright in his chair in the hope of discovering some answers.

"Well first, I should like to understand the facts, and then I shall tell you what I know," Westonhall added, sitting down and positioning his chair square behind the oak desk.

Henry placed an abridged report of the events at Trevelyan on the desk, written by himself and compiled with the help of the witness statements. Lord Westonhall, never one to be rushed, casually refilled his glass with more brandy and then leant back in his chair. He placed an old pair of pince-nez over the crook of his nose before picking up the report and beginning to read.

The three men waited patiently in silence, even Kian sat quite still, more than happy to relax after two long days in the saddle and eager to know if his assumptions regarding the Battle at Crowforth were correct.

Once Lord Westonhall had finished reading, he placed the report on the large oak desk in front of him and, removing his pince-nez, he leaned even further back in his chair before inhaling and exhaling loudly. He then rose.

"Before I tell you what I know," he announced, "first, there is something you must see."

He slowly made his way over to the bookcase on the opposite side of the room. Then very carefully he began to remove the books from the uppermost shelf, placing them carefully on a small side table.

"Sir, there is something else you should know, something I omitted from the report," Henry said, joining Westonhall at the bookcase.

"Oh yes," he replied, continuing to remove the books with care.

"Raven was seen in the Corridor, moments before the explosion."

"My son … Good God!" Westonhall froze, a sudden look of horror shot across his face.

"Yes sir," Arlen confirmed. "He was heading in the direction of the port and he was in quite a hurry and rather agitated. He has not been reported amongst the dead. I'm sure he must have reached the quayside before the first explosion. He said he was in the Corridor on an errand … For you sir."

Lord Westonhall didn't answer, he remained perfectly still, as if frozen to the spot, clutching a large leather-bound book in his hand. The blood literally drained from his face as he suddenly dropped the book to the floor with a thud and began frantically pulling at the other books from the shelf, tossing them wildly aside.

"Sir, what on earth is wrong?" Henry exclaimed, taken aback by his sudden erratic behaviour.

Westonhall ignored him and continued to madly pull at the books before reaching to the very back of the shelf, recovering a small wooden box. He swiped the books aside before placing it carefully on the side table, then, running back to his desk he rummaged around in a drawer and retrieved a tiny silver key. Upon hastily returning to the bookcase and swiftly opening the box, he gasped aloud. Henry snatched the box from the table, it was empty. He glared at Westonhall.

"Sir, please tell me what is wrong? What was in the box?"

"Iris," Westonhall muttered, staring past the men, who were all now stood up and opened mouthed, and through the large picture window towards the ancient Abbey.

The dim lights from the nave were just visible in the dark.

"Iris," Henry repeated, totally bewildered. "Sir, please, who on earth is Iris?"

"My daughter!" Westonhall yelled, instantly turning on his heels and running from the room.

The three men glared at each other utterly dumbfounded. Not one of them had any idea that Westonhall even had a daughter.

"Come!" Henry shouted to the two men as he fled from the study, hot on the heels of Westonhall.

Lord Westonhall had sped from the house in the direction of the Abbey. As he hastily approached, he observed that the ancient building was deadly quiet, nothing at all seemed amiss. He paused under the archway to the grounds, turning to face Henry, who had already reached his side.

"Please Henry, please allow me to enter alone, the nuns shall all be at evening prayer, I don't want to alarm them. I'm sorry Henry, you must think me quite deranged. I shall give you all an explanation for my sudden outburst, I promise. I can explain everything to you. It seems the time has finally come for the truth, but first I must know Iris is safe."

Henry nodded. "Yes of course sir, but are you sure you don't want me to accompany you?"

"Yes, quite sure thank you," Westonhall replied, glancing up at the Abbey once more. "All seems well, I'm just an overprotective father that's all, please forgive me Henry. I promise you, all shall become clear."

"Very well sir," Henry replied, looking unconvinced but stepping aside all the same to allow Lord Westonhall to go on alone.

Henry watched a little apprehensively as the old man walked up the pathway through the colonnade of the Abbey. His usual upright stance slumped forward slightly, his steps slow and considered. He briefly turned back around before entering, acknowledging Henry with a nod of his head before disappearing inside the ancient Abbey walls.

Just at that very moment women's terrified screams could be heard reverberating around the building. Henry bolted forward crashing through the large wooden double doors, his arming sword unsheathed. The two deeply unpleasant brutes from Winkhill stood glaring menacingly back at him, their swords raised and ready for combat. Arlen and Kian fled past Henry as they leapt into the fray. The sound of their singing swords flying through the air was followed by the deafening clash of steel, which echoed thunderously around the spacious nave as the two men skilfully set to. The terrified nuns were still screaming loudly, desperately pressing themselves further back against the wall as the vicious sword fighting played out precariously close in front of them.

Lord Westonhall lay injured, sprawled out on the ground just inside the entrance with blood gushing from a deadly wound to his stomach. Henry instantly fell to his knees besides him. Westonhall was barely breathing as he grappled for Henry's arm.

"Iris," he flinched, pointing a shaky finger in the direction of a side room. "Please Henry … Iris."

Henry was back on his feet in a flash and ran frantically towards the door, it was locked. He could just about make out the sound of a struggle and a woman crying. Using all his force he set his weight to the door, battering it with his shoulder. The woman screamed out louder. He doubled his effort, thrusting himself at the heavy wooden barrier once again, pulling the nails holding the old iron bolt out from the stone wall, finally forcing it open. Henry fell into the small side room. The man with the scar stood staring back at him. He had a young nun locked tightly in his arms. She was kicking and screaming, desperately trying to free herself from the man's bruising hold. Upon observing Henry, the man with the scar retrieved his dagger from its scabbard and pressed the keen edge firmly to the nun's throat.

"Move closer and I'll kill her," he snarled in a warning tone. He made it very clear that it was not an idol threat. "Drop your sword," he continued between clenched teeth.

Henry obeyed; carefully lowering his sword to the ground before raising his arms in the air. The young nun stared at him, terrified, her vibrant blue eyes wide and filled with tears, as if pleading for his help.

"Well, it seems we meet again," the man with the scar grinned, roughly dragging the nun backwards.

"Let her go," Henry barked. "Fight me like a man you coward."

"I am no coward," the man snarled, sounding angry at Henry's degrading words.

He pushed the nun forward, trapping her between himself and a table in the centre of the room. She cried out as her body hit the edge with a brutal force.

"Quiet!" he hissed, roughly yanking her head backwards and pressing the dagger harder to her throat.

"Your time will come Crown Knight, I can assure you of that," the man grinned menacingly, goading Henry with his sinister words and at the same time forcing the nun back down onto the table and pressing her face hard against the weathered wood. She whimpered; more terrified tears filling her eyes.

"Let her go," Henry growled, frantically glancing around the room for a way to perhaps gain the upper hand.

"No," the man laughed cruelly and placing his large hand to the nun's head, pressing it down further onto the table. She let out a petrified cry.

Beyond desperate, the young nun managed to place her hand onto the table, grabbing a small kitchen knife in her fingers just inches from her face. She gripped it tightly in her hand, just as the man with the scar forcefully yanked her upright again, dragging her backwards towards the door at the far end of the room. Henry had his dark eyes fixed rigidly upon the nun as she firmly clenched the small knife in her fist. She stared at Henry, her eyes wide. Predicting her next move he acknowledged it with a slight nod. She raised her arm and thrust the small knife with all her strength into the leg of the man with the scar. The man instantly recoiled, momentarily releasing his grip on the nun and allowing her just enough time to break free from his clutches and drop to the ground. The man grappled to get hold of her again as she frantically kicked back at him, managing to push herself away and roll beneath the table just as he brought his sword crashing down onto the cold stone floor right beside her. Henry had reacted like lightening, having already retrieved his sword from the floor he was now hurtling over the table in the direction of the man with the scar. The man raised his sword just in time to block Henry's attack, hastily stepping backwards and pulling at a stack of crates and tipping them over to block Henry's path. Henry madly pulled at the crates desperate to reach the man who was now exiting the Abbey by the door at the back, still with the small kitchen knife protruding from his leg. Henry eventually fell from the doorway just in time to observe the man with the scar riding away from the Abbey and into the darkness of the night.

"Arrh!" he roared in frustration, driving his sword wildly into the dirt.

Seconds later he returned to the side room where the young nun was still cowering under the table and extended his hand out in order to aid her, she instantly recoiled.

"Iris," he spoke softly. "You are Iris?"

"Yes," she replied hesitantly, staring up at him frightened, shaking like a leaf.

"What you did Iris was very brave, but you must now come with me, your father, he needs you."

Iris tentatively held out her hand to Henry as he aided her from under the table. He could feel her trembling as he gently embraced her in his arms.

"It's alright Iris, you are safe now I promise you," he whispered reassuringly, before leading her back towards the nave.

Arlen and Kian had efficiently finished off the two thugs with impeccable speed. Their dead bodies now lay in pools of blood, sprawled out across the nave floor. The nuns were sobbing uncontrollably, desperately clinging to each other for comfort. Arlen was trying unsuccessfully to console them just as a priest appeared at the far end of the room. He had clearly heard the commotion and had been running, sweat dripping from his forehead.

"What in heaven's name has happened here?" he cried out, staring in horror at the sight before him.

Arlen gave up with the nuns and made his way over to the priest to explain the carnage. Kian began hauling the dead bodies out, flinging them unceremoniously into a ditch at the side of the Abbey.

Henry dropped back to his knees besides Lord Westonhall and gently lifted the old man's head onto his lap. "She is safe sir, your daughter is safe," he whispered, motioning for Iris to come closer.

Iris fell to her knees beside Henry, weeping at the sight of her injured father, grabbing his hand tightly in hers.

"Oh, Father, please no," she sobbed, holding his hand close to her heart.

"Iris my darling please don't cry; you must be brave," he breathed, his speech terribly faint and strained.

Lord Westonhall turned and made eye contact with Henry, blood bubbling from his mouth, it was clear he had merely seconds left to live.

"Henry," he said, flinching, "I don't have much time."

"No, sir please," Henry begged, desperately not wanting his friend to succumb to his injuries.

"Henry, grant Iris Crown protection, she is in great peril … promise me."

"I promise," Henry replied, without any hesitation, even though he had no understanding of the reason for the request.

"Take this," he continued, removing a small emerald ring from his finger and placing it in Henry's hand, feebly closing his own around it.

"You must take her to the East, to Ivan Lorimer, he can explain everything, he knows …" Lord Bennett Westonhall did not finish his last sentence, he gently slipped away in Henry's arms.

Henry sat leant up against the wall on the wet grass outside the Abbey grounds. He ran his fingers through his thick dark hair, struggling to make any sense of what had just happened. Lord Westonhall was dead, he could hardly believe it. Now he, like Arlen, wanted revenge. He wanted to kill someone, he wanted to kill the man with the scar. He thumped the ground with his fist, cursing and blaming himself, *I should never have allowed Westonhall to enter the Abbey alone, I should have been better prepared; I am a Crown Knight for God's sake.* Thumping the ground again several times in pure frustration he drew blood from his knuckles. Lifting his hand in the air, he watched as his blood trickled down his fingers and over the emerald ring, turning the stone black.

The priest stood under the Abbey archway discreetly watching Henry from a distance as he anguished on the grass. Iris had relayed her father's last words to him, he gently rubbed at the grey stubble covering his chin in silent contemplation.

Chapter 6

Henry stood all alone in Lord Westonhall's study, the small wooden box still on the side table next to the bookcase. He picked it up and threw it in fury against the wall, then he swiped the contents of another table to the floor before doing the same to the contents of the large oak desk, roaring angrily as the books, papers and glasses crashed loudly to the ground. He stopped at the sideboard containing the brandy, picked up the decanter and lifted it in the air ready to throw it into the fireplace. He stopped and poured himself a large glass instead, and slumped down heartbroken and downcast into one of the chairs.

Sometime later the priest entered the room; he also poured himself a glass of brandy before sitting down opposite Henry.

"I don't need your prayers Priest," Henry growled, wanting nothing more than to be left alone. "You should return to your nuns," he said, downing the contents of his glass.

"I'm not here to pray for you Lord Morton," the priest replied, observing Henry closely as he sipped on his brandy.

"Then what do you want?" Henry snarled, refilling his own glass.

"I think perhaps I may be able to help you," the priest replied. "I know what Lord Westonhall asked of you."

"Well Priest, unless you can tell me what was contained in that box?" Henry snapped, pointing to the small wooden box on the floor. "Or, what the hell happened here tonight, or how on earth I'm going to bring a nun to the East, then I'm sorry Priest, but I am not in any way interested in anything else you have to say," he added and gulped down another large glass of brandy, running his fingers through his dark hair in frustration.

"The contents of the box, who those men were and why they wanted Iris, no, that is not what I can tell you. How to get to the East, yes, Lord Morton, that I can tell you."

Henry glared at the priest. He had an old, battered appearance and his face was full of scars with missing teeth and thinning hair. Henry surmised he had once been a soldier, not always a priest. Once a strong powerful man that was clear to see, but life had not been so kind to this man of God sat before him.

"Alright, Priest, you have my attention," Henry replied behind crossed arms, casually leaning back in his chair.

"I have not always been a man of God; you may have already guessed that by my appearance," the priest smiled. "When I first arrived here in Mercia my name was Edward Maddock, I wanted a different life to the one I had been born into. I was strong, handy with a sword, desperate to please. I became a soldier … no, not a soldier, a killing machine – an assassin for hire. I would despatch anyone for the right price. Very soon I came to the attention of King Charles and I committed unspeakable acts, all in the name of the so-called Crown. After the civil war I could not go back to being Edward Maddock. I needed to somehow atone for my many sins, so I became a priest; Father Peter. I returned here to Baines Abbey," he paused, lost in thought for a brief moment, sipping on his brandy. "Edward Maddock was born in Corstir."

"Forest dwellers are a myth," Henry laughed. He thought, at first, that the priest must be joking, but he was quite insistent.

"I can assure you Lord Morton they are not," Father Peter replied, his expression deadly serious.

Henry studied the priest closely. "If what you say is true, Corstir Forest is impenetrable, many have tried to navigate its dense terrain but none have succeeded."

"True, no man from Mercia has succeeded," Father Peter replied, "but I am from Corstir and I can assure you milord, I have travelled between the West and the East many times. It is not an easy journey; it will take several days, and of course you will be expected to pay for a safe passage."

"Money!" Henry exclaimed. "Money is not a problem."

The priest laughed, showing his broken teeth. "No, milord not money, the forest settlement has no use for money, hard labour."

"Hard labour, I don't understand," Henry replied quizzically, now sitting upright in his chair, he was becoming increasingly intrigued with what the priest had to say.

"The population of Corstir has dwindled over the years, many of the young men don't want the forest life, they crave adventure, money and to discover all the things Mercia can offer a young man and Corstir cannot. The settlement is in desperate need of repair. They need manual labour, tools, men with strong backs able to work and build, for this you will receive safe passage."

"And for how long would we be required to work?"

"Four or five days, no more. A simple task will be set and once completed you will be allowed to continue on your way. Total secrecy will of course be part of the agreement. Inviting strangers into the settlement is rarely allowed, I have to ensure you can be trusted. I do believe however, that I can trust you Lord Morton," the priest replied. "You have my word, hard labour for a safe passage – there is no other way to navigate Corstir. Unless you can enter via the Corridor, it is the only way to get to the East and Ivan Lorimer."

Henry had already been considering travelling to the East via the Corridor. He could almost certainly gain access from the Mercia side, but no Eastern soldier would allow a Crown Knight over the border into the East, not to mention the fact it would draw a lot of unwanted attention. Questions would be asked, many questions, and then there was Iris Westonhall. It was now more than evident that Raven Westonhall was involved in some way with the explosion in the Corridor, but he was certainly not working alone. Knowing the man as Henry did, he supposed he had been tricked or coerced in some way. Who could Henry trust? The less people that knew about this the better.

Arlen and Kian entered the study, diverting Henry's attention. They had been busy aiding the nuns clear up after all the mayhem at the Abbey. Kian poured them both a large glass of brandy before settling himself down into a chair.

"Oh, Father Peter, the Abbess is looking for you – she wants to bring Iris home, but she is refusing to leave her father. Strong willed that one, not at all like any nun I have ever met before," Arlen said sounding amused and accepting a glass of brandy from Kian and pulling up another chair.

"She is not a nun," Father Peter replied. "She has not yet taken her vows; it was only her father's wish that she entered the church. Iris has been resisting it for months now, she is, as you say, wilful," the priest explained, raising a knowing eyebrow.

"Tell me Priest, I have known Bennett Westonhall all my life and he never once mentioned having a daughter, why all the secrecy?" Henry asked, rising from his chair and retrieving the small wooden box from the floor. "He said she was in peril. Why would that be?"

"I don't know," the priest replied, shrugging his shoulders, but with perhaps a sudden hint of doubt in his voice.

"Whatever was in this box, we have to presume Raven took it. It must have had something to do with the explosion – that is evident. The man with the scar did not come to kill Iris, he had ample opportunity. He was attempting to abduct her. Perhaps she knows what was in the box," Henry mused, placing it carefully upon the desk, tracing his finger over the brass inlay.

"Iris has been corresponding with her brother in secret for a while now," the priest added. "I overheard her speaking with her maid. Iris is very close to Kate; they are clearly in cahoots with each other. I do believe Iris was intending to flee Baines Abbey in order to join her brother in Kingslea."

"Kian, speak with the maid, get me those letters," Henry commanded, his tone sharp.

"Now?" Kian moaned, rolling his eyes.

"Now!" Henry barked, sounding cross.

Kian stood up tutting loudly. Henry ignored him, so, swallowing down the remains of his brandy, he made for the door.

"Kian, wait, I shall take you to Kate," the priest said, rising from his chair. "I need to return to the Abbey. Lord Morton let me have your decision regarding Corstir in the morning."

Henry nodded as the two men briskly left the room.

"What decision?" Arlen asked curiously.

"Wait for Kian to return and I shall explain," Henry replied, cupping his head to his hands.

Henry spent the rest of the night in the study, drinking brandy, reading and rereading Raven's letters to his sister. There was no mention of the box, the Corridor or Trevelyan. Just idle promises of bringing Iris to Kingslea, buying her new dresses, dancing and other such nonsense. After too many glasses of brandy and utter exhaustion, Henry finally succumbed to sleep and slumped unceremoniously across the desk. Kian found himself a bed, whilst Arlen returned to the Abbey to watch over Iris. She remained in silent prayer with her father's body until late into the night, until she finally surrendered to exhaustion. Arlen found her asleep on the stone floor of the nave, so, carefully picking her up, he carried her to a small bedchamber. The Abbess thanked him and promised to watch over her for the rest of the night. Father Peter then relieved Arlen of his post, allowing him to return to the house for some much-needed rest.

The following morning Henry felt surprisingly clearer headed. He allowed a maid into the study to clear away the broken glass, books, and papers from the floor. She worked efficiently, before bringing in trays of fresh food and ale for breakfast. Arlen and Kian joined him.

"Tell me Arlen, what do you know of Lady Westonhall?" Henry asked, tucking into a plentiful plate of food.

"Raven and Iris's mother?"

"Yes."

"Nothing, I'm afraid, why do you ask?"

"I have been wondering if she may have had some claim to the throne. It might explain Westonhall's desire to keep Iris in relative secrecy, not wanting her to be used as a pawn. Particularly in these uncertain times we find ourselves in with the lack of any heir. She would indeed be a valuable asset."

"Surely if Lady Westonhall had such a claim, we would know it. Raven would never be able to keep such a secret, and besides, would that not mean he also had a claim?"

"Perhaps," Henry mused, considering the idea for a moment.

"Have you made a decision, Henry, do we travel east?" Arlen asked.

"Yes, I have already spoken with the priest, Kian and I shall travel east. Arlen, I need you to return to Kingslea. I have already despatched a letter to Edwin informing him of your return. I need you to find Raven. Ask Edwin for assistance. It is imperative that we conceal the truth from the Privy Council; the fewer people that know of Iris the better, at least for the time being, until we fully understand the situation. I'm unsure of who we can trust – this treachery may run deep. I shall also need you to be back in Trevelyan, if the priest is to be believed. I have calculated that we should be ready to return from the East within a fortnight and we shall endeavour to exit via the Corridor. I will need you at the border control in order to expedite a speedy re-entry to Mercia."

"Yes, of course, Henry. When do we depart?" Arlen asked, slightly disappointed he was to return to Kingslea.

"We depart tomorrow morning; we shall travel south together before Kian and I continue east to Corstir. Kian, please speak with the priest, there is much to do and we need to be fully prepared. I need to speak with Iris Westonhall."

Kian nodded, but not before filling his mouth with a large piece of bread and cheese.

Kian and Arlen promptly left the study after they had finished off their breakfast and, after finding Father Peter, they set to work at once preparing for the long journey ahead. Henry remained in the study; he wrote several letters. His non-attendance at court would not go unnoticed, he needed to fabricate a reason for his absence without creating too much attention. He also wrote a precise and accurate account of the events at Baines Abbey for the King's eyes only. Once finished, he leaned back leisurely in his chair, yawning loudly. The small wooden box with its brass inlay still sat on the desk in front of him. He picked it up and began to ponder Iris.

According to the priest, it seemed she had spent all her life at Baines Abbey in relative obscurity, with her father encouraging her to join the church. Father Peter had said that Lord Westonhall doted on Iris, indulged her even. He had referred to her several times as wilful and impulsive, a trait that worried Henry. She had recently become very dissatisfied with her life – refusing to take her vows and requesting permission to visit her brother in Kingslea. Lord Westonhall had flatly refused. Tensions between father and daughter had reached crisis point in the last few weeks, which was almost certainly the reason for her secret plans to quit Baines Abbey and join Raven. The prospect of navigating halfway across Mercia, let alone through an impenetrable forest with a flippant young woman, vexed Henry greatly. But it seemed if he were to uncover the truth behind the explosions in Trevelyan, he had no other choice.

Iris kissed her father a final farewell, momentarily glancing back at his cold dead body as it lay laid out peacefully in the nave. Her beloved father was now gone, mercilessly taken from her in the most violent of ways. She wiped away the last of her tears on her soiled habit before turning to exit the Abbey for the last time. Her emotions were a bubbling cauldron of grief, anger, fear, and anticipation. For the first time in her life, Iris's future was uncertain, but she now had the freedom to make her own choices. She mused to herself as she slowly descended the hill towards the grand house; first release Lord Morton from his promise and then join Raven in Kingslea. She had dreamt of going to Kingslea for so long. Raven's letters described the city in such magical detail. *Kingslea*, she thought, *where anything was possible.*

Iris deliberately avoided her father's study as she was not quite ready to confront Lord Morton with her plans. Instead, she headed directly to her bedchamber in order to wash and change. She was still wearing her nun's habit, stained with the blood of her father – a terrible reminder of the horrific events from the night before. Her maid Kate was frantically pacing up and down the room as she entered.

"Kate what on earth is wrong?" Iris asked, embracing her fondly.

"Oh, miss, I'm so sorry," the young girl sobbed. "I wanted to come to you at the Abbey, but Mrs Parker wouldn't allow it."

Mrs Parker was the Baines Abbey housekeeper; she was not a terribly nice woman, particularly to the other servants under her employ.

"Kate, it's alright … I'm alright, please don't cry."

Kate was two or three years younger than Iris, no more than five feet tall, with a small, pleasant face and mousey brown hair. She had arrived at Baines Abbey as a mere timid scullery maid, having, most disapprovingly by other members of the household staff, been elevated to lady's maid at Iris's request. The two girls formed an awfully close bond, Kate being the closest person Iris had to a friend and Iris protected her vehemently whenever she could.

"Oh, miss, I have to tell you, the man with the red hair, he said I was to lay out travelling clothes. I told him you din't have none, I din't know what I was to do."

"Don't worry Kate, I shall wear my new dress; the one Raven sent me. Kate, I'm going to Kingslea, to Raven and I want you to come with me. Pack all our things, we are finally leaving Baines Abbey and going on an adventure," Iris smiled, grabbing hold of her maid's hands and spinning the young woman wildly around the room. The two women giggled innocently with excitement.

Kate smiled broadly. "Oh miss, how exciting, you really mean me to come with you?"

"Yes, of course I do Kate. I could not imagine going without you," Iris smiled back, placing a kiss to Kate's cheek. "Now hurry, I want to depart first thing in the morning."

"Yes, miss," Kate replied, overjoyed by the news, she turned to leave the room then suddenly stopped and turned back around.

"Oh, miss, I forgot to say, that man with the red hair, he took your brother's letters. I tries to stop him, but he be havin' none of it. He took 'em to that right important Lord who bin sat in your fathers study."

"What?" Iris exclaimed, annoyed by the blatant disregard of her privacy. "He took my letters? How dare he," she hissed, furiously pushing past Kate.

Iris was indeed really rather impulsive. She suddenly felt quite invincible. Now free of all restraint and now her own woman to come and go as she pleased – how dare anyone take her private letters! Iris was also immensely naive.

Henry was leaning back in the chair behind Lord Westonhall's desk when Iris appeared in the doorway to the study. He rose immediately.

"Miss Westonhall," he said, with a deep bow.

"Milord," she replied, with a curtsy and a look of irritation running across her face.

Henry moved his position from behind the desk to the front, towering over Iris's small frame. His dark eyes surveyed her as she stood in front of him, still wearing her soiled nun's habit. Iris had a pleasing face, even considering her large vibrant blue eyes were red and swollen through crying, her long wavy auburn hair was just peeping out from under a wimple.

Iris was under no illusion, the man stood in front of her was an extremely important and powerful man who obviously commanded obedience, just like her father. His dominant presence was intimidating.

"Tell me Miss Westonhall, do you know what was in this box?" he asked, picking it up from the desk and holding it out in front of her.

"No milord, I have never seen that box before … whose is it?"

Henry believed she was telling the truth; she showed no emotion upon seeing the box. It clearly meant nothing to her.

"Never mind," he replied, waving his hand as if to dismiss her, he was not in any kind of mood for pleasantries. "Oh, and Miss Westonhall, we depart for the East at sunrise tomorrow morning, be sure to be ready. I shall not tolerate any delays."

Iris was left with no doubt that was an order. It was now or never, she thought to herself. Taking a deep breath, with Henry's dark brooding eyes still fixed firmly upon her, she bravely made eye contact with him and spoke with as much confidence as she could muster.

"Milord, my maid informs me that you have taken my letters, from my brother. I want them back … now." Her tone brisk and sharp; she was clearly annoyed with him.

"I beg your pardon," Henry replied, sharply, taken aback by her insolent request.

"I think you heard me quite clearly milord," she continued, her courage building, feeling quite empowered. "Oh, and whilst I'm here, I might as well tell you. I'm not travelling east with you, I'm going to Kingslea, to my brother. I release you sir from your promise."

Henry could hardly believe her audacity, he had never been spoken to in such a way, and certainly not by a woman.

"I don't think you quite understand madam, you have no choice in the matter," Henry replied, the tone of his voice leaving Iris in no doubt at all that she had angered him greatly.

Iris was thrown off balance for a moment. She hesitated, unable to maintain eye contact much to her annoyance. This man was clearly not a man to be trifled with, however she was not going to give way quite so easily, forcing herself to resume eye contact with him once again.

"I am not a child, milord, I am a grown woman and you have absolutely no authority over me."

Henry's patience was beginning to wear very thin. His gaze upon Iris was so intense that she could not help but lower her eyes, suddenly becoming a little nervous and beginning to tremble, yet she was still undeterred.

"Milord, I demand my letters back at once and I say again, I shall not be traveling east with you; your services are not required." She spoke with as much authority in her voice as she could muster, although the words faltered slightly towards the end.

Henry remained silent; his temper rising and struggling to maintain his calm composure. *Who is this silly, disrespectful slip of a girl?* He thought to himself, *speaking to me in such a discourteous manner.*

"Will you not answer me milord?" Iris hissed through tight lips, exasperated by Henry's refusal to reply.

"Answer me, damn you!" she shrieked, completely losing her patience with him.

The silence became deafening. Henry stepped closer towards Iris; he had not taken his eyes from hers throughout their exchange.

"Answer me!" she screamed louder.

Unable to control his temper with her any longer, his expression darkened as he finally spoke – his tone now razor sharp. "You will be ready to leave in the morning madam, or I shall drag you kicking and screaming by your hair if I have to. Either way you are traveling east."

Iris's frustration totally got the better of her and she screamed again. "You cannot speak to me that way!" Raising her hand, she slapped Henry so hard across the face that the palm of her hand stung. Henry hardly flinched; so, she furiously lashed out at him again, but this time Henry was far too quick and grabbed her arm, firmly holding it up in front of them both.

"You're hurting me," she winced, trying desperately to pull away from his bruising hold.

"If you ever do that again I shall take my belt to you. Do you hear me?" Henry roared angrily, harshly jolting her arm down to her side before releasing it. "I suggest you return to your room and regain your composure madam."

Iris was having none of it. After the events of the last twenty-four hours and the cauldron of emotions bubbling away inside her, she finally snapped.

"You brute," she spat out the words, lurching at Henry once again and viciously swiping her sharp fingernails down his cheek, drawing blood.

Henry had taken just about enough of her impertinent behaviour, grief stricken or not she needed to be taught a lesson. He immediately, and without warning, grabbed her towards him and forcefully pushed her down over the oak desk. Iris kicked and screamed and slammed her foot into his shins several times, struggling to break free from his iron grasp. Henry was far too strong and completely overpowered her. He held her down firmly across the desk with one hand, whilst unbuckling his belt with the other. The frogs slipped from the leather strap as his sword and dagger crashed to the floor. He was just about to lift her skirts when a loud voice pleaded from the doorway.

"Lord Morton … Please," Father Peter implored, desperately clasping his hands together.

It had the desired effect. Henry hesitated before finally releasing his hold on Iris. She crumbled to the floor in a heap. Henry slowly backed up, his belt still in his hand. Iris hastily scrambled to her feet, positioning herself safely behind the priest, still furiously angry and visibly shaking.

"Bring her under control Priest, I shall not hesitate again I promise you," Henry roared, turning his back on the pair of them.

Father Peter hurriedly ushered Iris from the study as quickly as possible before she could say something that they would all regret, sighing deeply to himself, knowing only too well this was far from over.

Kian entered the study, having witnessed the exchange. Henry was busy refastening his belt.

"Fuck me!" Kian exclaimed, observing Henry's bloody face. "She is one hell of a wild cat."

"Whatever or whoever she is, the sooner we bring her to Lorimer the better," Henry groaned, running his fingers through his hair; exasperated by the whole unpleasant incident. It seemed their journey east was going to be even more difficult and vexing than he had first imagined.

Chapter 7

Father Peter tentatively made his way to Iris's bedchamber the following morning, in the hope that she had calmed down after yesterday's quarrel with Henry. He had tried desperately hard the previous evening to explain the seriousness of the situation, which proved difficult given the fact that he wanted to spare her the truth, particularly of her brother's involvement. She could not or would not understand why he insisted that she travelled east with strangers instead of being allowed to go to Raven in Kingslea. Tired and frustrated he had eventually given up and had took himself off to bed. Thankfully upon being granted entry to her room, he found her up and dressed and in a much-improved mood. Although he was slightly taken aback by her flamboyant appearance. The dress she was wearing was not at all suitable for the long arduous journey ahead, but he decided against making any negative comment and was just relieved that she was ready to leave.

"Good morning, Father Peter," she smiled. "Do you like my dress?" she beamed, swirling around the room.

"Very nice," he replied, anxiously. "They are waiting for us Iris, are you ready?"

"Almost," she replied, whispering something in Kate's ear. The two women giggled.

Father Peter felt evermore uneasy.

Iris's dress of pale pink satin was embroidered with green ivy leaves and bordered with the most exquisite delicate lace. It fitted tightly to her slim figure; a cincture hung from her waist. Her maid then placed an emerald green velvet cloak over her shoulders as she slipped into a pair of elaborately decorated brocade shoes.

"May I ask how you acquired such a beautiful dress?" Father Peter asked, watching her nervously.

"Raven," she replied joyfully, "he sent it to me from Kingslea, is it not splendid?" she said, admiring herself in the mirror.

Kate finished off the look by fastening a pink chiffon veil, tied with a velvet ribbon over her long wavy auburn hair which had been plaited loosely at the back and entwined with even more ribbons.

"Are you sure you want to wear it today; it would be an awful shame if it were to be ruined?" The priest asked, in the faint hope she might be encouraged to change.

"Don't worry, Father Peter," she replied, kissing him on the cheek before skipping towards the door.

Father Peter was worried; he had an awful feeling the day was not going to end well and they hadn't even left Baines Abbey yet.

Henry, Arlen and Kian were already mounted on their horses and were waiting patiently at the front of the house when Iris and Father Peter appeared at the entrance. Henry glared furiously at Iris as she descended the steps in the ridiculously inappropriate pink satin dress. He considered, for just a moment, dragging her back up the stairs to change. He was still enraged by her arrogant contempt towards him the previous evening. He decided against it, not wanting to create any more unpleasantness and instead turned his horse and rode on up the hillside. Kian and Arlen could not help but smile. Iris was small of stature with a delicate pretty face; she did look rather lovely, however unsuitable her choice of attire – quite a transformation indeed from her nun's habit. Iris was all smiles and was looking relaxed. The altercation with Henry was seemingly forgotten, it appeared she had thankfully accepted her situation with good grace.

The riders all finally left Baines Abbey and headed south. On the brow of the hill Iris stopped and turned, looking down upon the grand house that had been her home for almost eighteen years. *Every step I take from this point on will be my first*, she mused silently to herself before picking up her pace to a canter and catching up with the rest of the travelling party.

Iris thought it wise to ride up front with Father Peter and Kian for the first leg of their journey, to be as far away from Lord Morton as she could manage, chatting and laughing as if without a care. Father Peter talked of Corstir; its history and people. Kian was especially interested and quizzed the priest intensely about the mysterious forest settlement. Father Peter began to suspect Kian may have been there before, when he was a young child perhaps. Kian said he was unable to remember much before his time at the orphanage. The priest suggested that he may recall more once they were actually there.

It was a beautiful warm sunny day, and the riders were making suitable time. Iris eventually plucked up the courage to relieve herself behind a bush on one of their refreshment stops, unable to prevent it any longer. Kian welcomed her back with a raucous cheer, causing her to blush scarlet red.

"Well done!" he cried. "You will be pissing with the rest of us before long."

"Really, Kian," Father Peter scolded. "A little decorum please."

Kian winked wickedly at Iris; she smiled back, still blushing and feeling a little self-conscious. She dared a glance over at Henry, he had not spoken to her all morning; in fact, he had hardly spoken a word to anyone all morning. He looked even more grand and imposing in his full Crown Knight livery, with a deadly serious expression. He caught Iris's eye, causing her to look away instantly and blushing scarlet once again.

As the travellers continued along the way, Henry and Arlen remained riding behind in silence. Henry briefly removed his tricorn hat in order to run his fingers through his hair. Arlen suspected something was wrong.

"What's wrong Henry?" he asked, certain that they were out of earshot of the riders up front.

"She is up to something," Henry growled with annoyance in his voice and glaring over at Iris.

"What do you mean?" Arlen asked, rather surprised, believing Iris to be more than content.

"Well, that bloody ridiculous dress for one."

"Oh, come on Henry, she has never set foot outside Baines Abbey in her life, she is just naive that's all. She looks lovely and if it makes her feel better, then what harm can it do? This cannot be easy for her, you know, it's only natural she would want to go to her brother. You have to admit that after what she did in the Abbey and the way she spoke to you last night; the girl certainly has spunk."

"Yes, I agree she was very brave in the Abbey, but it also proves she can be reckless, and as for the way she spoke to me, well, any man would have been arrested for less."

"Henry Morton, I do believe your pride has been dented, and by a young woman no less. It seems you may have finally met your match," Arlen laughed.

"Laugh all you like Arlen, but I'm telling you, naive she may be, but she is also clever and cunning and I suspect she is definitely up to something."

"Well, if that is true my friend, I'm more than thankful that she is your problem and not mine," Arlen grinned, rather amused by the whole thing.

"Umm," Henry muttered, women had never been 'problems' for him in the past and it was causing him much vexation. Henry demanded control and order, not disobedience and uncertainty. *The sooner they reached the East the better* he thought to himself.

As it fast approached midday, with the sun beating down mercilessly on the riders, it was time to get off the road to rest the horses and take refreshments. Much to Henry's relief Iris continued to appear more than happy with her situation, she was certainly enjoying the attention from the labourers in the fields, who cheerfully whistled to her as she rode past.

"Wychway ahead," Kian bellowed finally, picking up his pace slightly, his stomach rumbling.

They had been riding for around six hours when they reached the Wychway, an aptly named Inn situated next to a crossroads. This was where they would bid their farewell to Arlen as he continued his journey to Kingslea. Dismounting from their horses, Iris insisted on helping Kian lead them to the stables which were situated at the rear of the building. Henry, Arlen, and Father Peter promptly made their way inside to order much needed hot food and ale. Henry paid for a private room, away from prying eyes. Kian followed them about ten minutes later.

"Where the hell have you been?" Henry snapped. "How long does it take to stable horses?"

"For Christ's sake Henry, I've been for a fucking shit if you must know," Kian grunted back, annoyed by Henry's tone.

"Then where is Iris?" Henry asked, glaring past Kian towards the door.

"For fuck sake, she said she wasn't hungry so I left her in the stables."

Henry immediately shot from his seat; the three men hot on his heels. "She's gone!" he shouted, hurriedly running back from the stables. "Priest, you stay here. Arlen, Kian with me."

"Fuck!" Kian moaned, placing his hand to his head. "Where the fuck would she go?"

"Is it not obvious?" Henry yelled furiously, pointing a finger to the milestone in the centre of the crossroads, '*Kingslea 60 miles.*'

Arlen hastily ran back to the stables in order to retrieve the horses. "She's removed the saddles, the cunning little minx," he announced, quickly leading them out.

"I told you she was up to something didn't I?" Henry yelled, absolutely enraged. He had grown up riding bareback on the wild ponies that roamed the salt marshes on his families land on the west coast of Mercia. He swiftly swung himself up onto his horse, galloping fast along the road in the direction of Kingslea.

Kian followed not far behind him. Arlen, having never ridden bareback in his life, rushed back to the stables in order to retrieve his saddle and bags. Father Peter remained standing outside the Inn, anxiously clasping his hands together. "Oh, Iris what on earth have you done, you silly girl?" he muttered under his breath, lowering his head in prayer.

Iris was riding hard along the road to Kingslea, desperate to put as much distance as she could between herself and Henry Morton. The landscape looked vastly different from that of Baines Abbey, it was flat, no hills or thickets – she suddenly felt very exposed. Glancing over her shoulder several times, thankful that there was no sign of any riders on the road behind her, she breathed a deep sigh of relief.

Iris was a skilled horsewoman; she confidently continued to ride on hard, pushing her horse, three or four miles along the road, when suddenly she was forced to pull up. A flock of sheep were blocking her way and an old shepherd was furiously shaking his whip at her.

"Hey, you, pull back, you be frightening me sheep," he yelled at her angrily beneath his chaperon.

"I need to pass," she called over to him. "Please sir, it's very urgent."

"You ain't hurrying me sheep miss, no matter the urgency," he replied, still shaking his whip in the air.

There were stone walls either side of the road and Iris considered for a moment whether she could jump them. Concluding it was definitely possible, she began backing up her horse for a longer run up. All of a sudden she heard a rider on the road behind her. Not daring to look back, she kicked hard and her horse lifted its head to assess the wall before gathering power. Just as Iris loosened the reins, allowing the beast to raise its head and shorten its last stride, it suddenly dug its front hooves into the dirt, lurching forward before coming to a dead stop. It took Iris all her strength to remain seated. She had hardly time to catch her breath before Henry had reached her side, he roughly grabbed hold of her arm and pulled her from the saddle, unceremoniously throwing her to the floor.

"Don't you dare move," he snarled, glaring down at her, seething before striding off in the direction of the shepherd.

"Whip," he ordered to the old man, holding out his hand.

The shepherd handed it over without any hesitation.

Henry tapped it hard across the palm of his hand, "Good," he murmured to himself.

Iris watched in horror. She had absolutely no intention of staying put and, scrambling to her feet, she ran swiftly back along the road. Kian pulled up, stopping dead in front of her. She glanced back at Henry who looked so immensely angry and was now heading fast in her direction.

"Kian," she pleaded, desperately grabbing at his leg. "Please Kian, I'm sorry, don't let him …"

"Sorry miss," Kian replied, rather tersely, "you should not have run off like that, just grit your teeth lass and it will soon be over."

Before Iris had the chance to protest further, Henry had her pinned to the ground, lifting her skirts as he mercilessly delivered six punishing strokes. Iris sobbed uncontrollably as Henry picked her up off the floor and effortlessly hoisted her up on to Kian's horse.

"Take her back to the Inn," he ordered sharply, before leisurely strolling back towards the shepherd and handing back the whip.

"Thank you," he said with a brief smile, before throwing the old boy a sixpence.

"Thank you, milord," the shepherd replied, tipping his cap, before going on his way.

Arlen nodded to Kian as they passed on the road. He didn't need to ask what had happened. Iris was crying and she lowered her head despondently. Arlen continued further along the road until he reached Henry leaning up against the stone wall, running his fingers through his hair, holding Iris's pink chiffon veil.

"Are you alright?" he asked, jumping from his horse and joining Henry at the wall.

Henry shrugged his shoulders, running the chiffon veil through his fingers.

"You had no choice Henry," Arlen said, placing his hand to Henry's shoulder. "She needed to be taught a lesson, she could have put us all in danger."

"Yes, I know, but it doesn't make me feel any better … I knew the very moment we left Baines Abbey that she was up to something … Oh, Arlen, she made me so very angry."

"Well, let us hope she has finally learnt her lesson; I don't imagine she will be running off again in a hurry."

"No, quite, in fact I doubt she will be able to ride anywhere today. I'm afraid I didn't hold back; her backside will be smarting for days. Nobody has ever caused me to lose control in such a way before."

Arlen observed Henry closely. Iris Westonhall was certainly testing his friend to the very limit.

"What will you do now?" he asked.

"We shall have to remain at the Wychway tonight, although she will have to endure a few hours in the saddle tomorrow morning. But once we reach the forest, we shall be on foot the rest of the way … Anyway Arlen, enough about that, what about you? There seems little point in you returning to the Wychway, but you shall still need to rest your horse, it is a long ride to Kingslea. Do you have everything you need?"

"Yes thankfully, I already thought about that," Arlen replied, pointing towards his saddle bag. "I shall stop at the next Inn, don't worry about me … Henry, are you sure you know what you are doing going to Corstir?" Arlen asked with real concern in his voice.

"No, not really Arlen, but what choice do I have? I do trust the priest, I'm not sure why, but I do," Henry replied, turning to face his friend. "Arlen, you will be in Trevelyan, won't you?"

"Yes, of course Henry within the fortnight, I promise."

"Good … Thank you," Henry replied, exhaling loudly.

The two men embraced fondly before bidding each other farewell with hopes of a speedy and safe journey for both of them. Henry remained leaning against the wall; he watched as Arlen disappeared out of sight riding west. Then, tucking the pink chiffon veil into his pocket, he mounted his horse and, with Iris's horse in tow, slowly headed back towards the Wychway.

Father Peter was still waiting anxiously outside the Inn when Kian returned with a dejected Iris. He aided her in dismounting, supporting her as best he could – it was obvious she was in a lot of discomfort.

"Come," he whispered softly, "let's get you inside."

"I'm sorry Father," she sniffed, holding tightly onto his arm, the backs of her legs and buttocks stinging profusely.

Kian re-stabled his horse, muttering something obscene under his breath, before following the pair back inside the Inn. Iris couldn't sit down so remained standing in the corner of the private room; her head lowered, quietly weeping. Kian plonked himself down at the table, picking up his spoon. He lingered over his cold bowl of stew.

"Fuck!" he grumbled aloud.

Henry arrived back a while later and immediately ordered fresh hot food and ale, before sitting down beside Kian. Iris turned her back to him, feeling utterly ashamed and embarrassed.

"How is she?" he asked, removing his outer garments.

"Well, she has finally stopped fucking crying at least; she is going to need something for her sore arse," Kian grunted under his breath. "She certainly won't be able to ride any further today, that is unless you intend to punish her further."

"No, I do not. See if they have rooms will you, we shall stay here overnight," Henry replied. "Oh, and Kian, ask if they have any ointment and perhaps a clean dress."

"Fuck, Henry, anything else whilst I'm fucking up there?" Kian grumbled with a miserable scowl running across his face. He dropped his spoon into the cold stew before sauntering off towards the bar.

Father Peter joined Henry at the table. "Did you have to be quite so hard on her?" he asked.

"What would you have me do, Priest?" Henry snapped back. "She needed to be taught a lesson and she also needs to know the truth about her brother to put a stop to this bloody foolish notion she has of going to him in Kingslea."

"Yes, you're right, I'm sorry Henry. I should have told her the truth last night. She may not have been so reckless. I shall speak with her directly. I think we have all had quite enough of her silly ideas and we have a long arduous journey ahead even without all this unpleasantness."

"Good," Henry replied, eagerly tucking into his bowl of steaming hot stew. If nothing else, the episode had given him quite an appetite.

"They only have one room," Kian announced, throwing a key at the priest. "We shall have to sleep in the fucking stables. The Innkeeper's wife will bring a dress," he added, carefully placing another jug of ale and large jar of soothing ointment on the table.

"I'll take her up then," the priest declared, picking up the jar.

Henry nodded before leaning back in his chair and swallowing down a large cup of ale, relishing the taste of the robust flavoured bitter liquid. He allowed himself to finally relax for the first time all day.

Father Peter took hold of Iris's arm, leading her from the small private room up the stairs, which were situated at the rear of the Inn, to a small sparsely furnished, yet clean bedchamber. Even the soft linen chemise beneath her dress felt like tiny needles piercing her bruised buttocks and legs as she walked. Father Peter quickly ushered her inside the room and handed her the ointment.

"Here, you shall need to apply this, liberally," he said sharply. "You should be thankful Henry has agreed to remain here overnight, he could have insisted we continued on our journey today. I shall fetch you some food and once I return there is something very important that I have to say to you."

Iris nodded, feeling evermore dejected. She knew she was in serious trouble when even Father Peter struggled to converse with her in a civil manner. Once the priest had left, she took the jar of ointment and very carefully patted it tentatively on the back of her legs and buttocks, flinching at every delicate touch. Each punishing stroke of the whip had left a raised welt on her soft skin. The greasy substance did however have a cooling effect and soothed her injured body. Iris moved towards the window, which ironically overlooked the crossroads at the front of the Inn. She stood peering down at the milestone in the centre which was cruelly tormenting her. Tears began welling up in her eyes once more; she was beginning to feel really rather sorry for herself.

Father Peter returned directly carrying a tray of piping hot stew and a small loaf of bread and jug of ale.

"Here, you must eat," he said sternly, placing the tray on the table beneath the window.

"I'm not hungry," Iris murmured back, sounding morose.

Father Peter could delay no longer, unfortunately it was time Iris heard the truth about her brother.

"Well Iris," he began, "I had hoped to shield you from the truth, but after today's reckless behaviour, well, Lord Morton has insisted you know."

"Know what? What truth, what are you talking about?" Iris asked, crossing her arms defensively.

"The truth about your brother Iris. The men that came to Baines Abbey were not just bandits that happened upon the Abbey to cause mayhem and havoc in the hope of stealing some silver. Like I told the Abbess, they had come specifically to abduct you, Iris."

"What," Iris cried out, "What do you mean? What has this got to do with Raven?"

"There was an explosion in a town called Trevelyan on the south coast of Mercia. The cause is still unknown, but your brother was seen there moments before as well as the man with the scar at the Abbey. Lord Morton came to Baines Abbey in order to speak with your father as he quite rightly believed he could throw some light on these recent awful events. Your father was moments away from revealing the cause of the explosion when he was so brutally murdered. Whatever was contained in that small wooden box somehow held the key to this mystery. Your brother is the only person that could have taken the contents, he is most certainly involved in some way and whether his involvement is a consequence of purely innocent actions or he is complicit, that we do not know. But one thing is for certain Iris, it has resulted in putting you in extreme danger. Your father realised this at once, why on earth do you think he asked Lord Morton to grant you Crown protection? The explosion was like nothing ever seen before. If your brother and these men still have the means to cause such devastation, who knows what other untold atrocities they could wreak upon Mercia."

"But why on earth would they want me? I don't know anything." Iris whispered, still stood beside the window, staring down at the milestone.

"We don't know why; perhaps they believe your brother confided in you in some way, you had been corresponding with him in secret after all."

"Yes, that's true," Iris replied, suddenly realising why Lord Morton had been so interested in her brother's letters. "But I swear to you Father, I know nothing of what you speak. Raven wrote nothing of these events."

"Whatever the reason Iris, these men came for you. They are brutal murderers. Hundreds of innocent people lost their lives in Trevelyan; the carnage was unprecedented. If you were to go to Raven, presuming you were even able to find him, you would be throwing yourself at the mercy of these men, is this what you truly want Iris? Do you really think your brother can protect you, more so than Lord Morton?"

"I can't believe it, Raven is not a violent man, he is so kind and gentle," Iris whimpered, mortified by the priest's words.

"Yes, I agree with you Iris, but he is also extremely gullible and easily deceived, you know this to be true. How many times had your father had to intervene in one of his ludicrous schemes? Perhaps he got himself tangled up in this quite by accident, but the fact remains his actions have put you in great peril. What you did today was foolish and reckless, the situation could not be more serious. Iris you are better than this, where is the bright, intelligent young woman I know so well? What do you think your father would say if he could see you now? His dying words were to ensure your safety, asking Lord Morton to place you in Crown protection, and today you have so casually dismissed his wishes. Oh, Iris I'm so disappointed."

Iris remained staring from the window, she had never been scolded in such away before. Father Peter's harsh words pierced her heart. She suddenly felt so stupid and ashamed, what on earth had she been thinking? Of course, her father would never have insisted on Crown protection unless he feared for her very safety. Raven was an utter fool, she knew this to be true – she had always known this. However, her blind determination to quit Baines Abbey for a new life had, it seemed, caused all intelligent reason to temporarily desert her. After several minutes of silent contemplation, she turned sorrowfully to face the priest.

"Oh, Father I'm so sorry, I have been such a fool, haven't I? I have behaved no better than a silly spoilt child. Can you ever forgive me?" she whispered, tears filling her eyes.

"Oh, my dear child, I blame myself. I should have told you the truth right from the very start, but after losing your father so cruelly I thought only to protect you. Oh, Iris I'm sorry too … please pray with me."

Iris gently lowered herself to her knees, her tears now flowing freely. Father Peter gently placed his hand to her head as the pair both began to silently pray.

It was almost dusk, with the sun setting below the horizon in the west. Iris had been left alone in her room for the entire afternoon. She had used the time wisely reflecting on the last three days; the stew on the tray beneath the window untouched and stone cold. She thought of her father and how they had argued so in the weeks before his death. He had been absolutely right not to allow her to go to Raven. She had been blinded by her brother's letters describing life in Kingslea as if it were some magical fairy tale, encouraging her to abscond from her life at Baines Abbey. How stupid she had been to believe in his fantasies. She wished she could go back and tell her father how sorry she was and how very much she loved him. Tears welled up in her eyes once more. However, determined not to cry again, she sniffed and wiped her eyes on the sleeve of her silly satin pink dress which was now all torn and soiled. Her buttocks were beginning to sting once again; a constant reminder of her stupid, reckless behaviour. She blushed ashamedly as she recalled Lord

Morton whipping her in the road, tugging furiously at the dress to pull it from her shoulders – but the laces that fastened her gown ran down the back. She growled, cursing angrily to herself and admitting it would serve her right if she were to be trussed up in pink satin forever. Resorting to ruching up her skirts once more, she tentatively applied another layer of greasy ointment before standing beside the window peering out over the entrance to the Inn.

It was a lovely balmy evening and many of the customers had taken their seats outside to enjoy the pleasant warm air. Iris observed Lord Morton and Kian laughing together, drinking ale. Lord Morton appeared happy and relaxed, chatting away when he suddenly glanced up at Iris in the window. Iris quickly stepped back out of sight, not wanting to be seen. Moments later she dared to peer down at him once again, but he had gone.

A knock to the bedchamber door diverted her attention.

"Yes," she replied as cheerfully as she could, expecting it to be Father Peter.

Lord Henry Morton opened the door. He was smiling, his handsome features softened. The harsh scratch to his cheek still visible – another reminder to Iris of her unbecoming behaviour. *What must he think of me?* She thought to herself.

"Father Peter said you asked to see me," Henry spoke in his usual authoritative tone. "May I come in?"

"Yes," Iris replied, stepping back nervously, she was certainly not going to deny him entry.

She was however rather shocked by his presence and had not been expecting him to speak with her today, believing that he was far too angry.

"Please, you don't need to be afraid of me," he said, his tone now a little softer. He could clearly see she was frightened of him. "I understand Father Peter has spoken with you?"

"Yes, milord," Iris nodded, grateful for his calm demeanour. "I'm sorry Lord Morton. I'm sorry for my reckless behaviour today and I'm sorry for my blatant disrespect of you at Baines Abbey. I have no excuses for my actions, please forgive me," she blurted out as if her life depended on it.

Henry observed her closely. Her cheeks were flushed and her blue eyes were wide and dazzling in the dim candlelight. She looked defeated and so melancholy standing in her torn satin dress. After having been so furiously angry with her earlier in the day, Henry now felt quite sorry for her. After all her whole life had just been turned upside down in a matter of days.

"I accept your apology madam and I can promise you I shall not rest until I uncover the truth and know you to be safe. I am bound to protect you Miss Westonhall, which I will, with or without your approval. All I can say is that the journey east will be far less vexing if I have it."

"You do have it milord," Iris replied quickly, still uneasy in his presence.

"Good, I'm very pleased to hear it," he said with a smile.

A moment of awkward silence followed; Henry finally spoke. "How is your … how are you feeling?" he asked, awkwardly in an attempt to alleviate some of the tension between them. Henry was not good with polite conversation.

"Sore," Iris replied, blushing scarlet.

"Good … I don't mean good, I mean …"

Iris understood his meaning at once. "It's alright milord, I can assure you, I shall not delay our journey any longer."

"Good," Henry repeated, relief in his voice.

Another moment of awkward silence followed, as they both had their eyes fixed firmly upon each other.

"Oh, I have a dress for you," Henry said, breaking their gaze. "It's nothing special I'm afraid, but perhaps a little more practical." He handed Iris a plain grey woollen dress donated by the Innkeepers wife.

"Thank you," she replied, accepting the dress with a small curtsey.

"I shall bid you goodnight then. Oh, and please call me Henry, Crown Knights and Lords of Mercia are not welcome in the East … perhaps I may call you Iris?"

"Yes, of course, thank you Milor … Henry."

Henry smiled again, before turning to leave the room.

"Please wait," Iris asked her cheeks still burning.

Henry stopped; he turned back around to face Iris. Her melancholy gaze alluring.

"Can you help me?" she asked, squirming around, pointing to the laces that fastened her dress from behind. "I can't get out of this ridiculous dress."

"Oh, yes … yes, of course," Henry replied, slightly taken aback by the odd request.

Iris turned around, allowing Henry access to the laces at the back of her dress.

"Keep still," he said, gently moving her long auburn hair over her shoulders, then carefully using the tip of his dagger, he slowly cut through the laces. The sensation caused Iris to quiver. She pulled the dress from her shoulders, allowing it to drop to the floor. Then turning back around to face Henry, standing in only her under garments, she picked the pink satin dress up from the floor and held it out to him.

"Will you burn it for me please?"

"Yes, of course," Henry replied, taking the dress from her, their eyes locked again for just a fleeting moment.

Henry then gave a small bow before turning and leaving the room, closing the door firmly behind him. He stood on the landing outside the room, staring down at the pink satin dress in his hands. He held it to his face; it was still warm. *Who is this beautiful young woman that has been thrust upon me, testing and tormenting me, yet so utterly alone and innocent?* he mused to himself.

It was sunrise the following morning and Henry was in the bar talking with the Innkeeper, as Iris descended the stairs. The grey woollen dress was far too big for her, the hem dragged along the floor. Henry resisted smiling at her comical appearance and instead asked the Innkeeper for a belt or cord.

"Good morning," he said cheerfully through a smile, as she approached, hoping to start the day far less vexing than the day before. "Did you sleep well?"

"Not very, I'm afraid," she murmured softly, still looking rather melancholy.

Henry suspected her sore backside had something to do with that. "Have you eaten? We are leaving soon," he added.

"I'm not hungry, thank you," she replied, taking a belt from the Innkeeper and fastening it tightly around her waist and blousing the material over so the skirt didn't drag along the floor.

She glanced at Henry and smiled; he smiled back. "That looks much better," he remarked.

"We're ready Henry," Father Peter called from the doorway, breaking their gaze.

Henry was no longer dressed in his navy blue Crown Knight livery, instead he wore black breeches, a leather doublet over a simple white shirt and a black woollen cloak. His usual clean shaven appearance was now showing signs of stubble, his dark hair, all ruffled, contained strands of straw from a night in the stables no doubt.

Henry and Iris joined Kian and Father Peter outside. Henry immediately headed over towards Kian who was busy inspecting the horses. Iris watched him intensely, he looked so much younger without his Crown livery. He was still smiling and his manner was much more relaxed. He glanced back over towards Iris, catching her eye – she looked away blushing.

"It seems you may have tamed the wildcat," Kian commented, curiously observing his friend watching Iris.

"Umm," Henry mused, "Perhaps, or perhaps not, she may just be licking her wounds. We shall have to see."

"Does a leopard ever change its spots?" Kian added.

"Yes, quite," Henry replied, his eyes still fixed firmly upon Iris.

A scrawny young boy called Simon, who was the Innkeeper's nephew, was joining them on their journey, at least as far as the edge of the forest. He had been employed with strict instructions to deliver the horses to Blackmore Barracks once they had entered Corstir. Henry had paid him four crowns along with a letter containing instructions to pay him a further four crowns once he had fulfilled his commission, with a promise that if he ever spoke of it to anyone, Henry would find him. That thought alone was petrifying and it had resulted in rendering the poor boy dumb.

Kian was rather more miserable than usual this morning; having not had a lot of sleep. It seemed that he had engaged with other residents of the Wychway in a game of cards that had lasted almost the entire night, which resulted in Kian losing a lot of money and having very little to no sleep. Henry had absolutely no sympathy for him whatsoever as the pair exchanged a few choice words. The upshot was peace and quiet as they continued on their journey south, before turning east towards the forbidding forest.

Henry relished the silence; he began to wonder about Corstir. He had grown up hearing stories of gruesome forest dwellers, with large red eyes and fanged teeth that ate all the naughty children of Mercia. *They must be quite primitive people*, he thought to himself, *to survive in such a hostile environment.*

They were travelling heavily loaded; laden with tools, linens, brandy and numerous other offerings. He hoped the priest was as good as his word and four or five days hard labour would be all the payment required for their safe passage to the East.

His thoughts were then abruptly interrupted as Iris suddenly slumped forward in her saddle before very slowly slipping from her horse and landing on the ground hard. Father Peter instantly jumped from his mount and ran to her aid.

"She's fainted … I don't think she has eaten for days," he muttered, gently lifting her head onto his lap.

Kian handed him a flask of water. "Here, get her to drink," he moaned, still grumpy.

Iris very slowly came to, opening her eyes. Father Peter encouraged her to sip the water. After a short while he attempted to get her back on her feet, but she was still very unsteady – stumbling backwards and falling against him.

"She can't ride like this," he declared, holding her up in his arms.

"For fuck's sake," Kian growled, clicking his tongue. "More fucking delays," he muttered under his breath.

"Priest, lift her up, she shall ride with me," Henry insisted, pulling his horse around to their position.

Father Peter obeyed, lifting Iris onto Henry's saddle with ease. Iris groaned in a feeble protest, but Henry had already wrapped his arm tightly around her waist, holding her firm. Feeling far too weak to resist further, she conceded and leant back to rest her head against his chest. The smoky odour of his leather doublet, mingled with a sweet smell of vanilla was comforting. After the events of the previous two days, she felt surprisingly safe in his arms. She listened to the faint beat of his heart and could feel his warm breath against her neck.

"You must eat," he ordered, passing her a parcel containing a small loaf of bread.

Father Peter passed her the flask of water again and she took a few more sips before handing it back and opening the parcel to nibble on the bread.

After a couple of hours Iris finally began to feel a little better, the food and water had been welcomed and her head was beginning to clear. Her sore buttocks however were not. They were starting to uncomfortably sting once again, having not been able to apply any soothing ointment since leaving the Wychway. She began to annoyingly fidget in an attempt to get comfortable, irritating Henry as he pressed his hand hard against her waist.

"Keep still!" he insisted his tone sharp.

"I cannot," Iris snapped back at him, "I'm too sore, perhaps if you hadn't been so hard on me."

Henry glared down at her frowning. "Perhaps you shouldn't have run off," he said sternly. The wild cat was stirring it seemed. "Besides, we are almost at the edge of the forest," he said, his hand pressed firmly to her waist.

Iris lay her own hand over his and, leaning back against him, she looked upwards at the mighty Corstir Forest that loomed up in front of them. The trees were packed so closely together, they formed a thick canopy – there was nothing but black beyond the outer edge. The wind had picked up, whistling around them and the horses began to spin, their tails swishing. They certainly had no intention of getting much closer. Iris could not blame them. Her sore buttocks all but forgotten, she sat very still, pressing herself back against Henry as he tightened his grip around her waist for reassurance.

"Fuck me!" Kian exclaimed, turning his horse around to face Henry. "Are we sure about this?"

Henry stared up at the enormous mass of trees in front of him, packed together so tightly, all competing for sunlight as their canopy of leaves blocked out any hope of life on the ground. He had to admit he was not sure about anything anymore.

"No," he replied, "but we have no other option."

After dismounting the horses and removing all their belongings, Henry sent young Simon on his way. He was more than happy to quit the eerie surroundings. Kian looked glum as he watched him disappear into the distance, it was a long way on foot in any direction they decided to take from here on.

"Well, that's that!" he exclaimed. "What now Priest?"

Father Peter was busy heaving his bags onto his shoulder; he was keen to get moving. Navigating the dense outer edge of Corstir was the most arduous part of their journey.

"I shall lead you through the dense outer edge of the forest which encloses a steep-sided gorge, I can only take you so far, before I must leave you …"

"What the fuck?" Kian shouted, cutting the priest off mid flow.

"Kian, please, before I must leave you, for only a brief time, I have to descend alone, in order to gain permission to enter the settlement. You shall be quite safe, I can assure you. When I return, we shall be escorted the rest of the way; you will of course have to relinquish your weapons."

"Henry, for fuck's sake," Kian protested, loudly, throwing his arms up furiously into the air.

"Kian, please calm down, what use will our weapons be anyway? We shall be at their mercy as soon as we enter the forest. All they need do is abandon us, we would not survive more than two or three days at most," Henry said, placing his hand to Kian's shoulder in an attempt to pacify him.

"What happens if you are refused entry?" Henry asked.

"I would never be refused," the priest assured him with a broad smile. "My brother is chieftain."

"Father Peter," Iris whispered, nervously, "you would never abandon us, would you?"

"Oh, my dear child, never, I promise, trust me. Please all of you, trust me," he implored, clasping his hands together as if in prayer.

Henry ran his fingers through his thick dark hair, pausing for a moment and glancing over at Iris.

"Alright then Priest, lead the way," he said, gesturing towards the forest and collecting his belongings from the ground.

Kian reluctantly nodded in agreement, flinging his bags over his shoulder. Iris stepped backwards, glaring up at the great forest. She looked over at Henry, frightened and shaking.

"Come," he said softly, holding out his hand. "We shall enter together."

Iris gripped his hand tightly and, surrendering herself to Henry completely, followed him into the darkness of Corstir.

Chapter 8

Arlen arrived in Kingslea in the early hours of the morning and made his way directly to Barlett House. The Barlett family town house was located in the heart of Kingslea, a stone's throw from the Kilve Palace. He startled the young hall boy who fell from his perch beside the door, before climbing the stairs and immediately taking to his bed, utterly exhausted after the long journey from Baines Abbey. When he did finally awake it was early in the afternoon. The excellent May weather was holding and the sun was streaming through the window, warming his face. He had dreamt of Harriet; it had been nine days since the explosion and so much had happened. Slowly rising from his bed, he pulled the cord for the housekeeper. Wrapping himself in a red velvet embroidered housecoat, he sauntered over to the window and looked out over the bustling city. He began to wonder what Harriet might have made of the place; they had talked many times of visiting Kingslea. Arlen had promised to bring her, he had promised to buy her a new dress and take her to the Royal theatre. *How beautiful she would have looked* he thought to himself, watching the folk going about their business on the street below.

"You rang, sir," came a woman's terse voice from behind him, interrupting his thoughts.

Arlen quickly spun around. Mrs Brooke, the formidable Barlett housekeeper, stood in the doorway, her hands clinging to her hips, looking extremely irritated.

Mrs Brooke was an older woman. She had been in the Barlett employ for over forty years, after first arriving as a young shy scullery maid, working, at the time, for Arlen's grandparents. She was small in stature with sharp pointed features, her grey hair was always tied up high on her head and covered by a white lace cap. She was clearly annoyed by Arlen's unexpected arrival. Running the Barlett House with impeccable efficiency, her diminutive appearance was a disguise for the mighty Vikrin warrior that lay beneath.

"I'm sorry for my unscheduled arrival Mrs Brooke, are my father and brother in town?"

"Yes, sir, they are aware of your arrival, they left early this morning for court. I am expecting them both back for an early dinner this evening," she replied sounding cross, still with her hands clinging to her hips.

"Thank you, Mrs Brooke. Please may I have some food?" Arlen asked, turning his back on the woman, not daring to keep eye contact with her, "and perhaps some clean clothes … and a bath?" he cringed bravely beneath gritted teeth.

There was a moment of awkward silence. "Yes, sir," finally came her stern response.

Arlen swore he could feel her eyes boring holes into the back of his head and he sighed with relief once he heard the door close firmly behind her.

"Christ, that bloody woman is scary," he muttered quietly to himself.

Scary she may be, but there was no doubting her efficiency. Arlen's room was soon a buzz of activity; a young maid brought a tray of meats, bread and preserves along with a jug of fresh ale. Two burly young boys carried in the bath, rushing backwards and forwards filling it with steaming hot water. Arlen felt slightly uncomfortable demanding such excess in the middle of the day, but he was desperate to soak his aching limbs. Finally stepping into the large wooden tub, lined with linen cloth, he quickly sank down into the soothing hot water.

Having barely had time to close his eyes, the door to his bedchamber suddenly flung wide open. Startled, Arlen jumped up causing water to spill out all over the wooden floor.

"Christ, Arlen," Edwin bellowed loudly, from the doorway, certainly not expecting to see his brother standing stark naked in a bathtub.

"For God's sake Edwin, you could have knocked. Mrs Brooke shall be even more intolerable once she sees this mess. I already have scorch marks in the back of my neck when I asked for the bloody bath," Arlen moaned, staring down at the soaking wet floor.

"You're a braver man than I," Edwin laughed, making his way over to the bed. "By the way your wound seems to have healed nicely," he commented, observing Arlen's left thigh.

"Yes, thankfully," Arlen groaned, sinking back down into the hot water.

"I wouldn't get too comfortable, Father is waiting downstairs and wishes to speak with you."

"Oh, Christ," Arlen muttered, immersing his head beneath the water. "What have you told him?" he asked, finally coming up for air and shaking his hair furiously before placing his arms around the rim of the bathtub and leaning back against the linen cloth.

"Nothing. He suspects I know more than I am prepared to say. I imagine with your unplanned arrival he will at least be expecting some answers."

"Westonhall is dead," Arlen muttered with his eyes closed, still relaxing in the warm water.

"Christ Arlen, what the hell happened at Baines Abbey?"

Arlen eventually stepped from the bathtub and relayed the events of Baines Abbey to his brother as he dressed in clean clothes, courtesy of Mrs Brooke.

"So, what are you going to tell Father?" Edwin asked, leisurely lying back on the bed.

"That we travelled to Baines Abbey to enquire about Crowforth and to find out if there could be any connection to Trevelyan. I shall say that Westonhall was fatally injured by Northern raiders hours before we arrived, and that Henry has travelled further north in pursuit of the bandits."

"So, no mention of Iris Westonhall?" Edwin asked, curiously.

"No, Henry was quite insistent that her existence must remain a secret, at least for the time being," Arlen replied, now ready and waiting to go. "There is one other thing Edwin. Henry has issued an arrest warrant for Raven Westonhall. Can you possibly aid me in coordinating enquiries into his whereabouts, with only the most loyal of men?"

"Yes, of course, I understand your meaning. Crown Knight business only."

"Yes, exactly," Arlen nodded.

"Aid you or take charge?" Edwin asked with a broad grin.

"Oh, Brother you know you are far better at these kind of things than I am," Arlen replied with a huge smile.

"Very well little Brother," Edwin smiled back, placing his arm to Arlen's shoulder as the two brothers headed for the stairs.

Lord Douglas Barlett was standing next to a side table, on which a decanter of brandy sat, as his two sons entered the drawing room of Barlett House. He smiled with immense pride, considering himself a most fortunate man to have two such strong, strapping sons and both Crown Knights. Lord Barlett was a muscular looking man of average height. His once wavy fair hair was now thinning and tinged with grey. It was abundantly clear to see his sons had inherited his ruggedly handsome features. The Barlett boys were certainly strong, masculine, no nonsense men. Barlett was not only Lord President of the Privy Council but also a valued advisor and friend to the King.

"Arlen my boy," he beamed, embracing his son lovingly and stepping backwards to inspect him further. "You look tired, here take this," he said, passing Arlen a large glass of his finest Vikrin brandy.

"Hello, Father," Arlen replied, accepting the glass before settling himself down into an easy chair. "It has been an unusual few days to say the least," he sighed deeply.

"Yes, I can imagine. Your brother has quite eloquently relayed the events at Trevelyan to the Privy Council, but I am certain he knows more than he is letting on. I don't suppose you can enlighten me further?" his father asked, passing Edwin a glass of brandy.

"I'm afraid not," Arlen replied, slightly uncomfortable at not being able to bring his father into his confidence, but Henry had been most insistent.

Lord Barlett made no comment, he trusted his sons implicitly. He had faith in them and Henry Morton and believed that when the time was right, they would bring him into their confidence.

Arlen hastily relayed the erroneous account of Lord Westonhall's demise, passing his father a full report of the events written by Henry for the Privy Council.

"I do have another letter, Father" he added, hastily swigging down his brandy.

"Oh yes," Lord Barlett replied, eyeing his son curiously.

"It is for the King; I have been instructed to hand it to him personally."

"My, my, Henry Morton, does not trust anyone it seems," Lord Barlett mused, fully understanding Henry's cautiousness. He himself had an awful feeling the treachery inflicted on the Corridor was unfortunately much closer to home than anybody dared to imagine. "This is most irregular Arlen," he continued. "But I shall see what I can do. It does so happen that the Privy Council reconvenes later today. The King has negotiated an audience with an Ambassador from the East, he is due to arrive in Kingslea tomorrow. The decision, as you can quite imagine, has caused much vexation within the council. I may have the opportunity to speak with the King afterwards, he shall most certainly be interested to hear the views of the council on this particular matter."

"An Ambassador from the East?" Edwin asked, rather astonished. "For what purpose?"

"The King wishes to open negotiations with the Howards," Lord Barlett replied, rising from his chair in order to refill his glass with more brandy.

"Negotiations regarding the succession?" Arlen asked, as astonished as his brother. "Father, could this have something to do with the explosion in the Corridor?"

"Yes, this was Henry's theory right from the start," Edwin added.

"Yes, quite possibly. However, if it was, the plot failed, negotiations are still taking place."

"But Father, what if another attempt is made?"

"Calm yourself Arlen, I can assure you that every precaution is being taken and besides, if the explosion does relate to this matter, then it wasn't the Ambassador they were after, it was Lord Lorimer."

Arlen went to speak; his father raised an authoritative hand to stop him.

"I've said too much already, you concentrate on apprehending the perpetrators of the explosion and I shall deal with the Eastern Ambassador. One thing I can say, Henry Morton is quite right not to trust anyone."

It was by this time already late in the afternoon. Lord Barlett had requested an early dinner due to the reconvening of the Privy Council; Arlen and his brother had no objections, they were always ready for a tasty meal at Barlett House. The cook, like Mrs Brooke, was a master of her craft, she certainly knew how to feed hungry men. The three men eagerly sat down to a hearty dinner; they enjoyed roasted lamb followed by the cook's secret recipe for gingerbread, served warm with thick cream. Arlen deliberately kept his head down when Mrs Brooke enquired about the damp floor in his bedchamber. His father and brother roared with laughter once she had left the room. Douglas Barlett admitted that the woman also terrified him and had done since he was a young boy. However, according to his mother, and now his wife, good housekeepers were extremely hard to find and there was certainly no doubting that Mrs Brooke knew how to run a house.

"It is so good to have my boys here in Kingslea," Lord Barlett announced, casually leaning back in his chair and patting his full stomach. "It has been too long since we all dined together. Your mother will be so disappointed that she insisted on remaining at Wenlock Hall when I inform her that you are both here in town."

Ann Barlett was ten years younger than Douglas. A dainty woman, who was charming and unassuming. Their wedding had been arranged by their prospective families; Ann being betrothed to Douglas from birth. Over the years they had grown to love each other very much; their marriage was a happy one.

"Unfortunately, I shall have to take my leave," Lord Barlett announced finally. "The Privy Council waits for no man," he said, slowly rising from his chair. "Whatever you know, or do not know, please take care, your mother would never forgive me if anything were to happen to either of you. Oh, and Arlen, I shall attempt to secure an audience with the King," he added, making his way towards the door.

"Thank you, Father," Arlen replied, respectfully.

Lord Barlett then promptly finished off the last of his brandy and placed the empty glass on a side table near the door before bidding his two sons a good evening and swiftly leaving the room.

"Come Arlen," Edwin said the instant their father had left and hastily jumping to his feet. "We should go also; we need to make some discreet enquiries I believe?"

"Yes, indeed Brother, lead the way," Arlen replied, popping the last slice of gingerbread into his mouth.

"Hey, I had my eye on that," Edwin joked, placing a friendly punch to his brother's shoulder as they exited the dining room.

The two men walked the short distance from Barlett House to the Crown Knight headquarters located in the grounds of the Kilve Palace. A practical group of long buildings consisting of administration offices, apartments for Crown Knights stationed at Kingslea and barracks for the Crown Soldiers. Edwin, being the most senior Crown Knight at court with the absence of Henry, had more than a full workload. The men all jostled for his attention as he entered. He raised his hand dismissing them all and instead directed his gaze towards a Crown Knight stood behind one of the desks at the far end of the room.

"Phillip, please join me in the office," he said, heading for a private room to the right of the administration area.

"Phillip, you know my brother," Edwin said, gesturing towards Arlen and firmly closing the office door behind them.

"Yes, sir," Phillip replied, nodding his head at Arlen.

"Oh, of course you do, how foolish of me, he's marrying your sister," Edwin laughed loudly.

"Hello Phillip," Arlen replied, also with a nod of his head.

Phillip Ainsworth was the twin brother of Beatrice and the second son of Lord Hagan Ainsworth. A man of average height, with a stocky build. His raven black hair was worn long and swept back on the top of his head, the sides cropped short; his hair colour was the only real resemblance to Beatrice. Phillip had a reputation of being rather a callous man, not liked by many of the other men who tended to keep their distance from him. Edwin however rated his no-nonsense approach and found him to be quite amenable – he certainly got a job done, which made him more than suitable for the task in hand.

"Phillip, I shall get straight to the point," Edwin continued most efficiently. "Lord Henry Morton has issued an arrest warrant for Raven Westonhall. I would like you to select a handful of our most loyal men to ascertain his whereabouts post haste. It is also imperative we act with the utmost discretion."

"Yes, of course sir," Phillip replied, a hint of hesitancy in his voice.

Arlen thought Phillip appeared slightly troubled by the order, as he had turned a little pale. He continued to observe him closely as Edwin relayed a brief account of the known facts, omitting any mention of Iris and, of course, Henry's true whereabouts. What he did hear seemed to put him at ease. Arlen thought his reaction was a trifle bizarre.

Once Edwin had finished speaking, Phillip turned to leave.

"Oh, and Phillip, put the word out with some of the young urchins, will you?" Edwin added, throwing him a leather purse full of coins. "A few crowns might help to speed things up."

"Yes, sir," Phillip replied, before giving a small bow and promptly leaving the room.

"Now we wait," Edwin declared, sinking into the chair behind the desk.

Arlen stared around the room. It was so obviously Henry's office – there was a place for everything and everything was in its place. He could not help but smile to himself at the excessively neat and precise order. It was no wonder, he thought to himself, that his brother looked so at home sat behind the desk.

"What are you smiling at like a fool?" Edwin asked, eyeing his brother quizzically.

"Nothing Brother," Arlen replied, deliberately sitting down at the edge of the desk and disturbing the neat piles of paper.

"Move," Edwin snapped most indignantly, pushing his brother from the desk and immediately bringing it back to order.

Arlen grinned to himself, then after skulking around for a while doing nothing more than annoying Edwin, he decided he may as well head home – Edwin was more than thankful to get rid of him. He had a mountain of paperwork to trawl through and he promised to inform Arlen as soon as he had any news.

Arlen curiously spied Mrs Brooke bobbing up and down looking most perturbed in the doorway of Barlett House as he hastily approached.

"Mrs Brooke, what on earth is the matter?" he asked, racing to the bottom of the steps.

"Oh, Master Arlen, your father has just sent word, you are to attend court this very instant, the King … the King!" she blurted out with excitement, her pointed nose twitching. Mrs Brooke appeared flustered. She hadn't called Arlen 'Master Arlen', clearly a term of endearment, for a very long time. It took a King no less to penetrate her hard exterior. Arlen smiled.

"Thank you, Mrs Brooke, I shall go directly," he replied, a little taken aback at the rapid response, but more than pleased all the same.

Lord Douglas Barlett was waiting impatiently, pacing the grand hall of the Kilve Palace as his son eventually arrived. The lavish space was exceptionally large and imposing with an impressive ornate coffered ceiling. Colourful tapestries, depicting images of the civil war, hung from the walls. Long tables lined the outside edge, with court clerks furiously scribbling in notebooks, chatting and debating. Other members of the royal household staff were milling around cleaning and clearing the tables. Arlen was relieved to see there were no other members of the Privy Council in attendance.

"Arlen, good," Lord Barlett exclaimed, upon observing his son. "Hurry," he said. "The King has agreed an audience, he is waiting for you in the watching chamber, make haste, it is late," his father implored, gripping hold of Arlen's arm and literally pulling him along.

"I was not expecting such a swift decision Father," Arlen declared as the two men hastily raced along a wide corridor just off the grand hall.

"I have to admit I was rather surprised myself, but the King was most insistent," his father replied, still clinging to Arlen's arm.

Lord Barlett then suddenly stopped in his tracks, pointing towards a court guard. "Go," he said, hastily pushing Arlen forward. "Hurry!"

Arlen nodded to his father, feeling slightly nervous before following the guard in the direction of the grand watching chamber. They passed many other rooms with their colourfully painted doors firmly closed as they continued, heading deeper into the heart of the Kilve Palace. Two Crown Knights stood to attention at the chamber entrance, controlling all access. Only visitors of high rank or by order of the King himself were granted entry. Upon eyeing Arlen, they immediately knocked three times before opening the large intricately carved double doors. The court guard stopped, motioning for Arlen to continue on alone. He now suddenly felt extremely nervous, clutching Henry's letter in his sweaty palm.

The grand watching chamber was much smaller than the grand hall, however the decoration was breathtaking. The ceiling and elaborately panelled walls were gilded in the richest gold, with mouldings of roses painted red and white. A row of stools either side of the room were upholstered in the most sumptuous red velvet, which matched the red velvet carpet covering the centre floor and leading to raised steps and a canopy draped in purple silk damask. A large decorative hanging frame holding well over one hundred candles sent an arc of brilliant gold dancing off every surface. Arlen could not help but gasp at the brilliant splendour.

King Osbert sat directly opposite the large double doors. Draped in a rich purple cloak trimmed with sable and lined with miniver. His throne, gilded in gold, was also upholstered in rich red velvet. A high back adorned with a pair of mythical winged creatures, their forked tails entwined around the arms of the magnificent chair. Osbert was slender, his appearance attractive yet frail. A shy, sensitive man possibly due to his stammer. He wore his dark hair long, well below his shoulders and immaculately curled. He sported a goatee beard and an impressive handlebar moustache. He gently pulled at the tip of his beard as Arlen approached.

Arlen gave his deepest bow. He had observed the King on many occasions, but only from a distance, never so close and so intimate; he felt extremely privileged to be in his presence.

"Your Majesty," he said, holding Henry's letter aloft.

The King remained silent as he rose from his throne and slowly descended the steps. His high-heeled purple shoes were encrusted with jewels that sparkled in the candlelight, reflecting colourful rays over the red velvet carpet.

"You m-m-may r-rise," he instructed, coming to a stop in front of Arlen.

Arlen handed him the letter and stood to attention and waited.

The King appeared to read and re-read the letter several times. Arlen observed him very closely, watching as his face seemed to turn pale as if in shock, his breath quickening. Turning back around to ascend the steps, he stumbled forward. Arlen reacted instantly, steadying the King and aiding him back to his throne.

"T-t-t-thank you … you were at B-B-B-Baines Abbey?" the King enquired, still looking terribly pale.

"Yes, your Majesty," Arlen replied, wondering what on earth Henry could have written in the letter to cause the King such distress.

Arlen knew Henry had relayed a precise, exact account of the events at Baines Abbey. He was also aware that Lord Westonhall had been a lifelong friend to the King, but even so, the King's apparent anguish was quite odd indeed.

"I w-w-w-want to know the m-m-moment Raven Westonhall is apprehended," the King demanded, dismissing Arlen with a wave of his hand.

"Yes, your Majesty," Arlen replied, quickly bowing himself out of the room.

* * *

Raven Westonhall impatiently paced up and down a gloomy and drab room at a cheap boarding house in Goring End. A rundown area of Kingslea on the east of the River Rame. He had been hiding out here for the past week, having quit Trevelyan, fearful and in a hurry. Picking up his third bottle of brandy in as many days and emptying what was left of the contents into a glass, he anxiously glared from the window. Raven was becoming increasingly frantic at the lack of word from his lover, to whom he had so willingly aided in bringing about the dreadful events in Trevelyan. He continued to pace up and down the room, pausing every few minutes to peer from the window onto the street below in the faint hope of catching sight of his lover returning to him.

"Where are you?" he cried out, gulping down the last remains of the brandy.

Raven had become acquainted with his lover via a friend, a young man calling himself Charles three months earlier in the Corridor. Charles wasn't his real name, but Raven cared little as they had been instantly attracted to each other. Spending an entire week together holed up at an Inn overlooking the ocean in Trevelyan, they made love and consumed large amounts of alcohol laced with poppy tears. Raven became very quickly infatuated with Charles, happy to bend to his will, acting blindly to his many demands without question or any hesitation.

"Where is who?" Came a familiar silky voice suddenly from the doorway.

Raven spun around startled, dropping his brandy. The glass shattered into tiny pieces all over the floor.

"Clumsy," said a handsome young man, smiling back at him.

"Oh, Charles, where have you been?" Raven demanded, throwing himself at the young man, embracing him tightly and showering him with kisses. "I have been so worried, I kept imagining you had been killed in Trevelyan."

"My darling Raven, you know it is not so easy for me, I got here as soon as I could," the young man replied, throwing off his outer garments and placing a new bottle of brandy on the table beside the bed.

"The explosion," Raven exclaimed. "What have we done? I would never have agreed if I had known the extent of the devastation, please tell me you didn't know?"

"Calm yourself my darling, of course not, how could I? But Raven it is done now, please, you must not fret. Nobody has any idea who caused the explosion or how. We must remain calm, it can only play to our advantage. You will see, all will be well," the young man replied, placing a lingering kiss to Raven's lips. "You do trust me don't you Raven?" his lover asked, gently cupping his face in his hands.

"Oh, yes, yes of course Charles, of course I do. It's just that I have been here all alone, worrying, longing for you to come to me. I love you Charles, I've missed you so much."

"Well, I'm here now, and I have missed you too, desperately," the young man whispered seductively, pulling Raven towards the bed.

Charles sat down; Raven remained standing. Charles smiled up at Raven from the bed then very slowly began to untie the laces of his breeches.

"Well, well, I can see you are indeed very pleased to see me," Charles grinned, cupping his hands around Raven's buttocks, pulling him even closer before taking him gently into his mouth.

The two men spent the rest of the night making love, in between drinking large amounts of brandy laced with poppy tears.

"I love you, Charles," Raven whispered, sometime during their third encounter, kissing his lover passionately. "All will be well, won't it?" he asked again.

"Yes, my love, of course it will. Admittedly the explosion was far more immense than we could have ever imagined, but it is done now. The Crown fumbles around in the dark, they know nothing believe me … Now please Raven stop this continual fretting, I don't like it and besides, it's so unattractive," Charles snapped, becoming exasperated by Raven's persistent need for reassurance.

Raven managed a smile, for appearances sake only, before rising from the bed in order to relieve himself; he was trying desperately hard to dismiss the dreadful images from the Corridor that continued to whirl around his head and wishing beyond anything else he had not involved his sister in this most grim affair. It seemed Raven Westonhall had got himself mixed up in something quite serious and he doubted that even his father would have the ability to bail him out this time.

"Raven, what are you doing?" his lover called out. "Come back to bed."

Raven obeyed and climbed back into bed and into the arms of his lover. At least now with Charles here he felt safer as the pair finally drifted off to sleep in the early hours of the morning.

Chapter 9

It was barely light when a soft tapping noise came from the boarding house bedchamber door. Raven stirred, but Charles was already up and dressed in only his rich silk shirt. He bent down over the bed, kissing Raven gently on the lips. "Stay in bed my love, I shall see who it is," he whispered softly with a smile.

Upon opening the door, Charles briefly glanced back at Raven – he was no longer smiling as he stepped from the room out onto the landing and firmly closing the door behind him. Raven stretched leisurely in the bed, his nerves finally beginning to settle a little. Reaching for the bottle of brandy on the table, he poured himself a large glass, straining to hear what was being said outside the door. He wondered to himself who on earth it could be, he thought only he and Charles knew about Goring End. Whoever it was they seemed to have an awful lot to say. Raven very quickly became impatient. Rising from the bed and wrapping himself in a sumptuous velvet housecoat he moved towards the door, just as it reopened.

"Wait here," Charles said to the visitor sounding cross, before stepping back inside the room and closing the door behind him.

"Who is it, Charles?" Raven asked, concerned by the serious look on his lovers face.

"I have some unwelcome news, I'm afraid," Charles replied gravely. "It seems your father is dead, and your sister has disappeared."

"What … how … my God, no this cannot be," Raven muttered, overcome with anguish at Charles's dire words. He staggered backwards, falling down upon the bed.

Charles remained silent, seemingly in contemplation, and gave Raven an indifferent shrug of his shoulders. Raven hadn't observed his lover's strange reaction to the news. Charles slowly moved towards the window, picking something up from the dresser as he passed.

"There is more," he said, his tone cold as he stared absently from the grubby, cracked window down onto the busy street below. "There is a warrant out for your arrest, issued by Lord Henry Morton."

"What!" Raven screamed, now suddenly beginning to tremble. He swiftly rose from the bed and joined Charles at the window.

"It seems Morton was with your father when he was killed."

"What do you mean? Does Henry think I had something to do with the death of my father?" Raven cried out, visibly shaking. "I shall go to him at once … sort this out … find out what is going on."

"He is not in Kingslea, we don't know where he is, and he must have taken your sister," Charles replied, gently stroking Raven's face and staring deep into his tearful eyes with a mock sympathy. "You were seen in the Corridor my darling."

"No!" Raven protested, turning quite pale at this latest revelation. "Oh, I feel sick," he declared, cupping his hand to his mouth.

"Yes, it is true my love. Sir Arlen Barlett was with Morton at Baines Abbey, he saw you in the Corridor."

"Yes … yes, he did," Raven sniffed, recalling his brief conversation with Arlen. He shivered from the chilly air whistling through the broken window. "But he cannot link me to the explosion. Besides I shall deny it, you said yourself the Crown are fumbling in the dark."

"Perhaps they cannot link you to the explosion my darling, but they can certainly link you to me," Charles whispered, placing a cold kiss to Raven's lips.

"But I would never betray you Charles," Raven declared with sincerity in his voice. "Never … I love you."

"I know you love me, Raven; I know you would never willingly betray me, but you are weak, and they have ways of making weak men talk."

"What do you mean?" Raven implored, desperately clinging to Charles's shoulders. His blood ran cold.

Charles laughed a cruel, sinister laugh. "Torture you ridiculous fool," Charles replied, Raven was now nothing more than an object of his ridicule.

"No … it's not possible; we no longer condone torture in Mercia."

Charles laughed again, loudly and even more mockingly. Raven froze. It finally dawned on the simple fool that this man who stood in front of him, calling himself Charles, didn't love him at all, he had merely used him for his own wicked end.

"Oh, Raven, you really are utterly absurd, aren't you?" Charles grinned just before ruthlessly driving a dagger hard between his ribs, twisting and thrusting it deep into Raven's slender frame.

Raven let out a high-pitched scream, his pitiful eyes wide, helpless and betrayed. Charles continued to hold him tightly in his arms, callously kissing his lips until he felt Raven's body slump as he finally breathed his last pathetic breath.

Charles then promptly released his hold, allowing Raven's body to heartlessly drop to the floor with a thud and casually pulled out the dagger and wiped it clean on his sumptuous velvet housecoat.

He hurriedly returned to the door, flinging it wide open and allowing the waiting visitor on the landing to step inside the room.

"The Landlord?" he said, hastily dressing himself.

"He won't talk," the other man replied, eyeing Raven's dead body beneath the window. Raven had once been his lover too.

"Good … Insurance!" Charles demanded, holding out his hand.

The other man passed him a letter, the seal having already been broken. He hastily placed it on the table beside the bed, propping it up against the near empty bottle of brandy. The two men then took a final look around the room before exiting and closing the door firmly behind them.

* * *

The Lords on the Privy Council were all assembled after abandoning the meeting the previous evening due to too many frayed tempers. Unfortunately, the privy chamber was again filled with the raucous sound of council members all competing to be heard. Lord Barlett, the Lord President of the Council, was attempting to bring the room to order, unsuccessfully. Finally he resorted to slamming his fist down on the table, causing the glasses to shake and clink precariously together.

"Gentleman, please," he bellowed. "The King shall be here directly; can we please bring this meeting to order."

The men thankfully all began to quieten, taking their seats at the long oak table, which was piled high with papers at the centre of the room.

"Thank you, gentlemen," Lord Barlett said with a huge exasperated sigh of relief and wiping his brow on a handkerchief. He took his seat at the far end of the table. "As you are all aware," he continued, "an Ambassador from the East shall be arriving here today. I have already received word that he safely entered Mercia yesterday via the Corridor. His name is Sir James Ripley. He is uncle to Lord Sebastian Howard, on his mother's side."

"What else do we know of this man?" one of the other members shouted out across the table.

"Not very much I'm afraid," Lord Barlett replied, "We know he fought in the civil war, for the East, obviously. He was severely burnt at the battle of Crowforth and his injuries are quite disfiguring by all accounts, which cause him to wear a leather mask in order to conceal his face. Only his left eye is visible, having unfortunately lost the right. Ripley has been guardian to Sebastian since the boy was eight years old, following the death of his father – the King's cousin, Lord Matthew Howard."

"Why on earth is the King entertaining an audience with this man?" Lord Gilmore complained.

"Thomas," Barlett replied, "You know why, the King wishes to know of Sebastian."

"To reinstate his claim to the throne no doubt," he hissed, most indignantly and throwing his arms up in the air.

"Perhaps," Barlett replied. "As you know we have been unable to agree a line of succession; Mercia needs to know that the Crown is secure and that we have future stability. We are vulnerable without it. The Vikrin Ambassador already writes of uncertainty and turmoil, a united Mercia can only ensure our strength."

"And how do we know what the Vikrin Ambassador writes?" another member shouted loudly.

"Because I read all his letters before they are despatched," Barlett replied, knowing only too well that the council relied upon it.

A disapproving groan rumbled around the room; Lord Barlett completely ignored the blatantly false disapproval by his fellow Lords.

"But can we trust the East? Ivan Lorimer still rules, what word from him? Has he not just blown-up hundreds of his own people in that disgusting Corridor market. Not to mention the many good people of Mercia caught up in this foul atrocity?" Gilmore growled, frantically raising his arms up and down, rousing support from the other council members.

"We have no evidence that Lorimer was responsible for what happened in Trevelyan," Barlett roared over the din of raised voices. "Gentlemen please!"

"And we have no evidence to say he was not. However, I have to say, if I had had the means, I would have done it years ago," Gilmore scoffed, with a huge grin plastered across his face, now playing keenly to the room.

"Lord Gilmore, some compassion please for all those lost innocent souls," Douglas Barlett complained, becoming evermore exasperated as the proceedings threatened to spiral into chaos once more.

"Compassion!" Gilmore protested, followed by murmurs of agreeing Lords.

"Gentlemen, please!" Barlett objected vehemently, eventually bringing the room back to order. "I am sure the perpetrators responsible for the atrocity in Trevelyan will soon be apprehended, it is only a matter of time. We cannot allow falsehood to influence our decisions," he implored to the grumbling Lords.

"Our decisions or the King's," Gilmore snarled, still attempting to court attention. "Who is this young man Sebastian? He cannot be more than a child. To even consider him as our future King is ludicrous. You talk of stability, but we shall be even more vulnerable than ever."

"Yes," another member shouted, "What does this boy know of Mercia? Ludicrous indeed."

"Sebastian is twenty years old milord, he is no child," added Barlett, beginning to lose his patience.

Gilmore was certainly gaining support from the older members of the council who were cheering his comments with enthusiasm.

The Privy Council appeared more divided than ever over the great matter regarding the succession. Lord Gilmore, it was agreed, had a genuine claim to the throne having traced his family bloodline back to King Alfred, Charles's grandfather. Hatred for Lorimer and the East was still prevalent at court, but Gilmore was unpopular too. Lord Barlett believed that if push came to shove Gilmore would win out amongst the members of the Privy Council. Unfortunately, the King did not favour this decision at all. The King, rarely at odds with his advisors, had been the primary instigator in bringing about the arrival of Sir James Ripley to Mercia, having written firstly to Lorimer and his aunt, Margaret Howard more than a month previous. Lord Barlett was beginning to suspect that the King had already made his decision; bringing James Ripley to court was but a formality. If this was truly the King's wishes then Barlett hoped to be able to finalise arrangements sooner rather than later as a resolution needed to be agreed post haste. All this suspicion and infighting within the council was causing him much vexation.

The large double doors to the Privy Chamber suddenly swung open and all the Lords rose to their feet at once. King Osbert walked briskly into the chamber, looking rather gaunt but with a certain bounce in his step. He sat in the large elaborately carved chair at the head of the table indicating for everyone to sit.

"Your Majesty," Lord Barlett said with a deep bow, "I have received word. Sir James Ripley arrived safely in Mercia yesterday. He should be arriving in Kingslea within the hour, do you require any specific arrangements?"

"N-n-no, thank you Douglas," the King replied, pulling at the tip of his beard. "Oh, Douglas, p-p-please ask your s-s-son to j-j-join us in the w-w-watching chamber."

"Yes, of course your Majesty," Barlett replied, somewhat surprised, but not needing to ask which son. Henry Morton's letter seemed to have had quite an unusual effect on the King.

The King then immediately rose and departed the privy chamber as quickly as he had arrived and made his way to the watching chamber, in preparation for the arrival of the Ambassador. Members of the Privy Council followed in hot pursuit.

"Why does the King want Edwin in the watching chamber?" Thomas Gilmore hissed, grabbing at Barlett's arm and forcefully holding him back.

"Not Edwin, Arlen," Lord Barlett replied, promptly removing Gilmore's arm and leaving the arrogant little man opened mouthed and with no other explanation.

Arlen was skulking around Henry's office at the Crown Knight headquarters, becoming increasingly frustrated at the lack of any information regarding the whereabouts of Raven Westonhall. Edwin was keeping himself busy by deputising in Henry's absence and cursing Arlen for getting under his feet. Totally fed-up, Arlen decided to head back to Barlett House just as a young fresh-faced court guard burst into the administration office. Crown soldiers reacted to the intrusion by swiftly unsheathing their swords, causing the young boy to fall to the ground quivering in terror.

"Please, I'm here for Sir Arlen Barlett," he blurted out, cowering miserably on the floor.

"You stupid bastard, we could have killed you," a Crown soldier growled, holding his hand out in order to aid the boy to his feet.

The young boy turned scarlet red – made worst by the roar of laughter from the other soldiers present.

"I'm Barlett," Arlen replied, standing in the office doorway. "What do you want?"

"The King, sir, he requests your presence, immediately, in the watching chamber," the young boy blurted out.

Arlen glanced over at his brother, both men shrugging their shoulders, bewildered by the strange request.

"Please sir, come at once," the boy insisted, urgently dancing up and down on the tips of his toes.

"Yes, yes lead the way," Arlen replied, grabbing his tricorn hat and hastily following the boy towards the door.

When Arlen had been in the grand space the previous evening it was empty, this afternoon it was literally bursting at the seams. Finally spotting his father over the other side of the room he skilfully made his way around the perimeter virtually unnoticed, sidling up to his side. Lord Gilmore however had spotted him at once, having been waiting for his arrival. He glared at Arlen suspiciously.

"What's going on, Father?" Arlen asked, sensing the air of excitement and anticipation whirling wildly around the lavish space.

"The Ambassador from the East, Sir James Ripley, is here," his father replied, patting his son affectionately on the back, thankful he had arrived so swiftly.

"Why am I here?" Arlen asked, unable to understand the need for his presence.

"I have absolutely no idea," his father replied. "I was hoping you could tell me."

Arlen shrugged his shoulders. "Not a clue," he said, shaking his head, baffled.

The room suddenly hushed as the occupants all moved backwards from the centre allowing the herald to announce the arrival of the Ambassador.

Sir James Ripley confidently strode into the crowded room. He was a tall and a well-built physically strong looking man. Impeccably dressed, he wore an embellished doublet trimmed with gold and containing pinking which revealed a crimson silk. His surcoat depicted the emblem of the Lorimer family; a coat of arms supported by two white horses and the motto '*servus fidelis*', which meant faithful servant. The black leather mask covering his entire face bar one eye added yet another layer of mystery to the man, causing a hushed gasp to ripple around the room. Standing tall in front of the King, Ripley placed his hands to his side and lowered his head in the deepest of bows.

"Your Majesty," he said, his voice low and commanding.

"Sir ... Ripley," the King replied, slowly and deliberately so as to reduce the symptoms of his stammer. He raised his hand, indicating for Ripley to rise. "You ... are ... most ... welcome," he continued.

"Thank you, sire. It is a great honour to be granted such an audience with your Grace. Lord Lorimer and Lord and Lady Howard also send their most gracious thanks," Ripley replied, not once taking his eye from the King.

Lord Barlett pushed himself forward and stood at the foot of the steps to the throne.

"Sir Ripley, my name is Lord Douglas Barlett, if you would be so kind as to follow me, the King wishes to speak with you in his private chambers."

Grumbling murmurs of disapproval rippled throughout the room; the King stood up, instantly suppressing the sound. He slowly descended the steps muttering something in Barlett's ear before exiting the watching chamber into his private rooms at the back.

"Please Sir Ripley, if you would follow me," Lord Barlett requested, frantically signalling for Arlen to join them.

Lord Gilmore was utterly beside himself with anger, furiously elbowing past the other Lords, before storming from the grand room in fury.

Arlen hurriedly followed the three men, entering into another spacious corridor at the rear of the watching chamber. Lord Barlett nodded to his son with approval before leading Sir Ripley into yet another room further down the corridor. The King held back; he approached Arlen.

"T-t-t-tell me," he asked inquisitively, "the W-W-W-Westonhall girl, how o-o-old is she?"

Arlen stood utterly dumbfounded, why on earth was King Osbert asking about Iris Westonhall? He tried very hard not to portray the astonishment on his face. "I'm not sure, your Majesty, possibly seventeen, eighteen," he replied, after giving the question some thought.

"And her a-a-a-appearance?" the King continued, staring at Arlen intensely, causing him to feel extremely nervous.

"Umm, she is pretty, she has large vibrant blue eyes, long wavy auburn hair, she is small in stature ... wilful, yes definitely wilful and headstrong," he added with a smile.

"Wilful?" the King asked curiously. "How so?"

"Oh," Arlen hesitated, suddenly recalling Iris bolting from the Wychway. Deciding it perhaps prudent not to mention that, and the fact that Henry proceeded to chastise her in the road. "She took a bit of persuading to travel east, your Grace."

"I see ... t-t-t-thank you," the King replied with a half-smile, leaving Arlen standing alone in the spacious corridor, even more bewildered than he was already,

Arlen eventually managed to navigate his way out of the warren of corridors inside the Kilve Palace and back to the Crown Knight headquarters. He was at an utter loss to understand the King's interest in Iris Westonhall. She had lived at Baines Abbey all her life in relative obscurity, now it seemed the whole of Mercia had an interest in her. *Perhaps Henry was on to something,* Arlen thought to himself, *I shall endeavour to find out what I can about Lady Westonhall* he mused.

Edwin was still busily working away in Henry's office when Arlen returned from the palace and relayed the strange events of the afternoon. Edwin suggested he speak with Linus Eves, an old academic and genealogist, who had recently aided Thomas Gilmore in his relentless quest to prove his claim to the throne.

"If anyone knows about Mercia nobility, Eves is your man," Edwin suggested, knowingly.

Arlen, now feeling a little deflated after the earlier excitement, sat down opposite his brother and casually started shifting through the numerous letters on the desk; one particular letter caught his eye.

"Is this Florence's hand?" he asked, picking up the letter and examining the handwriting closely.

"Yes," Edwin replied, cheerfully. "We have continued to correspond after the events in Trevelyan. She is an excellent letter writer, extremely witty and very observant of people. She wrote all about your recent visit to Moorgate, it sounded as if you had a real ball."

"Christ, I hope not everything," Arlen cringed, recalling Kian's broad grin whilst holding Lady Ainsworth's key aloft.

"What do you mean?" his brother asked, curiously.

"Kian."

"Why? What on earth did Kian do?"

"Oh, never mind, it's better you don't know, I wish I didn't," Arlen replied, shaking his head and pulling a face of disgust.

Edwin laughed. "Well, I can assure you Florence wrote only very complimentary things of Kian, so you are probably right, it is better that I don't know."

The two men remained in the office idly chatting for a while, when Phillip Ainsworth and his older brother Steven knocked at the door.

"Aha Phillip, any news?" Edwin asked, inviting the two men in with a wave of his hand.

"No, nothing yet sir," he replied, rather matter-of-factly.

"Oh well, never mind … Hello Steven, what brings you to town?" Edwin asked, pulling up a couple of chairs.

Steven Ainsworth was of average height, slim and fair; more resembling his sister Florence. He was elegantly dressed in an embroidered doublet trimmed with gold and looking rather like a dandy. Steven had not attended Chesterford like his younger brother, instead opting to study the law in Langland. He now very successfully ran his father's wood mills in Cambrian.

"Hello Edwin, Arlen," he said, nodding at the two men in turn. "Business," he added with a smile.

"You look tired Steven," Edwin commented, gesturing for the men to sit as he arranged for refreshments.

"Yes, rather a rough night I'm afraid," he groaned, briefly glancing over at his brother Phillip.

"I'm sorry to hear that," Edwin replied. "Anything we can do to help?"

"No, thank you Edwin, all taken care of. Some difficult decisions are best tackled head on, don't you agree?"

"Yes, indeed I do," Edwin replied, directing his gaze towards Arlen.

Arlen pretended not to hear them.

It was by now early evening and the air was extremely close. The conversation very quickly turned to Arlen's impending wedding; he remained noticeably quiet on the subject. Edwin, knowing of his brother's continued struggle regarding his impulsive proposal, skilfully changed the subject. The four men all tucked into a feast of meats and candied fruits, and were chatting freely when a sudden confident knock at the office door diverted their attention.

"Yes," Edwin replied, rising from his seat, behind the desk.

A young Crown soldier entered the room. "Sir, one of the town urchins has reported seeing a man matching the description of …" he momentarily paused, observing Steven Ainsworth. "A boarding house in Goring End," he continued.

Arlen immediately jumped to his feet.

"Thank you," Edwin replied, to the Crown soldier. "Please wait outside, we shall join you directly."

"Yes, sir," the soldier replied, bowing himself from the room.

"Well, well, it sounds as if you three have confidential Crown business to attend, I shall take my leave," Steven said, smiling and nodding to the men in turn.

"Yes, thank you," Edwin replied. "It was very good to see you, Steven."

"Yes likewise, I look forward to seeing you all at the wedding then," he said, patting Arlen on the back. "Later then Brother," he nodded to Phillip as he left the room.

Phillip nodded back with a broad smile.

"Come," Edwin commanded as soon as Steven had gone. "We should make haste."

The Crown soldier thankfully had the foresight to bring the horses around to the front of the building, saddled and ready to go as Edwin, Arlen and Phillip appeared from the entrance of the Crown Knight headquarters. Mounting their horses, they hurriedly rode in the direction of East Kingslea.

The sight of Crown Knights and Crown soldiers riding through the streets of Goring End raised a lot of nervous attention in the area, with local folk scurrying off the streets in all directions. Crown Knights never came to Goring End unless they had a particularly good reason. An extremely poor neighbourhood, situated on the banks of the River Rame, a stone's throw from the docklands. It was an area full of cheap boarding houses, brothels and unscrupulous Inns – a place for illegal traffic and trade in the well-run underground economy. The Crown generally ignored the goings on here unless it spilled out into the rest of Kingslea. For all the unlawful activities there was an unwritten code between the criminals that ruled these streets, however the presence of Crown Knights would certainly send shock waves through the unsuspecting residents.

They very soon reached the rundown boarding house that was situated right on the edge of the river; it was entered from the street at the front with steps at the side, leading down to a dilapidated old boathouse in the basement. There was an unpleasant rancid smell running through the property as they entered. The proprietor sped into the hallway at the intrusion, only to freeze on the spot at the sight of the men entering his establishment.

"Gentleman," he mumbled nervously, closing the door on his wife and a handful of small dirty-faced children. "What can I do for you?"

"This man, is he here?" the Crown soldier asked, pushing an identification drawing of Raven Westonhall in the man's face.

The proprietor didn't even look at the picture, just nervously pointed his filthy finger towards the stairs.

"Second floor, room at the front. I knew he was fucking trouble," he muttered under his breath.

The Crown soldier remained in the hallway with the quivering proprietor. Edwin, Arlen and Phillip made their way up the stairs to the small grubby room.

"Christ!" Edwin exclaimed upon entering, holding his hand to his face to mask the foul stench. Raven's dead body was instantly visible from the doorway. Dressed in nothing but a velvet housecoat, he was caked in dried blood that appeared almost black in the dismal, dark room. Phillip quickly retrieved some candles as the three men stood staring down at the cold, dead body of Raven Westonhall. It was clear from his stiff body that he had been dead for at least twelve hours.

"A single knife wound to his abdomen, thrust upwards," Edwin concluded, crouching down over the body, pulling the housecoat open to reveal the fatal wound.

Peering around the room, it was evidently very clear that Raven had been entertaining. The bedclothes were all disarranged and there were two empty brandy glasses on either side of the bed. Raven's clothes were casually scattered about the floor as if he had undressed in a hurry. As well as the foul damp, musky smell, the room also reeked of opium.

"Phillip, speak with the landlord, ask if he saw anyone else here, man or woman. Raven was certainly sharing his bed with someone," Edwin ordered, picking up a letter that had been propped up against a brandy bottle on the side table beside the bed.

"Yes, sir," Phillip replied, quitting the room at once, glad for some relief from the horrendous stench.

"What have you got there?" Arlen asked, observing his brother with a letter in his hand.

"Look," Edwin said curiously, holding the letter up to the candlelight, "the seal."

"Gilmore!" Arlen exclaimed. "Christ, Edwin what on earth does it say?"

R,

The fireworks were spectacular, better than I could have imagined.

I am recalled to town as expected, with hopes of a favourable decision from the old men.

Regrettably, your sister will not be accompanying me. This should not give you any cause for concern or alter our arrangements in any way as I am confident that she shall very soon be joining us.

I look forward to concluding our business in due course.

I hear the riverside is most pleasant at this time of year.

T

"Good God!" Edwin exclaimed. "Can this really be?"

"Thomas Gilmore!" Arlen gasped, utterly astonished. "I know he has always been opposed to the Corridor, but this is absolutely unbelievable," Arlen declared, snatching the letter from his brother's hand and hastily rereading it.

Edwin returned to the window, staring down at Raven's bloody, dead body which lay sprawled out on the floor.

"Is Lord Gilmore capable of this?" he mused aloud, "Surely he would never have left such an incriminating letter behind."

"Perhaps it was one of Raven's many lovers. He clearly had someone in his bed. Folk in Goring End don't read or write. No one around here would have given a letter left on the table a second thought. We may have arrived before Gilmore had the chance, it does bear his seal. Surely that is evidence enough?" Arlen declared.

"Perhaps," Edwin replied, but was not totally convinced.

Phillip returned to the room. "There was a young man here, but he left early this morning apparently. The old bastard said it was not one of the local boys, he had never seen him before. He has given a description, but it could be almost anyone in Kingslea."

Arlen handed Phillip the letter to read, noting that his reaction was curiously indifferent.

"What are we going to do?" Arlen asked his brother, still observing Phillip closely.

"I shall take it to the King, at once," Edwin sighed, staring from the window, still unable to comprehend the severity of the situation.

"Phillip, arrange to have the body moved, will you? ... Arlen with me," Edwin ordered, promptly striding from the room.

The King sat upon his gilded throne in the grand watching chamber calmly and patiently, pulling at the tip of his beard. Lord Douglas Barlett and his son Edwin stood at the foot of the steps. All three men waited in silence, which was broken only by the sound of faint chatter coming from the courtyard below the window. Moments later, footsteps could be heard in the corridor before three confident knocks sounded on the large double doors. Lord Thomas Gilmore confidently strode into the grand watching chamber, his chest all puffed out, full of self-importance. The buttons on his expensive doublet strained under the pressure. The two Crown guards who had accompanied him followed him into the room, closing the double doors behind them.

"Your Majesty," Gilmore beamed, giving his deepest bow.

The arrogant little man looked excessively pleased with himself, falsely believing that being summoned at such a late hour could only be news advantageous to his cause. He quickly concluded that the audience with Sir James Ripley had not gone as well as the King had hoped. The King remained silent glaring at Gilmore, his face expressionless; Edwin slowly moved forward and handed Gilmore the crumpled letter adorned with his family seal.

"What is this?" he asked, curiously taking the letter from Edwin.

"That is your seal milord?" Edwin asked, stepping back to assume his previous position.

"Yes ... yes," Gilmore replied anxiously, hastily opening the letter and reading it.

"What is this? I did not write this letter!" he protested most vehemently, his eyes wide, staring first at the King, then at Lord Barlett, before returning his gaze back towards the King.

"Your Majesty, this is not my hand, I implore you your Grace, what is this?"

"Not your hand, but your seal, milord, how is that possible?" Edwin asked, his tone sharp.

Gilmore shifted nervously backwards and forwards on his feet as he glanced behind him at the Crown guards, beads of sweat forming on his forehead.

"I have no idea," he mumbled, desperately wiping his brow, studying the seal in more detail.

There was no doubt at all, it was genuine. He lifted his hand up in front of him, staring down at the finger with his ring on that contained his seal, his hand shook uncontrollably.

"No ... no ... this is not possible," he whimpered, his words faltering as he spoke to them. "I never take my ring off."

"Yet there it is, Thomas," Lord Barlett replied, eyeing Gilmore curiously. "Tell me Thomas, who is 'R'?"

Gilmore glared down at the letter once again and began shaking his head furiously, "R, I have absolutely no idea, I did not write this letter, please you have to believe me, Douglas, please, your Majesty," he begged, falling desperately to his knees, clasping his hands together.

The King it seemed had heard quite enough. "T ... t ... t ... take him away," he commanded, with a casual swipe of his hand.

"No, your Majesty, please, I beg you. Douglas please," Gilmore begged, as the two Crown guards roughly grabbed him under his arms before effortlessly lifting the pathetic man to his feet. They efficiently whisked him away under more desperate declarations of innocence.

The King rose from his throne. Lord Barlett and Edwin bowed as he silently retired from the grand watching chamber back to his private apartments.

"Well Father, do you believe that Gilmore wrote that letter?" Edwin asked, once they were alone.

"I do not," his father replied confidently. "Gilmore may be cunning and devious, but he is certainly not stupid or reckless. He would consider it to be utterly beneath him to get involved with a malleable young man such as Raven Westonhall. And to record any such acquaintance is beyond foolish, which Gilmore is most certainly not. However, the fact remains, Gilmore's seal is on that letter. I shall question him further in the morning. A night in the tower may help him to recall who he has imprudently allowed access to his seal. Come Edwin it is late, let us retire, besides, your brother will be anxious to hear our news."

"Yes, thank you Father, I think it is also time Arlen and I entrusted you with all the facts. I am confident Henry Morton would approve."

"Thank you, Edwin, I too shall relay all I know. We must discover who is behind this treachery and fast. It is vital."

Chapter 10

Henry, Kian, and Iris had just spent what they believed to be their third night together in the darkness of the Corstir Forest. It was difficult to know whether it was day or night as the thick canopy of leaves shielded any possible view of the sky above. There didn't seem to be any life on the damp forest floor other than the small insects accustomed to the dark, humid conditions. Father Peter had left them hours before. Henry and Iris were sleeping and Kian was stoking the small campfire, their only source of light. The food and fresh water supplies were running low, and he was becoming increasingly anxious for the return of the priest.

Glancing over at Henry and Iris he smiled. Iris was neatly snuggled under the crook of Henry's arm, her head resting against his chest. Henry had his arm wrapped tightly around her, a position they had adopted for the last three nights. The pair certainly had chemistry, although Kian doubted that either of them had realised it quite yet – it did seem rather bizarre after their initial meeting and subsequent altercation. Iris was certainly very naive and innocent in many ways, but she was also extremely intelligent and witty. She challenged Henry, subtly teasing him and forcing him to share himself by revealing tiny glimpses of his true thoughts and feelings. Kian grinned to himself, thinking how good they could be for each other, if only they allowed themselves to realise it.

"What are you grinning at like a fool?" Henry asked, opening his eyes and observing Kian watching him.

"Just considering what a handsome couple you both make," he smiled.

"Don't be a bloody fool," Henry snapped, abruptly sitting up causing Iris to stir.

"Whatever you say Henry," Kian said with a laugh, returning his attention back to the fire.

Iris opened her eyes and looked up at Henry, smiling.

"Good morning," she whispered.

"Is it?" he replied sharply, "I wish I knew. Where are your stockings? Your legs are all scratched and bruised, you should be wearing them."

"They kept falling down when I snagged them and I got fed up with trying to keep them up," she replied, sitting up and rubbing her hands up and down her sore legs.

"Where are they? You should tie them around the bottom of your legs like bandages. If you were to get an infection in one of those scratches it could turn nasty."

Iris pulled her soiled stockings from her bag and began wrapping them around her legs as Henry had instructed. It seemed Henry was in an irritable mood this morning.

"No sign of the fucking priest then?" Kian scoffed, still poking at the fire. "You know Henry, I think we are going to die in this fucking godforsaken place."

Henry ignored him, however he was beginning to wonder if Kian might be right. After tucking into what was left of the food, Kian stood up, stretching and yawning loudly.

"Give me some slack on the rope will you, I need a shit," he declared.

"Kian, please," Henry moaned, throwing him a disapproving look.

"We all do it," Kian laughed, winking at Iris and causing her to blush.

"Yes, but the rest of us do not feel the need to announce it in quite such a crude manner," Henry scolded, shaking his head.

Kian ignored him and just pulled on the rope, disappearing into the darkness.

Father Peter had insisted on tying them all together on a long robe as an added precaution; it was extremely easy to get very quickly lost within the forest. Iris was still blushing. She had had to get used to living in close proximity with these men; modesty was a luxury none of them could afford. Henry gave her an apologetic smile.

Kian returned a short while later and promptly went to sleep. Henry kept the fire burning. Iris remained close to his side. They sat for a while in silence when she suddenly shivered. Henry wrapped his arm around her shoulders, pulling her closer.

"Are you warm enough?" he whispered, his mood seemed to have softened.

"Yes," she replied, smiling, lying her head against his chest, the familiar smell of musky leather and vanilla made her feel safe. She very quickly drifted back off to sleep.

Time stood still in the forest. Henry glanced down at Iris as she slept in his arms. He could hear her soft breath. She looked beautiful with the light from the fire dancing off of her rosy cheeks. He thought about what Kian had intimated earlier. He had certainly never met another woman quite like Iris before. She was undoubtedly a handful, but he had to admit to himself that he was beginning to rather enjoy her company.

Henry heard Father Peter moments before he appeared out of the darkness accompanied by two much older looking men.

"Thank God!" he exclaimed, startling Iris and waking Kian.

"Father Peter," Iris cried. "How glad we are to see you at last," she said, jumping to her feet and embracing the priest fondly.

"My dear child, I promised you that I would return, didn't I?" he replied, kissing her affectionately on the forehead.

"About fucking time," Kian grumbled, more than relieved at the sight of the priest.

"Nice to see you too, Kian," Father Peter grinned, placing a gentle hand to Kian's shoulder. "Come, gather your belongings, we need to make haste if we are to reach the settlement before dusk."

"What time is it then, Father?" Iris asked, busily stuffing her bag with all her things.

"It is around midday. It is only a short walk from here and the forest will open up, you shall soon be able to see the sky once more," he explained.

"Thank fuck for that," Kian added, swiftly hauling his bag over his shoulder.

Henry shook his head, exasperated.

"What?" Kian laughed, winking at Iris. She giggled. Henry rolled his eyes.

After gathering all their belongings together, they reluctantly relinquished their weapons to the two weather-beaten men from Corstir. Kian however kept a small knife concealed in his boot; he was not in the habit of leaving anything to chance.

Just as the priest had promised, they reached a point in the forest where the trees began to thin out. The sky was blue and cloudless, the sun strong. It took a while for the three travellers to adjust their eyes to the light, all sighing with relief and taking in deep breaths as if inhaling the sunlight. They found themselves stood atop a steep rocky wall looking down upon a narrow valley with a river running central along the bottom.

"It's beautiful," Iris declared, admiring the spectacular view. Henry and Kian both had to agree with her.

"Look there," Father Peter said, pointing down, to the spot where the river curved away, "Corstir."

A large cluster of basic rectangular wooden cottages with pitched roofs encircled a much larger building, also built of wood. Smoke billowed from the central chimney. Wooden fences marked the boundaries around the houses and it was just possible to make out the people and animals milling around, going about their daily chores. The settlement was surrounded on either side by the steep rock wall. Father Peter pointed out a winding pathway that led all the way down to the valley floor.

"Come," he said, "your arrival has caused much excitement, they are already preparing a welcome feast."

Iris smiled broadly with excitement, glancing over at Henry. He smiled back at her affectionately, *she has a beautiful smile* he mused to himself.

Father Peter paused, turning to look at the weary travellers. "Henry," he said, "I may have intimated to the folk in the settlement that you and Iris are married."

"What?" Henry replied, puzzled, "Why on earth would you do that?"

"Men are scarce in Corstir Henry, if they believe you are married you will not attract any unwanted attention … if you understand my meaning. I hope I have done the right thing. I thought perhaps …"

"Yes, Priest," Henry interjected, momentarily glancing over at Iris.

"I'm sorry Kian; you shall have to bear it I'm afraid," the priest continued.

"Christ, Priest you don't need to worry about me," Kian added with a broad grin. "Lead the fucking way."

Father Peter laughed; Henry shook his head; although he could not help but smile to himself at the sight of Kian charging off in pursuit of the two Corstir men. He observed that Iris was looking slightly bewildered. He smiled at her, holding out his hand.

"Come on let's go," he said softly, gripping hold of her hand tightly as they followed closely behind Kian towards the steep pathway.

"What did you tell them was our reason for travelling through the forest?" Henry asked the priest as they began their descent.

"They have no interest in why you travel, only that while you are in Corstir you respect their ways and work hard. There is much to do in the settlement, it is in desperate need of repair."

"Why did you tell them Henry and I were married?" Iris asked, still feeling slightly confused.

The priest glanced over at Henry, raising his eyebrows. "It's just better that way, trust me Iris," he replied, reassuringly.

Henry nodded in agreement, gently squeezing her hand.

"Oh, and Kian," the priest continued, as they finally caught up with him. "There may be more reason for celebration than the abundance of women."

"Oh, yes Priest, what do you mean?" he asked, still grinning broadly.

"Patience Kian," Father Peter teased.

"Fucking priest," Kian grumbled, casually draping his arm over Father Peter's shoulder.

From the top of the gorge the distance to the settlement had looked short but the pathway down was long and precarious. Iris was beginning to tire and held tightly onto Henry's arm until they finally reached level ground. Henry passed her what was left of the fresh water and insisted that they rest for a while. Father Peter reluctantly agreed as he reassured Henry that it was only a few more miles walk. It was late in the afternoon by the time they reached the settlement, it seemed the whole of Corstir had come out to welcome them. Father Peter had been right, women outnumbered men by quite a way. There were also, surprisingly, a lot of children. The priest led them directly to the large wooden hall in the centre of the village, the smell of roasting meat utterly mouth-watering as they slowly approached. An older man stood in the enormous doorway; it was unmistakeably Father Peter's brother, the resemblance was clear to see.

"Welcome," he beamed, "Welcome to Corstir, my name is Arthur Maddock. I am Chieftain here, if you come in peace, you are more than welcome."

"We do," Henry replied, stepping forward. "And we thank you for granting us permission to enter your settlement."

"Excellent, excellent," he bellowed. "Brother, make our guests comfortable will you, then later we shall feast," he announced as a group of young children merrily circled around him. Henry suspected that they were all his own children; Corstir was certainly a paradise for the handful of men that lived here.

Father Peter quickly ushered them in the direction of a small unoccupied hut to the rear of the central hall. A stream of young children followed behind them, curious for a glance at the three strangers. Father Peter joyfully shoed them all away.

The hut comprised of two rooms. The main living area had a central hearth for a fire, a couple of chairs, a table and a small cot. The second much smaller room was situated at the back and was partitioned off by a reed screen. It contained a wooden framed bed covered with skins, a table holding a bowl with a jug of water and another smaller reed screen concealing a bucket.

"Here we are," Father Peter exclaimed. "Henry, Iris, you shall stay here, basic I know, but it's not for long and it's a relative palace compared to the forest, don't you agree? … Ah, look they have already brought fresh water for you to wash," the priest declared.

Iris glanced around the room. It looked comfortable enough. She agreed with the priest that it was definitely a palace compared to the forest.

"I shall leave you both now to rest. They shall sound a horn to announce the feast. Henry we can discuss what will be required in terms of work later … Kian," the priest continued, "you shall be staying somewhere else," he smiled, draping his arm over Kian's shoulder.

"Are you sure you are alright with this Henry?" Kian asked, quickly surveying the modest hut.

"Yes, it's alright Kian you go, we shall speak later."

"Very well," Kian replied, allowing the priest to lead him away.

Once Father Peter and Kian had departed, Iris stood awkwardly in the main living area, not quite sure what she should do.

"Go and lie down," Henry insisted. "You must be dreadfully tired; it has been a long day and I have a feeling it is going to be an even longer night."

"Where will you be Henry?" Iris asked, tentatively peering behind the reed screen and observing the bed.

Henry turned to face her; she looked a little frightened.

"You will be safe here Iris," he reassured her. "I shall be right here," he said, pointing to the cot.

"Won't you lie with me Henry?" she asked, her gaze alluring. "I don't want to be alone."

Henry observed her closely. If he didn't know better, he would have considered her a temptress and would have been more than happy to be seduced. Her look upon him was bewitching.

"No, Iris it's not appropriate for me to lie with you," he replied, shaking his head.

"But we have lain together in the forest for three nights."

"That was different."

"But …"

"No, Iris."

An awkward silence followed before Iris disappeared behind the screen. Henry sat down on the cot, burying his head in his hands. He suddenly realised that he wanted nothing more than to lie with Iris in the bed. He was beginning to have romantic feelings for her.

Father Peter had led Kian to a cottage on the outer edge of the settlement. The land surrounding the wooden structure was neatly fenced, housing goats and chickens. To the right there was a well-tended cottage garden with an abundance of produce. The river ran at the back of the property, with the water flowing into a large ditch and creating a natural pond.

"Do you know Priest, if I didn't know better, I would have sworn I had been here before," Kian declared, staring intensely at the cottage before spinning around and taking in the rest of the surroundings.

"Well Kian, that is exactly why we are here. On our journey from Baines Abbey, when I spoke of Corstir, something you said made me suspect you had been here before. You said that you knew your name was Munro because you remembered it was your father's name, Harold Munro, right?"

"Yes, that's right," Kian replied quizzically, turning to face the priest.

"You said you didn't remember much before the orphanage at Elmbridge, but you did mention one other place before that. Well, I believe what you talked about was right here in Corstir," the priest replied, observing Kian closely as he turned back around to look upon the quaint cottage, with its weathered wood front door and a trail of wildflowers growing along the pathway to the entrance.

"Fuck!" Kian exclaimed, hardly able to believe his eyes. "Yes, Priest I think you may be right, I do remember this cottage … this was my home … I do remember."

"Come Kian, there is someone inside you should meet," Father Peter said, gesturing for Kian to join him inside.

Before they entered Kian observed a cross carved into the far left of the door. He slowly traced his finger over the image.

"I did this," he muttered under his breath. "Christ Priest, I can't believe it."

Almost as soon as Kian stepped inside the cottage even more memories began to flood back. He suddenly felt transported back in time to when he was a young boy. His eyes bounced around the spacious living area utterly mesmerised; familiar objects, long forgotten were dotted around just as he remembered. The homely smell of delicious stew. Lavender and thyme were contained within the rushes and flowers that covered the floor – Kian was finally home.

An older woman stood with her back to the two men. She was carefully stirring a large pot beside the fire which was bubbling away above the flames. The lady was of average height with strawberry blond curly hair tinged with strands of grey and worn loose over her shoulders. Her simple grey woollen dress was well-worn with numerous repairs, old and new.

"Anna," the priest said softly, causing her to jump and drop her ladle into the pot.

"Oh, my! You frightened me!" she exclaimed. "Why Father Peter what a pleasant …" She stopped, her eyes fixed firmly upon Kian. The room fell deadly silent, even the bubbling stew seemed to settle in the pot. Anna stumbled forward gripping on to the back of a chair to steady herself. She could not take her eyes from Kian. He instinctively knew who she was. For the first time in his life, Kian Munro was completely speechless.

"Kian, is it really you?" Anna whispered, desperately clutching to her old apron and moving closer towards him.

Kian nodded, still dumbstruck.

"Do you know who I am Kian?" she asked, raising her hand to gently touch his face.

Kian nodded still unable to speak, still unable to believe his eyes. He took in every tiny detail of the woman stood in front of him. Her soft features, her beautiful curly hair, her vibrant green eyes; older eyes but unmistakably the same green eyes that watched him as a child, kissing and tucking him safely into bed every night. His own eyes began to fill with tears.

"Oh, Kian," she whispered, finally placing her hand to his face. "My beautiful boy."

"Mother," Kian muttered, barely above a whisper.

Anna instantly burst into floods of tears. Flinging herself up at her son and throwing her arms tightly around him, she wept uncontrollably. Kian joined her, his tears now rolling freely down his cheeks, embracing his beautiful mother for the first time in eighteen years.

A young woman and a small boy entered the room behind Father Peter. The young woman stared in bewilderment at Kian and Anna embracing and weeping together in each other's arms.

"Father Peter?" she asked quizzically, staring at the priest.

"Anna, Kian," the priest interrupted the emotional reunion for just a moment. "Kian, this is Katherine, your sister and her son Little Kian," he continued, pointing to the bewildered pair stood in the doorway.

"My brother!" Katherine gasped, unable to believe her eyes; he was just as she imagined he would be.

Kian turned, flabbergasted. Katherine appeared to be about eighteen or nineteen years old. Taller than the average woman, her long wild red hair framed her beautiful face and ivory complexion. She also had the most dazzling vibrant green eyes, just like their mother. The little boy stood beside her was no more than two or three years old, his hair fairer in appearance but still with an enormous mop of curls. He had the most adorable, mischievously cheeky smile. Kian and Anna instinctively opened their arms inviting the pair into their heartfelt loving embrace.

The priest took one final look at the Munro family before deciding to leave them in peace and allowing them to reunite in private. He smiled to himself with an air of satisfaction as he headed back towards the hall.

The sound of a loud horn filled the air, breaking the early evening silence as day turned to night. The folk of Corstir began emerging from their homes, heading towards the meeting hall for a night of merriment.

"Iris, it's time to go," Henry called out from behind the screen.

Henry looked refreshed having shaved and put on a clean shirt that had been provided by a young girl who had called at the hut earlier with a handful of useful items. Iris stirred, stretching out on the bed. She still felt incredibly tired.

"Must I go?" she asked, yawning loudly. "I'm so tired Henry. I feel as if I could sleep for days."

"Yes, you must," Henry replied. "Here, they have brought you a clean dress," he said, placing it on the only other piece of furniture in the bedchamber. "It's not much of a dress I'm afraid, it more resembles a long linen shirt and there are no under garments. It seems the women of Corstir care little for appropriate attire. You shall need to wash out that grey woollen dress before we leave, the good folk of Mercia would presume you to be out in your nightclothes if you were to wear this dress in the East," Henry added sounding amused, he turned to face Iris. She still had her eyes closed, deliberately ignoring him and curling up into a tight ball on the bed.

"Now, Iris," he boomed.

"But I …"

"Now, Iris, I shall not repeat myself again," he said sharply, pre-empting her next words. "We are guests here and besides, you need to eat."

Deciding against protesting further Iris slowly rose from the bed, stretching once again. She tipped her head slightly and gave Henry a coy smile. He shook his head at her, rolling his eyes.

"I shall wait outside," he said, leaving the bedchamber and allowing Iris to wash and change.

Henry observed Kian waiting patiently at the entrance to the hall as he and Iris approached. He was stood with two women and a young boy brimming with glee. Henry gave him a quizzical look as they drew nearer.

"Kian?" he asked, seeing his friend with his arm draped casually over the older woman's shoulder. All four of them had varying shades of curly red hair.

"Henry, Iris," Kian beamed, hardly able to contain himself. "You are never going to fucking believe this."

"Kian," the older woman scolded. "Language!" motioning towards the young boy.

Kian cringed. "Sorry," he replied, placing a loving kiss to the woman's cheek.

"Henry, Iris, I would very much like you to meet my mother, Anna … my sister Katherine … and my nephew Little Kian," he announced, glowing with pride. He wore the most enormous smile as he pointed towards his family.

"Christ!" Henry exclaimed, taken aback. He was certainly not expecting that. "Is this really true? My God Kian, this is absolutely amazing," he said, embracing his friend lovingly and joining Kian in rejoicing in this most incredible news.

"It is true Henry, even though I can still hardly believe it myself," Kian replied, struggling to hold back his tears of utter joy.

Kian quickly relayed his earlier conversations with Father Peter and how he had instantly recognised his family home. He reintroduced them all once again with lots of laughter and more tears as he was unable to prevent them any longer, and lots and lots of loving embraces. Katherine insisted on being called 'Kat.' Little Kian climbed up onto his uncle's shoulders, pulling at his wild red hair as Kian spun him around in excited circles. Henry observed Kian with such loving affection. He had never seen his friend so happy and joyful. It surely was the most magical of moments.

"This journey we find ourselves on is truly full of surprises," he declared, turning to see Iris already chatting with Kat as though they were old friends.

He smiled. Iris caught his eye and smiled back as they kept eye contact for just a moment longer. Iris too was now beginning to have romantic feelings for Henry, although she was a little uncertain what that actually meant, she just knew she wanted to be close to him.

"Come," hollered a loud voice from the doorway. Father Peter was stood at the entrance, frantically beckoning them all inside.

The hall was exceedingly long and wide with an enormous fire burning at the centre. A boar was slowly roasting above the flames on a spit. Tables and benches lined the sides of the room with one large table at the far end. Arthur sat at the centre of the top table in a throne-like chair covered with furs and adorned with animal tusks. He beckoned for his brother and the men to join him. The hall was raucous with people talking and laughing loudly. Numerous plates of food were being passed around, accompanied by jugs of ale and sweet wine. A musician began playing a lyre with a handful of young girls singing a song of love. *More than apt for the occasion,* Henry mused to himself. Henry and Kian joined Father Peter at the top table with Arthur. Iris sat with Kat, Anna, and Little Kian on one of the side tables nearer the door. A plate of food piled so high that it fell from the sides was passed down the table, along with a jug of Corstir wine.

"Be careful with that, it's very strong if you are not used to it," Kat warned, passing Iris a jug and cup.

"It tastes really nice," Iris replied, tentatively sipping the sweet wine.

"Yes, it does," Kat smiled, gulping down a whole cupful. Iris followed suit.

Iris and Kat instantly bonded with each other; Kat was a confident, no-nonsense straight-talking woman who resembled her tall and athletic brother. Along with her beautiful red hair, all curly and wild, she also had the most mesmerizing vibrant green eyes. Iris continued to drink large amounts of the wine as she attempted to keep pace with Kat. It made her feel good. She very quickly relaxed and, with little effort, Kat was able to encourage her up onto the table to dance together to the sound of the lyre. Henry watched her from the top table. He thought how beautiful she looked. Her long auburn hair worn loose, was bobbing up and down around her shoulders and she was dancing and laughing as if without a single care in the world. Her large blue eyes sparkled, and her cheeks were flushed from the wine. The donated linen dress did not leave much to the imagination as she twirled around in the soft candlelight.

After a couple of hours of eating, drinking and celebration, Henry eventually made his way over to Iris's table. She and Kat were still drinking and dancing, whereas Anna and Little Kian had already retired a while ago.

"Iris, I'm leaving with Father Peter, we have things we need to discuss. Do you want me to walk you back to the hut?"

"No thank you, I should like to stay a little longer, if I may?" she asked, holding her arms out for him to aid her from the table.

As Henry effortlessly lifted her down, she stumbled forward. Even though she had clearly drunk too much wine, she immediately reached for another cup. Henry snatched it from her hand.

"No more wine," he insisted. "You have had enough, it will make you ill."

"But I like it," she protested, attempting to take the cup back. She fell against him and wrapped her arms around his waist.

"No more Iris," he said in a warning tone. "Promise me."

"I promise," she sulked, leaning against his chest and breathing in the familiar seductive scent.

"I mean it Iris, or I shall take you back to the hut now," he added, his dark eyes intense.

"I promise Henry," she cooed, glancing up at him all silly and doe eyed. "Kiss me?" she said, closing her eyes and puckering up her lips.

Henry was momentarily taken aback by her bold request. He could quite easily have kissed her there and then – God knows he wanted to. *What is this woman doing to me?* He thought to himself.

He resisted the urge. "No, Iris you are drunk," he replied, his tone a clear reprimand. Then, loosening her grip from around his waist he promptly left the hall without saying another word.

Iris slumped down onto the bench feeling rejected. Kat jumped from the table and joined her.

"Are, you alright? " she asked, having observed the exchange.

"Yes," Iris sighed, reaching for another cup of wine.

"How long have you been married?"

"We are not married," Iris confessed, "Father Peter said it would be best, for Henry, although I don't really understand why."

"To keep the other women from pestering him I should imagine," Kat smiled.

"Pestering?" Iris asked, shrugging her shoulders.

"Yes, you know what I mean. Men are scarce in Corstir and Henry is very handsome, they would undoubtedly want to share his bed."

"Share his bed … what for?" Iris asked, naively.

"To make love, silly," Kat replied with a laugh, observing Iris closely. Kat suddenly realised Iris had absolutely no idea what she was talking about.

Iris blushed scarlet. "I'm sorry Kat, I don't understand," she replied, embarrassed by her innocence.

"Hey, no need to feel uncomfortable, I understand," Kat replied. "You like Henry, don't you?"

"Yes, I do. I didn't at first, I hated him in fact, but … well, I don't know, I can't explain it Kat," Iris confessed, her cheeks now burning.

"And do you think he likes you?" Kat asked, smiling sympathetically.

Iris shrugged her shoulders and reached for another cup of wine and gulped down the contents.

"Kat, will you tell me what it means to make love?"

"Yes, of course," Kat smiled cheerfully. "But not now, tomorrow. Come let us dance some more," she said, pulling Iris up from the bench and swirling her wildly around the spacious hall.

As it got late, the hall began to quickly empty. Henry had not returned and Kian was nowhere to be seen. Iris suddenly slumped forward over the table; she felt extremely nauseous.

"Come on," Kat announced, seeing Iris with her head on the table. "It's time for bed. I shall take you back to the hut. Henry must be wondering where you are."

"I don't think I can walk," Iris declared, her vision blurred. She was struggling to contain the urge to vomit.

"You best try, the fresh air might make you feel a little better," Kat replied, attempting to aid Iris to her feet.

The two women very slowly managed to navigate their way outside, just in time before Iris collapsed to her knees, violently vomiting all over herself and the floor.

"Oh, Christ," Kat muttered under her breath. "I had better fetch Henry." She rushed off in the direction of the hut, leaving Iris sprawled out on the floor as the last remaining revellers casually stepped over her as they made their way home.

Henry was still in deep conversation with Father Peter as Kat hastily approached.

"I think you best come," she shouted over to him. "It's Iris I'm afraid, she drank more wine."

Henry shot back in the direction of the hall, already annoyed that Iris had disobeyed his order regarding the wine. Upon observing her on the ground covered in her own vomit, his temper rose further.

"You drank more wine," he shouted down at her angrily.

"I shall leave you," Father Peter sighed, shaking his head in disapproval. "We better let Henry deal with it now," he said, signalling for Kat to join him.

"Get up," Henry bellowed. "Now!"

Iris slowly managed to stagger to her feet; everything was spinning. Then, without warning Henry roughly grabbed her by the arm and unceremoniously marched her the short distance back to their hut.

"You're hurting me," she whined, attempting to pull away from his grasp.

Henry, almost throwing her into the hut, was not in any kind of mood for her feeble protests. Once inside Iris stood as still as she was able, her head bowed with her eyes to the ground. Her clean linen dress now soiled, stained with wine and vomit.

"What did I say to you before I left the hall? … No more wine," Henry growled. "Are you totally incapable of following any order? … Well?" he yelled, his voice now raised as well as his temper.

"I'm going to be sick again," Iris whimpered, cupping her hand to her mouth.

Henry hastily retrieved the bucket from the bedchamber and shoved it towards Iris, just in time as she once again collapsed to her knees violently vomiting.

Henry paced the room, running his fingers through his hair. He glared down at Iris furiously, as she knelt on the floor with her head in the bucket, contemplating what on earth he was going to do with her as she continued to test him in every way possible.

"Please," came a soft voice from the doorway. "I've brought another clean dress and fresh water. Please just leave her soiled clothes outside and we can wash them all out tomorrow," Kat declared, handing Henry the dress and water.

"Thank you," he replied with a brief smile. "You are most kind, although I'm not sure she deserves it."

"She is not the first and she certainly won't be the last. Corstir wine is very strong, she is not used to drinking I think?" Kat asked, sighing at the sight of Iris with her head still in the bucket.

"No, she is not," Henry confirmed. "Thank you again."

"Don't be too hard on her then," Kat said with a sweet smile before turning and disappearing into the darkness.

Henry returned his attention back to Iris, who was still on the floor, although she had thankfully taken her head from the bucket.

"Please, Henry, I'm sorry, please don't scold me," she pleaded, looking up at him and trying very hard to appear innocent.

"Give me one good reason why I should not?" he snapped, glaring down at her still annoyed.

"Because I'm still sore from the first time," she whimpered.

"That is not a good enough reason Iris, you obviously have not learnt your lesson." he added with a scowl.

"I have Henry, I did …"

"But you disobeyed me again. I specifically said to you before I left the hall 'no more wine, it will make you ill' and you clearly dismissed that order. I do not ask anything of you that is unreasonable, but you continue to insist on testing me … for Christ's sake Iris."

Fearful of saying anything that might infuriate him further, Iris decided it prudent to sit in silence with her head bowed and wait for Henry to decide her fate.

Henry rubbed his hand over his face, shaking his head in sheer frustration. He didn't want to punish Iris again – after all he had picked Kian up off the floor many a time after an overindulgence of ale or wine and Kian should certainly have known better. Iris dared to look up at him hoping to read a little sympathy in his face. She was crying. Henry knew full well it was only self-pity, but she was obviously suffering enough.

"Come on, stand-up," he said softly, aiding her to her feet.

"What are you going to do?" she asked fearfully, pulling away from him.

"Wash your face and get you into bed," he replied with a smile.

Iris cautiously rose, afraid the urge to vomit might overwhelm her again. Henry soaked a cloth in the clean water, first wiping away the tears and then the vomit from her face and hair. He was very gentle; Iris dared a smile.

"Come on, let's get you out of this soiled dress, the bad head you shall have in the morning will be punishment enough," he said, promptly turning her around to face the reed screen before grabbing the hem of her dress and pulling it up over her head. Having no under garments, Henry was able to observe the faint red marks on her legs and buttocks from her earlier indiscretion.

"I'm sorry," Iris whispered, now standing completely naked in his presence, but only ashamed by her current intoxicated state.

"Get to bed," Henry replied, hastily removing the dirty dress from the floor and throwing it from the hut.

Iris obeyed without question, sinking down onto the soft skins and pulling a woollen blanket over her body. Henry followed moments later. He removed his doublet and boots, then, after loosening his shirt, he lay next to her on the bed. Leaning over to gently remove her hair from her face, he kissed her tenderly on the forehead. Iris turned to face him and, placing her arm across his chest, she shifted closer towards him, snuggling under the crook of his arm. Henry wrapped his other arm around her tightly, pulling her even closer. The pair then fell fast asleep, wrapped up together in each other's embrace.

Chapter 11

Iris awoke to a soft tapping noise on the reed screen. She lay on the bed covered only by the woollen blanket and Henry was nowhere to be seen. The room was spinning.

"Iris, can I come in?" Kat called out from the other room.

"Yes, of course," Iris replied, slowly sitting up. Her head was pounding and her mouth was as dry as a bone. "Oh, I feel quite funny," she declared, rubbing her sore head.

"I'm not surprised, you drank far too much wine. Here I have brought you something to drink, it will make you feel better," Kat smiled, handing Iris a wooden beaker.

"What is it?" Iris asked, looking down at the slimy liquid.

"Just drink it down quickly, it will make you feel better, I promise."

Iris obeyed, swallowing down the gooey green substance. It made her retch.

Kat laughed, "I know disgusting, isn't it?" she said, filling the bowl with fresh water. "But it will make you feel better. Come on, you had better get up, we have a lot to do today – cleaning all your dresses for one," she joked sounding amused.

Iris, tentatively rose from the bed, her head still pounding dreadfully. She blushed at the fact that she wasn't wearing any clothes, knowing full well Henry must have seen her this way. She quickly splashed the chilly water over her face and used the cloth to wipe down her naked body.

"Here," Kat continued, "I brought you another clean dress last night, you best put it on. Did Henry scold you very much?"

"No thankfully. He was exceedingly angry at first, but then he softened," Iris replied. "He lay beside me," she muttered, turning scarlet.

Kat grinned. "Come on, hurry up and get dressed, I think perhaps there is something we need to talk about."

Iris smiled back and quickly pulled on the dress, her cheeks now burning.

Henry and Kian had been up since sunrise as they had been tasked with replacing the rotten wood on the settlement meeting hall. Kian was already up on the roof, whilst Henry was busy planing new planks. It was a balmy day for outside manual work, but they were both more than content in their labours. Having both removed their shirts, they were displaying muscular torsos and were creating quite a bit of attention from the women of Corstir. Kian was more than happy to play to the crowd.

"I hear the wildcat overindulged last night. Has she got another fucking sore arse this morning?" Kian asked, tipping a cup of cold water over his head in order to cool down. He furiously shook his wild red hair.

"No, just a sore head," Henry replied, following Kian's lead.

"You're going fucking soft Henry Morton," Kian joked, jumping from the roof to refill his cup.

"No, not at all I merely concluded that some lessons are best learnt by your own mistakes."

"You like this girl don't you Henry?"

"Yes Kian I do, absurd, isn't it?"

"Why absurd?" Kian asked, observing his friend very closely.

"Oh, I don't know Kian … I really don't want to talk about it," Henry sighed, turning back to his work bench.

Kian skilfully changed the subject and instead he talked of his newly rediscovered family with such pride and affection. Henry was more than happy to listen to him rambling on and on, occasionally getting lost in his own thoughts, which were becoming increasingly occupied by Iris. The hours quickly ticked by as the men worked efficiently and made excellent progress. It had been a long time since either of them had engaged in any kind of manual work, but, surprisingly, they were both enjoying the task in hand. Finally, as the sun began to set and dip below the mighty Corstir that encased the forest settlement, Henry and Kian made their way to Anna's cottage for a much earned home cooked meal. The men leisurely bathed in the natural pool whilst the women prepared the food. Iris brought clean clothes before watching from a distance as the men relaxed in the cool water and washing away the days sweat and grime. Kat had, as promised, enlightened Iris in the finer details of lovemaking earlier in the day. She now observed Henry with a renewed interest as he emerged naked from the water.

After enjoying a delicious meal, Little Kian insisted on sitting on his uncle's lap refusing to go to bed until eventually, Kian lifted him high in the air and carried him off with a promise of a story. About half an hour later and, once Kian was confident the boy had eventually fallen fast asleep, he quietly ushered everyone outside to sit so as not to wake him. Carrying their chairs outside, they all sat around a warming fire pit. Kat proceeded to pass around the Corstir wine which Iris flatly refused, blushing. Kian teased her mercilessly, whilst Anna promptly fetched some fresh water infused with elderflower and patted Iris affectionately on the shoulder.

"Take no notice of him my dear." she said, throwing her son a stern look. "Corstir wine is very strong, here drink this it tastes just as nice and won't give you such a terrible sore head."

"Thank you," Iris replied, glancing over at Henry and giving him a sweet smile.

He smiled back and considered how alluring she looked with light from the fire bouncing off her flushed cheeks.

The conversation effortlessly flowed; Kian had many questions for his mother and sister. It seemed that his father had left Corstir with Kian when he was around five years old. They were only supposed to be gone a few weeks; Anna had only just given birth to Kat and the family were in desperate need of new tools and linens. When Harold and Kian did not return Anna of course had feared the worst. Kian was unable to recall the exact circumstances surrounding his father's death, only that he had ended up in an orphanage near Elmbridge and was rescued, as he put it, by Lord Morton, Henry's father.

"Where is the boy's father?" Kian asked Kat, tilting his head towards the house.

"Dead," Kat replied with a grunt. "He was a traveller who decided to remain in Corstir. He told me he loved me, but he was a liar. When I realised I was with child he fled. I found him dead in the forest four days later."

"Bastard," Kian hissed, wrapping his large arm around his sister's shoulders.

"Indeed," Anna agreed, beaming with pride at her daughter and long-lost son.

Corstir, it seemed, was also having a positive effect on Henry; He felt at ease with the Munro family, chatting freely and relaying many stories of when he and Kian were younger, which made everyone roar with laughter. Anna was overjoyed, thankful her son had found real friendship in Mercia, she even began to cry at one point. Kian instantly jumped to his mother's aid in order to comfort her.

"Tears of joy, my son, only tears of joy," she sniffed, embracing him lovingly.

Iris found herself unable to take her eyes from Henry for almost the entire evening. She considered how handsome he looked laughing and smiling and being so very relaxed. A total transformation from the imposing, immensely serious man she had first encountered at Baines Abbey. She longed to be alone with him.

The time very quickly ticked by and as it got late it turned rather chilly. Iris struggled to keep her eyes open at one point, trying unsuccessfully to disguise a yawn.

"Time your husband took you to bed my dear," Anna smiled, wrapping a shawl around Iris's shoulders.

"Thank you," Iris replied, blushing. "But he's not my husband."

"Oh, I'm sorry, Father Peter told us you were married, he is your lover then?"

Iris turned scarlet.

"No, not quite Mother, I'll explain it all later," Kian grinned broadly at Henry and Iris whilst embracing his mother.

"Oh, very well," Anna laughed, happy to be enveloped in her son's strong arms again.

Henry promptly stood up. He thanked Anna and Kat for their hospitality before holding out his hand to aid Iris to her feet. Then, after bidding the Munro family goodnight, they left the cottage and headed back towards their small hut.

"Kian is so happy," Iris mused, as they slowly walked along the calming riverbank.

"Yes, he is," Henry replied. "In fact, I don't think I have ever seen him so happy. I believe he will struggle greatly once it is time to leave."

"I think I could live here forever too, it's so beautiful and Kat is so very nice. I have never had a real friend before."

"Yes, I can see you are very happy," he said, wrapping his arm around her shoulders as she shivered slightly from the cold breeze whirling around the settlement.

As they reached their small hut, Henry allowed Iris to enter first before following her inside.

"Goodnight then Iris," he said, standing just inside the doorway.

Iris turned around to face him, her face flushed. She tentatively gripped Henry's hand in hers.

"Henry, please come to bed with me … I would very much like you to make love to me."

Henry was completely taken aback by her latest bold request. He had certainly not been expecting that.

"Iris, I …"

Iris cut him short by blurting out, "I know we haven't known each other awfully long Henry and I know that I vex you greatly, but Kat has explained everything to me, and she said that you know when it is right, and it is right Henry. I have all these strange and most wonderful feelings whirling around inside me. I can't stop thinking about you."

Henry cupped her face in his hand. She looked so beautiful, so innocent; she was incandescent with excitement and anticipation.

Henry longed to take her into his arms, to kiss her perfect full lips. Standing for just a moment and staring deep into her dazzling blue eyes, he had never wanted a woman more than in this very moment. But for the first time in his life Henry didn't know what to do. Casually bedding other men's wives was one thing, making love to Iris was something quite different; this would mean a commitment, a betrothal in fact.

"Iris, I cannot," he replied hesitantly.

"You don't want me?" Iris gasped, releasing his hand and looking terribly hurt by his unexpected reaction to her heartfelt request.

"Iris it's not that I don't want you … Christ Iris, I do, God knows I do."

"Then why Henry?"

"Your feelings for me are confused, I understand, I too am struggling. The way we have been thrown together under such unusual circumstances, this burning desire we have for each other. But we must know it to be real Iris. You are the daughter of a great Lord, it would mean betrothing ourselves to each other and committing to a life together. You do understand, don't you? I cannot make love to you Iris, not until I know you are absolutely sure this is really what you want."

"But I am sure Henry … I love you," Iris replied, standing on her tip toes and reaching up to kiss him gently on the lips.

Henry pulled away. "I have to be sure too, Iris," he said, turning and disappearing from the hut.

It was still exceedingly early the next morning, even though Henry and Kian were already hard at work on the hall, when Iris and Kat approached. Henry and Iris had not spoken since the night before and there was a certain air of tension between them.

"We are going hunting," Kat declared cheerfully, fully aware at what had occurred and hoping to lighten the mood slightly. "Henry, I have asked Iris to join me, she said she needs your permission."

"Permission … Well, that's a fucking first," Kian laughed, jumping from the roof of the hall.

Kat threw her brother a disapproving look as he promptly tipped a cup of water over his head and furiously shook his hair.

Henry glanced over at Iris, running his fingers through his hair. She looked immensely cross.

"Well?" she snapped sharply, her blue eyes piercing his.

"What do you hunt?" Henry enquired, quickly redirecting his gaze towards Kat.

"Wild boar," she replied. "There is not much else in the woods, perhaps some rabbit if we are lucky."

"Boar hunting can be deadly; do you promise to listen to Kat's instructions?" Henry asked, turning to look at Iris once more, his tone also sharp.

"Yes," she snapped again.

"Very well," he snorted back, abruptly turning his back on the women and returning to his workbench without another word.

"Come Iris, we need to find you something more suitable to wear," Kat declared, catching Kian's eye with an exasperated expression on her face.

Henry looked up from his bench, watching as the women headed off towards the river. He was struggling with his feelings and was questioning his choice of abstinence. Kian had suspected something was wrong as Henry had been so tense all morning. His cold exchanges with Iris confirmed his suspicions.

"What has that wildcat gone and done now?" he asked, refilling his cup with more water.

"She told me she loved me and asked me to make love to her," Henry replied exhaling loudly and placing his hands to his face.

"What!" Kian exclaimed. "Fuck, she certainly knows how to surprise that one. Christ Henry that does seem rather bold even for the wildcat … Well, what on earth did you do?"

"Nothing, I said I couldn't make love to her."

"Fuck, no wonder she is so pissed … But why Henry, you have already admitted to me that you like her?" Kian asked, bewildered by his friend's decision.

"It's not that simple is it Kian? She is Lord Westonhall's daughter; she is a virgin for God's sake. I cannot just casually make love to her, in the heat of the moment."

"But you wanted to?"

"Christ, yes, of course I wanted to. I've never wanted a woman more. It's driving me insane."

"Then why not pledge yourself to her Henry?" Kian asked, placing his hands to Henry's shoulders. "Her lively, fervent spirit – I know it stirs your every emotion the like of which I have never witnessed in you before. You need to take a leaf out of Arlen's book my friend and listen to your heart for once in your life, you won't regret it I promise you."

"Oh Kian," Henry groaned, releasing Kian's hands from his shoulders. "I'm sorry I can't have this conversation with you." He turned back to his workbench.

Kian knew better than to push him further, so smiling broadly to himself he said no more on the matter – at least for the time being anyway.

The young women of Corstir who were attending the hunting party were all scantily dressed in animal skins and resembled an ancient warrior tribe. They were all carrying spears fitted with cross guards as well as an assortment of brutal looking hunting knives.

Kat handed Iris a spear. "Here take this, just in case, make sure you stay behind me," she said, having just finished binding Iris's hair up with leather straps.

"Are you sure about this Kat?" Iris murmured. She was beginning to think she was in over her head after her initial enthusiasm.

"Don't worry, you will be fine, hunting is thrilling, trust me," Kat replied, calming her fears.

"I do trust you," Iris said, tentatively following the women into the woods.

The woods on the valley floor were far less dense than the imposing forest that encased the settlement and the women were able to navigate it with relative ease. Leaping from tree to tree like young gazelles, they sprinkled the sweet Corstir wine on the ground as they moved deeper into the wooded expanse.

"Why are they throwing the wine onto the floor?" Iris asked, observing the women curiously.

"It attracts the boar, they like the sweet smell," Kat whispered, holding her finger to her lips and tilting her head for Iris to follow, in silence.

There was a real mix of excitement and urgency whirling around the women. Iris however felt more nervous than anything else and, sticking closely behind Kat, they manoeuvred skilfully through the trees. All of a sudden, a rustling of leaves could be heard right in front of them. Kat looked up, nodding to the other women. It seemed they finally had a boar in their sights. A hush rippled through the woods; only the sound of the trees swishing in the gentle breeze and tiny insects buzzing all around broke the silence. Two of the women began casually tossing food in the direction of the boar, attempting to tease it from its lair in order to lure the animal very slowly into their trap. The other women, including Kat and Iris, began to quietly circle the area, surrounding the unsuspecting beast from all sides – their spears were raised and ready. The boar was a large, powerful looking animal covered in grey-brown fur with sharp pointed tusks. It seemed oblivious to the women encircling it, grunting happily while foraging for food on the forest floor. Iris decided that it might be wise to stay well back at this point, not following Kat as she edged closer towards the enormous beast. Iris's heart was pounding as the tension rose. She was desperate to calm herself, fearing that the boar might smell her fear.

Iris watched in awe as the women worked skilfully as a team, the tension heightening as they stealthily crept in for the kill. At the very moment of attack, the noise became deafening as the boar suddenly realised it was being hunted. Iris struggled to see what was going on behind the bodies of the women jumping and running in all directions as they adeptly contained the animal within their tight circle. The animal's fierce growling could be heard over the din of the women who were furiously shouting orders to each other. All of a sudden one of the women jumped backwards, screaming as the boar charged forward and breaking free from their trap. It ferociously bounded directly towards Iris, its head down, much like a battering ram. Iris froze to the spot, closing her eyes in terror as the powerful animal lurched forward. Kat reacted like lightening, flinging herself on top of the beast and driving her spear hard into the back of the animal's neck. It let out the most horrific blood curdling cry before succumbing to its fate and falling dead on the ground, only inches from Iris. Iris tentatively opened her eyes; she thought her heart might beat right out from her chest as she shook her head in an attempt to bring herself back into the moment.

"Are you alright?" Kat shouted over to her. She now stood above the dead animal, one hand on her hip and the other still triumphantly clutching the spear.

"Yes," Iris nodded back eventually, still trying to bring her breathing under control.

"Another?" Kat asked.

"Another," Iris replied, energised by the experience.

The fearless women spent the rest of the morning in the woods tracking boar before emerging from the canopy of trees, further down the river. More than pleased with their morning's work, they rested near a beautiful waterfall, with crystal-clear water cascading down from the rocky wall into the river below. Lush green grass and patches of beautiful wildflowers lined the water's edge, creating an ethereal beauty. The women quickly rid themselves of their skins, jumping and diving into the inviting cooling water. They spent some time swimming and bathing. Iris had never had an opportunity to learn to swim before, so Kat attempted to teach her, unfortunately with little success. After much splashing around and roars of laughter, they retreated to the riverbank and basked in the late morning sunshine.

Corstir was liberating for Iris in every way as she leisurely stretched out on the soft grass unashamedly naked.

"I have been thinking," Kat declared a short while later. "Kian tells me Henry is especially important and he has a lot of responsibility in Mercia. It is only natural I suppose he would have behaved so honourably last night. You did rather put him on the spot."

"Yes, I suppose so … but I really wanted him to make love to me," Iris groaned.

"Yes, I know you did," Kat laughed. "I think perhaps you should speak with him later, and maybe get to know one another a little better first. Henry does not strike me as the impulsive type. "

"Umm," Iris mused, pulling a disappointed face.

"Iris Westonhall, you are quite the enigma, so seemingly innocent yet so openly brazen. No wonder you have Henry in such a quandary," Kat laughed. "Kian calls you a wildcat you know, and I think perhaps he might be right."

"Yes, he is," Iris admitted, grinning with a wicked glint in her eye. "A wildcat who is now free from restraint and I want to make the most of every precious moment. Who knows what the future holds for any of us Kat."

"Yes, you are right Iris, that is why I have decided to come with you to the East and then to Mercia," Kat announced with excitement in her voice.

"You have? That's wonderful," Iris replied, sitting up embracing her new friend lovingly. "But what about Little Kian?"

"My mother shall care for Little Kian; I have already spoken with her and Kian has agreed I can accompany you. Of course, I shall return to Corstir, but I need to see more of the world Iris, I want to see more of the world and I want to find love, just like you. You shall have to teach me many things once we are in Mercia," she added, clasping Iris's hand in hers.

"Me?" Iris laughed, "I'm afraid I shall not be able to teach you a thing. My life at Baines Abbey was very sheltered, as you well know. I am even more far less equipped for life in Mercia than yourself."

"You can teach me to ride a horse," Kat declared.

"Yes, indeed that I can do," Iris smiled. "And perhaps you can teach me to swim."

"Well then, between us we shall do very well," Kat concluded.

"Yes, we shall," Iris agreed.

The two women fell back down onto the lush grass still holding each other's hands tightly; Kat dreaming of Mercia, Iris dreaming of Henry.

Kian was still up on the roof of the hall when the hunting party strode back into the settlement; each woman carrying a brace of rabbits and collectively heaving two wild boar behind them.

"Christ, have I just fucking died and gone to heaven!" he declared, rubbing his eyes at the sight of the women marching towards the hall, clad in their skins.

Henry glanced up at Kian before spinning around to see what was so preoccupying his attention.

"Christ," he exclaimed, "that is certainly a sight you do not see every day."

The women promptly dropped their kill at the entrance to the hall where a handful of older women were waiting patiently to prepare the animals to cook. Kat and Iris made their way over to the men.

"Close your mouth brother, anyone would think you had never seen a woman before," Kat shouted up at Kian as he stood with his mouth wide open, glaring brazenly at the women.

"Well, not fucking dressed like that, I haven't. I thought I must have died and gone to heaven, " he laughed, jumping from the roof to join them.

"And what about you Henry, what do you think?" Kat asked, grabbing Iris's hand and spinning her around in order for Henry to admire her scantily dressed figure.

Iris blushed scarlet.

"A very impressive sight, I have to agree with Kian," he replied. "How was your first hunt Iris?" he asked with a smile, hoping to alleviate some of the tension between them and still admiring her dressed in her skins.

174

"I was a little nervous at first admittedly, but it was so thrilling Henry; I thought my heart would beat from my chest when the boar began to charge towards me," she replied, excitedly, thankful for his friendly tone. Iris had decided to take Kat's advice and speak with Henry later.

Henry raised his eyebrows, staring in Kat's direction.

"She was never in any danger," Kat replied, waving her hand, dismissing his concerns. "Come Iris, we need to clean down our spears," she said, grabbing at Iris's hand.

The two women turned to join the others who were already heading back in the direction of the river.

"Do we really have to leave Corstir?" Kian moaned, still grinning, catching the eye of one of the other women.

"I have to admit it is quite the paradise," Henry replied.

"It has certainly given Iris a womanly glow," Kian remarked, observing his friend who had yet to take his eyes from her as she walked away.

"Please don't Kian," Henry muttered, turning back to his work bench and picking up the planer.

After another hot and barmy yet productive day, the sun finally set on their third day in Corstir. Henry and Kian had arranged to meet with Father Peter and Arthur and had agreed to take dinner at Arthur's cottage. After a hearty meal Kian announced that he had a liaison with one of the women from the hunting party. Henry accepted an invitation from Arthur to stay the night after he produced a bottle of brandy. Henry thought it perhaps wise to allow a little space between himself and Iris, to allow the intensity between them to settle. He also doubted he would be able to refuse her a second time if she were to invite him to her bed. He had thought of nothing else all day.

Meanwhile back at the small hut Iris sat quietly on the bed, waiting anxiously to speak with Henry. She too had been unable to think of much else all day and now desperately wanted to tell him that she was sure, surer than she had ever been about anything else in her life. Rising from the bed she decided to sit on the cot in the other room and picked up Henry's leather doublet. She breathed in the musky smell of leather. It smelt of Henry. Clutching it to her breast she closed her eyes, longing for him to return.

The following morning, it was set to be another fine day in Corstir. The older women who had prepared the kill had all been up and about early and the fire pit in the hall was lit with one of the boars already beginning to roast above the flames. Some of the younger children had been gathering wildflowers to decorate the space and a handful of the older girls were practising a dance for the farewell feast. By midday Henry and Kian had finally completed their commission – successfully replacing the rotten wood from the hall. All that was left to do was clear away the old planks. Kian had just taken the first load down to the river when a young woman approached.

"Hello," she said to Henry. "I'm looking for Kian."

"He has just gone down to the river, he won't be too long," Henry replied, presuming she must be the woman with whom Kian had had the liaison.

"I'm Mary," she smiled, "I have brought some food and wine, there is plenty if you would like some?"

"Thank you, Mary," Henry replied, accepting a parcel of food as she busily filled him a cup of wine.

The pair continued to chat, smiling, and laughing while waiting for Kian to return. Henry thought Mary was rather charming, with a sweet smile, long golden hair and large beautiful blue eyes. He could clearly see why Kian had been attracted to her.

Iris had woken late that morning still lay atop Henry's cot. She was furious! He had not returned to their hut. She allowed her imagination to run wild and envisaged him spending the night with another woman. After having spent what was left of the morning with Kat and Little Kian, her agitated, melancholy mood was not conducive to the happy carefree day Kat had planned for her young son. So, as they all headed back towards the Munro cottage to take lunch Iris decided it better to leave them to enjoy their last day together alone. She was determined to speak with Henry once and for all so she decided to head straight for the hall. As she approached, she immediately spotted Henry chatting and laughing with another woman. Her blood began to boil. Instantly jumping to the wrong conclusion, she stormed up to them all wild and angry.

"So, this is where you were last night," she yelled, pointing an aggressive finger towards Mary.

"I beg your pardon," Henry replied, taken aback by her sudden uncomely outburst.

"You heard me," she screamed back. "How could you Henry? I waited for you all night. I wanted you and all the time you were with her … I hate you."

Kian had just arrived back from the river. Mary quickly moved towards him grabbing his arm, alarmed by Iris's wild rage.

"What the fuck is going on?" he snapped, staring at Iris.

"Ask him?" Iris screamed louder, now pointing her finger furiously at Henry.

"Kian, what is she talking about?" Mary asked, gripping tighter onto Kian's arm.

"Well Iris, what the fuck?" he growled, now with his arm draped around Mary's shoulder.

Iris glared at Kian, then at Mary. All of a sudden she realised her foolish error.

"You are with Kian?" she whispered, nervously stepping backwards.

Henry grabbed her arm in a bruising hold and firmly pushing her forward, positioning her right in front of Mary.

"Apologise," he roared, "Now!"

"I'm sorry," she muttered under her breath, lowering her head, utterly mortified by her ridiculous mistake.

"Louder," Henry growled, shaking her angrily.

"I'm sorry," she screamed, pulling away from Henry's grasp, spinning around and striking him hard across the face. "I hate you," she yelled before bolting in the direction of the hut.

Henry struggled to maintain his calm composure. He ran his fingers through his thick dark hair before turning and bracing his arms to his work bench, lowering his head in sheer frustration.

Kian whispered something in Mary's ear, she kissed him tenderly on the cheek before leaving the two men alone.

"What the fuck is going on?" Kian snapped, staring intensely at his friend.

"Nothing," Henry replied, shaking his head.

"Fuck nothing, she wants you and you want her, don't tell me you fucking don't, Henry."

"I have already told you Kian, it's not that simple."

"Not that simple, what the fuck? She is a Lord's daughter, you are a Lord, do you really think that once we bring her to Lorimer you will be able to walk away from her? Go back to Mercia fucking other men's wives for the rest of your life? I know if you bed her Henry, you are committing yourself to her, but for Christ's sake. Not one of those flighty young fucking ladies at all those fucking balls, that you never even fucking attend, would ever be able to ignite your passion and stir your emotions in the way that wildcat does. Admittedly, you will be taking your belt to her as often as your cock, but for God's sake Henry."

Henry stood up from his bench and ran his fingers through his thick dark hair once again, letting out a deep sigh.

"You are right Kian I do want her; I want her desperately. I am in love with her."

"Then go to her Henry – make love to her and commit yourself to her, to each other. She is so good for you. You are so good for each other my friend."

"Thank you, Kian," Henry replied, placing his hand to Kian's shoulder before heading in the direction of the hut.

Iris sat on the bed. She was angry at herself and she was angry at Henry. She pounded the bed with her fists, screaming aloud. Henry appeared from behind the screen, as she knew he would, after her violent outburst. Too angry to feign remorse and, knowing her fate was already set, she picked up her shoe from the floor and threw it directly at him.

"Get out!" she screamed, "I hate you!"

Henry remained in the doorway, watching as Iris continued to scream obscenities at him.

"You have been spending too much time with Kian," he said with a laugh.

"Don't you dare laugh at me Henry Morton," she screamed, picking up her belt from the floor and furiously throwing it at him. "Here, you will need this," she yelled, jumping to her feet.

Henry stepped over the belt and moved towards Iris. She was visibly shaking.

"I'm not going to beat you Iris," he said, wrapping his arms around her and holding her in a tight embrace,

Iris struggled to break free of his grasp, tears now welling up in her eyes.

"Let me go," she protested, "I hate you."

"Iris, I'm not going to hurt you, please calm down," he whispered, still holding her tightly.

"Then what are you going to do?" she groaned, still shaking.

"I love you Iris … I'm going to make love to you," he replied softly.

Iris suddenly stopped struggling and glanced up at Henry, tears still in her eyes.

"Can I kiss you?" he murmured, brushing his lips against hers.

"Oh Henry, yes," she breathed nervously.

Henry released his hold and cupped her face in his hands. He wiped away her tears before leaning down and kissing her passionately on the lips. Iris trembled.

"Don't be afraid Iris," he whispered, scooping her up into his arms.

They stood for a long while kissing and embracing each other before Henry stepped backwards and removed his shirt. He took Iris's hand and gently placed it to his naked chest. He felt so strong, a solid wall of muscle. Iris felt an excited anticipation coursing through her veins and she began to tremble again. Henry grabbed at the hem of her dress, ruching it up. Iris instinctively raised her arms and allowed him to pull it up over her head. He then stood back and admired her now naked body. Iris blushed and attempted to cover herself with her arms.

"You don't ever have to be embarrassed in front of me Iris," Henry whispered, tenderly kissing her reddening cheek. "You have the most beautiful body," he said, taking her hands in his. He pulled her close again, their bodies pressed tightly together. Henry continued to kiss her passionately, slowly moving his hands down her back and cupping her buttocks, pressing his hips to hers. Iris moaned softly to his gentle caresses as an intense erotic feeling built up inside her.

"Lie down," Henry whispered, finally releasing her from his embrace.

Iris obeyed and dreamily stretched out on the bed. Henry stood for a moment admiring her shapely figure once more, then, leaning down, he kissed her. First on the lips, then her breasts. Iris closed her eyes inhaling sharply.

"Do you like that?" Henry smiled glancing upwards, teasing her now hardened nipples with his tongue.

"Yes," Iris breathed, her body tingling with excitement.

Henry hastily kicked off his boots before removing his breeches. He stood for a moment at the side of the bed and allowed Iris to see his naked body, fully aroused. Iris turned scarlet.

Henry smiled tenderly, sliding down beside her, and continued to kiss and caress her breasts; sucking and biting at her nipples. Iris reacted to his touches, raising her body up and pushing herself seductively against him. Henry then ran his hand up and down the length of her naked body several times, before coming to a stop. Iris gasped as he skilfully massaged the intimate area between her legs, her whole body succumbing to his expert touch. Her muscles tightened as she pressed her head back against the bed.

"Oh Henry," she cried out, an explosion erupting inside her.

"Was that nice?" Henry murmured, kissing her mouth as his fingers continued to repeat the same action.

"Yes," she moaned, consumed once again, almost instantly.

Iris slowly opened her eyes. She was breathless with a pulsating aftershock between her legs.

Henry gently parted her legs wider then lifting himself up he positioned himself between her thighs.

"This might hurt a little," he whispered, kissing her lips before thrusting himself hard into her core.

Iris winced. Her whole body tensed at his solid presence deep inside her. Henry maintained a slow steady rhythm until he felt Iris's body relaxing beneath him.

"Move with me Iris," he breathed, desperately craving more and more of her.

Iris obeyed, raising her hips and meeting Henry's movements whilst gripping onto the skins beneath them as Henry thrust himself inside her harder and faster, moaning softly with pleasure to his increased rhythm.

"Christ, you feel so good Iris," he groaned, pushing her knees up further, driving himself deeper inside her.

Their bodies moved in harmony lost in each other completely, totally.

Several minutes later Iris cried out. "Henry … please … yes." Her body was shaking as she pressed her legs down and, as her muscles began to tighten, the wave of breath-taking pleasure washing over her once again. Henry joined her letting out a garbled groan. With one final push he emptied himself deep inside her as he too reached his climax.

"Are you alright?" he asked, still joined. "Did I hurt you?"

"Yes, at first … but I liked it," Iris smiled, with a glow of satisfaction lighting up her face.

"Oh Iris," Henry breathed, gently withdrawing from inside her. Iris let out a small gasp, she blushed.

Henry laughed, "Why do you blush so?"

"I can't help it; it must be the effect you have on me."

"Well from now on, every time you blush I shall have to make love to you, until you are no longer embarrassed in my presence."

"Then I shall never stop blushing," she grinned, gently pulling herself up onto his chest and leaning down to kiss him.

They lay together for a while, embracing each other, their naked bodies soaked in perspiration and tightly entwined. At some point later they both drifted off to sleep.

It was dusk when Henry finally awoke, he could hear the chatter of folk milling around outside the hut. He gently nudged Iris awake.

"We shall have to get up Iris and attend the festivities, it's getting late," Henry whispered in her ear, nipping it gently with his teeth. He was fully aroused.

"Must we," Iris replied seductively, feeling his erection pressing against her. "Make love to me Henry."

"We do have to go Iris."

"I know, but just not yet," she grinned, leisurely lying back on the bed.

"Christ woman, what on earth are you doing to me?" he groaned, pulling himself up and gently sheathing himself inside her once again.

The night's festivities were bittersweet as it was their last in Corstir. The evening was spent with Anna and Little Kian. Father Peter had insisted they leave before sunrise the following morning, so it was important for Kat to spend as much quality time with her young son as possible. It was late when they finally bid goodnight to Henry and Iris. Kian carried the young boy back to the cottage; he was fast asleep in his uncle's arms. Kian had grown very fond of the boy and had promised him that he would return as soon as he was able. After bidding an emotional farewell to Anna, Kian and Kat left the cottage and headed back to spend the night in one of the small unoccupied huts.

"We could have stayed the night you know," Kian said as they paused at the riverbank, looking out over the valley; the moon was reflected in the dark water.

"No, it is better this way," Kat replied. "He will be well cared for here and I don't think I could bear to see him cry if he were to see me leave."

Kian placed his large arm around his sister's shoulders, pulling her close.

"Nor I," he confessed, kissing her on the cheek. "I wish we had more time."

"Tell me Kian, what is it like in Mercia?" she asked, shivering and wrapping her own arms around her brother's waist for warmth.

"The countryside is much like Corstir, people work hard on the land for not a lot. The towns are quite different. Brick-built houses, enormous in size some of them, and an abundance of food, wines, fabrics – in fact everything you could possibly imagine. You wait until you see the ladies dressed in all their finery and the rich men who own the lands. Not always honourable though – vast wealth can make a man greedy and not just for money and power."

"Henry is rich, he owns land," Kat mused.

"True, he is, but he is one of the good ones, in fact one of the very best. I trust Henry with my life, he is my brother," Kian replied, reflecting on his long friendship for a moment.

"Will he marry Iris, do you think?"

"Yes, undoubtedly. He would not have bedded her otherwise. I believe he will ask Lorimer for her hand as soon as we reach Wicken Hall."

"Why Lorimer?" Kat enquired.

"We suspect him to be Iris's guardian, why else would her father have asked Henry to deliver her safely to him," Kian replied, "Arlen is never going to believe it. The last time he saw Iris she was sobbing atop my horse after receiving a sore arse from Henry," he laughed.

"Who is Arlen?"

Kian laughed louder, "Come on let us get you back to the hut and I shall tell you all about Arlen, you will like him, I am sure. He will meet us in the Corridor on our return to Mercia, well he better fucking had, that's for sure," Kian sniffed, turning from the riverbank and heading back towards the settlement.

The following morning the travellers were all stood atop the steep rocky wall, looking down on the narrow valley below. Henry stood behind Iris and wrapped his arms around her waist.

"Do you see it?" she said, pointing towards Corstir.

"See what?" Henry asked, tightening his grip.

"Our hut. Do you think we shall ever return?" she asked, turning to face him.

"Perhaps, one day, if you would like to," he replied.

"Yes, I think I would, one day," she whispered, leaning up and kissing Henry on the lips.

"For fuck's sake, I hope we're not going to have to endure you pair all loved up the whole way. I think I prefer you at odds with each other," Kian grinned, winking at Iris.

"No, Kian," Iris laughed, kissing Henry again.

"Come," Father Peter shouted, distracting them. "It is time, we must make haste; I hope to reach Haven Abbey within two days."

"Haven Abbey?" Henry asked.

"Yes," the priest replied. "We shall be able to take refuge there before continuing on to Wicken Hall, I know the abbess."

The travellers then all turned and hoisted their bags over their shoulders. The last five idyllic, carefree days behind them, it was now time to return to reality as they followed the priest, once again into the dark forbidding Corstir Forest on the final leg of their journey heading east.

Chapter 12

Lord Douglas Barlett sat in a small dingy office at the commoners' prison in the basement of the tower in Kingslea. He clutched a handkerchief to his nose in a desperate attempt to mask the dreadful stench coming from the filthy, disease-ridden prison cells. The sound of despairing, wretched men unsettled him greatly. It had been five days since Lord Thomas Gilmore had been arrested and left to the mercy of the unscrupulous prison guards in order to extract information regarding the murder of Raven Westonhall and the explosion in Trevelyan.

Lord Barlett, having petitioned the King unsuccessfully to take charge of the interrogation, had finally received an order granting permission. He was under no illusion that it was due to the fact that the prison guards had failed to gain any added information. Barlett was convinced that Gilmore was merely a patsy. He was expecting to see a broken man, but nothing could have prepared him for the sight of Thomas Gilmore being unceremoniously dragged into the dark damp office. The short plump pompous man was utterly unrecognisable. His face was so badly swollen that he was barely even able to open his eyes. He could not stand, much less walk, as the two prison guards abruptly dropped him into a chair. Gilmore slumped forward, desperately gripping the desk with his blood encrusted hands to prevent him from falling.

"Get out," Lord Barlett bellowed sharply at the two tormentors as they grinned through rotten teeth at the despondent Lord Gilmore.

They glared at each other blankly, not quite sure what they should do. "Milord, we were told …"

"Out, I say," Barlett growled, waving his hand furiously at the two men.

They promptly scurried away like filthy rats, without saying another word.

Barlett stared down at Gilmore, shaking his head in disbelief before pouring a glass of brandy. He handed it to the piteous man, only for it to instantly slip from his bloody fingers and shatter on the floor. Barlett observed Gilmore's hands. They were splayed as though crushed, his fingernails removed and his palms had been branded with irons. Immediately refilling another glass, Barlett gently lifted it to Gilmore's lips. He spluttered, unable to even swallow as the liquid dribbled from his mouth.

"My God, Thomas, what have they done to you?" Barlett whispered, utterly appalled at the barbaric treatment so cruelly bestowed, and on a Lord of Mercia.

Filling another glass of brandy for himself he gulped down the contents before stepping from the office, only to find the two prison guards skulking outside.

"Fetch the Constable," he bellowed, as the two men hurriedly fled off in opposite directions.

Barlett returned to the office, glancing down once again at the broken man in front of him. The smell of urine and excrement was overpowering and his expensive clothes resembled nothing more than rags, torn and smeared with his blood. Barlett held his handkerchief tightly to his nose once again.

"You asked to see me?" came a deep confident voice. Sir William Gee, Constable of the tower appeared in the doorway.

Gee was a courtier and administrator and had held the post of constable for the last twenty years. His keen facial features, large eyes and prominent nose seemed fitting to the surroundings. He was dressed all in black, save for a small white ruffle collar protruding from his surcoat.

"Yes, I did," Barlett replied with an air of authority. "Have this man taken to the private chambers above and fetch a physician, immediately!" he roared, leaving Gee in no doubt of his utmost displeasure.

Gee promptly summoned the two men who were still skulking outside the doorway. Under Barlett's watchful eye, they carefully lifted Gilmore from the chair, carrying him from the dingy office. Gee rushed off in order to summon a physician. Lord Barlett proceeded to follow the two prison guards to the private chambers above, thankful to leave the stench of death and decay behind. The private rooms were well furnished; still with bars at the windows, but clean and airy. The two guards gently lay Gilmore on a soft feather bed covered in red damask before hastily scurrying away. Gee returned directly, standing sheepishly in the doorway.

"A physician is on his way, milord … We did nothing we were not given permission to do," he declared, shifting nervously around on his feet.

"My God man, you have tortured him almost to death," Barlett growled, pointing towards Gilmore curled up on the bed. "Why was he not at least housed here in the private chambers, he is a Lord of Mercia?"

"The order came directly from the King, milord. I have the paperwork if you wish to inspect it?" Gee sniffed, attempting to defend his complicit actions.

"Get out," Barlett roared, absolutely furious and wanting nothing more than Gee out of his sight.

Douglas Barlett paced the private prison cell, waiting in silence for a physician to arrive, trying hard to comprehend the King's fury regarding Gilmore.

The King was usually such a compassionate man, opposed to any violence unlike his father. *This rage is unprecedented*, Barlett mused to himself. *It has to have something to do with Henry Morton's letter.* Arlen had informed his father that the King had turned quite pale upon reading it, and then there was his curious interest in Westonhall's daughter. *Why on earth should the King be interested in a girl nobody even knew existed a few weeks ago?* He rubbed his chin perplexed.

Thomas Gilmore had not moved an inch or made a single sound as he lay curled up on the bed. Barlett observed that the nails on his feet had been removed and his toes were splayed, having also been crushed. He turned from the bed to peer from the barred window, out onto the inner courtyard of the tower. It was eerily quiet.

Finally, after about an hour a physician arrived. Gee had struggled to find anyone willing to attend a prisoner from the lower cells due to the filth and disease, and more importantly lack of money. The physician was a jolly looking character but, as he bounded through the door, his expression altered instantly upon observing Gilmore on the bed. Clearly visibly shocked at the injuries to his patient's body, he set to work at once cleaning and dressing his numerous wounds. Barlett sighed aloud as he watched the physician efficiently working away. He knew it was not going to be possible to speak with Gilmore today, if at all, so he decided to take his leave. He promised to return the following morning, although he doubted Gilmore even knew he was there.

Edwin and Arlen were in the drawing room of Barlett House when their father finally returned from the prison. It was evident to the two men that he was deeply troubled.

"What is wrong Father?" Edwin asked, rising from his chair to pour his father a glass of brandy. "Is it Gilmore?"

"Yes, it's a wonder the man is still alive," Barlett murmured, sipping his brandy as he stood beside the large bay window looking out onto the street.

Edwin and Arlen glanced over at each other, raising their eyebrows. They remained silent to allow their father to gather his thoughts, neither being able to remember seeing him so profoundly unsettled before. Barlett eventually moved away from the window and joined his sons. He sat down in one of the easy chairs.

"Gilmore did not write that letter. I knew it at once, it was not even his hand. If he had, he would have confessed days ago. They have completely broken him, body as well as mind I should imagine. I thought we had progressed from the barbaric act of torturous interrogation in Mercia, clearly, I was wrong."

"Is the King aware?" Edwin asked.

"The King sanctioned it," Lord Barlett snapped angrily. Immediately, he began to apologise to his son. "I'm so sorry Edwin, please forgive me, I have allowed my emotions to get the better of me."

"It is quite alright Father, I totally understand," Edwin replied.

Lord Barlett's sons were able to count on only one hand the times they had witnessed their father losing his usual calm composure, this current state of affairs had clearly vexed him greatly.

The three men sat in silence for a while, drinking brandy, lost in their own thoughts. Mrs Brooke provided refreshments, which sat on the table untouched as not one of them had much of an appetite. Lord Barlett was the first to speak, his composure seemingly recovered.

"Arlen, when do you return to Trevelyan?" he asked cheerfully.

"The day after tomorrow sir, if Henry's calculations are correct. They should be ready to exit the East within the week. I also have some affairs to put in order; my lodging house for one. I left Trevelyan in such a hurry. It is paid up until the end of the month, but even so I would like to spend a…" Arlen paused, clearing his throat.

"Your friend still occupies your thoughts?" his father enquired.

"Her name was Harriet, Father, and yes, she does," he replied, staring aimlessly into his empty glass.

"I'm sorry my son," his father added, rising from his chair and placing a hand to Arlen's shoulder. "I shall need you to deliver a letter to Trevelyan House for me please. Lady Gilmore and her daughter are being held under house arrest. I should very much like them brought to Kingslea. Gilmore shall require a lot of care and attention if he has any hope at all of recovering from this monstrous ordeal."

"Yes, of course Father," Arlen replied.

"We do seem to have reached rather a dead end in our investigations," Edwin grumbled, also rising from his seat and pulling the cord for Mrs Brooke.

"Well, let us consider what we do know," Lord Barlett mused, settling back down in his chair with another full glass of brandy.

"After the King firstly extended his hand to the East, we know that Lorimer requested a private audience with Osbert and was due to arrive on the day of the explosion. We don't know the reason for this request and, fortunately for Lorimer, he was taken ill only hours before he was due to travel. We must therefore presume the explosion was meant for him. Either to put a stop to negotiations regarding Howard or something else entirely. Regardless, negotiations have taken place with the arrival of the Ambassador James Ripley. I am confident the King will very soon be extending an invitation to his aunt and Sebastian to join him here in Kingslea with a view to reinstating the line of succession. Raven Westonhall was murdered either because he was of no more use to the true perpetrators or he had become a liability. Having been seen in the Corridor by you Arlen, may have played a part in that. We must also presume that the men that came for his sister believed Raven may have confided in her in some way. We know they were corresponding with each other in secret and that perhaps she also knew what was contained in that box at Baines Abbey. Westonhall served under Lorimer in the Vikrin wars, and I know for a fact he was a valued friend of the King and had been for many years. Lorimer and Westonhall were also both at Crowforth, albeit on different sides, which may explain why Westonhall insisted that Henry travel to the East for answers regarding the explosion. We shall have to wait for Henry to return in order to enlighten us on that point. I believe there are two possible avenues of investigation we can take. Arlen, I have already made enquiries into Raven Westonhall. It seems he was a regular visitor to Trevelyan, so ask around whilst you are there. You know these people, find out where he went and what he was doing and more importantly who he was meeting. It does seem odd you had not encountered him before the day of the explosion, perhaps he travelled incognito. I shall attempt to speak with Gilmore again tomorrow, the prison guards were asking all the wrong questions. I am convinced he knows nothing of the explosion; I am more interested in who he inadvertently gave access to his seal – a whore perhaps or an unscrupulous servant. If we can find them, then maybe we can make a connection."

"It does not explain the King's reaction to Henry's letter or his interest in Iris though," Arlen mused.

"No, I have to admit that baffles me greatly, but I am hopeful Henry shall also be able to throw some light on that once he has spoken to Lorimer."

"Father, tell me who was to rendezvous with Lorimer in Trevelyan?" Arlen asked, curious to know who his father had entrusted with such an important commission.

"Phillip Ainsworth. I wrote to your brother for a recommendation. Ainsworth was instructed to rendezvous with Lorimer on the quayside at midday and bring him to a secret location just north of Trevelyan."

"Oh, I did rather wonder about that," Edwin mused. "Yes, Phillip Ainsworth would have been my choice, discretion is his middle name and tell me Father, what of Sir Ripley?"

"Ripley remains in Kingslea. He seems content enough. He wrote to Lorimer regarding Raven Westonhall. They are probably as anxious as we are to uncover the truth – Howard's future as King might depend upon it."

An idea suddenly popped into Arlen's head just as Mrs Brooke entered the room. She busily cleared away the plates of untouched food, clearly irritated and glaring at the three men with pursed lips before informing them that dinner would not be served for another hour.

"Christ, that bloody woman," Lord Barlett grumbled, leaning back in his chair and closing his eyes with a shake of his head.

Edwin and Arlen laughed aloud.

The following morning the three men were all up early and sat at the dining room table tucking into a hearty breakfast. Lord Barlett's mood had improved, having received a note from the physician informing him that Gilmore had spent a comfortable night and that he had actually managed to eat a little hot soup.

"I shall attend the prison again today," he announced. "Somebody got their hands on Gilmore's seal; we need to know who."

"Arlen, what are you up to today?" Edwin asked, now starting on his second bowl of porridge.

"I have some business in town to address, why?"

"I have received correspondence from Florence. She arrives in Kingslea today with her mother. I know she is desperately hoping to see you."

"I don't have time for all that," Arlen snarled indignantly.

"Brother, you are her betrothed and you hardly even acknowledge her existence; I have to wonder why on earth you asked for her hand in the first place," Edwin growled, annoyed by his brother's flippant response.

"Because I'm a bloody fool," Arlen snapped back, slamming his spoon down into his empty bowl of porridge.

"You are too cruel Arlen; Florence deserves far better," Edwin insisted, glaring furiously at his brother across the table.

"Well Brother, if you are that fucking concerned about her feelings then get her to release me and marry her yourself," Arlen yelled, immediately apologising to his father for his use of foul language at the dining table, before promptly striding from the room.

Lord Barlett and Edwin both let out a deep sigh as the breakfast dishes rattled on the sideboard as Arlen angrily slammed the door behind him.

"Oh dear, it seems your brother is in quite a dilemma," Lord Barlett muttered, with another deep sigh.

"Yes," Edwin agreed with a thoughtful look in his eyes. "He is indeed."

It was mid-morning when Douglas Barlett arrived back at the tower prison and the physician had just finished his latest assessment of Lord Gilmore.

"Good morning, Milord," he smiled, "I'm pleased to report that Lord Gilmore spent a comfortable night; I administered a little opium for the pain and it seemed to have done the trick. I do fear however perhaps this ordeal may have affected his mind, he seems rather troubled this morning, mumbling something about a gold pin or some such," he continued, quickly gathering up all his things from the table.

"Thank you, I shall sit with him for a while, please send me your bill," Barlett replied, pulling up a chair to the bed and bidding the physician a good day.

Lord Barlett decided it prudent to begin discussing insignificant things and general chit-chat in the hope that Gilmore might begin to engage with him. Lunging into direct questions relating to his seal might cause him to retreat back into himself. After about an hour of no responses at all, he rose from his chair and began hopelessly pacing the room, resorting to the pointed questions after all, desperate to gain any answers.

"Thomas, who could have gained access to your seal? A prostitute? A servant?" he repeated over and over again. His voice raised along with his frustration.

At length he resigned himself to the fact that he was completely wasting his time, Gilmore was too far gone. So, retrieving his hat from the table he proceeded towards the door.

"Black hair," Gilmore muttered, barely above a whisper. "She had black hair."

Barlett instantly turned on his heels and hastily kneeled beside the bed.

"Who did Thomas, who had black hair?"

"A pin, gold and black," he gibbered, his mouth dribbling blood and saliva.

"Who? Thomas, do you know her name?" Barlett implored, staring at the pitiful man, willing him to answer back. "Was she a whore?"

"A lady, she had raven black hair," Gilmore continued, repeating himself several times over until finally drifting back off to sleep.

Barlett stood up, rubbing his chin in deep contemplation. He stared down at Gilmore lying on the bed and, confident that he could not extract any further information from him today, decided to leave and return tomorrow to try again. It was not a lot to go on, but it was definitely a start. Although the fact it was a lady perturbed Barlett greatly – it seemed Mercia had a traitor deep within its midst after all.

Arlen was heading to the academic hotspot of the city, Langland. Boasting several universities and colleges, Langland was considered an area of excellence for those wanting to study the law, classics, and history. Arlen and Henry had both spent time at Oxwich College during their Crown Knight training, which was where Arlen was heading today. Oxwich was set in thirty-two acres of wooded grounds and included hothouses and a lake. The rectangular lawned quadrangle was surrounded by sizable multi-level buildings, one of which housed the oldest library in Mercia and was home to Linus Eves, a renowned genealogist. Upon entering the library, Arlen was instantly hit by the sweet musty smell of old leather. Hundreds upon hundreds of books lined the shelves and small tables were piled high. A central study table ran the length of the ground floor. A rather tall gangly looking young man wearing a pince-nez on a chain dangling from his neck, his fair hair already thinning, hurried over to greet Arlen as he stood at the head of the large table.

"Can I help you sir?" he asked politely, curious at the sight of a Crown Knight in the library.

"Yes, I'm here to see Linus Eves, he is expecting me," Arlen replied.

Arlen had visited the library days earlier and had made enquiries into Lady Clara Westonhall.

"Oh yes," said the gangly young man, "Sir Barlett, Mr Eves is expecting you, please come this way." He beckoned for Arlen to follow him up the small staircase at the back of the room.

The young man led Arlen to a spacious office on the second floor. Linus Eves was sat behind a large oak desk, overloaded with papers, scrolls and books. The walls around the room were lined with bookcases, all brimming with even more books – much more than the wooden shelves could handle, judging by their warped appearance. Linus Eves peered up from his desk. He was an elderly man with wispy white hair sticking up from the roots as if he were continually running his fingers through it and causing it to be permanently standing upright. It made Arlen smile as he thought of Henry, who also had the habit of running his fingers through his hair, and wondered if he might resemble Linus Eves one day.

"Arlen," Eves beamed, "how good to see you again my boy. Good Lord, you are the image of your father," he said cheerfully. "How is the old devil?"

"Very well thank you," Arlen replied, rather surprised that Eves and his father were acquainted.

Eves noticed Arlen's quizzical expression.

"Yes, my boy I know your father. I had the pleasure of teaching him while he was on loan from Chesterford," he laughed, sounding amused. "You are very much like him, I didn't notice when you visited the other day, but I feel I have been transported back in time, what, thirty years," he laughed again.

Eves continued to chatter on, fussing around his desk, papers and books spilling onto the floor. The young gangly man seemed to have a full-time job picking up after him.

"Well," he said finally, passing Arlen a neatly rolled scroll tied with a red ribbon. "A genealogical chart for Lady Clara Westonhall."

Arlen hastily unwound the scroll and placed it on a side table that was relatively empty of books and papers.

"As you can see," Eves continued, joining Arlen at the table, "Clara Westonhall was the daughter of a timber merchant from Cambrian, quite an advantageous marriage to Bennett Westonhall. She produced one son, Raven, who as we now know met a premature death only days after his father. Bennett has a sister who married a Lord from Norland and she produced three sons. I have already despatched communication to Norland informing her eldest son, umm Richard I think his name is," Eves mused, circling around Arlen to check the name on the scroll. "Yes, Richard, that he is now Lord of Baines Abbey."

"What about Clara's daughter?" Arlen asked, still curiously staring down at the scroll.

"Berwyn, Berwyn," Eves shouted loudly to the young gangly man stood patiently beside the large oak desk. "A daughter, did we miss a daughter?"

Berwyn instantly scurried over, hurriedly placing his pince-nez on the bridge of his nose and glared down at the scroll, his face turning pink.

"I'm sorry sir, there was no mention of a daughter. I shall of course check the records again," he blurted out, his pince-nez slipping from his nose.

"Apologies, Arlen, daughters can sometimes be missed, we shall of course double-check the records," Eves confirmed. "Do you perhaps know of a daughter?" he asked, glaring at Arlen, slightly puzzled.

"No, not really, just hearsay," Arlen squirmed, conscious not to say too much.

"That will be it then," Eves replied, smiling, content with Arlen's explanation. "But of course, we shall make absolutely sure, right Berwyn?" he said, nodding at the young man.

Berwyn nodded back, his cheeks now scarlet.

"Is there anything else we can do for you?" Eves asked, busily returning to his desk and running his fingers through his sparse white hair.

"Yes, there is in fact, I would like a genealogical chart, as a gift for my future wife. Florence Ainsworth … a wedding gift," Arlen declared, slightly embarrassed by his phoney request.

Linus Eves looked disappointed; he was obviously hoping for a more interesting commission. Arlen was sure if Eves knew the real reason for the request it would have piqued his interest no end. Arlen was fully aware of his father and brother's regard for Phillip Ainsworth, but he could not shake a certain feeling he had. Phillip's indifference upon reading the letter at Goring End, and the fact he was privy to Lord Lorimer's planned visit to Trevelyan, which provided him with precise locations and times of arrival, bothered him. A wedding gift for Florence seemed a more than plausible reason for commissioning a geological chart allowing Arlen to investigate the Ainsworth family connections without drawing any unwanted attention.

"Yes, of course, we shall set to work at once, how soon do you require it?" Berwyn asked. Eves already had his head down in his books, not at all interested in Arlen's latest request.

"How soon can it be ready?"

"A couple of days no more, the family are well connected," Berwyn replied confidently.

"I am away from town tomorrow, but shall return within the week. Can you arrange to have it sent directly to Barlett House?" Arlen asked, retrieving some coins from his purse.

"Yes of course sir, and I shall also confirm the misunderstanding regarding the Westonhall daughter," Berwyn replied, flushing pink once again.

"Excellent, thank you," Arlen replied.

Their business concluded, Arlen bid the two men good day and decided to take dinner in an ale house en route. He didn't want to return to Barlett House too soon as he was worried that Edwin may have invited Florence for dinner. Even though he knew he was going to have to face her sooner or later and make a decision regarding the impending wedding, today however was not the day. It was well after midnight when he finally returned home, the house all in darkness. He let out a deep sigh of relief before quickly and quietly making his way up the stairs and climbing into bed.

Chapter 13

It was late in the afternoon when Father Peter finally stepped from the dense outer edge of the Corstir Forest and into the far east of Mercia. The rest of the weary travelling party were following not far behind. The weather had taken a distinct turn for the worse; they were greeted by driving rain and swirling winds. The priest had pushed them hard through the forest and they were all utterly exhausted. They had quickly wrapped themselves in cloaks and blankets to shield as best as they could from the awful weather. Father Peter pointed towards a dilapidated old grey building, just visible through the torrential rain, less than a mile from the forest.

"Haven Abbey," he called out, beckoning for them all to follow him.

As they drew nearer it was clear to see that the Abbey was in desperate need of repair. Although once an impressive fortress, it was now a miserable looking building flanked by four watch towers, one of which had collapsed many years ago, that enclosed an inner keep. Lights were lit inside the other three towers and lanterns burned at the main entrance. Father Peter banged his fist on the enormous wooden door several times, waiting patiently for someone to answer. Eventually creaking open, a middle-aged nun appeared at the entrance holding a candle up to her tired visitor's face.

"Father Peter," she beamed, pleasantly surprised. "It has been such a long time since we have seen you, come in, come in," she bellowed, flinging the door wide open and ushering everyone inside a large gatehouse with a welcoming roaring fire burning away in a grand fireplace. The travellers immediately gravitated towards the fire, desperate for a little warmth. They quickly rid themselves of their sodden outer garments.

"Sister Bridget," the priest declared, clasping the woman's hands in his. "It is so good to see you, how are you?"

"As well as can be expected," she replied, smiling fondly at the priest. "The people of the East have cared little for God and the Abbey in recent years. Times are very hard Father; the young crave the freedom of Mercia. We heard about the dreadful explosion in the Corridor, news still travels this far off the beaten track you know," she smiled, momentarily glancing at the priest's travelling companions. "Is that why you are here?" she asked curiously.

"In part, yes," the priest replied. "We are here to see Lord Lorimer. We hope he can provide us with some information if we may beg food and a bed for the night. Perhaps some fresh clothes and horses if you can spare them, we can pay, handsomely," he continued.

"The bed, food, and clothes you are welcome to, for no charge. The horses I'm afraid I cannot help no matter how handsomely you pay. We sold all our horses months ago; we do have an old ox and cart you are more than welcome to take."

"We thank you for whatever you can spare," the priest replied, still clasping her hands tightly.

Sister Bridget was of average height and was probably in her late fifties. Her white cotton cap framed her friendly, round, rather jolly looking face with blue-grey eyes and hooded lids. A rosary and large bunch of keys hung from a belt around her rotund middle. It was abundantly clear she was more than pleased to see Father Peter again.

Hot food was quickly provided for the travellers, along with loaves of fresh bread and jugs of weak watered-down ale. Kian pulled a disgusted face. Henry glowered at him to keep silent as they all tucked into the meagre feast. Iris and Kat were provided with clean, plain woollen dresses complete with much needed undergarments and sensible shoes, whilst the men were provided with coarse linen shirts. Sister Bridget seemed to be in her element bustling about and issuing orders to the other nuns, none of which appeared to speak. She efficiently arranged for rooms to be prepared with fires lit, which provided much needed comfortable accommodation for their unexpected weary visitors.

"Please Sister," the priest implored, "you don't need to go to so much trouble, we are used to far less," he said, encouraging her to sit with the others around the fireplace.

"We don't get many visitors, Father, I assure you it is no trouble," she beamed, thoroughly enjoying the diversion.

Finally conceding, Sister Bridget sat down, this time observing her visitors carefully one by one, smiling and nodding in turn. Upon seeing Iris however her face changed. The jolly expression faded as she suddenly turned quite pale. Henry and Father Peter noticed at once.

"Why Sister, what on earth is the matter, you look as if you have seen a ghost?" the priest asked, catching Henry's eye.

Sister Bridget ignored him; her eyes still fixed firmly upon Iris. "What is your name child?" she asked.

Iris hesitated to reply and glanced at Henry for support. He nodded back, confirming that she could answer.

"Iris Westonhall," she replied tentatively.

Sister Bridget appeared to be in shock and continued to stare at Iris for the longest time. Henry broke the awkward silence.

"Sister Bridget," he said in an overly authoritative voice.

It had the desired effect and the nun broke her gaze, apologising profusely.

"I'm so sorry my dear, it's just that you remind me of someone I knew a very long time ago, please forgive me," she mumbled, hastily scurrying off in the direction of the Abbey chapel.

"Christ," Kian muttered under his breath. Kat punched him hard on the leg.

"Hey, what was that for?" he moaned at his sister. "Bloody hell Iris, what the fuck was all that about?"

Henry shot Kian an angry glare, before smiling at Iris and squeezing her hand for reassurance. Nevertheless, he too was wondering the exact same thing as Kian.

After a short while another much older nun entered the gatehouse and indicated for the travellers to follow her as she made her way towards a winding staircase in the first of the towers to their freshly prepared bedchambers.

Henry decided it prudent to stay close to Iris and, returning to her room once the nun had departed back down the stairs, helped her to undress. She was utterly exhausted and could barely stand. He lifted her into the bed. Then undressing himself he slipped in beside her, pulling her close. She was cold and shivered in his embrace, so he wrapped his arms around her tightly. He kissed her tenderly before they both very quickly fell fast asleep.

Iris was first to wake, she had slept surprisingly well snuggled with her back to Henry and his arms still wrapped tightly around her. She could feel his warm breath on her neck and the sound of his soft breathing in her ear. She felt so safe and warm in his embrace. Having not made love since leaving the forest settlement, she yearned for him to take her again and tilted her hips back suggestively. Henry stirred; Iris pushed back a little further until she felt his hard erection pressing against her.

"Good morning," he whispered in her ear, nipping it gently with his teeth. "And what might you want wench?" he sniggered.

Iris giggled, tilting her hips back again. Henry without another word effortlessly rolled her over and gently settled himself firmly between her thighs.

Several minutes later as they lay together after their lovemaking, Iris spoke. "Henry, I'm afraid," she whispered, placing her head to his chest.

Henry gentle lifted her head so as to face her. "Why are you afraid Iris?" he asked, planting a lingering kiss to her lips.

"I'm afraid of what Lord Lorimer might say."

"You don't need to be afraid of anything Lorimer may or may not say Iris, I am here to look after you, always," Henry replied, cupping her face in his hand and kissing her passionately, their naked bodies pressed tightly together.

"Do you promise Henry?"

"Yes, I promise Iris," he purred, burying his face in her naked breasts.

Kian and Kat had already been up for a while when Henry and Iris descended the stairs. They were sat beside the fire in the gatehouse tucking into bowls of creamy porridge laced with honey.

"Well, we don't need to ask what you two have been up to," Kian remarked, observing Iris's flushed cheeks.

"Keep your voice down," Henry warned, eyeing one of the silent nuns.

Kian let out a silly mischievous laugh. Henry shook his head, tutting loudly.

It was still relatively early and Father Peter was nowhere to be seen. Another silent nun brought in more porridge and handed Henry and Iris a bowl. She replaced the empty water jug with a full one before quickly scurrying away.

"Where is the priest?" Henry asked, tucking into a bowl of porridge.

"We haven't seen him," Kian moaned. "Or the nun from last night, the others don't speak," he replied, shrugging his shoulders and helping himself to more porridge. "This is fucking delicious," he mused, cheerfully filling his mouth.

Iris sat down next to Kat and the two women quietly chatted to each other as Henry and Kian sat in silence enjoying their breakfast. As the time continued to tick by, and with no sign of the priest, Henry began to get a little impatient and resorted to pacing up and down the gatehouse running his fingers through his hair. Finally, and much to his relief, Father Peter and Sister Bridget appeared at the entrance. Both completely soaked through as the harsh weather persisted. Hastily shaking off their wet outer garments, they proceeded to warm themselves beside the fire.

"Ah, good," the priest declared. "You are all up and fed."

"Where have you been?" Henry snapped, still a little irritated, observing the priest's mudded boots.

"To the village, I have managed to procure some horses. I'm afraid they cost rather a lot of money, I hope you don't mind Henry, I took it from your purse," he replied, stamping his mudded boots on the ground. "I had to round them up myself from the field because the owner refused to leave the warmth of his home." He accepted a large bowl of creamy porridge topped with honey from one of the silent nuns.

"No, not at all," Henry replied, thankful they did not have to travel by ox and cart. "When do we depart?"

"The roads are waterlogged I'm afraid, it would be foolish of us to venture far in this rain. I suggest we wait for a break in the weather."

"How far to Wicken Hall then, Priest?" Kian grumbled. He was more than anxious to get moving and back to Mercia.

"A good day's ride, perhaps we should delay until tomorrow, what are your thoughts, Henry?"

Henry's attention however had been diverted by Sister Bridget who was once again staring unsettlingly at Iris.

"Yes, whatever you think Priest," he murmured, not really listening as he was too busy glaring at the nun.

Sister Bridget caught his eye and hurriedly scurried away.

"Well Priest," Kian moaned, jumping to his feet, stretching and yawning loudly. "If we are to stay put, I shall need an occupation. I cannot sit around all day with nothing to do."

"Come Brother," Kat laughed, pulling at his arm, "I shall find you an occupation. You need only to look around to see they are in desperate need of a good cart horse," she joked, smiling broadly.

"Hey less of that," he complained. "You aren't too big to go over my knee, you know."

Kat laughed louder. "Oh Brother, just you try. Now come along and less of your idle moaning," she said, pulling Kian reluctantly in the direction of the kitchens.

"Priest, a word if you please," Henry insisted, throwing Iris a smile as she finished off her breakfast.

Henry gestured for the priest to follow him; leaving Iris quite alone. Once he was sure they were out of earshot he turned to face Father Peter.

"What is wrong with the nun, why does she stare at Iris?"

"I cannot tell you Henry, I have asked her the very same question myself. All she will say is that Iris reminds her of someone from her past. Someone she failed a long time ago; it is nothing more than an old woman with a muddled mind I'm sure of it. I've known her many years, don't make yourself uncomfortable, we are quite safe here."

"Very well Priest, but you had better be right," Henry warned him, not entirely convinced by the priest's explanation.

After finishing her porridge and observing that everyone seemed to have deserted her, Iris decided to make her way to the Abbey chapel were she found Sister Bridget at the altar praying. As she drew closer, Iris noticed the nun was clutching a small leather-bound book to her breast. Too small to be a bible, it was bound with a faded pale blue ribbon keeping it firmly closed.

"May I join you, Sister?" she asked, smiling down at the nun.

The nun broke off her prayers. She had been crying; the trail of tears were still visible on her cheeks.

"Why, Sister what on earth is wrong?" Iris asked concerned, kneeling down beside the old woman.

"Nothing my child, I'm just thanking God for his many miracles," she sniffed, clasping Iris's hands in her own, "Will you pray with me my dear?"

"Yes, of course Sister," Iris replied, as the two women bowed their heads in silent prayer.

Henry had followed Iris to the chapel. He observed the two women curiously from the doorway, careful not to be seen. He was overprotective of one, suspicious of the other.

Kian and Kat spent a productive morning in the kitchens clearing out the numerous store cupboards. Kian was indeed an excellent cart horse, removing and rearranging all the furniture on Kat's orders. Kat had set about cleaning down the many shelves. The majority of the occupants of Haven Abbey were older women, with only a handful of younger nuns – although they were probably in their forties. They worked hard alongside Kian and Kat in silence;

even so, it was evident that they were enjoying the jolly company with Kian being continually scolded by his sister for his use of foul language inside the Abbey walls. The nuns may not have spoken but they certainly knew how to smile. Kian, as always, was lapping up all the attention.

The harsh weather finally broke by mid-afternoon. Henry and Kian ventured outside to inspect the horses in preparation for their journey to Wicken Hall. Kat continued her quest to put some order back into the extensive kitchens. Iris remained with Sister Bridget, who was encouraging her to talk of her childhood and growing up at Baines Abbey. Sister Bridget listened intensely to every word. Iris liked the old woman and felt a certain connection to her in some way. Henry continued to observe the pair from a safe distance, careful not to alert either of them of his interest.

After a modest dinner of rabbit stew and honey cakes and with much hope that the storm had finally subsided, Henry declared that they should not delay their journey any longer and insisted that they all be ready to leave by sunrise the following morning. With little else much to do other than drink the watered-down ale, the travelling party decided to retire early in preparation for their long journey to Wicken Hall and Lord Ivan Lorimer.

Henry lay in the bed watching Iris as she spun about the room, dancing and chatting. The nun had evidently made quite an impression on her. Henry's earlier concern waned slightly as he listened to Iris relaying some of the old woman's stories. She looked so immensely happy and contented; her long auburn hair, worn loose, was bobbing over her shoulders as she moved around the roomy bedchamber. Her cheeks were flushed from the fire and, wearing only a thin linen chemise, her naked body was visible beneath. Henry longed to take her, but resisted calling her to their bed, just for a short while as she continued smiling and dancing about the room.

"Come to bed," he said finally, unable to contain himself any longer.

Iris quietened and smiled, "I love you, Henry Morton."

"And I love you too Iris, now come to bed woman, I want you," he grinned, pulling her beneath the covers.

Thankfully the rain had not returned and the travelling party were all up and ready before sunrise, anxious to get on their way. Iris however felt a little apprehensive. If Lord Lorimer was indeed her guardian as suspected, then she hoped he was a kind man who would approve of Henry. She searched the Abbey in order to bid farewell to Sister Bridget who, for some reason, was nowhere to be found. She asked some of the silent nuns but to no avail as they just shrugged their shoulders at her.

Kian suddenly burst into the gatehouse, red faced and flustered. "One of the horses has gone," he growled, glaring at Henry.

"The nun," Henry hissed, throwing the priest an angry look. "I knew something was not right."

"What do you mean Henry?" Iris asked, shocked by his dismay regarding Sister Bridget.

"It's alright Iris, nothing for you to worry about," he replied, glancing up at Kian who already had his hand firmly wrapped around the hilt of his sword.

They were going to need their wits about them it seemed. Kian passed his sister a dagger, which she quickly concealed under her skirts.

"Henry you are frightening me," Iris continued, grabbing his arm.

"The nun, she recognised you I am sure of it. I should have trusted my instincts," he grumbled, glaring in the direction of the priest once more.

"Please Henry," Father Peter implored. "Sister Bridget would not do anything to harm anyone, I promise you, there will be a reasonable explanation I'm sure of it."

"We shall see," Henry growled back, spinning around to face Iris. "I shall not let anything happen to you Iris, I promise. Come, you shall ride with me, let us make haste."

Iris sat atop Henry's horse with Henry's arm wrapped tightly around her waist. Leaning back against him, she could feel that he was tense. No longer the tender, gentle man she had woken up with this morning, now the hard, fearless Crown Knight that she had first encountered at Baines Abbey, although this time she was grateful for the fact.

They continued their journey travelling further east with Father Peter silently leading the way. The bleak and sombre wilderness of the area seemed a fitting setting for the mood of the travellers. The East had always been known as the wildest extent of marshland in Mercia, even before the civil war. Today it was ghostly, forbidding and, in places, dangerous. The priest navigated them over the spongy ground with peat bogs surrounding them in every direction. They stopped for only the shortest of time to rest the horses, relieve themselves and to take light refreshments. They were utterly exposed in this open expanse. As the midday sun began moving west, they began their journey south. Kian breathed a loud sigh of relief.

"Thank fuck for that," he whispered in Kat's ear. "I was beginning to think if we travelled any further fucking east we would end up in the wild ocean."

"And south is the right direction for Trevelyan, yes?" she asked her brother.

"Yes, the sooner we get out of this fucking godforsaken place the better."

The ground became firmer as they continued their journey south. As they had hardly met a soul thus far, Henry relaxed slightly, although he remained vigilant. He tightened his grip on Iris's waist, leaning down to kiss her neck. She lay her own hand over his and leant back against him, becoming increasingly anxious of what may lie ahead. As late afternoon approached, Wicken Hall finally appeared on the horizon, as if majestically rising from the ground as they slowly approached.

Wicken Hall was a large, stately residence with high walls and flanked by lookout towers; it resembled a castle more than a grand house. As they drew nearer, four Eastern soldiers rode from the fortified gatehouse to intercept their arrival.

The travellers stopped, staring up at the high walls. Henry transferred Iris onto the priest's horse, much to her disapproval.

"No, Henry," she said stubbornly, gripping hold of his arm in protest.

"Do as you are told Iris," he said, leaving her in no doubt that it was an order. "Now is not the time for disobedience," he added sternly.

Kat slipped from Kian's saddle, allowing him to join Henry as the two men rode on towards the four soldiers. There was an air of tension swirling around the men as they approached the gatehouse.

"What is your business here?" a ruddy faced soldier shouted, clearly in charge.

"We are here to see Lord Ivan Lorimer; I have been sent by Lord Bennett Westonhall,"

Henry replied, making eye contact with the soldier.

"You are from Mercia?" the ruddy faced soldier enquired, rather surprised.

"Yes, we are," Henry replied.

The soldier nodded to the man on his right who immediately pulled on his reins and headed back inside the hall.

All five men waited in silence. Henry continued to keep eye contact with the ruddy faced soldier, whilst Kian was busy weighing up the other two men. You could cut the tense atmosphere with a knife.

Moments later the door to the gatehouse reopened and Sister Bridget appeared in the entrance. Henry glanced over in her direction, gripping the hilt of his sword tightly. Sister Bridget nodded up at the fourth soldier before disappearing back inside the hall. The man rode back to their position, nodding to his commander as he retook his place at his side.

"It seems you have been granted an audience. You must surrender your weapons if you wish to enter," he demanded, now glaring at Kian.

Henry unsheathed his sword and passed it over, along with his dagger. Kian hesitated, but Henry nodded for him to comply. Kian reluctantly obeyed, relinquishing his weapons. One of the other soldiers rode over to Father Peter and the women and instructed them to follow him as they were all hastily ushered into the depths of Wicken Hall.

Not only resembling a castle from the outside, the travellers were not disappointed from the inside as they were first led into a large inner bailey before being directed towards the grand hall.

Sister Bridget stood in the doorway. Henry gave her an angry look as he gripped tightly onto Iris's hand.

"Please forgive me my Lord," she whispered, "I had to ensure you were granted safe entry, all shall become clear. I promise you," she said, smiling at Iris tenderly.

Upon entering they all marvelled at the majestic grand hall; the floor, tiled in Vikrin marble of black and white, resembled an enormous chess board and the oak panelled walls were adorned with an extensive collection of weapons and suits of armour from a bygone time. The fireplace was a large structure made of stone with elaborately decorated wood carvings adorning the mantle. The roaring fire sent a golden glow into the dark space as the visitors tentatively entered. Lord Ivan Lorimer sat at the far end of the hall on what could only be described as a throne. He looked old and frail, not the powerful, fierce warrior from civil war history. His once dark hair was now streaked white and his blue eyes were tired and sunken. Dressed in a plain velvet housecoat, it was clear that he was an extremely ill man. He watched intensely as his visitors approached; his eyes fixed firmly upon Iris. Sister Bridget joined him and stood at his side. He very slowly rose from his chair, stumbling slightly on the steps as the nun held his arm in order to steady him.

"Caroline," he muttered, barely above a whisper and moving towards Iris.

Henry stepped forward, positioning himself between Iris and Lorimer. The soldiers shifted closer, their swords drawn. Kian turned to face them with his arms raised. The tension heightened within the room as Kat discreetly ruched up her skirt and pressed her hand firmly against the dagger hidden beneath.

"Enough," Lorimer shouted with as much authority as he could muster. "Leave us," he commanded to the soldiers, waving his hand to dismiss them.

The ruddy-faced soldier hesitated for a moment then, beckoning to his men to stand down, they all then quit the room at once, closing the large oak doors behind them.

"Caroline," Lorimer whispered again, raising his hand to touch Iris's face.

Henry adjusted his position, blocking Lorimer's path.

"Please," the old man muttered, "I would never hurt her. I have waited a lifetime to look upon her face."

Iris stepped from behind Henry. She glanced up at him with a warm smile before allowing Lorimer to gently touch her face, his eyes filled with tears.

"Who is Caroline, my Lord?" she asked softly, gently placing her own hand over his.

"My daughter … your mother," he murmured with tears now rolling freely down his face.

Lorimer stumbled backwards, the emotion of the moment overwhelming him. Sister Bridget tried to steady him, unsuccessfully. Iris reacted instantly and grabbed his other arm as the two women helped him back to his grand chair.

"Look my dear," Sister Bridget said, pointing to a large portrait hung above the grand fireplace.

Everyone turned simultaneously. It was a picture of a beautiful young woman with auburn hair and deep blue eyes. She was holding a single blue iris in her hand. A muted gasp reverberated around the grand room; the portrait was the image of Iris.

"I recognised you at once, my dear," the nun declared. "I could hardly believe my eyes, you are the true image of your mother. I apologise for my earlier deceit, but your grandfather is very unwell, his heart is weak. I feared the shock may have been more than he could bear. I had to arrive ahead in order to prepare him and ensure your safe entry. After the suspected attempt on his life in the Corridor, tensions run extremely high here in the East. I could not risk anything happening to you at the hands of zealous soldiers."

"My darling Caroline," Lorimer whispered, bowing his head into his hands.

Iris stood very still, staring up at the picture, transfixed upon the image. So this was the woman of whom Sister Bridget spoke from her past.

"Sister Bridget, is it my mother of whom you spoke at the Abbey? You said you failed her."

"It was my dear and there is not a day goes by that I don't think of her."

"Tell me about my mother," Iris asked, tearing herself away from the portrait.

Sister Bridget produced the small leather-bound book wrapped in the pale blue ribbon from under her habit. Iris had not been able to see it clearly back at the Abbey. It was adorned with gold embossed initials on the cover, 'CL' along with the words 'Hope & Faith'. Sister Bridget held the book out to Iris.

"Your mother's journal my dear, she can tell you in her own words how this story began, with much hope, faith, and love. And I shall tell you how it ended in tragedy and betrayal."

"Please Sister Bridget will you read it aloud?" Iris asked, moving back towards Henry and clutching his hand in hers.

The travelling party all settled down onto the benches that lined the walls of the grand hall, anxious to hear what secrets the journal held.

The nun nodded. "Yes of course, my dear," she replied.

Father Peter remained standing; he had turned quite pale as a sudden wave of realisation swept over him. He already knew the ending to this story, he was there. Henry noticed the priest's odd reaction and suspected something was amiss.

Sister Bridget pulled up a stool next to Lorimer and gently squeezed the old man's hand for reassurance. She then very slowly unbound the pale blue ribbon from the small book and placed an old pair of pince-nez over the bridge of her nose.

"The story begins at the end of June, nineteen years ago. Caroline was eighteen years old and she was preparing to attend her first Mercia Ball in Kingslea. She was full of excitement and hope for the future; a beautiful, intelligent young woman stepping out into the world for the very first time."

Chapter 14

Extracts from Caroline Lorimer's journal.

22ⁿᵈ June

Today is my eighteenth birthday, I have been given this beautiful little book by my dearest mother and I already have the most exciting news to report. The annual Mercia balls will take place on the 1st of July, in just over one week's time, after a two-year delay, firstly for the Vikrin wars two years earlier and then the awful sickness that spread through the land last year. Father has procured rooms at the palace for our entire stay. I am so giddy with excitement. Mother is also thankful, declaring I am already an old maid, which made Father and I roar with laughter. I am but eighteen years old I declared, she reminded us that she attended her first ball at sixteen and was married only three months later. Father returned from court laden with the most beautiful fabrics. The dressmaker is already hard at work on my new wardrobe. We depart for Kingslea tomorrow, but how can I sleep? Father informs us the prince will open the first ball of the season; Mother shrieked with elation, he is quite the most handsome man in the whole of Mercia she declared. Father scolded her most vehemently for she has never even set eyes on him, how we all laughed once more.

I have had the most wonderful of days, I love you Mother, I love you Father.

26ᵗʰ June

It is extremely late; we have only just arrived at our apartments within the Kilve Palace. I am afraid I did not travel well, so have been unable to write. The city has an awful stench about it which does not aid my current delicate disposition. Father said you do get used to the smell; I hope with all my heart he is right. Mother is worried my pale complexion shall diminish my chances of attracting a husband, which at this present time I have to admit is the last thing on my mind.

27th June

Thankfully, I felt much better today, Mother insisted I ate breakfast; I did nibble on a small piece of dry bread. The dressmaker has been here all day, I was utterly enamoured by the designs. Mother was quite delirious with excitement at the sight of me in the pale blue satin embroidered with iris flowers. Father has promised a corsage of fresh irises, Mother scoffed at him saying the best of the irises have gone over and it was quite impossible, but Father never makes a promise he cannot keep. I have managed to eat a little more at dinner. The awful smell of the city still lingers in my nostrils as I sit beside the open window of my room writing. My room overlooks the enormous inner courtyard of the palace, I declare I have never seen so many people in my life, and they never seem to sleep. I am becoming a little nervous as the night of the first ball draws closer.

28th June

Today the hairdresser has pulled at my hair so furiously trialling the latest styles that I have a throbbing headache. If all my hair were to fall out, I would not be surprised. I favour a simple style, but Mother is insisting on an intricately braided updo. Father brought rose and lavender to fragrance the rooms, I have to say the heady scent is most welcome.

29th June

Father insisted we dined in the city. The weather was glorious though I am sure it aids the dreadful stench, although I am beginning to become accustomed to the smell and with a growing sense of anticipation for the ball it certainly helps to take my mind from it. Dinner was fresh trout from the River Rame followed by fresh fruit and the most delicious marzipan sweets that Mother rationed, claiming they turn your teeth black. I did however manage to smuggle one into my purse which I am savouring as I write.

30th June

The day has been frantic, Father brought me a beautiful book of poetry.

1st July

I cannot sit still so therefore cannot write, for I am so excited.

Father has secured the most exquisite fresh irises; Mother was totally flabbergasted.

2nd July

Last evening was magical, all my nervous anticipation melted away as soon as I entered the grand ballroom, I danced every dance, the last two with the prince. He is so handsome and shy, I think he may have a slight stammer, it was endearing. He told me irises were his favourite flower. The whole room watched as we whirled about the floor, the other dancers moving aside. I felt like a princess. Mother was beside herself with joy; Father tried hard to calm her but to no avail, I have only managed to have a few hours' sleep, I shall never forget my first ball.

Two dozen blue irises have just been delivered; Mother is having palpitations. They are from Prince Osbert; I must remain calm.

3rd July

Prince Osbert called at our apartments early this morning. Thankfully, I was up and suitably dressed. He stayed for over an hour and Mother left us alone for a full twenty minutes on the pretence of urgent business. I knew full well it was merely a ruse and suspect Osbert did too. But no matter, Osbert talked nonstop once she had gone, his stutter almost non-existent. I have to say I was mesmerised. He promised to call again tomorrow and he asked for permission to escort me around the palace. Mother agreed but did insist on accompanying us, never mind I know she can be discreet when she wants to. Osbert kissed my hand before he left, my heart skipped a beat. Mother is beside herself with glee.

Poor Father he looked so tired when he returned from court. I heard him later refer to the King as a despot, Mother scolded him profusely declaring it was treason and he should take heed, particularly inside the palace.

4ᵗʰ July

Osbert conducted me around the palace today, Mother was an angel and allowed us space. Osbert insisted on filling my dance card for the next ball declaring he would never dance with another ever again. He held my hand as we stood beside the impressive fountain in the extensive gardens, then we got lost in the maze together, vexing Mother greatly. How we laughed.

Osbert kissed me on the lips. I declare I am in love with him.

Sister Bridget paused to sip on a glass of wine and clear her throat. She shuffled on her little stool; the whole room was transfixed and waited patiently for her to continue.

"My dear," she said, directing her gaze towards Iris. "This is how your mother's story begins, with your permission I shall continue at the end of the Mercia Ball season. The relationship between your mother and Prince Osbert has progressed and they are both now very much in love."

Iris nodded. "Yes, thank you, Sister Bridget." Desperate for her to continue.

27ᵗʰ July

Osbert has asked Father for my hand, and of course he has given his permission. I am quite the happiest, luckiest woman in the whole of Mercia. The final ball of the season is in three days, we then return to Wicken Hall. How shall I bear to be parted from Osbert, even if it is for only a brief time? We hope the wedding shall take place as soon as possible. Osbert promised to speak with his father the King tomorrow in order to set a date. I think I shall wear my pale blue satin dress to the ball once again, the hothouses in Langland have promised to supply the fresh irises.

28th July

I sat beside the window all day waiting for a glimpse of Osbert but to no avail. I have received no word from him today and my daily flowers from the hothouses did not arrive. Mother said Father has been occupied with the King all day, they discuss urgent Crown business. Tensions are running high throughout the land; Mother said the King has raised taxes once again which is never welcome news. I must believe this has delayed Osbert speaking with his father, how I long to see him once more, how I long for his loving embrace.

29th July

It is late, there is still no word from Osbert. Father has not returned to our apartments. Mother keeps a cheerful face and tries to occupy my mind; I have struggled to sit still all day. Where are you, my love?

30th July

Father returned this morning, he looked tired and worried, although he insists all is well. Osbert has been sent on urgent Crown business to Vikrin. We are to attend the final ball as planned. I must admit I would prefer to remain in my room, but Father insists. The King will be closing the season and wishes to become acquainted with me. Mother has been overly attentive, even sending out for a tray of marzipan sweets. I think she may have eaten most of them herself though as they seem to have disappeared and I have no appetite.

* * *

The King paid me a lot of attention tonight, he made me feel extremely uncomfortable. He is not a comely man; his breath smells foul and he eats far too many marzipan sweets. I asked about Osbert, but my questions were ignored. I can hear Mother crying, I long to be back at Wicken Hall.

1st August

It seems I am to marry the King in three weeks, we remain at court, and nobody will speak to me of Osbert. I spend all my time in my room, my eyes swollen through crying. I wish I had never come to Kingslea.

217

Sister Bridget paused, once again sipping more wine and clearing her throat. Lorimer placed a gentle hand to her shoulder and softly spoke.

"When Prince Osbert asked for Caroline's hand, she was so very happy, they both were – two young people so much in love," he said in a disheartened tone of voice. "It was the last time I ever saw her so; Osbert had, as promised, gone directly to his father to ask permission to marry Caroline. The King, unsurprisingly, was in a foul mood, which was not unusual. He was the cruellest and most oppressive ruler Mercia has ever known. Rumours of an uprising in the East had fuelled his fury. The people were protesting against the high taxes being imposed on the landowners and poor alike. Charles held me solely responsible, citing anarchy. He accused me of lacking strength of character, weak like his son he said. And if Osbert were to marry the daughter of a weak man, then they would only produce weak children, which would jeopardise the DeBowscale dynasty. Osbert protested admirably of course, demanding that his father grant permission to marry Caroline. I promised to address the unrest in the East, begging the King, but he flatly refused and becoming quite animated in fact. He left us both under no doubt of his displeasure, he was a dreadful tyrant. Osbert was forcibly removed from court. Charles sent him to Vikrin on the pretence of marrying him off to one of the emperor's daughters. He cruelly announced he would marry Caroline himself, laughing as he described in graphic detail how he would 'break in Osbert's young filly.' I was powerless, trapped. Offer my daughter to a monster or face his retribution, knowing full well he would take Caroline regardless. Little did I know that that day sparked a chain of events that ultimately ended in civil war."

Lorimer finished speaking and turned to Sister Bridget, nodding for her to continue reading. She smiled back at Lorimer before returning to the journal. The rest of the room waited with bated breath for the next instalment.

16th August

Less than a week until my wedding. I thank God that I have not had to see Charles since the night of the farewell ball. Father has returned east in an attempt to quell the unrest in the region. Mother has been trying hard to raise my spirits but to no avail. She declared it necessary to educate me in the more intimate details of married life. The thought of it with Charles repulses me beyond belief, I declare I should rather die. Mother sobs and then I sob, we are quite certainly the most miserable women in all the land. I have had no word from Osbert, I can only assume he no longer loves me, perhaps he never did. I still love him desperately. I only wish that I could have been a better person to have him love me as much as I love him.

* * *

Whilst sitting in my room pondering my future the strangest thing has just occurred. Mother is out on her daily turn about the park. A single blue iris has been delivered with a note attached requesting me to attend Kilve Abbey at midnight. My heart is pounding.

Unbeknownst to the King, Osbert has returned from Vikrin, he loves me. I am to pack only the smallest bag and meet him again tomorrow night, we are to be married in the Abbey before travelling north. I must not breathe a word to anyone, the deceit however breaks my heart; Mother will be distraught. I shall write to her as soon as I am able. Osbert loves me, surely that is all that matters now.

Sister Bridget paused, the occupants of the room all breathed out loudly as if they had been holding their breaths and hanging on to the nun's every word.

"Caroline did go to the Abbey the following night and she and Osbert were married, in secret. They travelled north, moving from town to village and finally settling in modest rooms on the outskirts of Glen Ivor. They lived for a long while in obscurity. There are pages and pages in her journal, she was extremely happy, they were both happy. Even with the constant threat of discovery not far from their minds, they managed to carve out a comfortable life for themselves."

20th November

Ossy brought a nun from the local Abbey to attend me this morning. I have been feeling rather nauseous of late, he is such a love and has been fussing around me so. She examined me asking about my monthly courses, I have not bled for a few months believing it was nothing more than the stresses. She congratulated us both, confirming I am with child. Ossy declared that he should write to his father, after all I am now carrying an heir to the throne of Mercia. We have confided in Sister Bridget; she has promised to keep our secret and attend me regularly.

21st November

Sister Bridget visited again today; she has advised Ossy not to write to the King. Apparently, he is still outraged at our elopement, having sent scouts to every corner of Mercia in order to discover our whereabouts. Sister Bridget said there is a large bounty on our heads for anyone with any information. The King has also raised taxes further in the East and tensions are reaching boiling point. Some say the King has gone quite mad. Sister Bridget fears for our safety. After she left, I persuaded Ossy to delay writing to his father, we decided it might be wise to wait until the baby is born, a grandchild may temper his mood. I fear for my father and mother, and how our reckless actions may have affected them. The King is not a merciful man. I shall write to them, let them know we are safe, perhaps Father can approach the King. I am sure all will be well; I am convinced we shall have a son; the King could never deny a grandson.

Sister Bridget paused reading again. "They remained in Glen Ivor for several months; however, the money was beginning to run short, Osbert had never had to consider money before. He was constantly treating Caroline, bringing her fine fabrics, fresh flowers, the best food and wine. It was also attracting a lot of unwanted attention. Caroline did write to her father. I promised to have the letter delivered but I did not. I was fearful it would betray their whereabouts and that no good could come of it. There is not a day goes by that I wish I had sent that letter; the outcome could not have been any more tragic than what was to eventually occur. I betrayed her. Caroline waited every day for a reply from her father that never arrived, adding to her increased anxiety, along with the constant fear of being discovered, as the birth of their child drew evermore closer. Charles's net was rapidly closing in on them. The Master of the Crown Knights stationed in Glen Ivor was called Quinn. He was a ruthless man, keen to elevate his status at court. He had scouts all over the city, convinced Osbert and Caroline were there having traced their journey from the south."

25th April

I grow bigger every day; Sister Bridget believes I have less than six weeks before the baby comes. It is becoming increasingly difficult to get comfortable at night. I have had no word from my father, I fear for his very safety and there are murmurings of war. We considered writing to the King once again. Ossy grows evermore anxious of us remaining in Glen Ivor, we find ourselves jumping at the shadows. Rumours are rife and scouts are everywhere in the city, it is only a matter of time before we are discovered. Sister Bridget leaves for Baines Abbey in a few days, she urges us to join her.

Ossy brought me some early irises today, they smell earthy, I close my eyes and I am safe back at Wicken Hall. I love him so much. I encourage him to consider Baines Abbey.

3rd May

Ossy has agreed, we are to accompany Sister Bridget to Baines Abbey; I have been busy all day preparing. Ossy went out earlier. I wait besides the window watching for his return. I feel a little melancholy leaving our humble rooms, we have been so happy here, living a simple life. I always knew it could not last, I shall never forget Glen Ivor. The baby is kicking, so I read poetry aloud from the little book given to me by my father in Kingslea, and it settles the baby. Ossy sings to my enormous bump every morning, still insisting it is a girl, he has already named her Iris.

15th May

I am here at Baines Abbey alone. Ossy did not return to our rooms the day before we were due to depart Glen Ivor. Sister Bridget came to me in the middle of the night informing me that Ossy had been apprehended by Quinn, he has been taken back to Kingslea. He had refused to give up my location, but Sister Bridget said it was only a matter of time before I was discovered so we fled that very night. The Abbey houses both nuns and monks, it is an impressive building but not more so than the adjacent house which is quite a magnificent sight. I have been introduced to Lady Clara Westonhall; Sister Bridget announced me as a young widow from Glen Ivor. Clara is most kind. Being with child herself she is sympathetic to my plight. She receives regular correspondence from her husband at court which, unbeknownst to her, eases my anxieties as he writes of Osbert. He is safe and well, although the King has him watched constantly under house arrest. I pray he shall soon be able to join me. News of my father is not so favourable; he has been banished from court and exiled to the East. Lord Westonhall writes that he fears dire consequences from the King's actions. Clara is a welcome friend and we spend most days together; she is more than content here at Baines Abbey with only her young son for company, she dislikes the political and cultural complexities of court life. I find I envy her situation.

19th May

The weather was glorious today, I found myself in the extensive gardens here at Baines Abbey. I sat amongst the blue irises and the baby settled inside me, she must enjoy the earthy scent as do I. Closing my eyes, I dreamt of Osbert, I long to see him, to embrace him.

Clara found me later she had received another letter from her husband. She enjoys reading the correspondence aloud. I am secretly grateful, although it is not always welcome news. The King continues his search for me, I have been cited as a witch and a whore, and he declares that Osbert is under my spell – blaming his struggle to recover from the ordeal as cause for his absence at court. My hope for a speedy reunion diminishes upon hearing these words.

Clara defends Caroline Lorimer which aids my melancholy state, I would like to confide in her but fear for her safety if I do.

20th May

Clara is unwell, Sister Bridget has insisted she remains in bed until the birth. She is most obedient. I do declare I would not be so. I have promised to visit her daily. We are quite the sight with our swollen bellies. I entertained her by waddling like a duck, how we laughed. Sister Bridget scolded me for exciting Clara so. I have taken to reading poetry aloud, which Sister Bridget more than approves of, saying it calms the babies as well as us. We laughed aloud once more when she had gone. I secretly long for another letter from Lord Westonhall.

21st May

Clara looked most unwell today, I pray for her.

25th May

Lord Westonhall arrived at Baines Abbey today, not for Clara but for me. Osbert has confided in him, revealing my location. Once the baby is born, I am to be sent to Norland, to Lord Westonhall's sister. Osbert has promised to join me as soon as he is able. He wrote me a poem. I have tucked if safely inside my little journal, the paper already crumpled for I have read it repeatedly. I love him so much.

Clara is not much better; Sister Bridget is most concerned. I sat with her this afternoon, finally revealing my true identity and relaying my adventures. Clara seemed to recover slightly and enjoyed a little refreshment, my tale a welcome diversion. Lord Westonhall attends her constantly, they are clearly very much in love. I pray for Clara.

28th May

Clara looked better this morning; I spent the day with her lazing in her room. I have started to have pains, I think perhaps the baby comes. Sister Bridget is occupied with Clara so I shall wait a little longer before I make a fuss. I am so nervous, I wish Ossy was here with me, I feel quite alone.

Clara's baby comes, the wait is exhausting, and my pains increase also. Osbert, I love you.

Sister Bridget closed the little book, retying it with the pale blue ribbon, and carefully removed her old pince-nez, placing them both on her lap.

"That was Caroline's last entry in her journal," she sighed. "Clara Westonhall gave birth to a stillborn daughter and the house went into mourning. Lord Westonhall was utterly devastated and Clara was quite delirious. Caroline returned to the Abbey alone, to pray; she had not mentioned that her pains were becoming stronger and more regular. We were all so occupied at the house, we did not even give her a second thought. When Clara finally fell asleep, Lord Westonhall cradled his dead daughter in his arms. He was bringing her to the Abbey to lay her to rest when a messenger arrived from Kingslea. Lord Westonhall recognised the man at once and they talked only briefly before he frantically ran towards the Abbey in search of Caroline. We found her in her room; she had given birth all alone, the baby's cord still attached. She had delivered a beautiful healthy girl … you Iris," the nun sniffed, smiling at Iris tenderly and holding back her tears for just a while longer.

"The messenger had informed Westonhall that Quinn had discovered Caroline's whereabouts and the King had employed an assassin to 'take care' of her and her child. Time was of the essence. Lord Westonhall had relayed the dreadful truth and there was no time for any delay. Caroline's fate was sealed, but her daughter's was not; Lord Westonhall held out his dead child to Caroline. She understood his meaning at once and without hesitation. She kissed her own child, you Iris, before so bravely passing you over. 'Her name is Iris' she whispered. She also gave Westonhall the emerald ring from her finger – the wedding ring given to her by Osbert. I hurriedly cleaned up the blood from the bed and Westonhall departed, immediately returning to the house. He could not risk being seen at the Abbey for fear of being accused of complicity in concealing Caroline's location. I waited with Caroline in silent prayer. She didn't speak, or cry, she just lay quite still clutching Clara's dead daughter to her breast. A menacing looking man arrived a short time later, as we knew he would. He casually strode into the small Abbey bedchamber. 'Are you Caroline Lorimer?' he had snarled through a clenched jaw, his demeanour hostile. 'No, I am Caroline DeBowscale,' she replied, defiant to the very end. Then without another word he mercilessly snatched the baby from her arms, so speedily that he had absolutely no idea that the child was already dead, and snapped its tiny neck as if it were nothing more than a brittle twig. Caroline refused to take her eyes from the assassin; he beat her ferociously hard across the face in order to divert her gaze before brutally and horrifically snapping her slender neck with the most savage of ease."

Sister Bridget broke down, sobbing uncontrollably.

"She was so brave," she wept, "so very brave."

Iris broke down in floods of tears. Henry instantly embraced her in his arms, trying to bring her a little comfort as best he could. Kat also began to cry, hugging her brother tightly as the combined grief consumed the grand room at Wicken Hall. The only sound to be heard was the soft whimpering of the three women and the crackle of the fire in the hearth.

Chapter 15

A quiet hush eventually settled within the room; time seemed to stand still in the grand space at Wicken Hall as the truth about Iris began to slowly sink in. The sorrowful quiet however was soon abruptly disrupted as Father Peter suddenly cried out and prostrated himself on the ground, his arms stretched wide and his face turned to the floor. Everyone jumped up startled. Henry positioned himself between Iris and the priest and Kian hastily pulled Kat backwards, feeling for the dagger concealed beneath her skirts.

"What is the meaning of this?" Henry bellowed, furiously staring down at the priest on the floor.

"Forgive me?" he muttered pitifully into the ground.

"Forgive you for what Father?" Iris sniffed, wiping away her tears on the sleeve of her dress and gripping tightly onto Henry's arm.

Henry understood his meaning at once. "It was you, was it not? You all but told me so, describing yourself as a monster, a killing machine for Charles. You said you returned to Baines Abbey. In order to return implies you had been there before. You were the monstrous assassin?"

"Yes, it was I, Edward Maddock," the priest confessed in total submission.

"I don't understand," Iris cried out. "Father Peter, what are you talking about?"

"He is the assassin who snapped your mother's neck Iris," Henry confirmed, his arm outstretched and holding Iris back from approaching the priest.

"No," Iris muttered, collapsing back down onto the bench and burying her face in her hands.

"Kian," Henry shouted over to his friend.

Kian understood Henry's meaning at once and retrieved the dagger from beneath Kat's skirts. Then, fiercely grabbing the priest and pulling his head up by his grey hair, he forced him onto his knees with the keen edge of the dagger pressed firmly against his throat.

"It is true Iris, he killed your mother," Henry snarled, now facing the murderous priest, "and he would have killed you too, without mercy, without remorse. He is no priest; he is nothing but a vile deceiver."

Sister Bridget moved closer to the man kneeling on the ground, staring horrified at his face, a face she thought she knew so well, a face full of scars and bloodshot eyes that now filled with tears. She clasped her hand to her mouth in utter disbelief.

"It cannot be," she murmured. "You have been my faithful friend for so many years, please tell me this is not true."

"It is true," the priest gurgled under the pressure of the dagger pressed hard against his throat. "Charles sent me and I obeyed without question, without mercy. Henry is right, it was me, forgive me," he swallowed, as Kian pressed the dagger harder, drawing blood. "What I did was monstrous, it weighed so heavily on my conscience. After the war I had to return to Baines Abbey to in some way atone for my sins. I became Father Peter and every day I have prayed at the grave of the unknown mother and child buried in the grounds there. I deserve no mercy, do with me what you will," he declared, laying his hands out in front of him fully prepared to meet his maker.

Kian stood poised, ready to slit his throat at Henry's order.

"Kill him!" Lorimer roared, stumbling forward just as Sister Bridget turned to steady him. "Kill him!" he repeated, fuelled by hatred and contempt. "Kill the evil bastard."

"Yes," Henry confirmed, nodding for Kian to finish the deed.

"No," Iris screamed, forcefully pushing past Henry and desperately falling to her knees in front of the priest.

Henry instinctively grabbed at her arm in order to pull her away.

"No," she protested, struggling to shake him off. "Henry please, no more bloodshed. Has there not already been enough?" she pleaded, placing a gentle hand to the priest's face and peering deep into his sorrowful eyes. "I have known Father Peter most of my life, he brought us here did he not?" she whispered, relinquishing her gaze upon the pitiful man and staring up at Henry, pleading with him. "Please Henry, no more bloodshed, not in my name, please sir," she implored, turning to face Lorimer, her grandfather. "Please, both of you I beg you."

Henry glanced over at Lorimer. After a short pause, he reluctantly nodded back in agreement.

"Very well," Henry replied, finally aiding Iris to her feet. "But he shall have to remain under house arrest. He will have to pay for his crimes at some point Iris."

"I know Henry, but not here, not now," she sobbed, wrapping her arms around him. Henry nodded over to Kian to release his hold upon the priest. Kian pushed him hard back down onto the floor, where he remained silently prostrated on the ground in front of them.

A quiet once again fell over the room whilst everyone slowly returned to their seats, still focused on the erroneous Father Peter.

After several minutes, the peaceful silence was again cut short as the large wooden doors to the hall suddenly flung wide open. An elderly noble woman and a strange looking little man stood inquisitively in the doorway, staring mystified at the occupants within.

Lady Margaret Howard and her loyal secretary Jasper Drake stood in the entrance to the grand room at Wicken Hall. Lady Howard was a short plump woman with a large nose and round cheeks. Her white hair was hidden under a green velvet headdress that was adorned with pearls and her matching green gown, encrusted with precious jewels, highlighted her full bosom around the low square neckline. Her regal look was finished off with a sumptuous velvet cloak, trimmed with fur and lined with miniver, which was casually draped over her shoulders.

"Is she the queen?" Kat whispered to her brother, open mouthed at the sight of the grand lady. She had never seen a woman dressed so splendidly.

"No," Kian whispered back. "But she must be someone fucking important though."

"Lord Lorimer?" Lady Howard said, her tone questioning. Glancing first at the old man before darting her eyes around the room. Jasper Drake shuffled beside her, his expensive surcoat, adorned with the Howard crest, hung from his small slender frame giving the illusion of encasing the tiny man in rich navy-blue brocade.

"Lady Howard," Lorimer replied with a tilt of his head, acknowledging the woman's presence. "Guards," he added, indicating for them to enter the room. "Take him away and lock him up," he commanded, motioning towards the priest still lying stretched out on the floor.

He then diverted his attention back to Lady Howard. "To what do we owe the pleasure?" he asked, surprised and a little irritated by her unexpected arrival.

The guards roughly pulled the priest from the floor and hurriedly dragged him from the room. Iris watched with great sadness as they departed, closing the doors behind them.

"Please don't let them hurt him," she pleaded, peering up at Henry with sorrowful eyes.

"I won't, I promise," he confirmed, wrapping her up in his arms.

"Well Ivan?" Lady Howard declared, more than conscious of the fact that she had interrupted something particularly important. "I was concerned after your sudden illness; I see however you have improved a little. Will you not introduce me to your guests?" she asked, glancing around the room once again.

Lorimer obliged. "Lord Henry Morton," he said, tilting his head towards Henry. "May I introduce Lady Margaret Howard."

"Lady Howard," Henry bowed his head to the old woman knowing her to be the King's aunt.

"Lord Morton," she replied, nodding her head in acknowledgement. "And the others?" she asked, raising a questioning eyebrow.

"Kian and Katherine Munro," Henry replied, pointing towards Kian and Kat. "And this is …" He hesitated for just a moment, "Iris DeBowscale."

Lady Howard glared at Iris expressionless, although Henry thought perhaps her cheeks reddened slightly.

"Ivan," she asked, observing Iris very closely. "Do my eyes deceive me?"

"No, they do not. She is my granddaughter and your great niece," he replied, the words faltering slightly as he spoke.

"Henry, I think I need to lie down," Iris muttered, feeling a little faint as she gripped tightly onto Henry's arm. "Please forgive me Lady Howard," she whispered, politely giving a small curtsy.

"Not at all, my dear, I can clearly see you have endured a lot. I am right in thinking you have come from Mercia?" she asked, directing the question towards Henry. "Through the forest perhaps?" observing their dishevelled appearances.

"Yes Madam, you are correct," Henry replied, "It has indeed been a taxing journey."

"I am impressed Lord Morton," she said, wide eyed, wrinkles forming on her forehead.

"Come my dear I shall take you to your room," Sister Bridget declared, holding out her hand in order to aid Iris. "Here my dear you should also have this," she said, holding out Caroline's journal.

Kat joined the women, briefly glancing over at Henry patting her skirt, indicating that the dagger was safely replaced beneath. Iris clutched her mother's journal tightly to her breast as the three women slowly left the grand room.

"Well, Ivan will you not apprise me of the situation?" Lady Howard inquired, promptly seating herself near the fireplace after removing her fur trimmed cloak and throwing it over the empty table. She was more than curious to understand what on earth was going on. Drake busily fussed around her making her comfortable, his shifty eyes darting between Henry and Kian.

Lorimer obliged and relayed the bare facts. He spoke slowly and deliberately, pausing often to catch his breath. The effort was evident, he was clearly an extremely sick man. Lady Howard sat expressionless, listening intensely to his every word. She was a noble woman, well-bred and accustomed to concealing her true feelings. Henry observed her closely, she gave nothing away.

"I am right in thinking, am I not Ivan, that you knew of her existence?" she enquired, after Lorimer had finished speaking.

"Yes, I did," he replied, a certain sadness in his voice. "Westonhall came to me. I had strived hard to quell the unrest here in the East, only just gaining an agreement from the landowners, Lord Howard included, to reconsider a war against Charles. I knew Osbert had been apprehended as he wrote to me in secret informing me that Caroline was to be sent to Norland and that she was well, he mentioned nothing of a child. Fearful perhaps his letter may have been intercepted. Anyway, after Westonhall informed me of Caroline's brutal murder and the fact she had given birth to a daughter only moments before, I no longer cared for peace; Charles had pushed me too far this time. The East was hungry for retribution and now so was I. I enthusiastically rallied the men as war against the tyrant was declared. The news of Caroline's death destroyed my wife. She doted on Caroline. Her senseless murder caused Mary to withdraw into herself, her fervent spirit broken beyond repair. She died of a broken heart merely six months later. I never told her of Iris. Charles had taken everything from me, he could never know of Iris's existence. Osbert was told that Caroline had died giving birth to a stillborn child. It was agreed Iris should remain with Westonhall at Baines Abbey, to be brought up as his daughter – it was the only way to guarantee her safety. Westonhall retained the marriage certificate between Osbert and Caroline. He also had the Abbot produce a birth certificate for Iris in the event that her true identity could one day be revealed."

"I believe those documents were kept in a small wooden box at Baines Abbey," Henry added. "The perpetrators that blew up the Corridor must have them. They intended to abduct Iris and they killed Westonhall in the attempt. He asked me to give her Crown protection as he lay dying, I was to bring her here to you."

"You are a Crown Knight, my Lord?" Lady Howard asked, rather surprised.

"Yes, I am Madam, a master ... My Lord," he continued, directing his gaze back towards Lorimer. "Do you also know what may have caused the explosion in the Corridor? There was something else contained in that box at Baines Abbey?"

"Yes, I do," Lorimer sighed, eventually descending the steps and slowly making his way over to the fireplace. He seated himself in one of the easy chairs and pulled a blanket over his lap. The strain of the movement was noticeable on his pained face.

"Westonhall served under my command during the Vikrin wars over twenty years ago. Mercia was ally to Vikrin, fighting against the Mechlers. It was a pointless, bloody war, much like our own. There were great losses on both sides. We eventually, over time, succeeded in pushing the Mechler forces back; the war was all but over. However, we prematurely let our guard down – we were overconfident. A Mechler troop made one final surprise attack. The Crown Prince Hakim was captured and Emperor Nasir was given five days to surrender the whole of the Vikrin southern region to Mechler or Hakim would be executed, his body to be impaled with the stake following his spine so as to prolong his agonies – the most gruesome of deaths. The Emperor was more than willing to surrender his lands for the safe return of his son, but the Mechlers could not be trusted. We were certain that Hakim's fate was already set. Westonhall offered to lead a detachment of able men in a brave attempt to rescue Hakim. They successfully infiltrated the Mechler camps, risking their lives, to bring the prince home. Vikrin and Mercia then proceeded to rain down terror on the Mechler forces, almost annihilating their whole army. Emperor Nasir rewarded Westonhall with six precious pearls as a tribute for the safe return of his son. Vikrin pearls are extremely rare, not at all like pearls you find in the sea – they are stones found in the mountains of Vikrin. Skilfully cut and polished by royal lapidaries over months and months of intricate processes. The stones have this inner iridescence and appear quite opaque in normal light, but held up to the sun it is possible to see their inner glow. Every Crown Prince is given six Vikrin pearls when they come of age as they are thought to protect them from harm. An unknown truth is that exposed to fire they create a massive explosion, the like of which cannot be explained. The fact they ignite in such a way was discovered quite by accident; to merely throw the pearls into a fire is one thing, but if the pearls are placed inside a vessel and thrown into a fire, they slowly heat and culminate in an enormous explosion. Emperor Nasir revealed their power to Westonhall."

"Were the pearls used at Crowforth, Sir?" Kian asked, fascinated by the story.

"Yes, young man they were. The civil war was lost for the East. We sustained great losses, but the men were too proud and refused to surrender. I requested a parley with Westonhall and asked him to use the pearls to end the war. My men would have no choice but to surrender against such force. Westonhall lit the fires containing the pearls. I held my men back, waiting for the explosion – it was like nothing we had ever seen before. I fabricated reports proclaiming great losses, however, we did not lose a single man or sustain any injuries. It did however have the desired effect. The East surrendered and the civil war ended."

"You said Westonhall was given six pearls?" Henry asked.

"That is right, two were used at Crowforth and it seems that two have been used in the Corridor. Whoever took those pearls still has the means to cause much more devastation in Mercia. When Osbert first wrote informing me that he was considering reinstating Sebastian's claim to the throne, I could not shake Iris from my mind. I am dying it is no secret and I thought that if any good could come of Caroline's death, then perhaps her daughter, my granddaughter, could reunite Mercia once and for all – a true heir to the throne. I know how Osbert struggles to name a successor. I foolishly and without regard for Iris or Westonhall requested a secret audience with Osbert. I intended to inform him of Iris's existence. I hoped it could finally bring peace to the whole of Mercia and I could look upon her face at least once before I die. I was a complete fool. I was due to enter the Corridor on the day of the explosion. It was clearly meant to silence me. Whether they knew about Iris or it was to stop negotiations regarding Sebastian, I do not know but hatred still consumes Mercia it seems. To even contemplate exposing Iris to this world and putting her life at such risk, I am so ashamed of myself; I thank you Henry for bringing her safely to me."

"Who else knew Westonhall had these pearls?" Henry asked, hoping it might throw some light on who could have taken them.

"A handful of men, all now passed except myself. Nothing was ever recorded, or at least not to my knowledge."

"Who knew that you intended an audience with the King?" Henry continued.

"My Ambassador Ripley and a handful of my most loyal soldiers. But I never once mentioned Iris to anyone. As far as they were aware I was to negotiate on behalf of Sebastian, nothing more. We have recently received news from Mercia that Lord Thomas Gilmore has been arrested for the atrocities in Trevelyan. Raven Westonhall was found murdered in a boarding house in Kingslea, I presume he must have taken the pearls and documents from his father."

Henry sighed deeply, "Yes, of that we are certain. Iris shall need to be told; she loved her brother very much."

"He was not her brother," Lorimer snapped indignantly. "And do not forget Henry, he betrayed her in a most heinous way."

"Yes, he did … tell me milord who was to meet you in Trevelyan?"

"I was to rendezvous with a Crown Knight on the quayside at midday. I know nothing more of the plans from there on. I have since sent Ripley to negotiate on behalf of Sebastian. He arrived in Mercia without any complications and has since written that negotiations with Osbert went well. He believes the King will very soon extend an invitation for Sebastian to join him in Kingslea."

"I can assure you Lord Morton, Sebastian will not step one foot in Mercia until these murderous traitors are apprehended," Lady Howard added. She was fearlessly overprotective of her grandson.

"No madam, you are quite right to be cautious, but I however must return to Mercia without delay," Henry declared.

"And Iris?" Lorimer asked, fearful for his granddaughter's safety.

"She shall remain here. It is clearly not safe for her in Mercia, not until we have retrieved the remaining Vikrin pearls."

"She's not going to like that Henry," Kian frowned, shaking his head.

"No, she will not," Henry replied, a hint of regret in his voice. "But unfortunately, I see no other alternative."

It was still dark when Iris awoke, she was cold. She shivered lying atop a large bed. Kat slept silently lying beside her under the covers. Iris silently rose, pulling her cloak tightly around her shoulders before picking up her mother's journal. She crept from the bedchamber and made her way to Henry's room. Almost as soon as she had entered he woke with a start, clasping at his dagger beneath the pillow. He let out a sigh of relief upon realising it was Iris. Iris slipped between the bedclothes and pressed herself up against Henry, still clutching her mother's journal to her breast.

"Hold me," she whispered, shivering in his arms.

Henry embraced her tightly, pulling her close.

"Are you alright my love?" he whispered. "You are so cold my darling."

"Yes, please just hold me Henry," she replied, leaning her head against his broad chest, safe once again in his strong arms.

They lay together for a while in silence. Henry kissed her tenderly on the forehead.

"Iris, there is something I need to tell you."

"Oh, yes."

"Your brother; he has been murdered in Kingslea ... I'm so sorry Iris."

Iris began to weep. She thought of Raven and she thought of her father. Several minutes passed before she finally sniffed away her tears, pressing herself closer to Henry. "Oh Henry, it seems my whole life has been nothing more than a deception. What we have together, please tell me it is not false?"

"No my love, we are truer than anything, I promise you but I'm afraid there is something else I must tell you."

Henry continued to relay Lorimer's account regarding the Vikrin pearls, their tremendous power, and the fact that there were still two remaining somewhere in Mercia.

"I understand Henry, you wish me to remain here in the East do you not?"

"Regrettably my love, I do," he replied, slightly taken aback by what appeared to be her rational acceptance of the situation.

He smiled, moving to face her. "Oh Iris, you never cease to amaze me. Thank you, my darling. You do know if there was any other way, I would have considered it. You shall be safe here with your grandfather, it is my only consolation. I love you so much Iris."

"I love you too Henry, please put an end to this nightmare so that we may be together, you will return for me, won't you?"

"Oh yes, of course I will, I promise Iris," he whispered, placing a gentle lingering kiss to her lips. "Once this nightmare as you put it is over, I shall ask the King for your hand. We shall be together soon Iris I promise."

A while later, and still clutching the small journal close to her breast, Iris crept from Henry's room back to her own bedchamber before the rest of the household awoke. She had persuaded Henry to allow her to travel south with them as far as Rothtir Hall, which was home to Lady Howard, where they would spend their last night together before Henry returned to Mercia and Iris back to Wicken Hall and her grandfather. She also managed to convince Henry to allow Father Peter to travel with them. Even though she now knew of his terrible involvement in her mother's death, she trusted the priest. He had been on their incredible adventure from the beginning and it made her feel closer to Henry in some way.

Kat was still fast asleep when Iris entered their room, stirring slightly as Iris began to wash herself at the basin.

"Good morning," she yawned loudly, eventually opening her eyes and stretching out on the bed.

She observed Iris at the wash basin still with her cloak draped over her shoulders.

"Where have you been?"

"With Henry," Iris smiled. "It seems we only have one night left together, at least for a while anyway," she mused, sadness in her voice.

"What … what do you mean?" Kat asked, rather astonished and sitting upright in the bed.

Iris enlightened Kat of the Vikrin pearls and Henry's decision for her to remain in the East.

"Oh, Iris, I'm so sorry."

"It is for the best and besides, I still travel with you as far as Rothtir Hall. I shall be safe here in the East and I would like to spend some time with my grandfather. I fear he does not have long and I should like to learn as much as I can about my mother."

"What is Rothtir Hall?" Kat enquired, extremely disheartened by Iris's news.

"The home of the grand Lady that arrived last night, Lady Howard. She is my great aunt by the way. It is only half a day's ride from the Corridor border control," Iris replied, trying awfully hard to put a brave face on things.

"Oh, Iris, I shall miss you greatly," Kat muttered, "I hoped we would discover Mercia together."

"And we shall Kat," Iris promised, sitting beside her on the bed. "I promise. Please don't do too many exciting things without me."

"Iris, I've been thinking."

"Oh yes."

"You do know you are a princess, don't you?"

Iris smiled, nodding, wishing for all the world she was just an ordinary woman like Kat.

All of a sudden Lady Howard burst into their bedchamber, causing the two women to jump.

"Fuck," Kat blurted out at the intrusion, immediately apologising for her use of foul language.

"I'm sorry, I have been spending too much time with my brother," she laughed apologetically.

Lady Howard glared at her disapprovingly for a second before smiling broadly, ushering in a maid laden with clothes, ribbons, and various other women's apparel.

"Ladies," she beamed, looking excessively pleased with herself. "I noticed last night that the pair of you were in desperate need of new clothes. I have managed to find some items more suitable. They are not the latest fashions I'm afraid, but they will do very well until we reach Rothtir," she grinned triumphantly.

"You are most kind," Iris replied, not at all interested in the new clothes. She was more than happy with her old woollen dress.

The maid efficiently lay the dresses out on the bed and waited patiently for her next instructions.

"Very good," Lady Howard proclaimed, "Sarah here will help you dress, excellent, excellent," she smiled, leaving the room as swiftly as she had arrived.

Kat immediately jumped up from the bed and excitedly shifted through the colourful dresses like a young child unwrapping a present.

"Are these really for us?" she beamed, holding a green velvet dress against her. "Iris, which one do you want?"

"You choose first Kat," Iris replied, pleased to see that the clothes were making Kat so happy.

Kat finally chose a crimson velvet dress trimmed with tiny pearls. Sarah fashioned her wild hair, entwining it with cream ribbons – although a few unruly red curls managed to spring free from their restraints. She also chose a pair of intricately embroidered shoes in a dark red brocade. Iris chose a much simpler design made of wool in a sombre dark blue. She was however pleased to have a decent pair of shoes at last and allowed Sarah to loosely plait her hair and entwine it with a pale blue ribbon.

Kian's mouth literally fell open as the two women entered the grand hall, Henry smiled. "You look beautiful ladies," he said, giving a deep bow.

"Thank you, milord," Iris replied, with a sweet smile and a deep curtsy in return.

"Shut your mouth Brother," Kat grinned broadly, patting down her full skirts. "I do scrub up rather well, don't I?"

"You look absolutely beautiful Sis," he declared, following Henry with a deep bow.

Kat then proceeded to spin around the room to show off the full effect of her dress. She was truly resplendent in crimson velvet.

"I'm not sure about these though," she muttered, coming to a stop in front of the men and promptly lifting her skirts to reveal the tops of her stockings.

"Put your fucking skirts down woman," Kian screamed, hastily glancing around the room to ensure nobody else had observed his sister's unsophisticated manner.

Henry and Iris roared with laughter.

Henry spent the next few hours with Lorimer alone. It took quite a bit of convincing for him to agree to allow Father Peter to join Iris at Rothtir and then to accompany her back to Wicken Hall. Finally conceding as it was Iris's wish and Henry was more than happy to vouch for the priest as he confirmed that he had been nothing more than a valued aid on their journey from Baines Abbey. Lorimer did however draw a line on allowing him entry to the hall, insisting that he confine himself to only the chapel and gardens. Henry understood and agreed to Lorimer's terms.

By late morning, an opulent coach was brought around to the front of the hall in readiness for their journey. Kian chose to ride up front with four of Lorimer's men, including the ruddy faced soldier who turned out to be a rather agreeable man. The women accompanied Lady Howard in the coach. Jasper Drake, who hardly ever spoke and seemed to lurk in the shadows and appear around every corner, sat with the coachman, much to Iris and Kat's relief. The women had both taken an instant disliking to the strange little man – Kat referred to him as Drake the Snake. Henry and Father Peter were content to follow on behind the coach. The travelling party finally left Wicken Hall just before midday, heading south to Rothtir.

Henry and the priest rode in silence for a long while. The weather thankfully remained dry and the roads were relatively good.

"I am trusting you to look out for Iris, Priest," Henry suddenly declared, his tone sharp. "If anything were to happen to her, I shall hold you solely responsible, do you understand?"

"Yes Henry, I shall protect her with my life, I promise. I genuinely believe God has given me this second chance. I shall not fail him or you."

"Had you absolutely no idea who she was?"

"No, how could I? I snapped the neck of a baby lying in what I thought was its mother's arms, how could I have known?" the priest replied, a sadness in his voice. "I never for a moment questioned it, why would I? Iris was about eight years old when I returned to Baines Abbey. I have always believed her birthday to be the 22nd of June."

"That was her mother's birthday. Westonhall thought of everything it seems, apart from the one thing he couldn't control of course, Iris's appearance. It does explain the reason he kept her in relative obscurity, not allowing her to attend court and instead insisting that she enter the church. Osbert would have been sure to recognise her and put two and two together."

"Yes, indeed," the priest replied.

Henry suddenly remembered the precise and accurate account that he had written for the King regarding the events at Baines Abbey. It was quite possible that he had already unwittingly let the cat out of the bag or, at the very least, aroused the King's suspicions. He let out a deep sigh of relief, thankful he had insisted that the report was for the King's eyes only.

Henry didn't speak for the rest of the journey, instead he used the time to reflect on the last few weeks and what might lay ahead for him, Iris and Mercia.

The ladies talked incessantly. Lady Howard encouraged both women to speak openly. Kat was a little more guarded and, careful not to divulge any information regarding the forest settlement, she claimed that she had merely travelled from Mercia as a chaperone for Iris. They were a jolly party, both women enjoyed Lady Howard's company and the many stories of Mercia past. The time passed quickly. It was soon late in the afternoon when Rothtir Hall came into view.

Rothtir, a magnificent mansion house, was situated in an outstandingly beautiful parkland. The house was originally built with a view to housing royalty, their retinue and their large entourage of loyal courtiers on a royal progress. Built only a couple of years before the civil war, apart from Lady Howard herself, the house had yet to receive any royal visitors.

"You have a very beautiful house, Lady Howard," Iris remarked, marvelling at the splendour.

"Thank you my dear, you shall be its very first royal visitor," she smiled, placing a gentle hand to Iris's knee.

"Oh please, Lady Howard," Iris replied, blushing.

"It is true my dear and please call me Margaret or Aunt, Lady Howard is so formal and we are family after all. And don't make yourself so uncomfortable, besides, you shall have to get used to the idea. Once Henry has returned west and informed the King, the whole of Mercia shall know of Princess Iris."

"I told you, didn't I? Oh, a princess this is all too magical," Kat beamed, leaning out of the carriage window to get a better view of the house.

Iris however seemed to be the only one not excited by the discovery of her true identity. For one, it was keeping her from Henry – that thought alone perturbed her greatly. The coach finally pulled up to the front of the impressive house with the riders following on behind. Father Peter and Lorimer's men headed directly towards the stables situated at the rear. A multitude of servants were already in attendance, ready to receive their mistress and her guests. Kat held tightly on to Iris's hand, both women a little nervous.

"Grandmother," bellowed a silky voice from the doorway. "Where the devil have you been?"

Lord Sebastian Howard, a young handsome man, tall and slender with dark shoulder length hair and dazzlingly deep blue eyes, stood on the front steps. His clothes oozed money. They were the finest silks and velvet, embroidered with gold thread. Henry immediately thought his manner and appearance seemed artificial and contrived. Sebastian was all smiles and over-exaggerated gestures as he bounded forward to aid his grandmother in alighting from the carriage.

"Well, what have we here," he declared, holding his hand out to Iris and Kat in turn, aiding them to alight from the coach, before giving the deepest bow. "Welcome to Rothtir Hall," he said cheerfully, kissing the hands of the women. There was no doubting he had a certain charisma.

"Fuck sake," Kian muttered under his breath. "If it was fucking raining, he'd have undoubtedly laid his cloak down for them to step over."

Kian was obviously of the same opinion as Henry. Henry however declined to comment.

"Iris, Katherine please meet my grandson, Sebastian," Lady Howard announced, beaming with pride. "Sebastian please meet Iris Westonhall, no wait, Iris DeBowscale and Katherine Munro."

"Ladies," Sebastian replied, giving them another deep theatrical bow.

The women giggled to each other, rather enjoying all the attention. Sebastian certainly put them both at ease. Henry and Kian promptly dismounted their horses and joined the party at the entrance to the house.

"Lord Henry Morton and Kian Munro," Lady Howard continued, gesturing towards the two men. "This is my grandson, Lord Sebastian Howard."

The three men acknowledged each other with a friendly nod of the head. Jasper Drake remained seated on the coach watching curiously with his beady eyes as everyone became acquainted with each other. Henry spied him suspiciously.

"How thrilling," Sebastian exclaimed in an over-excited manner. "We hardly ever get visitors and certainly not four so young and handsome. Did I hear you right Grandmother, Iris DeBowscale?" he asked, eyeing Iris curiously.

"You did my dear, but before I explain everything to you please allow our guests to enter, I'm sure they wish nothing more than to rest awhile before changing for dinner," Lady Howard declared, hastily ushering everyone inside the house.

An efficient housekeeper seemed to appear from nowhere and silently directed the other servants who were waiting patiently to show the visitors to their rooms. Iris and Kat asked to share a room as Kat wanted the moral support and Iris wanted to enjoy Kat's company a little longer, even though she didn't intend spending much time in her own bedchamber tonight. Hot water was promptly provided in every room, along with clean clothes for both the women and men. Henry was more than grateful to rid himself of the course linen shirt provided by Sister Bridget in exchange for a soft silk. The elegant velvet breeches also appealed to his sense of style. He momentarily contemplated leaving the thickening stubble on his face as Iris had indicated that she liked it, but finally decided to shave. He added a little essential oil to his water. A short while later Kian knocked his door and immediately entered before Henry even had the chance to reply.

"You smell like a whore," he sniffed, heading straight for the table containing a decanter of red wine and pouring himself a large glass before gulping down the contents in one.

"Fuck that tastes good," he announced immediately, pouring out another glass.

"Give me one of those will you?" Henry asked, adjusting the tie around his neck. "What do you make of the Howards?"

"Old money, must have been fucking hard for them after the civil war. Especially the old woman, being the King's aunt and all. They seem to have done alright for themselves though. Rather a nice set up they have here. Sebastian is a fucking pompous dandy; the ladies seem to like him. Kat's already cooing over him like a fucking dog on heat; she better not be getting any ideas … Anyway, isn't he, or was I should say, heir to the throne?"

"Yes," Henry replied. "And the King, it seems, had been considering reinstating his line of succession."

"Iris being the princess does rather change things for everyone now, doesn't it?"

"Yes, it does," Henry sighed, running his fingers through his hair.

"What's wrong Henry?"

"Watch Sebastian for me tonight, will you?"

"Yes of course," Kian replied, already on his third glass of wine.

"And stay fucking sober, will you?" Henry snapped.

"Fuck's sake, the first decent drink in weeks and you want me sober."

"It's important Kian; Lorimer trusts Lady Howard but …"

"But you don't?"

"No, I'm not sure I do. There was a real contempt in Lorimer's voice when he spoke of Sebastian. He certainly doesn't believe him worthy of the Crown, which is another reason why he was so willing to finally reveal Iris's existence to the King. Sebastian may masquerade as a man content with the current state of affairs, but is he really? In fact, what man would be, that's why I need you to watch him, listen to what he has to say and how he is around Iris."

Kian put his empty glass down with a thud. "Alright," Kian agreed. "I'll keep an eye on him, now are you ready to go down? I'm fucking starving and by the way you still smell like a fucking whore."

Henry shook his head exasperated and roughly pushed Kian from the room.

Iris and Kat were already downstairs as the men descended. Lady Howard had provided them with more new dresses; sporting the latest fashion for the low square neckline. They both looked splendid. Iris in pale blue and Kat in pale pink silk. Kat was beaming from ear to ear. Kian winked at her affectionately as he entered the room.

"You look fucking beautiful Sis," he whispered, giving her a quick peck on the cheek. Although not quite sure of the overly revealing neckline, particularly on his sister.

"I might not be a real princess like Iris, but I definitely feel like one," she replied, squeezing Kian's hand. "If this is only a grand house, I cannot wait to see the palace."

"You look beautiful Iris," Henry whispered in her ear, nipping it gently with his teeth. He rather liked the low neckline revealing the tops of her beautifully formed breasts.

Sebastian entered the room moments later accompanied by his grandmother. It appeared Sebastian was not only flamboyant in his behaviour but also in his choice of attire. He wore a dark purple doublet containing pinking, which revealed a rich cloth of gold with an enormous pure white silk ruffle and lace cuffs that framed his well-manicured hands. Purple was a colour usually reserved for royalty. He fussed and bustled around his grandmother, ensuring her comfort before turning his attention to his guests.

"Drinks?" he declared, with a broad smile and wave of his hand. A manservant immaculately dressed in the Howard livery, who had been standing patiently in the corner of the room holding a large tray of drinks, immediately stepped forward.

"Excellent," Sebastian beamed before raising a toast to Iris and insisting on referring to her as cousin.

Iris blushed scarlet. Jasper Drake stood conspicuously in the doorway watching the guests. Henry caught his eye. Drake acknowledged him with a nod of his head before turning on his heels and disappearing from the room.

Sebastian turned out to be the perfect host, rivalling Kian on his ability to work a room with a certain aplomb. After a sumptuous dinner of venison and orange followed by the most delicious, sweet jelly, he entertained them all by performing card tricks and reading romantic poetry, some of which was rather risqué and caused both women to blush and Lady Howard to scold him profusely. Henry felt uneasy with the stage-managed frolicking, so was pleased to accept an invitation to play a game of chess with Lady Howard, which ultimately ended in a stalemate.

"You are a worthy opponent my Lord," Lady Howard congratulated him with a smile. "Not many can beat me."

"But I didn't beat you madam. Perhaps next time," Henry replied, eyeing her curiously.

"Indeed," she replied, her usual blank expression giving nothing away.

Lady Howard retired soon after, bidding her guests a safe and speedy journey back to Mercia with a solemn promise to look after Iris as if she were her own daughter. Henry thanked her most graciously.

Kian reported back to Henry that Sebastian had shown no animosity towards Iris and, at one point, even declared that he was rather relieved that he would no longer be named successor but hoped to be invited to Mercia at the earliest opportunity.

"Does he protest too much?" Henry asked, watching Sebastian closely as he continued to thoroughly entertain the women.

"Perhaps," Kian mused, "he certainly likes to court a lot of attention. Are you having second thoughts about leaving Iris here in the East?"

"No, I don't think so. I will have a word with the priest though, make sure he accompanies Iris back to Lorimer as soon as we have left. I do believe she will be safe at Wicken Hall."

"Good, now can I have a bloody drink?" Kian grumbled.

Henry had already undressed and was wearing only a richly embroidered housecoat of the most sumptuous silk. He waited beside the large bay window in his bedchamber, sipping a glass of wine and waiting for the house to settle and for Iris to come to him. The window was east facing, which afforded a perfect view of the morning sunrise. He wished for a moment that he could wake up with Iris in his arms and appreciate such a view, instead of having to leave her here all alone. Moments later Iris slipped quietly into his room, gently turning the key in the lock before joining Henry at the window. They merely had a few hours left together. Henry wrapped his arms around her waist as she stood with her back to him, peering from the window.

"What do you look at?" she asked, pressing herself back against him.

"Nothing," he replied, staring out into the darkness. "I was just considering the excellent view of the sunrise from this position."

"Must you leave before first light; we could savour the view together?"

"Yes, I'm afraid I must Iris," he whispered, removing the small emerald ring given to him by Lord Westonhall from his little finger. "Here, I meant to give you this at Wicken Hall, your mother's ring," he said, placing it on Iris's finger and raising her hand to his mouth, kissing it affectionately.

"I have something for you too," she said, handing him a folded sheet of paper.

"What is it?" Henry asked, just about to read it.

"No," Iris whispered, closing her hand over his. "Don't read it now. It is the poem written by my father to my mother when they were separated. Read it when you are safely back in Mercia. It is everything I would wish to say to you."

"Thank you, my love," he replied, kissing her neck and gently cupping her breasts, teasing her nipples through the thin fabric of her nightgown.

Iris pressed back further against him, letting out little moans of pleasure as his one hand moved lower to between her legs.

"Oh, Henry," she breathed, succumbing almost instantly to his expert caresses.

"I want you Iris," he moaned, hastily ruching up her nightgown, "I want you here … now," he said, gently pushing her forward towards a table beneath the window.

Iris let out a pleasing giggle. "Here Henry?"

"Yes, right here, I'm going to fuck you, Iris," he said, throwing off his housecoat before swiping the contents of the table to the floor and parting her legs. Iris fell forward, gripping tightly to the sides of the table just as Henry thrust himself inside her hard.

She gasped. "Oh, Henry," as he gripped her hips, pulling her closer and plunging himself deeper inside her. The harder and faster he moved, the more Iris wanted from him. His rhythm was relentless as she urged him on, all the time teetering over the edge of a precipice between pleasure and pain; his manhood filling and stretching her to the very limit. She begged him not to stop as their lovemaking became intoxicating. The intensity of their passion was like a violent storm, destroying everything in its path, over and over again.

"Henry," she cried out again, as the all-consuming sensation became too much to bear yet at the same time not enough.

"I want to possess you Iris," Henry groaned, spiralling towards his own climax, his rhythm unabating.

Iris gripped tighter to the table as finally, and with one last exhilarating push, Henry exploded, finding his release deep within her core.

Iris's legs almost buckled beneath her as Henry gently withdrew from inside her.

"Are you alright?" he breathed, carefully lifting her from the table and turning her to face him.

Iris quivered in his embrace, her whole body spent and her insides throbbing.

"Yes Henry," she smiled, flushed and breathless. "How am I ever going to let you go?"

"How am I ever going to be able to leave you?" he replied, gently lifting her up in his arms and carrying her towards the bed.

On the opposite side of the bedchamber a flap to a tiny peep hole concealed in the wall flickered, Henry and Iris were being observed.

Chapter 16

Arlen had arrived back in Trevelyan four days earlier, having first visited Trevelyan House in order to deliver his father's letter requesting Lady Gilmore and her daughter be brought directly to Kingslea. He then made his way to his modest rooms in town. They were exactly as he had left them on the morning of the explosion in the Corridor; the unmade bed where he and Harriet had made love earlier that very morning, a pair of her stockings hanging over the mantle above the fire and a dish holding ribbons and ties that she used to pin up her beautiful dark hair. Arlen sat on the edge of the bed for a while running his hand over the sheet, closing his eyes and trying desperately to envisage Harriet still lying there, her ivory white skin so soft. Opening his eyes he sighed loudly before getting up from the bed and hastily gathering all her things into a small box. He sorted through the pile of correspondence on the desk and tucked them into his bag. Then he took a final look around the room before closing the door behind him. Leaving the small box at the foot of the stairs, he asked the landlady to dispose of it. He had intended to stay the night, but the memories were too painful. Instead, he decided to make his way to Blackmore Barracks. Henry had written to him from the Wychway the morning of their departure. He had requested that Arlen collect the horses and belongings that the young boy Simon had been instructed to deliver and pay back the four-crown debt on behalf of Henry. He would beg a bed and food for the night and hopefully be able to employ a couple of the young cadets to accompany him to the border control the following morning.

As it happened Arlen was not short of volunteers. There was a certain air of mystery surrounding the arrival of Lord Morton's horse and livery, particularly after the recent events – rumours were running rife. He asked the cadet sergeant to select two boys based on ability, obedience and discretion. This request alone caused even more excitement.

The following day after a substantial breakfast, Arlen and the cadets rode out of Blackmore heading towards Trevelyan with freshly laundered clothes and four horses in tow. As they approached the entrance to the Corridor, Arlen observed that it didn't look much changed. The stalls selling the fish on the quayside were as busy as ever, the stalls nearest to the entrance were still trading and the familiar smell of incense was wafting behind the coloured fabrics draping from the doorways. However, only a few yards in and it was evident to see the Corridor looked quite different. Almost all of the stalls that were still standing had been abandoned, their contents looted. Numerous carts were still being pulled up and down bringing out the last remains of the charred debris. The acrid and unpleasant smell of burning still lingered in the air. Arlen shivered as his mind flashed back to that fateful day. As they rode further up into the heart of the Corridor, signs of the explosion were evermore evident to see. Nothing remained of the stalls. The walls on either side of the Corridor were charred black and the ground was covered in mudded soot. The stench was overwhelming as they approached the site of the first explosion. Arlen requested that the cadets ride on, taking the horses with them. He dismounted his own horse, standing silently in front of what would have been the bakery. The wall at the back had completely collapsed; it had taken the full force of the first explosion. Nothing at all remained. Arlen stood for a while, quite alone, with only the eerie silence all around him. Closing his eyes, he spoke a loud, "Goodbye Harriet," with only tender thoughts of her filling his mind.

Moments later a horse and cart travelling back down the Corridor and loaded with debris clattered past, breaking the mournful silence. The driver tipped his cap as he went. Arlen nodded his head in acknowledgment before mounting his horse and, without looking back, he continued on his way.

The border control was a massive fortress with high walls curving around the tip of the Corstir Forest, which loomed over the west side of the building and connected the original Corridor wall to the East. Arlen stared up at the great forest as he drew nearer, wondering how on earth anyone could navigate such a formidable place, but praying that Henry had at least succeeded. There were four large watchtowers, two overlooking the East entrance and the other two overlooking the West into Mercia. The western wall was heavily guarded with a trench running around the perimeter that was filled with sharpened spears of wood positioned upright in the ground, which provided the fortress with a preliminary line of defence. The protection was rather excessive but it was considered crucial in the early days of the Corridor. The border crossing was quiet with only a handful of travellers passing to and from the East. Strict restrictions were now being enforced and nobody was getting through without the right documentation. The cadets had already stabled the horses and had had all the belongings sent to the private apartments in the tower which overlooked the eastern entrance. Lord Barlett had sent word on ahead, informing the commander in charge of his son's arrival. The rooms were prepared and the fortress was already on high alert, as rumours of another important person arriving from the East circulated. The first being Sir James Ripley several days earlier. Arlen made his way up the spiral staircase of the tower to the comfortable rooms at the top, which also afforded an excellent view of the eastern approach. He settled himself in to wait for the much-anticipated return of Henry and Kian.

It had been four days since Arlen had arrived at the border control and he was becoming evermore anxious for the safe return of his friends. Increasingly, he was spending most of his time pacing up and down the battlement between the two eastern watchtowers, hoping for a glimpse of Henry and Kian returning to Mercia. He had managed to keep busy until this point by making enquiries into Raven Westonhall. It seemed Raven was certainly well known in certain establishments within Trevelyan, but Arlen was unable to link him with the Corridor. It seemed he very much kept himself to himself, moving in a circle of mysterious tight-knit acquaintances. There was mention of one particular friend in recent months, a young man who called himself Charles. Arlen's informers were convinced Charles wasn't his real name, although they were pretty certain he came from money judging by his expensive clothes. None of the closely connected men however had been spotted since the explosion. Arlen's extensive investigations proving fruitless, which added to his agitated mood.

The morning sun rose high as midday fast approached. Arlen's mood was becoming more and more irritable. It was now three days past Henry's predicted exit from the East. Arlen was exceedingly worried. The border soldiers were deliberately keeping out of his way as much as possible. Just as he had decided to head back to the private apartments to take refreshments, he heard a horn sound from the other eastern watchtower.

"Riders ahead," one of the lookouts bellowed loudly.

Arlen immediately ran back onto the battlement, squinting into the late morning sunlight to see who was approaching.

"Thank God," he declared aloud, finally observing Henry and Kian on the horizon being accompanied by two of Lorimer's men; he recognised the livery. Strangely, there was no Father Peter and no Iris, instead another woman with vibrant red hair sat atop Kian's horse. Arlen watched and waited with much anticipation as they slowly drew nearer. Upon reaching the border control, the riders dismounted and Henry spoke briefly with Lorimer's men. The conversation appeared cordial and ended with handshakes. The men then mounted their horses, and took the reins of the other horses and immediately headed back east. Henry, Kian, and the young woman walked towards the border guard.

"Let them through," Arlen shouted from the battlement, waving eagerly at Henry.

Henry looked up and waved back. He looked extremely tired and exhausted.

Arlen bolted down the winding staircase of the tower and appeared at the bottom in an instant.

"Lord Morton how very pleased we are to see you," he grinned, giving a deep bow.

A muted gasp reverberated around the soldiers in attendance, who were now all standing to attention as the identity of the weary traveller suddenly dawned on them.

"Please follow me," Arlen continued, hastily heading back up the stairs.

"Thank God," he exclaimed, as they reached the private rooms at the top and embracing Henry fondly, "I was beginning to think I was never going to see you again."

"Arlen, it is so good to see you and to be back in Mercia, we have much to tell, but first I must freshen up."

"And you my friend … Yes of course," Arlen replied, gesturing towards the bedchamber.

"Thank you," Henry sighed, patting his friend on the shoulder before disappearing into the other room.

"Christ Kian, Henry looks absolutely exhausted. Where is Iris and Father Peter and who is this?" Arlen asked, pointing a quizzical finger towards Kat.

"Nice to see you too," Kian grumbled, dumping his bags onto the floor.

"I'm sorry Kian of course it's good to see you. It's just that I've been so worried, you should have returned days ago."

"Yes, well it has been a long onerous journey. I didn't think it at all possible to be so fucking pleased to be back in Trevelyan. Anyway, Henry looks exhausted because he was up all night fucking Iris. She is staying in the East with her grandfather, who is Lord Lorimer by the way. Father Peter, who murdered her mother, is staying with her to protect her. Oh, and this is my sister Kat," Kian grinned broadly before collapsing into a chair, already with a large glass of wine in his hand.

"What!" Arlen declared gobsmacked, firstly glancing down at Kian in the chair before turning his attention towards Kat.

Kat smiled sweetly, "Pleased to meet you Arlen. My brother has told me so much about you, but he omitted to say how very handsome you were," she said, pouring herself a glass of wine and collapsing into a chair besides Kian.

Kian huffed loudly, raising a disapproving eyebrow. Kat giggled.

"Christ," Arlen exclaimed, "I think I had better have one of those myself," he said, reaching for a glass.

Henry appeared from the bedchamber moments later having relieved himself and splashed water on his face in a feeble attempt to freshen up.

"Has Kian filled you in already?" he smiled, picking up a glass before filling it with wine.

"Well sort of," Arlen replied. "It sounds as if you have had quite the adventure," he added, feeling slightly envious.

"Yes, indeed, let's talk," Henry declared, "Arlen, tell us your news first. We have much to report and Kian wishes to spend the night in town. I shall remain here and travel down in the morning."

"Oh, you don't want to stay at the Fisherman's?" Arlen asked quizzically.

"No, not tonight, I'm exhausted," Henry replied, casually leaning back in his chair and momentarily closing his eyes.

"Yes, Kian said you were … with Iris."

"Did he?" Henry sighed, glaring at Kian and rolling his eyes.

Kian laughed. "Come on then Arlen, get started, I'm desperate for a fucking decent cup of ale."

The four of them sat in the private apartments at the border control for at least a couple of hours, listening, talking and debating. It seemed they had learnt so much over the last few weeks; answers to quite a few of the questions that they had been seeking. Nevertheless, they seemed no closer in discovering who was behind the explosion in the Corridor. Henry paced the room, running his fingers through his hair and exhaling loudly.

"Enough today," he announced finally. "I need to carefully consider what has been said, but first I need to sleep."

"Come on Sis," Kian declared jumping to his feet, "grab your stuff, it's going to take us a couple of hours to get down into Trevelyan," he said, stretching and yawning loudly. "Have they cleared the Corridor?" he asked Arlen.

"Yes, you shall be able to make good time."

"Aren't you coming with us?" Kat asked, a look of disappointment shooting across her face.

"Well, I …" Arlen hesitated, glancing over at Henry for approval.

"Go," Henry replied, "I'm only going to sleep and besides, you must have been here four days already. I suspect you are desperate to see the back of the place."

"Yes, I am rather," Arlen laughed, "As long as, you are sure?"

"Yes, go," Henry confirmed, "I shall meet you at the town gates at sunrise."

"Thank you," Arlen replied, throwing Kat a broad smile.

"Get a fucking move on then," Kian grumbled, already with his bag slung over his shoulder. "We are wasting valuable drinking time."

Henry walked out onto the battlements and took a deep breath, watching as his friends rode south down the Corridor. Once they were out of sight, he turned to face the East. Having retrieved Iris's pink chiffon veil from his surcoat pocket, his thoughts turned to Iris. He held the veil to his face hoping to breathe in her scent. *How easy it would be,* he thought to himself, *to mount my horse and return to her.* He felt inside his doublet pocket and pulled out the old, crumpled paper she had given him the night before. Carefully unfolding it, he read the poem.

Whilst I comest here and thou remain
Mine dreams doth turn upon thy face
To hold thee near, within warm embrace
Behold thy smile and hear thy voice
Thou knowest mine only choice
I shall my life with you to share
My body doth yearn thy gentle touch
No heart within doth beat as much

O'how, I love thee, I tell thee true
This absence doth take such painful toll
Thou' art mine body, mine life, mine soul
A hopeful heart haste thy journey home
Before thee child is but shown
Mine darling love I pray to reunite
For all thy passions mine heart ignite.

Henry reread the poem several times. Iris had been right, the words could not be more apt. He carefully refolded the brittle sheet, stowing it safely back inside his pocket. The wind suddenly picked up, causing the chiffon veil to slip from his fingers. It spiralled into the air and out of reach. Taken by the wind, it drifted east. Henry watched until it floated out of sight. He let out a deep sigh before returning to the bedchamber, collapsing onto the bed utterly exhausted.

Arlen was right, they did reach the quayside in good time. It was by now late afternoon and almost all of the stalls had closed for the day with only a handful of people still milling around. Kat gasped at the view. The two men followed her gaze, appreciating the beautiful scene for just a moment. Normally it was something they took for granted.

"Is this the ocean?" she breathed; her eyes wide, mesmerised. "It's beautiful. I can see the edge of the world."

Kian gently rested his chin on his sister's shoulder and lovingly kissed her cheek. "That's not the edge of the world Sis, the world goes on and on. One day I shall show you."

Kat gently leant back against him. "Do you promise?"

"I promise," he replied, wrapping his big strong arms around her waist. "I love you, Sis."

"I love you too Brother. Thank you for allowing me to accompany you."

Arlen watched the pair with affection, smiling to himself as the Munro siblings stared out over the vast deep blue ocean. Their wild red hair blowing in the breeze.

"Let's procure some rooms at the Mermaid," he announced, causing them to break their gaze.

"Not fucking likely," Kian sniffed, "the rooms at the Mermaid cost double what you pay in town."

"That's because the rooms have an excellent view of the ocean," Arlen declared. "Besides, I shall pay."

"Well in that case," Kian smirked, giving Kat a gentle squeeze, "lead the fucking way."

"Thank you," Kat said with a smile, glancing over at Arlen and winking suggestively. "I think I'm going to enjoy being in Mercia."

"Yes, I think you shall," Arlen agreed, smiling broadly.

After reaching the Mermaid Inn and procuring three of the most expensive rooms with a view, Kat stood on the small balcony of her bedchamber, which overlooked the ocean. She closed her eyes for just a moment, breathing in the fresh sea air. A single tear rolled down her cheek as she thought of Little Kian. *Oh, how he would love it here*, she mused to herself, missing her young son desperately.

A sudden knock at the door interrupted her thoughts. "Come in," she shouted, hastily wiping her eyes on the sleeve of her dress.

Arlen entered. He had observed her tears. "Are you alright?" he asked concerned, joining her on the balcony.

"Yes," she sniffed. "Just being silly and sentimental."

"Were you thinking of your son?" he asked sympathetically.

"Yes," she smiled, turning to face Arlen. "I was." Kat admired his ruggedly handsome features. "Do you know Arlen Barlett, I think I rather like you," she giggled, leaning over and placing a kiss to his cheek.

Kian then burst into the room without warning and Arlen hastily stepped backwards.

"What the fuck are you two doing?" he grumbled, standing in the doorway. "Come on, I'm parched?" he continued, immediately turning on his heels and heading for the stairs.

Kat gripped hold of Arlen's hand. "Come on then," she said cheerfully, "let's see what Trevelyan has to offer."

Starting at the Mermaid they continued to snake their way through the town, calling in at all Kian's favourite haunts. Arlen was more than impressed with Kat – she certainly knew how to hold her liquor. Finally, they found themselves at The Drovers Inn. Kian proudly showed off his sister to all the regular revellers at his favourite tavern in Trevelyan. As it started to get rather late, Kat began to tire and, with another full day in the saddle tomorrow, she asked Arlen if he would mind accompanying her back to the Mermaid. Arlen was more than happy to oblige. Kian announced that he was staying at the Drovers; Polly's husband was away from home. After lovingly kissing his sister affectionately goodnight he warned Arlen in no uncertain terms to take exceptionally good care of her, before promptly returning to Polly and his umpteenth jug of ale.

Arlen and Kat walked slowly back along the seafront towards the Mermaid Inn. It was a cool clear night, the sky was full of stars and the moon was reflected in the calm deep blue water. Kat paused for a moment, taking in a deep breath.

"The ocean. It's so magical isn't it, Arlen?" she beamed, utterly transfixed at the mass of water stretching out in front of them.

"I've never really considered it before," Arlen replied, more interested in admiring Kat. "But yes, you are right Kat, it is magical indeed."

Kat shivered in the cool breeze and Arlen quickly wrapped his cloak around her shoulders as they continued on their way. They didn't speak again, just silently walked along; Kat gripping onto Arlen's hand, squeezing tightly. Upon reaching the door to her bedchamber, she turned to face Arlen and then, leaning over, she casually kissed him on the cheek.

"Thank you, Arlen. I don't think I could have spent a more enjoyable first night in Mercia," she said, observing him very closely. "You know you are rather lovely," she said with a sweet smile before disappearing inside her room.

Arlen remained outside the door for just a moment longer, grinning to himself. *And I think you are rather lovely too*, he mused to himself before retiring to his own room.

Chapter 17

Henry was already waiting patiently at the town gates. Dressed in his full Crown Knight livery, he was creating quite a bit of unwanted attention from other early risers. He was well rested and looked completely refreshed. As he observed Arlen, Kian and Kat riding towards him, he was not surprised to see Kat sat atop Arlen's horse. He smiled to himself. They looked incredibly happy, chatting and laughing together. Kian also looked surprisingly jolly, particularly after a night on the ale.

"You all look surprisingly clear headed this morning," he remarked, as they drew nearer.

"As do you," Arlen added, "Sleep well?"

"Yes, very, thank you."

"Henry," Kat gasped. "You look … well. I was really rather impressed by Arlen in his Crown livery this morning … but I have to say you look very important."

"Thank you, Kat," Henry smiled at her innocent outspokenness. She was very much like her brother in many ways.

Arlen and Kian laughed aloud.

"Come," Henry said, pulling on the reins of his horse. "We should make haste, we have a long day's ride ahead of us. Thankfully the weather remains good. We shall rest up at Stockwood."

"What is Stockwood?" Kat asked, gently leaning back against Arlen.

"Stockwood," Arlen replied, "is the fruit capital of Mercia. There are acres and acres of orchards and fruit farms. This time of year they grow the most delicious strawberries, you would be hard pressed to find better."

"Strawberries?" Kat frowned.

"You have never tried strawberries?" Arlen enquired, rather astonished.

"No, never even heard of them," Kat replied, shrugging her shoulders.

"Well then young lady, you are in for a real treat. They taste deliciously juicy and sweet. The ancients believed they were sent from the Goddess of Love herself."

"Oh, they do sound delicious," she mused, pressing herself a little further back against Arlen.

Kian threw his sister a disapproving look, she ignored him. Henry laughed.

*   *   *

Meanwhile back on the quayside in Trevelyan, the man with the scar stood quietly looking out across the ocean – watching as the numerous ships and boats sailed into and out of the harbour. Raven's mysterious lover, Charles, quietly approached. The man with the scar remained perfectly still, his gaze unfaltering.

"Well?" the young man said, leaning back against the sea wall and eyeing the fisherman unloading their catch on the quayside.

"Morton has departed for Kingslea," the man with the scar said.

"What about the Westonhall girl?"

"She remains with Lorimer," the young man replied, "And the King?"

"The King is on his summer progress."

"Excellent," the young man replied, turning to face the ocean. "That gives us time. First we deal with Morton, then the girl. Come we should make haste."

Mounting their horses, the two men promptly left the quayside. They rode swiftly out of Trevelyan, also heading west towards Kingslea.

*   *   *

Kat ate a whole bowl of strawberries at Stockwood, turning her lips bright red.

"You were right Arlen, strawberries taste delicious," she said, suggestively licking her lips. "Umm, I taste of strawberries, see."

Quickly glancing around to ensure Kian was nowhere to be seen, she planted a kiss to Arlen's lips.

"Umm, you do taste good," he agreed. "I should very much like to taste more of you."

"Well, we shall have to see about that," she grinned, turning on her heels before rushing off in the direction of the horses, just as Henry and Kian appeared at the entrance to the Inn where they had stopped earlier to take refreshments.

"Ready to go?" Henry shouted over.

"Yes," Arlen nodded, licking his lips.

The weather remained good. Arlen and Kat rode up front and talked nonstop the whole way. Henry and Kian followed on, not far behind them.

"Henry, have you had any more thoughts after we all spoke yesterday?" Kian asked, at the same time keeping a keen eye on his sister.

"No, not really. I should like to try and speak with Gilmore if I can; I hope that with his wife and daughter in town he may have improved somewhat. And Phillip Ainsworth, although I do believe him to be most loyal, Arlen obviously has some doubts."

"Gilmore does seem to be our only link," Kian grumbled.

"Yes, indeed, we are still clutching at straws," Henry sighed. "I think perhaps it may also be prudent to speak with Sir James Ripley, after all he was privy to all Lorimer's plans. He may even know of this mysterious lady with the black hair."

"Why do you say that?" Kian asked, not quite understanding Henry's meaning.

"This is not over by a long way Kian. What better way to get to Lorimer than through his Ambassador. This woman is undoubtedly a seductress and she may have already formed an acquaintance with Ripley, hoping for idle pillow talk perhaps."

"Oh, yes now I understand your meaning," Kian nodded in agreement.

As the sun slowly dipped below the horizon, Kingslea came into view – it sat atop a rocky outcrop overlooking the Rame Valley. Kat gazed in wonder. With the sunset framing the city so, even the three men admitted that it was a magnificent sight.

It was extremely late and dark as the riders finally rode into the Crown Knight courtyard within the Kilve Palace. A couple of stable lads came out to attend them. Edwin promptly appeared from behind the large wooden doors, happy and relieved to see his brother returned from the Corridor with Henry and Kian in tow.

"Lord Morton," he beamed, giving his deepest bow. "How very good to see you returned to Kingslea."

"Hello, Edwin," Henry replied, quickly dismounting his horse and acknowledging Edwin with a firm hand to his shoulder. "It is so good to be back, I have to say."

A handful of Crown soldiers on duty immediately rose to their feet as the travellers entered, standing to attention upon observing Henry.

"At ease men," Henry said, motioning for them to all sit back down.

"Christ, Henry really is important, isn't he?" Kat whispered, holding onto Arlen's hand.

Arlen grinned back at her, nodding his head. "Yes, he is."

Once safely inside Henry's private office, Arlen closed the door behind them.

"My God, it is so good to see you all," Edwin repeated, embracing the men in turn. "I was beginning to get worried … is this, Iris Westonhall?" he asked, directing his gaze towards Kat.

"No, this is Kat. Katherine Munro, Kian's sister. Iris remains in the East, with Lorimer."

Edwin looked confused.

"We have so much to tell you, Edwin," Henry continued, "but not tonight, it shall have to wait until tomorrow. I now urgently need to speak with the King."

"The King is on his summer progress Henry."

Henry's shoulders sank at the news. He ran his fingers through his hair. Edwin observed his obvious disappointment.

"Henry, Father and I join the King the day after tomorrow. Come to Barlett House for dinner tomorrow evening and you can apprise us on all your news, then ride out with us the following day," Edwin eagerly suggested.

"Yes ... yes that sounds good," Henry replied, a little frustrated with the delay, but agreeing that the plan made sense.

"Kian, please take Kat to my private apartments, will you? Ask my man to send a maid to attend her. I shall join you shortly," Henry said, observing Kat yawning. She looked absolutely exhausted, barely able to stand.

"Come on Sis, let's get you to bed," Kian smiled, placing his arm around her shoulder and leading her towards the door.

"I will see you tomorrow, won't I?" she asked, turning to face Arlen.

"Yes," he replied, with a smile. "I shall see you in the morning," he said, giving her hand a gentle squeeze.

Edwin noticed their affectionate exchange. As soon as Kat and Kian had left, he spoke. "Arlen, I must speak with you concerning Florence. It's important Brother."

"For fuck's sake Edwin, not now. I shall see you in the morning Henry," he grumbled before leaving the room, slamming the door behind him.

Edwin banged his fist hard on the table. "He might well be my brother but sometimes I could bloody well strangle him," Edwin hissed, banging his fist on the table once again. "I apologise Henry, please forgive me."

"Don't mind me Edwin. Is everything alright?"

"It will be, I'm only trying to help the stupid bastard," Edwin moaned, plonking himself down into a chair.

"Speak with him tomorrow, Edwin, we are all tired and it has been a very long day." Henry suggested. "Edwin, before I go, Phillip Ainsworth, is he on duty tomorrow?"

"Yes, I believe so, he has recently been away from town, in Trevelyan as it happens with his brother I believe. But yes, he will be on duty tomorrow. I expect you wish to speak with him regarding Lorimer?"

"Yes, that's right. Good, I shall call upon Lord Gilmore in the morning and then I have some urgent private affairs I must put in order. Please ask Phillip to attend my office tomorrow afternoon, let's say around four o'clock."

"Yes, of course Henry, I shall inform him first thing in the morning."

"Excellent, well I shall look forward to dinner tomorrow evening then. Goodnight, Edwin."

"Goodnight, Henry," Edwin replied, reaching for a large glass of brandy.

Kat awoke late the following morning; she had slept exceptionally well. The bed was extremely comfortable, her whole body had sunk down into the soft mattress and the silky sheets were smooth against her skin. Sitting up she noticed that her clothes had been neatly laid out at the end of the bed with a small table under the window containing a tray of food. She instantly spotted a large bowl of fresh strawberries. Jumping from the bed, she froze. The floor was covered in the most exquisitely woven fabric.

"Oh my, I am truly in a palace now," she mused, heading straight for the bowl of strawberries.

Picking them up, she promptly exited the bedchamber into an elegant drawing room, which was furnished with comfortable seating, intricately carved side tables, windows that were adorned with sumptuous drapes, and numerous portraits that hung from the silk-covered walls.

"Christ," she exclaimed aloud.

Henry appeared in the doorway of the study at the far end of the drawing room. At the sight of Kat standing in nothing more than her sheer linen nightgown, clutching tightly to a bowl of strawberries, he could not help but smile broadly.

"I assume you slept well?" he asked, "It is quite late."

"Yes, I did, thank you," she replied, popping another strawberry into her mouth. "Are you very rich, Henry?" she asked, proceeding to dance around the room.

"I am," he replied, still smiling.

"Richer than the King?"

"Probably." he grinned.

"Christ Henry," she giggled, continuing to swirl around the room.

"Never mind, Christ Henry," Kian roared, hastily pushing past Henry in the doorway. "Where are your fucking clothes woman?"

Arlen followed behind Kian and stood beside Henry in the doorway.

"Get dressed woman for God's sake, exposing yourself like that. You are not in the fucking forest now," Kian growled, hastily ushering Kat back inside the bedchamber.

"The women of Corstir don't have many inhibitions when it comes to nakedness. You should see what they wear to hunt, or perhaps I should say do not wear," Henry said with a laugh.

"I should have liked to have seen that," Arlen mused.

"You like Kat, don't you?"

"I do." Arlen replied. "She is a strong and evidently a very independent woman. Clever and witty too, yet there is a certain innocence about her that is quite alluring."

"What are you going to do about Florence? You need to be honest with Kat before it goes too far, she is clearly smitten with you. Kian will not hesitate to have your balls hanging around his neck if you hurt her you know."

"Oh Christ Henry, I'm in a fucking mess. I don't want to marry Florence, I never did," Arlen groaned, returning to the study and slumping himself down into a chair, burying his head in his hands.

"Then tell her so. Put an end to this sham once and for all. For God's sake Arlen, put us all out of our misery."

"Yes, you are right Henry. I shall, I shall do it today," Arlen declared with determination in his voice. "Florence is here in town, as my bloody brother keeps reminding me. I shall go to her this very morning; you are right I need to put an end to it once and for all."

"Good," Henry replied, placing a friendly hand to Arlen's shoulder.

A short while later Henry and Kian were just about to leave for the prison tower when Kat entered the study – suitably dressed, much to Kian's relief.

"Where are you going?" she asked, her lips stained red from the strawberries.

"Crown business," Kian replied. "You have to stay here. Don't go getting yourself into any fucking trouble. Ask the maid if you need anything and for God's sake don't go wandering around on your own."

"Must I remain here?" she grumbled, glancing over at Arlen and seductively tossing her red hair over her shoulder.

"I would be more than happy to accompany Kat on a tour of the palace," Arlen suggested, jumping from his seat.

"Oh yes, I would like that very much," she replied, with a huge smile.

"I thought you had an urgent prior engagement?" Henry enquired knowingly.

"I do … But it's nothing that can't wait," he said, casually shrugging his shoulders.

Henry raised a dubious eyebrow. "Are you sure Arlen?" he asked, shaking his head with disapproval.

"Yes, I promise I shall deal with the other matter later."

"Very well," Henry replied.

"Well Brother, can I go with Arlen?"

"I suppose so, but you had better behave yourself."

"I will, I promise," Kat beamed, planting a kiss to her brother's cheek.

"Get off me woman," Kian grimaced, jokingly pushing her away. Kat laughed, flinging her arms around him.

Lord Thomas Gilmore sat in an easy chair underneath the barred window of his prison cell. His wife and daughter sat at a nearby table quietly sewing and keeping the still extremely sick man company. They rose immediately upon Henry's entry.

"Lord Morton," Lady Gilmore muttered, surprised by Henry's presence.

"Lady Gilmore, Miss Gilmore," Henry replied, bowing his head to the two women. "I apologise for the unscheduled intrusion. How is your husband madam?"

Lady Joan Gilmore looked tired. The lines on her forehead and around her eyes were most prominent. This dreadful affair had obviously taken its toll on the woman. Her daughter Elinor also looked tired; she had a pleasing full-rounded face, although, unfortunately, she sported her father's piggy nose. There was a certain strength and determination behind her dark eyes as she stared intensely at the two men.

"Not at all Lord Morton, it is an honour I can assure you. His physical injuries improve daily milord, but I am afraid his mind does not. We fear he may have suffered a brain attack…"

"May I speak with him madam?"

"Yes, of course milord, we shall leave you alone," she replied, pulling at her daughter's arm. Elinor released her fixed look upon Henry and reluctantly followed her mother from the room.

Kian joined Henry at the window. They both stared down at Lord Gilmore slumped over in his chair. His face was still very badly swollen with traces of yellow-brown bruises. His hands and feet were bound with clean bandages. The right side of his face appeared to have dropped and spittle was dribbling from the corner of his mouth. He was mumbling something inaudible, over and over again.

"Fuck," Kian whispered, "What the hell did they do to him?"

"God only knows," Henry replied, appalled. He crouched down. Gone was the condescending, arrogant man he knew so well – his admirable sparring partner from the privy chamber. Before him now was only a pitiful broken wretch.

"Thomas," Henry whispered, observing Gilmore closely, hoping for at least a small acknowledgement.

Henry took hold of Gilmore's hand and squeezed it gently. "I shall find who schemed against you Thomas, I promise."

Henry felt Gilmore move his hand, very slightly. At the same time, a tear rolled down his bruised cheek.

"I promise Thomas," Henry repeated.

Henry and Kian remained for a short while in silence; Henry deep in thought with Gilmore still gripping tightly onto his hand.

Meanwhile back at the Kilve Palace, Arlen was conducting Kat on a grand tour. With few courtiers in residence due to being on the King's progress, they were able to access rooms that would normally be out of bounds. Kat was in total awe of the place, staring in wonder at the multitude of elaborately decorated rooms. Their sumptuous furnishings, the rich gilding on the walls and ceilings with treasures of gold and silver adorning almost every surface. Arlen was allured by Kat's childlike reactions to the splendour, things that he took every day for granted. As they eventually made their way out into the extensive formal gardens with its magnificent great fountain at the centre, Kat leisurely kicked off her shoes and raced across the well-tended lawn.

"Arlen, this is truly the most magical place," she beamed, dancing and spinning around the small perimeter wall of the fountain and kicking her legs up high in the air.

"From what I have heard, I don't think it can be any more magical than Corstir," he replied, gripping her waist as she twirled past him and pulling her towards him.

"I want to kiss you," he smiled, cupping her beautiful face in his hand. Her vibrant green eyes sparkling with excitement.

Arlen pulled her even closer, their lips almost touching.

"I have only ever been with one man," she mused, staring deep into Arlen's eyes. "Little Kian's father. It was an awfully long time ago. I loved him, but he didn't love me, well not enough anyway."

"I would never hurt you Kat, I promise," Arlen whispered, gently brushing his lips against hers.

"Then kiss me Arlen," she replied, pressing her lips tightly to his.

They stood for several minutes kissing passionately to the sound of the rushing water from the fountain, lost in each other's embraces. Moments later, Arlen held out his hand and asked, "Will you come with me Kat?"

"Yes," she replied without hesitation, taking his hand in hers.

There was an ever-growing sense of urgency between them as they reached the steps of Barlett House. Arlen paused. "You are sure, aren't you?" he asked, kissing Kat again and praying that she had not changed her mind.

"Yes, I'm sure Arlen," she replied, gripping tightly onto his hand, her heart pounding fast.

Arlen then, very quietly opened the door, breathing a sigh of relief upon eyeing the empty hallway before leading Kat up the stairs to his bedchamber. He had hardly time to close the door behind them before Kat was busy pulling at his outer garments.

"Get me out of this dress," she breathed, hastily unbuttoning his doublet.

Wriggling and shaking off all their clothes in haste and casually scattering them about the floor, Kat proceeded to release the ties on Arlen's breeches and yanked them down.

"My boots," he moaned, in between kisses and passionately caressing Kat's now naked body. Only her stockings remaining.

"Forget your boots," she groaned, as his breeches fell to his knees.

Arlen staggered backwards and Kat forcefully pushed him back on to the bed. She wanted him inside her now. He just about managed to wriggle into the centre before Kat hastily straddled his hips, gripping hold of his erection and guiding him between her legs. They both let out pleasant lingering moans as his length filled her. Arlen gripped Kat's hips, moving his own to her steady rhythm. She leaned down over him, her hardened nipples brushing against his naked chest. With their lips locked and their tongues entwined, they gently rocked together as lovers do. Moments later, Kat sat upright, throwing her head back, her beautiful red hair flowing down her back. She increased their rhythm.

"Yes," she moaned loudly as Arlen moved with her – the intense erotic feeling almost tipping her over the edge. "Oh Arlen … yes!"

It had been a long time since Kat had had a man between her legs and she intended on relishing in every pleasure Arlen had to offer.

Increasing their rhythm further and pressing down hard, she could feel every inch of him deep inside her. "Yes!" she cried out, spiralling once again.

"Kat," Arlen breathed, her intense enthusiasm causing him to hurtle fast towards his own climax. "Please slow down Kat, or I'm going to …"

The euphoria filling the room suddenly evaporated into thin air as the door to the bedchamber flung open. Lord Douglas Barlett stood in the doorway, glaring crossly at his son with what appeared to be a wanton red head straddled across him.

"Get dressed," he commanded, leaving Arlen under no illusion as to his displeasure. "Florence Ainsworth and her mother are downstairs," he said, closing the door firmly behind him.

Kat stared down at Arlen. "Who is Florence Ainsworth?"

Arlen remained silent, so Kat asked again, clearly very annoyed with him. "Who is Florence Ainsworth?"

"My betrothed," he muttered, under his breath.

"You bastard," Kat screamed, slapping his face hard and jerking herself off him – deliberately catching his manhood between her thighs.

Arlen winced in pain before desperately scrambling to his feet. "Please Kat I can explain. I'm not going to marry her. It's all a big misunderstanding, please Kat. I don't love her, I never did."

"You lied to me," she screamed, striking him again hard across the face before hastily gathering her clothes from the floor.

"Please Kat, please listen. I'm so sorry. I shall put this right, I promise you. Please Kat."

Without saying another word Kat disappeared madly from the room, slamming the door behind her. Arlen was left alone naked and dejected, clutching his sore ego in one hand and rubbing his bruised face with the other. His breeches were puddled around his ankles.

"Fuck … fuck … fuck," he yelled aloud.

Arlen quickly got dressed and reluctantly made his way down the stairs, his hair all dishevelled and sporting a bright red mark across his left cheek. As he entered the drawing room, the occupants all fell silent and turned to stare. His father, clearly annoyed and with his face like thunder, stood beside the window.

"Arlen at last," his brother beamed. "We were so pleased when Father said you were home. We have been wanting to speak with you."

Edwin was stood holding Florence's hand. Arlen looked at them a little confused.

"Florence and I have something very important to ask you," Edwin added, smiling at Florence.

"Please let me," she said, smiling back at Edwin sweetly before turning her attention to Arlen. "Why Arlen, your face?" she exclaimed, observing his bruised cheek. "Whatever have you done?"

"Oh, it's nothing," Arlen mumbled, embarrassed and raising his hand to his reddened cheek.

He could feel his father's eyes glaring at him. He didn't dare to look over in his direction.

"Well," Florence continued, clearing her throat. "Edwin and I have been corresponding for a while now, as I am sure you are aware. Quite regularly in fact, well … well, we have grown rather …" Florence paused, blushing nervously and looking to Edwin for support.

"What Florence is trying to say brother, is that I have asked for her hand in marriage and, with your permission, Florence wishes to be released from your engagement. She has assured me she will only accept my offer if she is certain and that you are in total agreement. She won't hesitate to keep her promise to you if you are not. I know you have strong feelings for Florence Brother, but I believe my love for her is far greater and I … no, we, very much ask for your blessing."

Arlen could hardly believe his ears. Was he dreaming? All this time he had been avoiding Florence and all she wanted to do was release him from their engagement. His mind instantly turned to Kat. He wanted to quit the drawing room at once and run after her. He felt such a fool.

"Well Brother?" Edwin asked, bringing Arlen back into the moment and pressing him for an answer.

"Yes … yes of course. I would never stand in the way of true love, of course I agree. Edwin is by far the better man," Arlen replied, trying awfully hard not to betray too much relief in his voice.

"Thank you, Arlen," Florence beamed, kissing him tenderly on the cheek.

"Thank you, Brother," Edwin smiled and lovingly embraced him.

The whole thing seemed so surreal. Arlen felt as if he were in some strange dream. He wanted to scream.

Lady Ainsworth was overjoyed of course. This now meant that her younger daughter would one day become Lady Barlett, Mistress of Wenlock Hall.

"The wedding shall take place as planned," she announced, embracing Florence and Edwin in turn. "We shall merely blame the printers for the error in the name," she laughed.

"You do agree Lord Barlett?"

"Yes, indeed I do. In fact, it is cause for celebration," he replied, pulling the cord for Mrs Brooke.

Arlen stood in silence, watching the four people in the room congratulating each other, smiling, and embracing. He wanted to run. He longed to escape, to find Kat and apologise – beg for her forgiveness. Mrs Brooke entered the room and asked how many for refreshments, Arlen saw his chance to escape.

"Not for me, thank you Mrs Brooke," he said, hoping to flee the room at once.

His father however had other ideas, "Arlen, you cannot possibly have anywhere else more important to be than right here celebrating with your brother?" he declared, glaring at Arlen. It was not a question but an order.

Douglas Barlett was evidently not in any kind of mood to let his son off so easily it seemed.

"No sir," Arlen replied at once, faking a smile.

"Good," Lord Barlett replied. "Five please Mrs Brooke."

* * *

Henry had just returned to his study in the Kilve Palace, having left Kian at one of the taverns near the Tower after they had taken lunch together. He was keen to clear his desk of correspondence before his meeting with Philip Ainsworth. He shifted through the enormous pile of letters, pausing for a moment to pull out the folded paper containing the poem from his pocket. He was about to unfold it and read it again when a knock at the door diverted his attention. Hastily, he placed it safely under a weight on his desk.

"Yes," he shouted. "Please come in."

The door opened very slowly. Henry was pleasantly surprised to see Beatrice Ainsworth standing in the doorway.

"Lady Bentley," he said, immediately rising from his chair and giving a bow.

"Oh Henry, surely we know each other better than that, Beatrice please," she smiled, with a curtsey.

"Yes, I'm sorry, hello Beatrice, how are you?"

Henry could not help but notice a large bruise across her right cheek.

"Are you alright?" he asked, concern in his voice. "That looks like a nasty bruise."

"Oh, yes," Beatrice sighed, gently touching her cheek and dismissing his concern with a wave of her hand. "It's nothing really."

Henry observed the same vulnerable, melancholy expression he had first noticed at Moorgate Hall. She was clearly very troubled. He suspected at once someone had given her the bruise intentionally.

"Would you like a drink?" he asked, in an attempt to lighten the mood.

"Yes please," she replied, moving closer towards him and positioning herself so that Henry now had his back to the door.

Henry poured a brandy and passed her a glass. She slowly took a sip. He considered for just a moment what an exceptionally beautiful woman she was.

"Henry," she whispered, briefly glancing up at him as if she was about to divulge a secret before quickly lowering her eyes.

"What is it, Beatrice?" he asked, placing his hand under her chin and raising her head to face him. "Are you sure you are alright?"

Henry's attention was then suddenly distracted, his eyes drawn to a small brooch on the shoulder of her scarlet red dress – enamelled in black and gold and in the shape of a bumble bee. He gently reached over, taking a curl of her raven black hair, and twirled it between his fingers.

"You," he gasped, stepping backwards. "It is you; you took Gilmore's seal."

"I'm sorry Henry," she blurted out, a look of horror shooting across her face. "Please forgive me."

At that moment, a sudden hard thud to the back of his head caused Henry to fall forward and collapse unconscious in a heap on the floor.

Chapter 18

Arlen sat in silence for what felt like hours, listening to Lady Elizabeth Ainsworth rattling on and on. He knew his father must have also been finding her continuous babble excruciating, but it seemed he was content to punish Arlen a little longer. Finally, and much to Arlen's relief, she announced that it was time to go. Edwin insisted on accompanying the women back to their apartments at the Kilve Palace. Arlen remained seated in the drawing room after they had left. He felt very much like a disobedient schoolboy waiting for the headmaster to determine his punishment. His father poured himself a large glass of brandy and moved towards the bay window and looked out onto the street below.

"I would appreciate it if you did not bring whores into my house," he said, his tone sharp.

"She is not a whore Father," Arlen replied, feeling really rather ashamed. "Her name is Kat; she is Kian's sister."

"And is Kian's sister accustomed to bedding young men in the middle of the afternoon," he asked, clearly still very annoyed.

"No sir, please don't speak of her in that way. If you must think ill of anyone let it be me, I am totally to blame."

"I'm disappointed in you Arlen," Lord Barlett mused, sipping on his brandy.

"I'm sorry sir, I disappoint myself. I let Harriet down, I have treated Florence abominably and now I have just lied to Kat, only moments after I promised I would never hurt her. I'm a bloody fool Father, I'm so ashamed," he groaned, burying his head in his hands.

Douglas Barlett remained silent and sipped his brandy. He was well aware of his youngest son's impulsive tendencies. The way he acted sometimes without thinking of the consequences and wearing his heart so boldly on his sleeve. Ann had always insisted Arlen should be allowed to find his own way; being a second son was not easy. His proposal to Florence was an attempt to do the right thing. Lord Barlett was immensely proud of both of his boys and if, as it appeared, his younger son was attracted to the more unconventional woman, then who was he to disapprove? More than anything he wanted both his sons to be happy.

"So, how do you intend on putting this right?" he asked finally, turning to face Arlen.

Arlen looked surprised by his father's question, not quite sure of his meaning.

"Sir?" he replied, quizzically.

"Well after what I have just witnessed in your bedchamber, I take it you like this woman, Kat?" his father asked.

"Yes, sir I do, very much."

"Well Arlen, it seems your brother has conveniently got you out of one sticky situation. You now have a golden opportunity to put things right with Kat, I suggest you take it."

Arlen let out a deep sigh of relief and he smiled. "Thank you, Father. I think perhaps I should start with the truth, then I shall apologise and beg for her forgiveness if I must. She is wonderful Father, she is from Corstir. She is so talented in many ways; hunting and fishing and is as accomplished as any man, yet there is a real innocence about her. You should have seen her face when she first set eyes upon the ocean. Every day she discovers new things. I want to be there with her when she does. I want to teach her to ride a horse, to read and to write. I want to show her the world." Arlen paused to catch his breath.

Lord Barlett could clearly see that his son was enamoured by this woman.

"She has a son, Father," Arlen added, watching his father's reaction closely.

"I see," Lord Barlett replied, still standing beside the window and sipping his brandy. He remained silent for several minutes in deep contemplation, until finally he spoke. "Go to her my boy."

"Sir," Arlen replied, shocked yet more than grateful for what appeared to be his father's approval.

"Life is short my son, you should grasp happiness with both hands. If this woman truly makes you happy then tell her so – be honest with her Arlen. I'm sure if she feels the same way she will forgive you."

"Thank you, Father, I do hope you are right; besides, I dread to think what Kian will do to me if she will not."

Lord Barlett laughed aloud. "Well, yes there is that."

"I shall go to her at once," Arlen declared, already with his hand on the door handle.

"Arlen," his father said, turning to peer from the window. "It seems you shall not need to, she has come to you." He observed Kat racing towards the house at great speed, her red hair wild and unruly and her skirts hitched up well above her knees, most unladylike.

Lord Barlett could not help but smile, *unconventional indeed* he mused to himself.

Kat burst into the drawing room of Barlett House, almost collapsing to the floor in front of the two men whilst desperately trying hard to catch her breath.

"Kat," Arlen blurted out, not giving her a chance to speak. "I'm sorry, please forgive me. I'm not marrying Florence; she is to marry my brother. I should have told you before we … I'm sorry, can you ever forgive me?"

"Henry has been taken!" Kat cried out in between deep breaths. She ignored Arlen's pleas.

"What!" he exclaimed, suddenly taken aback by Kat's grim words. "What do you mean?"

"Yes, I'm afraid it's true, after we … after I left," she breathed, "I went back to the palace and walked around the gardens for a while, contemplating cutting your fucking balls off," she paused to take another deep breath.

Arlen cringed at her crude remark and glanced over at his father, but he had yet to take his eyes from Kat.

"Anyway," she continued, still breathing heavily. "I decided to head back to Henry's apartments, when, just as I rounded the corner, I saw two men dragging Henry from his study. I couldn't see their faces. There was a woman with them too. She was wearing a scarlet red dress and she had black hair. One of the men was a Crown Knight." she paused again, catching her breath.

Lord Barlett handed her a glass of brandy. "Are you sure he was a Crown Knight my dear?" he asked, anxiously.

"Yes sir," Kat confirmed at once. "Quite sure he was wearing a Crown livery, just like Arlen's."

"They didn't see you?" he continued, concerned for her safety.

"No sir, I backed up against the wall, quick like. I hardly dared breathe for fear they would discover me," she sighed, gulping down the contents of the glass.

"Arlen," Lord Barlett exclaimed, observing his son looking preoccupied all of a sudden. "What is it?"

Arlen didn't answer. Instead he swiftly threw open the drawing room door and bellowed for Mrs Brooke at the top of his voice. The tiny woman appeared from nowhere with her usual efficiency; her pointed features twitching. She was clearly irritated at being summoned in such an abrupt manner.

"Mrs Brooke has anything arrived for me in the last week, from Oxwich College?" he asked, urgently.

"Yes sir, a scroll. It's in your father's study."

"Thank you," he replied, frantically dashing off in the direction of the study.

Lord Barlett and Kat were hot on his heels.

"What is it, Arlen?" his father enquired upon seeing his son furiously unravelling a scroll atop the large oak desk.

"It's a genealogical chart Father," he replied. "I went to see Linus Eves in Langland to discover more about Clara Westonhall, but nothing came of that of course. But I couldn't shake a niggling feeling I had when I first observed Phillip Ainsworth's indifferent reaction to the letter found at Goring End. Then, when you informed Edwin and myself that he was the Crown Knight who was to rendezvous with Lorimer in Trevelyan, I commissioned Eves to produce a genealogical chart for the Ainsworth family."

Arlen stared down at the superlative piece of work and scanned the details in haste.

"Nothing," he growled, banging his fist hard upon the desk. "Oh Christ, what are we to do now? Who on earth could have taken Henry? This is absolutely insane."

"Wait a minute," his father said, picking up a note from the floor that had been wrapped within the scroll. "What's this?"

"It's from Eves," he said and began to read it aloud.

Sir Arlen Barlett

Firstly, may I say Berwyn has assiduously reviewed the chart for Clara Westonhall. I can categorically assure you that there are no records of a daughter. I hope this news meets with your satisfaction.

I have enclosed the genealogical chart for Florence Ainsworth as requested. As it is a gift for your future wife, may I take this opportunity on congratulating you both on the impending wedding.

Upon preparing the chart, Berwyn discovered something that might interest you. We have not included it here, but of course we can make amendments if you so wish. It appears that Ambassador Ripley, who recently visited from the East, is not only the half-brother of the deceased Jane Howard, mother to Lord Sebastian Howard, but also her sister, Elizabeth Ainsworth, your future mother-in-law.

Please do let me know if you require the chart to be amended.

Yours Sincerely

Linus Eves

"I can't believe it. Sir James Ripley is Phillip's uncle," Lord Barlett cried out, hastily rereading the note in utter disbelief. "He never breathed a single word ... Arlen, I fear we may have been betrayed."

"Who has been betrayed?" Edwin asked, now standing in the doorway to the study and looking puzzled at the three occupants.

"We have Brother," Arlen snapped, angrily. "Phillip Ainsworth is nephew to Sir James Ripley, the Ambassador from the East. They are involved in the explosion somehow, I know it, and I believe they have just taken Henry from his study," he added sharply.

"What, this cannot be, this is madness!" Edwin exclaimed in utter shock. He looked to his father for confirmation.

"It appears not. Kat here witnessed Henry being dragged from his study only a short while ago by a Crown Knight, the other man could have been Ripley," Lord Barlett replied, his shoulders slumped. A treasonous Crown Knight was unprecedented.

"And the woman, of course, we have been so blind, it's his sister Beatrice." Arlen growled, chastising himself. "Beatrice, but of course. The gold and black brooch is a bumble bee and her hair is jet black. She is certainly capable of seducing an old man like Gilmore, she is strikingly beautiful."

Edwin's mind suddenly turned to Florence. *She couldn't possibly be involved in this, could she*? he mused to himself.

Arlen turned to face his father. "Father, what explanation were you given for Ripley wearing that leather mask?"

"We were told that he had been badly burnt, disfigured even, at the battle of Crowforth."

"Who told you?"

"Phillip Ainsworth," his father replied with an exasperated sigh.

"Well, that settles it. According to Henry, Lorimer told him that he lost no men at Crowforth and sustained no injuries – the battle was merely a ruse to end the war. The mask is to hide a scar. He is the man with the scar, the man from Winkhill. The man who attempted to abduct Iris from Baines Abbey."

"Edwin, where is Phillip now?" his father bellowed, regaining his son's full attention.

"He should be waiting in Henry's office," Edwin replied, shaking his head in disbelief and struggling to comprehend the seriousness of the situation. "Arlen if this is true, we should make haste."

"Yes," their father confirmed. "Time is of the essence if you are to find Henry alive. Please, I beg you both to be careful."

"We shall Father, don't worry but I have to find Henry," Arlen groaned, already moving towards the door.

"I'm coming with you," Kat declared, grabbing at Arlen's arm and preventing him from leaving.

"No, Kat it's far too dangerous," he replied, stopping in his tracks and turning to face her.

"Well at least let me find Kian, he needs to know what is going on. He is probably already back at Henry's apartments right now wondering where we all are."

Arlen hesitated. He placed a gentle hand to Kat's face.

"Very well, but you must be careful … I'm sorry I lied to you Kat. Can you ever forgive me."

Kat placed her hand to Arlen's shoulder and forcefully pushed him back against the door.

"If you ever lie to me again Arlen Barlett, I shall not just bruise your balls, I shall fucking cut them off," she scolded, before planting a lingering kiss to his lips.

"Is that a yes?" he groaned.

"Yes, you handsome fool. Now go, make haste and find Henry."

Arlen briefly glanced over at his father. He gave his son an approving nod. Arlen mouthed back the words 'thank you' and, with that, was gone.

Lord Barlett stood alone in the study, staring aimlessly down at the genealogical chart.

"Is everything alright milord?" Mrs Brooke asked, appearing in the doorway, her pointed features softened.

"I hope so, Mrs Brooke, I do very much hope so," he replied with another deep sigh.

*   *   *

Henry pulled on the chains that were wrapped punishingly tight around his wrists and holding his arms above his head. His muscles were stretched to the very limit, as his battered body hung over the icy water in what appeared to be a boathouse on the River Rame. His upper body was naked, bloody, and bruised from a ferocious beating that had already been rained down upon him. He felt a searing pain from a gash above his right eye. His nose and mouth were choked with blood and a gag was tied securely around his face, restricting his breathing and preventing him from crying out. He groaned as another powerful punch to his abdomen caused him to drop his head forward in agony, pulling on the muscles in his arms as he rocked backwards and forwards on the torturous chain.

"Look at me," his tormentor sneered, slapping Henry's face hard several times to get his attention.

Henry blinked, attempting to clear the blood from his eyes in order to focus on the man causing him such agonies. His face was covered with a mysterious black leather mask.

"Do you know who I am?" he hissed, pushing his face closer to Henry.

Henry tried desperately to pull away but the man hit him again hard. He groaned and fell forward. The man grabbed at Henry's hair and jolted his head back violently.

"Look at me," he jeered, pressing his masked face to Henry's.

Henry somehow managed to refocus and stared straight in front of him.

"Do you know who I am?" the man repeated, striking Henry hard again, this time to his side.

Henry winced, shaking his head. He was unsure how much more of this brutal beating he could endure.

"Perhaps this will help," the masked man hissed menacingly and slowly removed the black leather mask from his face.

The man with the scar stood triumphantly in front of Henry, grinning broadly. "Well Lord Morton, it seems we meet again," he cruelly laughed, landing another punishing blow to Henry's body. "Let me introduce myself. Sir James Ripley," he grinned, giving a deep sardonic bow.

"Enough, Ripley," came a man's authoritative voice from the shadows.

He was stood atop the landing stage that ran the length of the boathouse. He was not quite visible in the dim candlelight.

"We certainly don't want to kill him, at least not yet," he joked, his tone sinister.

James Ripley immediately jumped from the muddy riverbank. The water was already sloshing against the wooden landing stage and his boots were ringing wet.

"The river is rising fast," he said, loosening the rope that was holding the chains around Henry's wrists and slowly lowering him into the murky icy water. It reached his knees and filled his boots.

"Hello Henry," the man in the shadows purred. "How wonderful it is to see you again so soon."

The tall, slender frame of Sebastian Howard emerged into the dim light of the filthy boathouse, the candlelight reflecting in his dazzling blue eyes.

Henry groaned and pulled on the chains that were restraining his wrists, causing him to spin. Sebastian laughed. "Oh Henry, do calm yourself, it shall soon be over I promise. But first I thought you might want to know some of the answers to the many questions you have so courageously travelled halfway around Mercia to discover."

Sebastian paused and moved slowly further down the landing stage, hovering just above Henry's position.

"I have spent my whole life growing up in the miserable, God forsaken East. Every damned day, dreaming of a new life in Mercia. A life very much like yours in fact, a life that was callously stolen from me by that self-righteous bastard Lorimer when he raged war on King Charles and fucking lost. How wonderful I thought when King Osbert fell ill. Finally I saw my chance of a new life, not only a new life in Mercia, but what is rightfully and lawfully mine as King. When Osbert first corresponded with Lorimer and my grandmother I was overjoyed, my future seemed certain. Then the miserable old bastards on the Privy Council intervened; hatred for Lorimer was still prevalent it seemed. They had the audacity to consider an alternative, Thomas Gilmore of all people. Well Henry, you can imagine how I felt about that. Quite fortuitously in fact I had only just recently discovered numerous old letters and journals belonging to my father. He had served under Lorimer in the Vikrin wars and was a member of the detachment responsible for the courageous rescue of the Crown Prince Hakim. Imagine my surprise when I came across a particularly enlightening journal describing the rescue in fastidious detail, including the tribute of six Vikrin pearls and their immense power. How easy it was to seduce Raven. I was already acquainted with him of course, he had once been lover to my cousin, Phillip Ainsworth. Well, you know Phillip and his sister of course, don't you? In fact, you made quite the impression on Beatrice after your recent visit to Moorgate Hall. So much so that she had to be gently persuaded to distract you in your office earlier today – I imagine you observed her face. But I digress. Raven would have done anything for me. Do you know that he obtained the contents of the box from his father's study without question? Well, you can imagine my utter surprise when I read the two documents that had been safely hidden away for all these years along with the Vikrin pearls. When Lorimer requested a private audience with Osbert, excluding myself and my grandmother from his plans, I knew very well that he was intent on revealing Iris's existence; his contempt for me has always been evident. Ripley of course is my man. He always has been and Phillip was more than willing to aid his cousin, the rewards were just too irresistible. The explosion was intended for Lorimer of course. A last-minute change to the rendezvous, courtesy of Phillip, to right outside Roses' ensured that Lorimer would be right in the eye of the storm. Raven was more than willing to casually discard the vessels containing the pearls at the blacksmith and bakery on his way back down the Corridor. He really had no idea what he was getting himself involved in. He did it all for love. Gilmore of course was the perfect scapegoat. Kill two birds with one stone, or two in this case," Sebastian laughed. Ripley joined him in the joke.

"Things then rather annoyingly started to go awry. The old bastard Lorimer fell ill moments before he was to enter Mercia, and Raven was observed in the Corridor. Well, we all know how that ended, and, fortunately for me, Lorimer is now too weak to be of any real consequence – in fact I doubt he shall live much longer. And then there was the beautiful Iris. Enter Lord Henry Morton, her handsome knight in shining armour. How wonderful it was to see you turning up in the East, delivering her straight into the hands of the enemy you had so bravely protected her from. Imagine her face Henry, when I break the news of your violent death. She will be so very alone in this big bad world of ours with only myself to comfort her. I do have to admire your skills as a lover Henry – from innocent virgin nun to fucking like a whore in a matter of weeks. Oh, did I not say, the walls have eyes at Rothtir. I did so enjoy your little show, in fact I could not quite make up my mind which of you I was most envious of. You are a fine specimen of a man Henry. I do however very much look forward to re-enacting the whole thing with the charming Iris in the not-so-distant future."

Sebastian laughed louder, leaning over in front of Henry and cruelly taunting him.

Henry groaned, pulling on the chains that suspended him over the icy water, which had now already reached his waist.

"Quiet," Ripley hissed, reaching down and swiping the tip of his sword across Henry's upper chest and mercilessly ripping through his skin.

Henry swung back on the chains groaning louder. Blood poured from the open wound and into the black murky water.

"My Lord," came a voice from the river. A boatman had suddenly appeared at the end of the landing stage and was struggling to keep his small boat in position. "The river is rising fast, milord, we must leave at once, the current is too strong," he grumbled.

Sebastian glared furiously at the man. "Wait," he sneered before turning his attention back to Henry.

"You know Henry, I was going to allow Ripley here to slit your throat, but I think I shall allow the river to take you instead. Once the river rats smell your blood they will flock here in their droves. Your dead body will be unrecognisable once they have feasted on your flesh. You will be wishing to have had your throat cut well before the water takes you," he grinned, observing the river rising faster and lapping up at the slash to Henry's upper chest.

"Well Henry, I shall leave you now. I will allow you a few more minutes to reflect and to die knowing that you lost, Henry Morton. Mercia is mine, Iris is mine ... let us make haste," he sniggered, jumping into the small rowboat.

Ripley promptly followed as the boatman heaved the oars, skilfully pulling the small boat away from the landing stage. Henry closed his eyes. His broken, bloody body was numb. He was slowly being enveloped into the murky freezing water of the Rame. Henry knew he was going to die and there was nothing he could do to prevent it.

Chapter 19

Phillip Ainsworth was tightly strapped down into an old iron chair in the cold, dark basement of the Kilve Palace beneath the Crown Knight headquarters. His bruised blood-soaked face was unrecognisable after just receiving a savage beating. Arlen continued to pound his fists into the traitorous bastard's face knowing only too well that whatever he did, Ainsworth would not talk. He was a Crown Knight and his death was now inevitable. Arlen stepped back momentarily to rub his sore and bloody knuckles, desperate for Ainsworth to reveal Henry's whereabouts.

"Talk you fucking bastard," he yelled in sheer frustration, lurching forward again towards the iron chair.

Edwin furiously yanked him backwards, "Enough Arlen, you will kill him for God's sake."

"I want to fucking kill him," Arlen yelled, fighting to break free from his brother's vicelike grip.

All of a sudden, a woman's terrified scream rang out from the other room, diverting the men's attention. Ainsworth groaned wildly in the iron chair, tipping the legs precariously backwards and forwards as he fought to break free.

The brothers glared at each other before Edwin bolted towards the door, momentarily disappearing into the other room. The woman's screaming abated, only for her to shriek out loudly once again upon Edwin's return.

"Who is it, Brother?" Arlen asked, wiping his sweaty brow on the sleeve of his blood splattered shirt.

"Kian, he has Beatrice; he's threatening to slice out her tongue unless her brother talks." Edwin leant down on the arms of the iron chair, pressing his face close to Ainsworth's.

The renegade Crown Knight's eyes widened, staring in horror as he listened to his sister's blood-curdling screams coming from the other room.

Edwin spoke low and fiercely. "Do you hear her Phillip? Do you hear your beautiful sister? She will soon be unable to even scream when she is delivered to the sailors on the docks in order for them to take their carnal pleasure."

"Let Kian do it," Arlen growled, lurching at Phillip once again with his fists raised, "and I shall cut out your fucking tongue at the same time, you traitorous bastard."

"Wait, Brother," Edwin shouted, holding his hand out and preventing Arlen from getting any closer. He pressed his ear closely to Ainsworth's mouth. "He's trying to speak."

Edwin knelt down, trying desperately hard to understand what Phillip was trying to say over the din of terrified screams coming from the other room.

"I can't make out what he is saying, he's choking on his own blood." Edwin moaned, repositioning himself. "What are you saying Phillip?" he yelled.

"G … o … r … i … n … g," Ainsworth gurgled, blood seeping from his swollen mouth.

"Goring End," Edwin shouted, ably jumping to his feet.

Arlen strode over towards the iron chair and landed another punishing blow to Ainsworth's head, knocking him out cold. Blood had sprayed from his mouth up the damp, slimy cold walls of the basement room.

The brothers then both instantly turned on their heels and headed for the door.

"Goring End," Arlen bellowed, almost falling from the doorway in his haste to quit the basement. "Kian, I know where …" He stopped dead in his tracks, astounded at the sight that met him. The woman's screams had ceased. Kian and Kat stood there staring back at him. Kat's beautiful green eyes were sparkling in the candlelight, her face flushed from all the bogus screaming.

"Kat," he breathed, his mouth wide with surprise. "Where is Beatrice?"

"Fuck knows," Kian replied. "I knew Ainsworth wouldn't talk without encouragement," he grinned broadly. "It was worth a fucking try."

"Christ Kian … well it damn well worked, I know where Henry is," Arlen yelled, already heading for the stairs. "Edwin, take Kat back to Barlett House, Kian with me."

With that the two men fled the basement post haste, heading east in the direction of Goring End.

Arlen battered down the door of the cheap boarding house with impeccable ease, the proprietor immediately fell to his knees terrified at the sight of the two fearsome men storming his establishment. Kian right away thrusted his sword to the man's throat.

"Where are they?" he roared, pressing the tip into the wretched man's neck, drawing blood.

He pointed a shaky finger back outside. "The boathouse," he gurgled, "at the side."

With that Kian landed one almighty powerful punch to the landlord's face causing the miserable excuse of a man to fall back with a thud, his nose bloody and broken.

"Don't you fucking move," Kian snarled, swiping the tip of his sword down the man's filthy doublet, popping the buttons as another warning.

The two men then fled the grubby hallway. Arlen grabbed a lantern from the entrance as they sped around to the side of the boarding house and down some precarious wooden steps. The sound of the water sloshing beneath them and the stench of the filthy river was overbearing as they emerged into the dark water-filled boathouse at the bottom.

"Fuck," Kian yelled, immediately observing Henry's head barely visible above the water line and his arms clasped in chains and outstretched above him. "Arlen cut the rope!" he screamed, jumping straight into the icy cold depths without a second of hesitation.

Kian grabbed hold of Henry's frozen cold body and lifted his face above the water. Arlen swiftly sliced through the rope with his sword. Henry's chained arms fell down heavily into the river, pulling the two men back under the water. Kian kicked up hard, dragging Henry with him; the weight of the chains pulling against them. Arlen reached down and just managed to grab hold of Henry's arms and, with Kian hoisting him upwards, they managed to finally free him from the cold murky water. Kian scrambled back on to the landing stage as Arlen hastily removed the shackles from around Henry's bloody and bruised wrists.

"He's not breathing!" Arlen screamed, frantically feeling for a pulse and tilting Henry's head back in an attempt to open his airways.

"Blow in his mouth," Kian yelled, "I've seen it done, he needs air."

Arlen obeyed without question and leant over Henry's cold broken body, blowing hard into his mouth several times.

"Nothing," he groaned, falling back onto his ankles and feeling for a pulse once again. "Come on Henry, fucking live," he roared, pulling himself up and blowing into Henry's mouth again and again and again.

Eventually Henry spluttered, water spraying from his mouth; Arlen fell backwards in utter relief, resting himself against the slimy green algae boathouse wall. Kian joined him.

"Thank God," they both muttered simultaneously, staring down at their much beloved friend.

*　*　*

Edwin sat waiting patiently with Kat and his father in the drawing room at Barlett House, having left Phillip Ainsworth in the basement of the Kilve Palace under close guard. Lord Barlett stood quietly beside the window sipping a large glass of brandy. Mrs Brooke entered the room carrying a tray of meats and bread and carefully placed it down on the table.

"Do you require anything else milord?" she asked. There was an air of melancholy filling the room.

"Yes, Mrs Brooke," Lord Barlett yelled abruptly. "We shall require a physician … at once," he said, observing Arlen and Kian carrying the broken body of Henry Morton up the steps to the front of the house.

"Yes sir," she shrieked, turning like lightening on her heels and exiting the room.

Lord Barlett had never been more grateful for his housekeeper's irrefutable efficiency. Edwin immediately jumped to his feet and met Arlen and Kian at the door, aiding them to carry Henry up the stairs to one of the guest bedchambers. They carefully laid him down on the bed. He was barely breathing. His face and upper body was so savagely beaten; smeared in blood and bruises as well as the filth and silt from the River Rame. The sizable slash across his upper chest was bleeding profusely.

"Christ," Edwin moaned, visibly shocked by Henry's appearance. "What the hell have they done to him?"

Kat and Lord Barlett hurriedly followed the men into the room. Kat clasped her hand to her mouth, gasping in horror. Her eyes filled with tears.

"Oh, no Henry," she whimpered. "Please tell me he's not dead?"

"No, Sis but he's barely alive," Kian replied, wrapping his large arms around his sister to comfort her as best as he could.

Moments later the silent shock and sadness filling the room came to an abrupt end as a sharp authoritative voice sounded from the doorway. "Everyone out, except you," an extremely serious looking physician pointed his finger towards Kat.

Arlen and Kian turned, glaring at the man angrily.

"Do you want me to attempt to save this man's life or not?" he asked, not bothering to wait for a response, instead pushing past the men in order to assess his gravely ill patient.

"Mrs Brooke, lots of hot water and clean cloth please," he continued, still ignoring the men's muted objections as they were hastily ushered from the room.

Kat and Mrs Brooke came and went from the bedchamber several times during the night, whilst the physician worked tirelessly.

The two women silently removed the bloody, soiled cloths and replaced them with fresh ones as well as basins of hot water and bottles of brandy.

It was not until the early hours of the following morning when the exhausted looking physician finally emerged from the bedchamber, shaking his weary head, Kat followed him with tears in her eyes.

"I have done what I can," the physician sighed, dabbing at his dripping forehead. "Surprisingly, I don't think he has sustained any broken bones, but I'm afraid a violent fever has taken hold and, given his weakened state, unfortunately I cannot see him surviving much longer. I'm very sorry. I have done all I can, but I do believe it is now only a matter of time," he bowed his head despondently, wiping his bloody hands on a soiled cloth.

Kian fled the landing at once upon hearing the dreadfully distressing news.

"He's going after Ainsworth," Arlen groaned, cupping his face to his hands in despair.

"I'll go," Edwin sighed, hastily following Kian down the stairs, concerned for his safety if he were to be observed within the palace killing a Crown Knight.

Lord Barlett accompanied the physician from the landing and thanked him for all his efforts. The physician promised to attend again in a few hours' time but was confident it would all be over by then. Lord Barlett paid the man and thanked him again before showing him out. He returned to the drawing room and poured himself a large brandy, exhaling loudly before gulping down the contents of his glass in one.

Kat wrapped her arms around Arlen who stood motionless on the landing unable to comprehend what he had just heard. He buried his head into her shoulder and openly wept.

Kian arrived back at the Kilve Palace in no time at all. He was so fuelled with anger and rage that he knocked the young Crown soldier guarding the basement room so hard as he sped past that he laid him out cold with a single powerful punch. Ainsworth glared up in horror from the iron chair where he was still tightly bound, as Kian burst through the door into the dark, damp space.

"You fucking bastard," he screamed, lurching at Ainsworth with a tremendous ferocity. "You should have talked sooner, you fucking traitor. I shall make sure you never fucking talk again," he roared, pulling his dagger from its scabbard and gripping it between his teeth.

Kian proceeded to forcefully wrench Ainsworth's mouth open with such savagery that he broke the man's jaw under the pressure. Ainsworth, unable to move due to the strap around his head that held him firmly against the back of the chair, screamed over the cracking sound of his jawbone breaking. Kian grappled for his tongue, finally yanking it from his mouth before reaching up to retrieve his dagger and brutally slicing through it as if it were merely a slab of warm butter.

Edwin flew into the basement room moments later, just in time to see Kian discard the severed tongue onto the filthy damp floor and hold his hand tightly across Ainsworth's mouth, causing him to choke on his own fresh blood.

"Drown you fucking bastard," Kian yelled. "Drown in your own fucking blood."

"Enough!" Edwin roared, forcefully pulling Kian backwards and pushing him back hard against the wall. "Enough Kian."

Kian stared down at his blood-soaked hands that were still clutching the dagger. He felt overwhelmed with shock and despair; his thoughts only for Henry. Henry was his brother. He could not contemplate losing him as he slid down the wall to the floor, numb to any other feelings regarding what he had just done. Edwin hurriedly untied the strap holding Ainsworth's head against the iron chair. Phillip immediately fell forward, blood gushing from his mouth as he let out a spine-chilling scream.

"Kian, you cannot be seen here, you must go," Edwin insisted, observing the young Crown soldier stirring on the ground outside the basement door. "I shall deal with Ainsworth now."

Kian was certainly not going to argue. He hauled himself up off the floor and fled from the scene in a flash. The young soldier scrambled to his knees, instantly vomiting at the sight of all the blood. Edwin roughly grabbed him by the shoulders and effortlessly lifted him to his feet.

"Fetch a physician," he bellowed. "Now!"

Arlen remained at Henry's bedside, keeping a silent vigil and listening to the faint breath of his dearest friend dying on the bed. Henry was drenched in sweat from the deadly fever that had taken hold of his ailing body. Kat remained on the landing, sitting quietly on the top stair. She was completely exhausted. As she was contemplating slipping into Arlen's room to lie down, Lord Barlett ascended the stairs.

"Are you alright my dear?" he asked, concerned by her weary appearance.

"Yes, thank you sir, just very tired," she replied, rubbing her sore eyes.

"You should sleep my dear," he said, slowly sitting down beside her, "but before you do would you enlighten me on all you know of Iris Westonhall and the explosion in the Corridor. I am to join the King; he shall need to decide on the next course of action and I should very much like to relay all the facts as best I can, but I'm afraid I must leave directly so it cannot wait."

Kat nodded, "Yes of course sir," she replied. "Where would you like me to start?"

"Thank you my dear. At the beginning please."

Kat talked continuously for several minutes, hardly pausing to take a breath. Lord Barlett listened intensely without interruption, making a mental note of every word, only clarifying some minor details after she had finished speaking.

"Thank you, my dear, now please get yourself to bed ... Oh and Kat, just one more thing, please look after my son for me. He shall need you now more than ever," he sighed, raising from the stair and holding out his hand in order to aid Kat to her feet.

"I will sir, I promise," she replied, flinging herself up at him and wrapping her arms tightly around his waist.

Lord Barlett was slightly taken aback by her over familiarity and hesitated for just a brief moment before wrapping his own strong arms around her in a genuine fond embrace. Edwin appeared on the staircase seconds later, his clothes soaked with blood.

"Good God Edwin, what on earth has happened now?" his father sighed, releasing Kat from their embrace.

"Kian!" Kat gasped, clasping her hand to her mouth upon observing Edwin's disordered bloody appearance.

"Kian is fine," he assured them both. "Although I cannot say the same for Ainsworth."

"Is he alive?" his father asked, troubled by this latest turn of events.

"Barely," Edwin replied, "There is a physician with him now. I have issued arrest warrants for Beatrice Ainsworth and Sir James Ripley. I have also sent an urgent despatch to the border control instructing them to arrest Ripley on sight and detain any man sporting a scar to his face attempting to cross the border. We cannot allow him to return east. Father we must go to the King."

"Yes, we should make haste," his father replied. "I have already sent for the coach. Edwin you best change your clothes, we can talk on the way. Kat has furnished me with all the facts, there is much to discuss … and you young lady," he said, turning his attention back to Kat. "To bed at once."

"Yes, Sir," Kat nodded wearily, bidding the two men a safe and speedy journey before making her way to Arlen's bedchamber. She collapsed down atop the bed still in her soiled dress, marked with Henry's blood. With the quiet hum of the city coming to life outside the window and the comforting scent of Arlen on the bedclothes, she closed her eyes and very quickly drifted silently off to sleep.

Chapter 20

It was dawn as the first light appeared in the sky when Lord Douglas Barlett and his son Edwin finally left Kingslea. They were travelling north-west towards Wenlock Hall; a good five-hour journey by coach ahead of them. Lord Barlett had opted to travel by coach, in part so that he could discuss the facts with his son as relayed by Kat and, in part, because he hadn't slept and doubted very much that he could ride the distance due to fatigue. They stopped only a couple of times along the way in order to change the horses and take refreshment. The two men finally managed a little sleep after spending the first half of their journey deep in conversation. It was late morning when the coachman woke them with a start by banging his heavy fist on the roof of the carriage, indicating that Wenlock Hall was in sight.

Wenlock Hall, a modest country house, was surrounded by a stone enclosure. It had been extended several times over the years – linking a collection of smaller stone-built buildings to create a single property with a warren of varying sized rooms. A symmetrical formal garden lay to the left of the house as you approached with numerous outhouses and stables to the right. A coppice on the brow of the hill situated to the rear opened out on to a sizable lake and ancient apple orchard.

Lady Ann Barlett appeared in the doorway, smiling sweetly as the coach drew up to the front of the house, pleased by the return of her husband and sons from court. Ann was a dainty woman with blueish grey eyes and mousey brown hair, tied up and entwined with pale blue ribbons. It was difficult to believe, judging by her petite statue, that she had produced two such strapping sons. Her third pregnancy however had been complicated and had resulted in a stillborn daughter. Her tiny body did recover after time, although she was never able to conceive a child again. A fact that saddened her greatly.

"Hello, my darling," Lord Barlett beamed, alighting the coach in haste and embracing his wife lovingly. Lord Barlett loved his wife very much.

"Hello Mother," Edwin said cheerfully, kissing his mother affectionately on the cheek.

"Where is Arlen?" Ann asked, clearly disappointed that her younger son had not accompanied them home.

Lord Barlett let out a deep sigh, shaking his head.

"Oh dear," she groaned. "Please just reassure me he is well?"

"He is perfectly well my dear," Barlett confirmed, squeezing her hand for reassurance. "Come, I have much to tell."

"I'm going to stretch my legs," Edwin called out, already heading for the gardens. He felt the need for some time alone.

Edwin breathed in the fresh country air, pleased at least to be far from the stench of the city. He ambled around the extensive formal gardens for a long while deep in thought. Finally, he ascended the hill at the rear of the house and navigated himself through the coppice before finding himself at the edge of the sizable lake. He stood for a time looking out across the peaceful water with its mirror like reflection. A raft of ducks were basking in the reeds. His thoughts turned to the many idyllic summers he had spent here with his brother, fishing and swimming – the pair of them without a care in the world. Today he stood beside the water miserable and tensed. It was less than twenty-four hours since he had been celebrating his joyous engagement to Florence and looking forward to their future life together. He was hardly able to believe how circumstances beyond their control had thrown them fortuitously together. Almost from their first correspondence he had felt a real connection to Florence and, knowing his brother's indifference towards her, he had dared to allow himself to hope that one day they may be together. Now however he stood at the edge of the lake wondering whether or not she had been privy to the recent monstrous events plaguing Mercia – perhaps even involved in some way.

"No," he bellowed aloud across the calm waters, startling the ducks. "I refuse to believe it."

Hastily throwing aside his outer garments and boots he dove deep into the chilly depths; swimming amongst the reeds for over halfway across the lake before having to come up for air. He relentlessly powered himself backwards and forwards across the water until finally sheer exhaustion forced him to stop. He clambered up onto the bank, collapsing onto his back and closing his eyes in order to dry out under the hot June sun; only thoughts of Florence filled his mind.

Ann Barlett found her eldest son a while later. She smiled down at him asleep on the lush soft grass.

"Are you alright my darling?" she whispered, gently waking him from his peaceful slumber.

Edwin squinted up at his mother who stood peering down at him. He smiled back.

"You and your brother loved to swim in the lake when you were younger, blissfully racing each other from one side to the other. My two beautiful boys," she mused, closing her eyes for just a moment and relishing the hot sun on her face.

Edwin sat up. His mother sat down beside him, her pale blue silk dress trimmed with delicate lace spreading out all around her.

"Your father has relayed some of the recent dreadful events. Your thoughts must be for Florence?" she said, observing her son closely and taking his hands in hers.

"Oh Mother," Edwin sighed. "With all the unspeakable goings on that have occurred over recent weeks and now Henry lies dying, I confess my thoughts are preoccupied by my own lost happiness. I am so ashamed Mother."

"My darling boy, there is no proof of Florence's involvement, from what your father says she is quite different to her sister," Ann replied, squeezing his hand reassuringly.

"Yes, indeed she is," Edwin confirmed, "but nevertheless Mother, her family are now tainted. The King shall show no mercy, I am sure of it. You only need witness the torturous acts bestowed on Lord Gilmore to know what he is capable of. Once his daughter's identity has been revealed to him and the plot to abduct her, the whole Ainsworth family and their associates shall be purged from Mercia forever."

"Perhaps," his mother mused. "But we must have some hope my dear that the innocent shall not have to pay for the crimes of the guilty."

Edwin leant over and kissed his mother affectionately on her cheek.

"I do love you Mother," he smiled. "Very much."

"And I love you too, my son. I'm sure all will be well. Now please help your old mother to her feet. The King it seems has been delayed; your father is cursing most ashamedly. I conclude it is a blessing. You both need to rest and besides some of the food already prepared shall spoil before tomorrow, so we have the most enormous feast for dinner. You both look as if you need a decent meal, Mrs Brooke it seems has not been feeding you properly. I shall have to speak with her when I am next in town."

Edwin could not help but smile to himself as he aided his mother to rise, knowing only too well how much she respected and relied on the woman. Ann Barlett had been unable to find a housekeeper even close to Mrs Brooke's expertise to run Wenlock and periodically asked her to consider relocating, but the Barlett House housekeeper was Kingslea born and bred and was not willing to even entertain the idea, which vexed Ann greatly.

Early the following morning Wenlock Hall was a raucous hive of activity; the fanfare announcing the arrival of the progress could be heard way out into the distance as the King and his extensive retinue slowly approached. Lord Barlett squeezed his wife's hand reassuringly as they stood on the steps to the hall, waiting patiently for their royal visitor. The house was fully prepared. Ann Barlett had worked tirelessly for weeks to ensure that no detail, however small, was forgotten. Extra help had been brought in from the surrounding villages. The stables and numerous outhouses had been turned into temporary accommodation for the hordes of people accompanying the King as he descended on Wenlock Hall. Hosting the King on his royal progress was as much an honour as it was a curse, the expense alone was astronomical let alone the weeks of preparation involved. But for the King to select your home as worthy of a visit was indeed a huge privilege and highly coveted. He had visited Wenlock Hall many times over the years. Ann Barlett was truly adept in providing an enjoyable escape for the King. Nevertheless, the initial anticipation always made her feel a trifle nervous.

Osbert sat majestically atop his black jennet, leading the progress. He looked immensely regal, dressed resplendently in purple brocade trimmed with gold. His numerous courtiers accompanying him were followed by hundreds of servants and carts carrying all the paraphernalia needed in order to ensure a successful progress. Ann gripped her husband's hand tightly as the enormous circus drew nearer.

Quite unexpectedly, and within a few hundred yards of the house, the King suddenly broke free of his party and cantered towards the entrance of Wenlock Hall in haste, coming to an abrupt stop in front of Lord and Lady Barlett.

"Your Majesty," Lord Barlett said giving his deepest bow, a little astonished by the King's impulsive behaviour.

Ann Barlett curtseyed with the rest of the household stood behind her following suit.

"Douglas," the King smiled, dismounting his horse in haste. "Ann," he continued, greeting them both fondly on the steps and placing a friendly hand to Lord Barlett's shoulder.

"Please t... t... tell me you have news D... D... Douglas?" the King asked with urgency in his tone.

"I do sire," Barlett confirmed at once. "Much news in fact."

Osbert exhaled loudly. "Thank goodness," he muttered under his breath.

The King then instantly turned on his heels and raised his hand to the scores of people who were already assembling behind him. Barlett eyed Lord Ainsworth and Lord Bentley amongst the crowd along with other members of the Privy Council.

"W… w… wait here," the King commanded. "I wish to s… s… speak with Lord B… B… Barlett alone."

A muted groan echoed around the King's entourage with some of the courtiers at the back bravely voicing their disapproval. The King however ignored all objections and indicated for Lord Barlett and Edwin to lead the way inside the house.

The study was just off the main entrance hall down a narrow corridor; the door frames were rather low as they were a part of the original manor house. The three men had to inconveniently duck down, then step up into a spacious room that was a later addition. Lord Barlett's study was bursting at the seams with books, paper and scrolls. On first impressions you would have thought the space a chaotic mess, however at a second glance it was clear that there was a distinct order to the excessive stuff. The King sat down in one of the easy chairs under the window and Lord Barlett sat down opposite him. Edwin remained standing near the doorway. The remains of a fire had burnt out in the hearth, filling the room with the familiar smell of smoke mingled with the musty smell of the old leather-bound books lining the shelves.

"Douglas, t… t… tell me everything," the King urged, desperately impatient for confirmation on what he had for weeks secretly hoped and prayed to be the truth after reading Henry Morton's letter.

Lord Barlett obliged and continued without any delay, relaying in as much detail as possible everything they had learnt, including the most recent dreadful events and the fact that Lord Henry Morton now lay dying of a fatal fever back at Barlett House. The King listened intensely to every word. Once Barlett had finished he slowly rose from his seat. He remained silent, gently pulling at the tip of his beard; his countenance giving nothing away. He turned to gaze from the window. A handful of his entourage were already milling about the formal gardens. The King's minstrels playing a merry tune to the many court servants who were busy erecting the colourful and elaborately decorated tents on the well-tended lawn.

The King eventually spoke. "I was told C… C… Caroline died giving birth to a stillborn child. I never knew whether we had a s…

s… son or a daughter, nobody dared speak of it for fear of angering my f… f…father. It seems they were wise; he was truly a monster." The King's stammer ceased somewhat as if in defiance of his affliction. "I always knew in my heart of course we were to have a d… d… daughter … Oh, my darling Caroline," he exhaled loudly, with only thoughts for his beautiful young wife so cruelly taken from him and their daughter of whom he never even knew existed.

Lord Barlett and Edwin waited patiently for what felt like hours waiting for the King to speak again. He seemed lost in his own thoughts, staring absently from the window.

"Douglas," he said finally between clenched teeth. "Bring my d… d… daughter home and avenge her."

"Sire, I beg we act with extreme caution, the Vikrin pearls; the motive for Ripley and Ainsworth's actions are still not clear. Sire, would it not be prudent to leave the princess in the East with her grandfather where we know she is safe. At least until Ripley is apprehended and we have the remaining Vikrin pearls."

"No, Douglas," the King replied, steadfast in his resolve. "I have s… s… spent my whole life being cautious, no longer. Arrest Lord Ainsworth and Lord Bentley. Arrest their entire f… f… families, they shall all pay for these atrocities. Spare no expense Douglas, w… w… whatever you need to apprehend these other fiends post haste. But bring my d… d… daughter home safely and do it without delay. This evil was first engrained by my f… f… father and it has plagued Mercia now for so long and it shall no longer p… p… prevail here. I shall eradicate these traitors once and for all. We must bring Iris home Douglas, we m… m… must reunite Mercia and finally have peace throughout the land."

"Yes, sire," Lord Barlett replied, giving his deepest bow. He had never before witnessed the King so firm and decisive; he was altogether inspiring.

The two men quit the room at once, leaving Osbert alone to his thoughts. Edwin made his way directly to the Crown Knights who were accompanying the King. He issued immediate orders for the arrest of Lord Hagan Ainsworth, Lord Edward Bentley, and any other member of their household on the royal progress. The arrest warrants sent terrified shock waves through the King's entourage; courtiers were frantic and fearful of who might be next. The only explanation given for these sudden startling revelations were that of high treason.

Ainsworth and Bentley were both heavy-handedly shackled, chained and dragged to their temporary prison in the cellar of Wenlock Hall, until such time as they were to be escorted back to Kingslea and the tower. Lord Barlett spoke with the accused men briefly, setting out the full extent of the charges against them. Both desperately pleading their innocence and pitifully begging for an audience with the King, which was unequivocally denied. Barlett doubted either of them had any idea to what Phillip and Beatrice were involved in. The Ainsworth siblings had a lot to answer for it seemed.

Wenlock Hall, so full of excitement and celebration earlier in the day, was now a miserable, sombre place. Nobody wanted to stay but everyone was afraid to leave, fearful of creating suspicion if they did. Ann Barlett busied herself coordinating the feeding and housing of the extensive melancholy crowd. Lord Barlett spent much time with his son and other Crown Knights coordinating plans to bring Iris DeBowscale home. Edwin agreed to travel east. The King penned a letter petitioning Lorimer to grant permission for entry. Extending the invitation to Lorimer himself, Lady Howard and Sebastian to accompany Iris on her journey back to Mercia. Edwin sent two other urgent despatches, one to his brother informing him of the King's orders and requesting that Arlen join him in Trevelyan as soon as possible – hoping that Arlen would agree to aid Edwin in bringing Iris home. The other requesting four Crown soldiers from Kingslea to accompany him at Wenlock Hall without delay. Information regarding the pearls also circulated quickly, resulting in an overly cautious vigilance when lighting a fire. This terrifying fact alone was enough to send a second shock wave bouncing around the progress.

Messengers were deployed post haste to every grand house in every corner of Mercia.

It was in the early hours of the following morning when Lord Barlett heard a soft tapping noise at his bedchamber door, waking him from his light sleep. He rose from his bed and wrapped himself in a sumptuous velvet housecoat before slowly opening the door. Edwin stood on the landing clutching a candle in one hand and a letter in the other. He was pale.

"Father, I'm sorry for the intrusion at such an hour, but I have just received correspondence from Arlen, he has agreed to join me in Trevelyan."

"That's excellent news Edwin," his father replied, although a little confused as to why Edwin felt the need to inform him at quite so early an hour.

"Sir, I'm afraid there is more," Edwin sighed deeply and looking extremely upset. "Arlen also writes that Lord Henry Morton, most beloved friend, passed away peacefully yesterday due to the deadly fever that took hold after the brutal beating he sustained at Goring End. He never once regained consciousness."

Lord Barlett gripped hold of his son's arm. "I'm so sorry Edwin," he muttered, troubled by the tragic news and latest sad turn of events.

"I can hardly believe it sir; Arlen will be utterly devastated," Edwin whispered, he too visibly affected by the loss of such a dear and valued friend.

"Edwin, you must take care of your brother, do not allow him to do anything foolish. What news of Kian?"

"There is no mention of Kian in the letter, but Arlen agreeing to travel east so soon after Henry's death, I confess, vexes me greatly. They will both undoubtedly be fuelled by revenge."

Edwin passed his father the letter to read.

"Yes indeed, this is most distressing," his father replied, rereading the letter with much sadness. "Let us pray that Ripley is apprehended without delay."

"Yes, and at least with Arlen agreeing to join me I shall be able to keep a close eye on him."

"Yes, indeed," his father replied, squeezing his son's arm lovingly.

Lord Barlett returned to his bed and wrapped his large arms tightly around Ann.

"Is everything alright my love?" she whispered, snuggling beside him.

"Yes, my dear, go back to sleep, all is well," he lied, holding her very close.

Later that morning the King returned to the study at Wenlock Hall where he had spent all of the previous day alone, left to his thoughts. He asked again not to be disturbed after hearing the tragic news of Henry Morton's death. He sat in a chair gazing from the window out onto the gardens, sipping a glass of Vikrin brandy, his thoughts turning to Caroline once again. Every day of his life he had thought about his beautiful young wife of whom he had fallen so deeply in love with, so long ago. Ever since her death he had never once looked upon another woman in the same way. Caroline's existence had all but been wiped from history by his tyrannical father; their marriage annulled and her name never again to be mentioned. He desperately longed to set eyes upon his daughter. Lord Barlett informed him that she was the image of her mother. He longed to embrace her in his arms. Falling to his knees, he crossed himself and prayed for Iris, for Caroline and for Henry Morton.

Later that day Lord Ainsworth and Beatrice's old fool of a husband, Lord Bentley, were forcefully placed atop their horses with their hands securely bound and surrounded by Crown soldiers. Other members of their household were tied roughly together with ropes, ready to be mercilessly dragged along on foot for their long journey back to Kingslea and the tower. The wretched Lords continued to petition their innocence by begging for clemency, but their pleas fell on deaf ears. The subdued entourage ambled nervously around the hall, edgy and anxious for whatever may occur next. They were more than grateful when the order was given to quit Wenlock Hall.

The King finally joined Lord Barlett and Edwin at the entrance to the house, watching as the miserable convoy eventually moved off. They stood in silence until the last cart disappeared out of sight. A handful of courtiers and Crown Knights held back waiting patiently to accompany the King.

"T... t... t... thank you, Edwin," the King said most sincerely, placing his hand to Edwin's shoulder. "P... p... please bring my daughter h... h... home safely."

"I shall sire, I promise," Edwin replied, giving his deepest bow.

The King thanked Lady Barlett most graciously for her hospitality and apologised for all the unpleasantness. She dismissed any talk of inconvenience and thanked the King for gracing them with his presence. Lord Barlett, having agreed to accompany the King back to Kingslea, smiled at his wife and son before mounting his horse and sadly leaving Wenlock, so soon after only just arriving.

"You are to leave me too?" Ann sighed at the sight of a young groom leading Edwin's horse around to the front of the house moments after the King had departed.

"Yes, I'm sorry to say mother I am. I must attend Moorgate Hall before continuing on to Trevelyan," he replied, busily inspecting his horse in readiness for his departure.

"Moorgate Hall?" his mother enquired, rather shocked and looking quizzically at her son.

"Yes. Florence and her mother shall be escorted to Kingslea. I merely want to ensure they are treated well ... I have to do this Mother," he murmured, embracing her lovingly.

"I know you do my son, but please take care Edwin," she urged, kissing him on the cheek.

"I shall Mother, I promise, please don't worry."

Then without any further ado he mounted his horse, pulled on the reins and headed east towards Moorgate Hall with four Crown soldiers in tow.

Chapter 21

Florence Ainsworth sat at the dressing table in her bedchamber daydreaming, her thoughts drifting off to more personal matters as the day of her wedding fast approached. Her maid had just laid out a clean gown in readiness for her to change for dinner. She stood patiently beside the bed waiting for Florence to rise. Lady Ainsworth, red faced and flustered, suddenly caused the two women to jump by bursting into the room and breaking the calming silence.

"My dear there are riders approaching, one appears to be a Crown Knight," she screeched, heading towards the window in order to take a better look.

Florence shot to her feet and promptly joined her mother. "Perhaps they bring news of Phillip and Beatrice," she said, squinting to see who was descending fast upon Moorgate Hall.

"I think it may be Edwin," she cried out startled and turning to face her mother.

The two women stared at each other, both looking extremely worried and concerned. Beatrice had not returned as expected to their apartments at the Kilve Palace on the morning they were to depart. Florence had also sought to contact Phillip but was met with only blank expressions and shrugged shoulders at the Crown Knight headquarters upon enquiring of his whereabouts. It had been over a week since they had received any word from either of them. Florence favoured writing to her father, but her mother forbade it, citing him "too busy on the royal progress" for trivial matters. Florence was not so sure it was trivial and with Edwin now riding hard towards the house, the uneasy feeling she had regarding the situation mounted greatly.

Florence hastily rushed to change into her clean gown. She only just had enough time to allow her maid to loosely tie up her fair hair before flying down the stairs at speed to join her mother, who was anxiously pacing up and down the grand hall. Moments later they heard a loud knock at the entrance, along with angry raised voices before the door to the hall wildly swung open. Florence instinctively knew something was seriously wrong as soon as she observed Edwin striding into the room followed by four Crown soldiers.

"Edwin, how lovely to see you again and so soon," Lady Ainsworth blurted out nervously, gripping onto her daughter's arm for support.

The two women curtsied.

"We are not here on a social visit madam, we are here on Crown business," Edwin replied sternly, making eye contact with Florence.

"Edwin," Florence muttered, distressed by his forbidding countenance. "What on earth is wrong?"

"We are here to arrest you for high treason madam," he continued, a scowl running across his face.

"What?" Lady Ainsworth screamed, faltering at Edwin's grave words.

Florence swiftly grabbed hold of her mother's arm steadying her. Both women were now visibly shaking.

"Please, may my mother sit a moment?" Florence asked, glaring at Edwin in dismay.

He nodded. "Yes, but a moment only," he replied, finding the situation much harder than he could ever have envisaged.

"Edwin, please, of what are we accused?" Florence pleaded, carefully aiding her mother to a chair.

"Phillip and Beatrice were observed abducting Lord Henry Morton from his study at the Kilve Palace. Henry was found later having been tortured. He died as a result. They are also complicit in the explosion that took place in Trevelyan. Their accomplice is Sir James Ripley, your uncle," Edwin replied, his outwardly stern countenance unwavering.

"My brother," Lady Ainsworth mumbled. "That is not possible. I have not seen James since … why, twenty years or more. He is not even acquainted with Phillip and Beatrice. This cannot be," she groaned, holding on tightly to Florence for support, gibbering to herself.

"It is beyond any doubt madam, the evidence is irrefutable. Now please, you may gather a few belongings, but you must depart for Kingslea at once."

"Edwin please, surely we can wait until morning, we are not likely to flee," Florence pleaded bravely, standing her ground.

Her plucky courage did not go unnoticed. Edwin hesitated, catching her eye once again. She looked beautiful in pink silk, her face flushed. She was clearly very frightened. He longed to comfort her and tell her all would be well but he could not, he was a Crown Knight with a duty to perform.

"Very well," he replied finally, breaking eye contact with Florence and turning to converse with his men.

They all seemed rather relieved at Edwin's decision to remain the night, after all they had already spent most of the day in the saddle, continuing on to Kingslea tonight was an almost unbearable thought.

"We were just about to eat Edwin; will you not join us?" Florence asked tentatively, desperately attempting to defuse the air of tension whirling around the room, if only for her mother's sake.

Lady Ainsworth was now sobbing uncontrollably, muttering pitifully to herself.

"Please Mother, everything shall be alright, please don't cry," Florence pleaded, kneeling beside her mother and comforting her as best she could.

"No madam, I cannot join you," Edwin replied, his composure steadfast. "I suggest you eat in your room; we shall leave promptly at sunrise."

Florence nodded, tears welling in her eyes. Edwin showing no deviation from his strict duty and the job in hand.

"I'm not hungry Florence," her mother muttered as Florence slowly aided her to her feet.

"Come then Mother, let us get you to your room," she whispered, holding tightly onto her arm before guiding her from the room.

The Crown soldiers glared at the two women with disgust, tormenting them and refusing to move aside from the doorway until Edwin ordered his men to stand down and allow the women to pass. His heart sank further, knowing only too well this was only the start of the disrespect and contempt that the women would have to endure at the hands of the authorities in Kingslea.

Once safely back in her bedchamber, Lady Ainsworth rallied slightly. The women briefly discussed the accusations raised against them but it vexed Lady Ainsworth further, causing her to become quite hysterical at one point. Florence eventually managed to calm her mother down and administered a little laudanum to aid her sleep. She remained with her for a while, fearful that she might awake in hysterics once again. As the time ticked by it became evident that her mother was not going to wake now until morning, so Florence decided to make her way to her own room, mentally exhausted and deeply saddened. She had barely set foot inside her bedchamber when she heard a soft tapping noise at the door. Wearily turning to open it, she found Edwin staring back at her.

"May I come in Florence?" he asked, his manner now thankfully softened.

Florence didn't answer, she merely stepped aside and allowed him to enter before gently closing the door behind them.

"I'm so sorry Florence," he whispered, "Please forgive me, I cannot show any favouritism or kindness towards you in front of the other men. You have been accused of high treason and your situation is very precarious."

"And do you believe me guilty Edwin?" she asked, standing defiant and staring deep into his blue eyes. Her own eyes filled with tears.

"I do not Florence, please believe me when I say I came here and acted the way I did only out of sheer concern and my love for you. I feared you would not have been treated so well if I had not. The King is refusing any kind of mercy, I am powerless to help you Florence. My only consolation is being able to oversee that you are taken to Kingslea with at least a modicum of decency. What happens to you once you arrive, I cannot say. But rest assured my father oversees proceedings and he will at least ensure that you are treated fairly. I must continue on from here to Trevelyan tomorrow morning, I'm so sorry Florence."

Edwin held her face in his hands as a stream of tears began rolling down her cheeks.

"Oh Florence, my darling," he whispered, moving closer towards her, desperate to take her into his embrace.

"So, it seems my whole family must pay for my sister and brother's sins?" she sniffed. "And my brother Steven?"

"Yes, I'm afraid so. Steven will have been arrested in Cambrian. He is undoubtedly on his way to Kingslea as we speak."

"Am I to die, Edwin?" she murmured, wiping her tears on the sleeve of her dress.

"The punishment for treason is death Florence," Edwin replied, still cupping her face in his hands.

Edwin and Florence had not had any opportunity to spend time alone together. Although they had written daily, sometimes two or maybe three letters a day, in the handful of times they had actually been in each other's company Florence had always been accompanied by her mother.

"Will you kiss me Edwin," she asked with a tentative smile.

Edwin immediately pulled her into his embrace and kissed her passionately, running his fingers through her beautiful fair hair.

"Let us flee?" he breathed, in between kisses. "We could head north, to Norland, start a new life together." The words surprising him as he spoke them. Perhaps he was more like his brother than he allowed himself to believe.

"No," she smiled, lovingly. "You are a Crown Knight my love, your dedication and loyalty to the Crown and your passion for the traditions of Mercia are why I fell in love with you. I would never ask you to give that up, to ruin your family as mine has been. No Edwin, it seems the extraordinary circumstances that threw us so wonderfully together are now pulling us sadly apart. You must continue on to Trevelyan and fulfil your duty to the King and I shall go to Kingslea and face my fate," she paused for just a moment, staring deep into his eyes.

"Edwin, before we are so cruelly torn apart and if it is my destiny to die as a traitor, then I should wish nothing more than to know you, for just one night," she whispered, pulling at the tie on his cloak.

"Florence, I … Oh, Florence," he moaned, hastily loosening the laces that fastened her dress.

*　*　*

Sebastian Howard and James Ripley sat in an impatient silence in the parlour of an old fisherman's cottage on the west side of Trevelyan. Four swords for hire sat in the back room playing cards and tucking into plates of food and jugs of ale, laughing and joking with a raucous camaraderie. Howard and Ripley were waiting for Beatrice to return from town, desperate for news of her brother and other recent events that were rocking Mercia to its core. Things it seemed were not going quite as they had hoped.

"Where the hell is she?" Sebastian snarled, becoming evermore impatient for Beatrice's return. He angrily paced up and down the modest room, with its whitewashed walls and sparse weathered wood furnishings, peering from the cracked windowpane in between gulping down large glasses of disgustingly cheap brandy.

"Go easy on that," Ripley warned. "You need to keep a cool head."

"Arrh," Sebastian yelled, hurling his empty glass into the fireplace. It shattered into tiny pieces just as Beatrice nervously appeared in the doorway.

She was dressed as a dowdy fisherwoman in a dress of coarse woollen russet, her raven black hair hidden under a simple cloth wimple. She looked tired and disheartened. Her eyes were swollen through crying and the nasty bruise to her face was still visible.

"Where the hell have you been?" Sebastian yelled madly, slamming the door behind her.

"You know where I have been Sebastian," she replied tentatively, trying to keep her distance and moving as far away from him as the modest room would allow, fearful of his violent temper.

Beatrice had been instructed to discover news of Phillip. Sebastian and her brother were adept in forcing her to use her beauty in order to manipulate gullible men into revealing secrets. It worked extremely effectively on the impressionable young Crown soldiers.

"Phillip is detained at the Kilve Palace," she murmured, directing her gaze towards her uncle, hoping for his support. "It seems we were observed at the palace."

"Fuck sake," Sebastian hissed furiously, lunging at Beatrice. "Has he fucking talked?" he screamed, gripping her by the throat and pushing her hard up against the wall. She gasped for breath as Sebastian mercilessly squeezed her neck tighter.

"No, please Sebastian," she breathed, struggling to break free from his iron grasp, "he would never talk, never."

"Enough," Ripley growled, forcefully pulling Sebastian from Beatrice and pushing him down hard into a chair. "I said you need to keep a cool head."

"And you," he snapped, turning his attention to Beatrice. "What other news?"

"Arrest warrants have been issued for our entire family," she trembled, not daring to make eye contact with either man. "Even my mother and sister have been arrested. They are already on their way to Kingslea under Crown guard. The King vows no mercy. Trevelyan is on high alert, any man sporting a scarred face is being arrested on sight. An urgent despatch has been sent to Lorimer; the soldiers are in a frenzy to understand the meaning."

"What of Sebastian?" Ripley snarled, furiously raising his hand in order to quieten Sebastian who was hotly cursing in his chair.

"There is no mention at all of Sebastian. Henry Morton has been confirmed dead, he was found at the boathouse but never regained consciousness."

Ripley paced the room several times. He was seething but remained outwardly calm, well aware that the situation could quite quickly spiral out of control.

"Sebastian you must return east at once, Beatrice and I shall remain here. I knew we should not have deviated from our original plan and slit Morton's throat in his study instead of dragging him halfway across the city," he hissed, directing an angry gaze towards Sebastian. "The King it seems is taking every precaution. He must also know by now that we still have two Vikrin pearls, he will be desperate to bring his daughter home safely. I suspect he has written to Lorimer requesting her return. Sebastian get close to the girl when she receives news of Henry Morton's demise, she will be extremely vulnerable – it can only play to our advantage."

"And what of us Uncle?" Beatrice asked, trembling nervously and rubbing at her sore neck.

"We wait, see how this plays out. The girl is still our insurance. The King's judgement shall be clouded where she is concerned."

"And Phillip?"

"Phillip is already dead," Ripley snapped, turning to casually refill another glass with cheap brandy.

"No, I refuse to believe it," Beatrice screamed hysterically, fleeing from the cottage.

"Uncle, when she returns get rid of her, she is a liability. The Ainsworths have served their purpose," Sebastian said, his tone cruelly matter of fact.

"The Ainsworths are my family," Ripley replied, turning to face Sebastian and crossly narrowing his eyes at his arrogant nephew lounging in a chair.

"Yes, and so are the Howards, we cannot afford any more mistakes. If Beatrice were to be apprehended, she would almost certainly reveal everything in an instant, of that we can be sure. Without Phillip she is a loose cannon. I shall make this up to you Uncle I promise."

"Yes, Sebastian you will. I want gold and lots of it. If I am forced to quit Mercia, which seems more than likely given the current circumstances, then I shall only be content to live in Vikrin as a King, at least for a short while until my return … do you hear me?"

"Yes, Uncle I shall not let you down."

"No Sebastian, I can assure you that you will not."

"Don't worry I shall have Iris eating out of my hand I promise you and if not, then I still have the Vikrin pearls," Sebastian grinned menacingly.

*   *   *

It was early evening when Sir Edwin Barlett finally rode up the Corridor to the border control. He had just endured a long miserable wet journey. The fine June weather that they had been enjoying had made way for tremendous thunderstorms. He was literally soaked through to the skin. His thoughts turned to Florence, thankful he had allowed her and her mother to travel by coach to Kingslea. Upon climbing the winding staircase to the private apartments in the East tower, he was rather surprised, and shocked, to see his brother already warming himself by the fire.

"Arlen," he exclaimed, promptly dumping his heavy bag in the doorway.

"Hello Brother. I had the fire lit, I suspected you might need it," Arlen announced, observing Edwin wet through.

Edwin eyed his brother quizzically whilst he busily rid himself of his sodden outer garments and passed them to a manservant who had followed him up the stairs.

"Thank you," he said, dismissing the man before moving towards the fireplace and holding his hands aloft to feel the welcomed warmth.

"I'm surprised to see you Brother."

"Why?" Arlen asked casually. "You wrote for me to come."

"Yes, but I thought …"

"Henry."

"Yes, of course Henry."

"Henry would have wanted me to aid you in bringing Iris home safely, it is the least I can do for him now," Arlen replied, diverting his gaze from his brother and glaring aimlessly into the roaring fire.

"And what of Kian and Kat?" Edwin asked, vexed by Arlen's strange calm demeanour.

"Oh, they travelled with me. They are at my rooms in town," he replied, nonchalantly.

"I thought you had given up your rooms?"

"Yes, I had, but they remained unoccupied, so I have procured them for a few more weeks."

"I see," Edwin said, eyeing his brother closely. "Are you sure you are alright Arlen?"

"Yes, Brother, don't start fucking fussing around me for God's sake."

"Very well," Edwin replied, raising a dubious eyebrow. He knew his brother far too well, his lack of emotion regarding Henry was unsettling. He was definitely up to something and it was already causing Edwin much angst.

"What now then Brother?" Arlen asked, passing Edwin a large glass of brandy.

"An urgent despatch has already been sent to Lorimer asking for permission to enter the East, as soon as it has been granted we shall ride out. The King has also extended his invitation to Lorimer and the Howards, so it seems we might have quite the travelling party on our way back."

"Excellent," Arlen mused, casually settling himself down into an easy chair. "So now all we have to do is wait," he concluded, sipping on his glass of brandy.

"Yes," Edwin replied, glaring down at his brother suspiciously. "All we have to do is wait."

Chapter 22

Lord Ivan Lorimer, fierce warrior of civil war history and self-proclaimed ruler of the East, had passed away peacefully in his sleep the previous evening. One of his final acts was granting permission for Crown Knights to enter the East via the Corridor in order to escort his most beloved granddaughter, Princess Iris, home to Mercia. Iris had remained with her grandfather until the end. His final moments quietly slipped away as he gently clutched her hand. Iris was left torn between conflicting emotions, great sadness and regret for the grandfather she hardly knew but had given her so much in their short time together. They had both found solace in his stories of her mother and grandmother, laughing and crying in equal measure. And then there was the immense happiness and excitement she felt in anticipation for the much prayed for return of Lord Henry Morton, her handsome lover and the man who would finally bring her home.

Iris sat in a small area of the garden at Wicken Hall. It lay to the right of the formal grounds and she had named it the small wilderness. Once a beautiful rose garden established by her grandmother, it had been left abandoned over the years to overgrow wildly causing the rose bushes to grow tall and lanky and lacking any buds on many of the lower stems. Iris had thought to tidy them up but decided she liked it just the way it was. After the recent week of persistent torrential rain, she was pleased at last to be back in the garden, the sun shining and the roses smelling wonderful. Closing her eyes she breathed in the abundance of floral and fruity scents awakening her senses. Sat on an old stone bench that had all but crumbled along the one side, she reread her mother's journal; she had read it so many times over the last few weeks that she almost knew every word off by heart. Pausing for a moment she looked up from the book, suddenly feeling a little nauseous – an affliction that had plagued her for days. Dismissing it again as nothing more than the mixed emotions whirling around her head and the lack of much-needed sleep after keeping an almost constant vigil at her grandfather's bedside in his final hours.

Iris thought perhaps she had best try to eat something, believing it may aid her nausea. It was as it happened fast approaching lunch time, so closing her mother's journal and carefully replacing the faded pale blue ribbon she decided to head back towards the house.

"There you are my dear," Lady Howard cried out, observing Iris walking across the formal lawn.

Lady Howard was also residing at Wicken Hall; she had insisted on joining Iris soon after she had returned here from Rothtir. Iris was extremely fond of the old woman. She had turned out to be an excellent source of wonderful stories, not only of her mother and grandmother, but also of the civil war and the many hardships endured by the East in the years that followed. Iris hoped beyond hope that if any good could come from the horrific events that had occurred over the last six weeks, then perhaps reuniting Mercia again might possibly be one of those blessings.

"I have been looking for you," Lady Howard continued. "Sebastian has just arrived from Rothtir. Come, we shall all take lunch together. Word of your grandfather's passing is spreading rapidly; you must have noticed that people are already starting to arrive to pay their respects. There is quite a crowd assembled at the chapel. Father Peter will most certainly be earning his keep."

"Yes, I did notice. Should I be doing anything?" Iris asked nervously, hoping that the answer was no and that she would not be asked to address the pilgrims ascending on Wicken Hall.

"No, my dear, it is all taken care of. That is unless you wish to of course," Lady Howard smiled, casually linking her arm through Iris's.

"No, not really, unless you think I must."

"Let us wait and see," Lady Howard assured her as the two women made their way towards the dining room. Sebastian was already seated at the table as they arrived.

"Here she is," Lady Howard announced cheerfully. "She was hiding out in the gardens."

"Iris," Sebastian smiled, immediately jumping to his feet and kissing her fondly on each cheek. "I'm so very sorry for your loss my darling, if there is anything I can do you merely need only to ask," he said in his usual over-exaggerated manner.

"Thank you, Sebastian. How wonderful to see you again. Thank you for coming," Iris replied, grateful that she was not alone at this sorrowful time. "I believe your grandmother is taking care of everything for me. I am quite redundant but shamefully more than thankful for that fact."

"Why my darling girl you do look rather pale," Sebastian added, holding Iris at arm's length and observing her closely.

"I confess I do feel a little nauseous again this morning I have to say, but perhaps it is because I have not eaten."

"Well then, we shall have to remedy that at once," Sebastian replied, swiftly pulling out a chair for Iris to sit. "We cannot have you looking all pale and sickly, not with your handsome beau about to arrive at any moment," he grinned ominously to himself.

Iris had hardly sat down at the table when the smell of the food caused a sudden wave of nausea to overwhelm her.

"You shall have to excuse me," she cried out, running speedily from the room.

Sebastian and Lady Howard both instantly stood up from the table and observed Iris curiously.

"Oh dear, what on earth can be the matter? I hope she is not catching a chill, how awful if she were to fall ill," Sebastian said sarcastically, promptly sitting back down and tucking into a plate of food.

"Sebastian please," Lady Howard rebuked his cruel irony. *I wonder,* she mused to herself. "I think I shall attend her." She immediately headed out of the dining room in pursuit of Iris.

Sebastian smirked to himself as he casually swallowed down a large glass of Lorimer's excellent red wine.

The maid Sarah was just leaving Iris's room carrying a bowl covered with a cloth as Lady Howard appeared on the landing.

"Sarah," Lady Howard enquired, the smell of vomit unmistakable. "Is everything alright?"

"Oh, milady she bin sick again, that be twice yesterday morning and the day before. She ain't hardly eaten a thing for two days. I'm starting to become a bit worried milady."

"Tell me Sarah, has your mistress asked for any rags for her monthly courses whilst at Wicken Hall."

"Why, no milady she ain't ... why you don't think she's ..."

Lady Howard raised her hand and cut the maid off mid-flow. "Thank you Sarah, that will be all. I shall attend to your mistress now. I shall call if we require your assistance."

"Very well, milady," the maid replied, under no illusion that she was to keep her mouth shut. She curtsied before eagerly scurrying off down the stairs.

Lady Howard lifted her hand to tap on Iris's bedchamber door, pausing for just a brief moment and raising a half-smile. A sudden thought shot into her head. Recovering herself she confidently knocked and promptly entered the room.

"Oh, my darling girl, how you suffer," she declared, sitting down beside Iris on the bed and gently stroking her auburn hair. "I shall ask cook to prepare you a simple broth."

"I'm afraid even a simple broth would course me to vomit, just the smell alone is unbearable," Iris grumbled, leaning back against her cushions, her face worryingly pale.

"Well then a little dry bread, you have to eat something my dear ... Iris might it be possible you are with child?" Lady Howard asked knowingly.

Iris gasped, blushing scarlet at the mere thought.

"Well, my dear, the vomiting, your pale complexion. Tell me, when was your last monthly bleed?"

Iris sat up upright on the bed, shaking her head in utter disbelief. She thought for a second or two.

"Not since Baines Abbey, six weeks or more."

"And your breasts my dear, are they tender to the touch?"

Iris felt her breasts beneath her dress. They did indeed feel sensitive and sore.

"Can this really be?" she mused, open mouthed and placing a hand to her stomach.

"I think perhaps it may. I am right am I not my dear in concluding the father-to-be is Lord Henry Morton?"

Iris nodded, still blushing and feeling rather awkward and embarrassed with the subject matter. Lady Howard was indeed an extremely astute woman.

"Well, that has definitely put some colour back in your cheeks," Lady Howard smiled. "My dear child, Lord Morton shall be arriving here at any moment, you do know you shall have to marry him at once … you do love him, don't you Iris?"

"Oh yes, with all my heart, yes, I do. I love him so very much," Iris replied, now clutching both hands to her stomach. "He was all set to ask Grandfather for my hand but then we discovered the truth of course."

"Well then my dear, we have absolutely nothing to worry about, all shall be well," Lady Howard declared, embracing Iris fondly.

"You do not think ill of me?" Iris asked, still feeling a trifle self-conscious regarding her unrestrained sexual behaviour.

"Oh, my dear, not at all. Many a young lady has had to hasten her wedding plans, do not trouble yourself. At least your young man is honourable."

Iris smiled back. "Thank you," she replied, gripping the old lady's hands in hers. "Oh yes, Henry is honourable, very much so."

"There, your beautiful smile has returned. Now, please allow me to fetch some dry bread, you must eat something Iris, after all you are now eating for two."

And with that Lady Howard was gone. Iris gently lay back against her cushions, still clutching her stomach with both hands.

Oh Henry, a baby, she mused to herself, closing her eyes, overjoyed at the prospect of a child.

Iris managed to eat a little dry bread and a small bowl of chicken broth. By late afternoon she had begun to feel a little better and tentatively decided to venture downstairs to the grand hall. Sebastian and Lady Howard appeared content as they played a game of chess. An unseasonable fire was lit – the fires were always lit at Wicken Hall, even on the hottest summer's day.

"Oh cousin, there you are," Sebastian beamed upon eyeing Iris standing in the doorway. "Please, come and sit next to me, I need all the help I can get. Grandmother is the devil himself when it comes to chess. I'm afraid I'm losing abominably," he grinned, moving along the bench to allow Iris to sit down next to him.

"You look much better my dear," Lady Howard remarked, briefly glancing up at Iris before pondering her next chess move.

"I feel much better, thank you," Iris replied with a smile, some colour back in her cheeks.

"Excellent," Sebastian exclaimed, casually draping his arm around her shoulder and pulling her closer towards him.

"Grandmother said it must have been something you had eaten."

"Oh … yes … something I ate," Iris muttered, unable to help herself from turning scarlet with embarrassment.

Much to her relief Sebastian didn't look up from the chess board to notice her reddened face. She felt sure that he would have made a fuss or, at the very least, a remark if he had. He did still however have his arm draped loosely over her shoulder. Iris doubted Henry would much approve of his over familiarity.

Several minutes or so later the occupants of the room suddenly turned with a start to a loud knock on the large double doors of the grand hall.

"Yes," Sebastian bellowed from his seat and pulling himself upright, thankfully releasing his arm from around Iris.

The ruddy faced soldier promptly entered, giving a deep bow. "My Lord, Ladies, the Crown Knights approach."

"Excellent," Sebastian beamed. "Please show them in as soon as they arrive."

"Yes, milord," the man replied, departing the room and closing the double doors behind him.

Sebastian immediately rose from the bench and made his way over to the throne-like seat at the far end of the room. He beckoned for Iris and Lady Howard to join him before sitting down in the grand chair. Lady Howard smiled broadly at her grandson. Iris thought it rather presumptuous and disrespectful, but her thoughts soon turned to the Crown Knights descending fast upon Wicken Hall. Iris had missed Henry desperately; she suddenly felt a little dizzy. Bursting with anticipation and excitement, she tried to breathe slowly, fearful that she might be overcome with the urge to vomit; her stomach was performing somersaults. The wait was utterly excruciating, she could hardly keep herself still, so eager to see Henry again to tell him her most joyful news.

The large double doors to the grand hall finally swung open. Edwin and Arlen Barlett strode confidently into the impressive space.

Iris instantly made eye contact with Arlen. Her heart sank, he looked so very sombre. She knew at once something was dreadfully wrong.

Edwin meanwhile stared quizzically at Sebastian Howard sat in the throne-like chair.

"Please forgive me milord, you have me at a disadvantage. We were expecting an audience with Lord Ivan Lorimer," Edwin said, slightly perturbed. He gave a customary deep bow.

"Not at all sir, my name is Lord Sebastian Howard. I have the unfortunate duty in informing you that Lord Ivan Lorimer passed away peacefully in his sleep last evening after a short sudden illness, and you are?"

"I'm so sorry milord, please accept my sincere apologies and condolences for your loss. My name is Sir Edwin Barlett, and this is my brother Sir Arlen Barlett."

The two men bowed once again.

"Arlen!" Iris blurted out, unable to contain herself any longer. "Where is Henry?" A desperation in her voice.

Arlen had been unable to take his eyes from Iris since entering the room and was completely devastated by having to convey the tragic news relating to Henry's death.

"I'm so very sorry Iris … Henry is dead," he replied, a lump raising in his throat as he spoke the words out loud.

Iris instantly fell at Arlen's crushing words. He rushed forward in order to aid her, but his brother hastily pulled him back. Sebastian caught Iris in his arms.

"Oh, the poor child," Lady Howard cried out in dismay. "Sebastian, carry her to her room at once," she declared, patting her full bosom.

"Yes, of course Grandmother, please forgive me gentlemen." Sebastian responded by effortlessly carrying Iris from the room.

"No, not at all," Edwin replied, momentarily distracted by his brother.

Arlen glared furiously at Sebastian, his pursed lips curled in disdain, as he left the room with Iris in his arms.

"Arlen." Edwin rebuked his brother sharply under his breath. "Pull yourself together for God's sake," he hissed before turning his attention to Lady Howard.

"My sincere apologies milady. Our intention was not to break this most dreadful news in quite such an abrupt manner," Edwin sighed, throwing his brother another angry look.

"Calm yourself Sir Barlett, there is no easy way to deliver such heart wrenching news," Lady Howard replied. "Please would you relay to me the circumstances surrounding Lord Morton's death."

"Yes of course milady." Edwin then continued to furnish Lady Howard with all the facts.

Meanwhile upstairs, Sebastian lay Iris gently down on the bed in her bedchamber, removing the hair from her face just as Sarah appeared in the doorway.

"Can I fetch you anything milord?" she asked, concerned for her mistress's wellbeing.

"Yes, some brandy perhaps, she has had a terrible shock," Sebastian replied, smiling cruelly down at Iris on the bed as she slowly began to stir.

He remained at her side until Sarah returned, then, deciding to leave the maid to it, he proceeded to descend the stairs when he eyed Edwin and Arlen leaving the grand hall and heading outside. He thought perhaps it prudent to observe them both from a distance, so he followed a moment or two later.

The two Barlett men made their way to the Lorimer family chapel, which was situated in its own grounds not more than a few hundred yards to the left of the main hall. They had requested permission from Lady Howard to pay their respects to Lord Lorimer. The pungent smell of sweaty bodies did not distract from the beautifully decorated interior. The most intricate gilded mouldings adorned the walls, surrounding gold mosaic panels. Several colourful stained-glass windows, and a curved ceiling covered in the most breathtakingly beautiful paintings, dazzled the men as they entered.

"My word," Edwin muttered, taken aback by the grandeur of the place. It was not at all what he was expecting.

There was a steady stream of people filing past Lorimer's body, which had been placed in a shroud surrounded by herbs and flowers at the far end of the chapel. The pews were bursting with even more folk silently praying.

Lorimer was obviously well loved here in the East, Edwin thought to himself as a muted gasp reverberated around the chapel at the sight of the two men in their Crown Knight livery.

"It's alright, it's alright, nothing to worry about," came a soft comforting voice from the chancel, addressing the grieving congregation.

The crowd very quickly quietened and returned to their prayers. Father Peter enthusiastically beckoned for Arlen to join him.

"Father Peter," Arlen beamed, hastily making his way over towards the priest.

"Hello Arlen, how wonderful to see you again. I take it you have come to bring Iris home?" he asked, ushering the two men into the vestry for a little privacy and away from prying eyes.

Sebastian hovered near the entrance suspiciously observing the three men from a discreet distance.

"Yes, Father we have," Arlen replied, genuinely pleased to see the priest. "Please allow me to introduce my brother Edwin," he continued, gesturing towards his brother.

"Pleased to meet you, Edwin."

"Priest," Edwin nodded in acknowledgment.

"Arlen, where the devil is Henry?" he asked, surprised that he had not accompanied them.

"Henry is dead Father; he was abducted from the Kilve Palace only days after he arrived back in Mercia. He was brutally tortured. We did discover him still alive, but unfortunately, he never regained consciousness and finally succumbed to a violent fever. One of the perpetrators responsible has already been apprehended – he was a Crown Knight, the traitorous bastard. The other two I hope very soon will be. I have to say Father it has been a most heart wrenching time indeed."

"Oh, good Lord," the priest exclaimed, crossing himself furiously. "Does Iris know?"

"Yes, she has just been told."

"Oh, that poor dear child, her life has been filled with such tragedy."

Edwin and Arlen remained in silence for a while as Father Peter fell to his knees in prayer. The sorrowful silence was broken only by the soft footsteps from the nave as the mourners continued filing past the dead body of Ivan Lorimer to pay their respects to the great Lord.

"I should like to accompany you back to Mercia," the priest declared, finally finishing his silent prayers. "I swore to Henry that I would protect Iris. I should very much like to stay close to her if I may?"

"Yes, of course, Father. I have no objection and I'm sure Iris would wish it also," Arlen replied, glancing at his brother for confirmation.

Edwin nodded. "I have no objection," he confirmed.

"Thank you," the priest declared, clasping his hands together and shaking his head in earnest.

The two men remained with the priest, talking until late into the evening, when eventually Edwin and Arlen were requested to return to the house for dinner. Wicken Hall provided a sumptuous spread, which at any other time would have been most appreciated. As it was, dinner turned out to be a sombre affair with neither party having much conversation other than tedious chit-chat. Iris didn't attend and sent her apologies. Lady Howard had encouraged her to remain in her room. She didn't want Iris conversing with the two Crown Knights, not yet at least. Arlen struggled to even swallow his food and was desperate to quit the room. Finally, and much to his relief, his brother fabricated an excuse for needing to complete a report for the King, which allowed both men to escape the awkwardness of the situation they found themselves in.

Lady Howard remained in the dining room with her grandson after the Barlett men had retired. She joined Sebastian beside the fireplace as he stood aimlessly staring into the flames. She suddenly turned abruptly to face him and slapped him so hard across the face that his brandy glass slipped from his fingers and shattered all over the floor.

"Ouch, what on earth was that for," he seethed, glaring perplexed at his grandmother, shocked by her sudden violent outburst.

"Edwin Barlett enlightened me on the circumstances surrounding Henry Morton's untimely death. Apparently, he was found in a flooded boathouse in Goring End, still alive," she hissed, angrily pouring herself a large glass of wine from the decanter on the table beside the fireplace. "It was only by pure luck that he never regained consciousness and died from a subsequent fever … you were supposed to slit his throat at the palace – a quick in and out.

But no, your arrogance and conceit got the better of you. What was it, Sebastian? You wanted to gloat? Take pleasure in the fact that you held this man's life in your hands?" she snarled, her breathing increasing. She was utterly enraged at her grandson's stupidity.

"Grandmother, I'm sorry, I didn't think."

"No, that's your problem isn't it Sebastian, you don't think. Arrest warrants have been issued for Ripley and the entire Ainsworth family; although I am quite sure you are already privy to this information. This is what happens when you don't think," she groaned, struggling to remain calm. "When were you thinking of informing me of this latest dire turn of events?"

"I'm sorry Grandmother."

"Sorry is not good enough Sebastian. We are so close now to taking the throne and going back to Mercia after all these miserable years stuck in this godforsaken place. I shall not tolerate any more mistakes; do you hear me?"

Sebastian nodded and poured himself another drink before sitting down at the table. Lady Howard remained beside the fireplace, quietly regaining her composure and considering their next move.

"All is not lost," she announced finally, her inscrutable countenance returning. "The situation with Ripley and the Ainsworth's is unfortunate, but all wars have casualties. Thankfully, it seems they still have no idea at all that we are involved in any way. We shall accompany Iris back to Mercia. Sebastian you must remain at her side at all times. Do not allow her to speak with the Crown Knights alone – it is imperative. I need you to watch her every move."

"Yes of course, Grandmother, but for what purpose? Surely it would be better if she were dead. We could arrange for a surprise attack on the road. Osbert would surely turn to me and we could dispose of those two brothers at the same time," he grumbled, staring absently into his now empty glass.

"You think it so easy to kill two trained Crown Knights? It would take several strong men, and how would you explain us being the only survivors? No Sebastian, enough of your foolish notions, from now on you do exactly as I say without question. You shall remain at Iris's side at all times."

"But Grandmother I ask you again, for what purpose?"

"Because she is to be your wife," Lady Howard replied triumphantly and smugly refilling her glass with wine.

"Wife!" Sebastian exclaimed, dumbfounded. "Have you gone completely mad? She will never agree to marry me, not of her own free will." Highly amused, he dismissed his grandmother's ridiculous idea with a laugh and a casual wave of his hand.

"That is where you are wrong my boy. You see fate has finally dealt us a lucky hand. Iris DeBowscale is with child."

"What? … How do you know this? Are you sure?"

"Oh yes, and she will need to find a husband quickly. A princess of Mercia cannot be allowed to give birth to a bastard child. Not even Osbert could allow that, and Iris is not likely to give up Henry Morton's child for any Crown of Mercia."

"So, you want me to marry her and take on Morton's bastard as my own?" Sebastian scoffed, shaking his head in disbelief.

"The child is just a means to an end Sebastian, do you not see that? If she gives birth to a son, then she can have others, if it is a daughter, then no matter. She will do anything you ask of her once she becomes a mother; your Crown would be assured."

"How can you be so sure that she will agree?" Sebastian asked, still rather sceptical of the idea.

"She will agree, leave it to me," Lady Howard grinned, raising her glass to her grandson. "Oh, she will agree alright," she repeated, full of confidence.

Chapter 23

It was extremely late when Iris stirred as she lay atop her bed. Sarah shot from her chair beneath the window to attend her.

"Miss are you alright? Should I fetch Lady Howard?" she asked, looking most concerned.

"No thank you Sarah, please don't disturb her, not at this late hour. I wish to go to the chapel to pray," she whispered, slipping on a pair of shoes and wrapping a housecoat tightly around her.

"I'll come with you," Sarah replied, afraid to let Iris out of her sight.

Lady Howard had been most insistent that Iris should not be left alone.

"I'm perfectly well, please Sarah I wish to be alone," Iris declared, gripping her maid's arm and squeezing it affectionately. "But thank you for your concern," she smiled.

"Very well miss." Sarah replied reluctantly.

Iris made her way directly to the chapel. There was a ghostly chill in the air as she crossed the formal gardens before joining the path that led to the entrance. Candles were still burning brightly inside. She hoped that Father Peter would still be in attendance. Iris had grown extremely fond of the priest over the last few weeks, even though he had been her mother's assassin. He had brought her much comfort and that was what she craved more than anything else on this dark cold night.

"I have been waiting for you," he smiled as soon as she entered through the chapel doors. Iris ran to him. He opened his arms to receive her and embraced her lovingly.

"Oh, my poor child," he whispered, cradling her gently as she wept.

The pair stood for several minutes in silence; the only sound being Iris's soft whimper. The chapel thankfully had been emptied;

the numerous mourners had been dismissed for the evening on the instructions of Sebastian, in the pretence of allowing the immediate family private time. In truth, he was resentful at the public show of sorrow for a man he loathed so intensely.

"Come," the priest said softly, holding out his hand. "Let us pray together."

Father Peter led Iris to the chancel, where they both fell to their knees at the altar in silent prayer. After a short while, Father Peter felt Iris shiver beside him.

"Come my dear, you are desperately cold and you need to sleep. Arlen and his brother wish to depart early tomorrow morning and you are going to need all your strength for the long journey to Kingslea."

"You are coming with me?" Iris asked, gripping hold of the priest's hand.

"Yes, my dear, of course. I would never leave you Iris," he replied, embracing her once again.

The door to the chapel suddenly flung wide open. Lady Margaret Howard stood in the doorway, looking rather annoyed.

"Iris, my dear I was worried," she said, throwing the priest a stern look.

"She came to pray milady," he replied with a deep bow, instantly releasing Iris from their embrace and stepping backwards.

"May we have a moment alone?" she asked, making her way towards the chancel.

"Yes of course. I shall leave you," he replied, smiling at Iris. Before he took his leave, he retrieved a blanket from the vestry and wrapped it around her shoulders. He nodded to Lady Howard before leaving the two women alone to talk.

"Thank you, Father," Iris sniffed, sitting down on a pew.

Lady Howard joined her. She waited patiently for the door to the vestry to close before speaking. However, unbeknownst to the two women, Father Peter had ducked out of sight and had concealed himself behind the altar. He wanted to hear what was so important that Lady Howard felt the need to follow Iris to the chapel at such a late hour.

"Iris, my dear, I know you have had a dreadful shock losing Lord Morton so and under such terrible circumstances, but we must consider your situation," Lady Howard implored, wrapping her arm tightly around Iris in the pretence of comforting her.

Iris gently lay her head against the old woman's shoulder. "I cannot …" she sniffed, shaking her head. "I still can't believe Henry is dead. It is too awful to comprehend."

"But you must my dear, it is inescapable – you are carrying his child."

"Nothing can be done; it is quite hopeless. I shall have to confess my condition to my father, the King, and hope he is understanding of my plight."

"I have absolutely no doubt that the King would forgive you anything in a heartbeat my dear, but you must know that you will not be able to keep this child. It will almost certainly be taken from you at birth, to live quietly in the country no doubt, well cared for I am sure but you would never be allowed to acknowledge it as your own. The best you could hope for is a yearly visit on birthdays perhaps."

"No, my father would never take my child away from me, surely? Not after what happened to my mother."

"He may be the King my dear, but not even Osbert could possibly condone a princess of Mercia keeping a bastard child to bring up as her own. You must know in your heart that it is impossible. The scandal and stigma would be so damaging, not only to yourself but Mercia itself and, of course, Henry – he would be remembered only as a blackguard."

Iris broke down at Lady Howard's harsh words and sobbed uncontrollably. The old woman allowed the full extent of the dire situation to sink in and waited patiently for Iris to compose herself before she spoke again.

"I cannot and will not give up Henry's child. I shall do everything in my power to prevent it. I'll run far away if I have to," Iris cried out in defiance.

"Yes my dear, that is one option but somewhat foolhardy and doomed to fail don't you think? How on earth would you support yourself, let alone a child? Henry was not even aware of your condition so had no chance to make any provision. Iris listen to me. There is another way that you can keep your child and live as a princess, maybe even queen one day – your child would, therefore, be heir to the throne."

"How?" Iris replied questioningly, desperate to latch on to any suggestion that might aid her current predicament.

"If you were to marry and soon," Lady Howard replied, finally seeing her opportunity.

"I cannot possibly sit here contemplating marrying another man, only hours after losing Henry, it is quite impossible and besides who would even have me I am now soiled," Iris sniffed, her shoulders sinking at what she thought was a ridiculous idea.

"Sebastian would marry you," Lady Howard whispered, tentatively watching for Iris's reaction.

"Sebastian," Iris replied, startled. "Sebastian, marry me, take on another man's child, he would never agree, why would he?" Iris protested, shaking her head in opposition.

"My dear, I know this is extremely hard for you but let me assure you beyond any doubt that Sebastian is very fond of you. He has already confided in me that fact. I am absolutely certain he would agree. You must know the King was considering him as his heir. If you were to marry you could rule as King and Queen. My dear, Sebastian is young and reckless and he lacks any real responsibility. This arrangement would benefit him as much as it would you, believe me my dear, with you at his side, Mercia could prosper."

"And my baby?" Iris asked, clutching tightly to her stomach and allowing herself to consider the idea for just a moment.

"No one need ever know the truth. Edwin Barlett wishes to leave early tomorrow morning; we shall spend one night at Rothtir before traveling on to Trevelyan. Word of your engagement could be sent on ahead. I am sure the King would have no objections, not if you declared it your dearest wish."

"But I don't love Sebastian," Iris whispered, staring down at the emerald ring. The ring Henry had placed on her finger, her mother's ring.

"Love will come after time my dear, I am sure of it. You do at least like Sebastian, do you not?"

"Yes, I do but …"

"Iris, right now at this very moment you only need consider the baby. This way Henry's child will be given a name and be protected, loved and cared for by its true mother. And perhaps one day even heir to Mercia."

"Oh, Aunt I'm so very grateful for what you are trying to do, aiding me so, but I need more time to think. This is all too much to take in," Iris insisted, hardly able to believe what was being asked of her.

"My dear, you don't have the luxury of time. Sebastian would treat you very well my dear. But this child grows bigger every day, if he were to agree he would insist on the King and everyone else believing that the child is his, you do understand that don't you?"

"Yes, of course I do, but …"

Iris sat for several minutes in silence; deep in sorrowful thought and feeling desperately trapped as if in some horrid nightmare. But she was also no fool and she knew very well Lady Howard was right, she had to think of her baby – surely it was all that mattered now. Her heart was broken, but Henry was gone and with him all her dreams and hopes for the future. She could never give up Henry's child, it was all she had left of him. She knew she had to do whatever she needed to ensure that they remained together. Pulling herself upright on the pew, she straightened her dress and sniffed away her final tears.

She turned to face Lady Howard. "Very well," she said at last. "I agree to this arrangement."

"You have made the right choice my dear," Lady Howard smiled, satisfied with her night's work. "It is imperative however that you mention this to no one, it must be wholly believed that Sebastian is the true father."

"I understand Aunt, I shall not let you down I promise. After all it is for my child," Iris replied, lying her head against Lady Howard's shoulder.

Father Peter, still concealed behind the altar, shook his head in utter disbelief.

"This cannot be the only way," he muttered sadly to himself.

Chapter 24

Lady Howard gained immense pleasure in announcing the news of the engagement at breakfast and insisted that Edwin despatch correspondence to the King as soon as they reached Trevelyan. Iris and Sebastian stood together smiling, hand in hand. Edwin was most gracious and wished them both much happiness for their future life together. Arlen however could not hide his anger and contempt and quit the dining room abruptly without saying a single word. Beneath her false smiles Iris's heart was breaking in two. She wanted to run after Arlen and tell him how much she loved Henry, how much she longed for him and that his child grew inside her. It took all of her strength to hold back the tears. Despite being in a room filled with people, she felt so desperately lonely.

Wicken Hall very quickly descended into a flurry of activity with numerous travelling cases being brought out of the house as the coach and horses were made ready. Lady Howard and Sebastian coordinated the final arrangements for Lord Lorimer's internment. Iris joined them later and thanked the many mourners who were continuing to arrive by the hour in order to pay their respects. She remained at the chapel for a while longer after the Howards had quit; alone with the pilgrims in order to say a final sorrowful farewell to her grandfather. Sebastian remained close by, determined not to let Iris out of his sight particularly after the hostile reaction from Arlen Barlett regarding their engagement. He was all too aware of Iris's fragile state, the last thing he wanted was her breaking down and confessing the real reason for the hasty marriage.

As the time fast approached midday and their departure from Wicken Hall loomed, Arlen rode to the gatehouse entrance. He had already been sat atop his horse for a least half an hour waiting impatiently for the travellers to assemble. He was becoming increasingly annoyed. Edwin and Father Peter joined him directly.

"What the fuck are they all doing?" he snarled, enraged by the delay. "We shall not even reach Rothtir by nightfall at this rate."

"Good God Brother, what on earth is the matter with you? Iris is with her grandfather, give her some time … Have you spoken with her since breakfast?"

"No, I cannot. Henry is not yet buried and she is already throwing herself at another man. Sebastian Howard of all people, has the woman no shame … I don't know what the hell I'm doing here, I should never have come."

"Well Brother, women can indeed be fickle. Perhaps her feelings for Henry were not as strong as you all believed."

"Obviously not. I suppose you should know better than anyone Brother, how is Florence?" Arlen snapped, spitefully. Although shamefully regretting the words as soon as they had left his lips.

"I shall ignore that Brother, but if you ever speak of Florence in that way again, I shall not be so forgiving, do you hear me?" Edwin growled, leaving Arlen under no illusion as to his displeasure. "I knew it was a mistake to bring you so soon after Henry's death," he continued, throwing his brother an angry look before pulling on the reins of his horse and walking it away.

"Fuck," Arlen muttered under his breath, annoyed with himself for upsetting Edwin.

"Arlen, we must speak," Father Peter implored, clasping his hands together as if in prayer. "Please, hold back with me a while after the coach has departed, it is extremely important."

"Christ Priest, must I linger here any longer?" Arlen moaned, desperate to return to Mercia.

"It is important Arlen," the priest assured him.

"Oh, very well if you insist," Arlen replied, furiously walking his horse in circles around the entrance.

Iris and the Howards eventually appeared, ready to depart. Iris looked terribly pale and sickly, having hardly slept or been able to eat a thing due to the nausea returning. She had rallied herself at breakfast for appearances sake, however the contrived happiness regarding the engagement was not aiding her disposition; she still felt so desolate and bereft. Arlen eyed her curiously. *Something is not right*, he mused to himself, *this was not Iris; this was not the wildcat.* Finally, and much to his relief, the coach eventually pulled out of the gatehouse of Wicken Hall and headed south towards Rothtir.

"Well Priest, what is it that is so urgent?" Arlen asked, as the priest rode up to his side.

"Iris is with child," he blurted out, unable to contain himself any longer.

"What!" Arlen exclaimed, an awful pang of guilt washing over him.

"It's true. I overheard a conversation between Iris and Lady Howard in the chapel last night. Iris is quite desperate Arlen; she has been skilfully coaxed into marrying Sebastian by his grandmother. Lady Howard manoeuvred her into a corner, persuading her without doubt that there was no other way if she wished to keep her child."

"Oh, Christ," Arlen moaned, placing his hand to his face, "and I treated her with such utter contempt this morning, what on earth was I thinking, of course she would never have agreed to marry Howard without good reason."

"I have been thinking Arlen," the priest continued, "what if we were to fabricate a marriage between Iris and Henry? I am willing to swear it, so no one would ever know. Surely to God, she cannot marry Sebastian, she loves Henry … loved … Oh, Christ Arlen, what a terrible calamity, what on earth are we to do?"

"The sooner we get back to Trevelyan the better," Arlen moaned, picking up his pace slightly in order to catch up with the coach.

"But why what is in Trevelyan that can aid this dreadful situation?" the priest asked, hastily chasing after him.

"Nothing, Priest … It's just that I cannot think straight, not here in the East," Arlen groaned, still seriously annoyed with himself.

It was early evening when the impressive Rothtir Hall came into view. Arlen was desperate to speak with Iris alone, but Sebastian had not left her side at the Inn when they stopped earlier in the day to take refreshments. He was keeping an awfully close eye on her it seemed.

Hordes of servants promptly appeared at the entrance as the travelling party all drew around to the front of the grand house. Jasper Drake, Lady Howard's strange little private secretary, stepped from the shadows of the doorway, his beady eyes fixed firmly on the Crown Knights. Sebastian promptly jumped from the coach holding out his hand first to aid his grandmother to alight from the coach, followed by Iris. Lady Howard immediately headed over to Drake and ushered the tiny mouse-like man back inside the house, already deep in conversation. Iris still looked terribly pale and melancholy and kept her eyes lowered. Arlen's heart sank at the sight of her. He wanted to rush over and reassure her that all would be well, but he could not. He turned away frustrated and powerless.

Arlen and his brother dismounted their horses and Father Peter joined the grooms as they headed towards the stables. He knew very well he would not be welcome inside the house, so he decided to head directly towards the chapel.

"Father Peter," Iris called after him. "I should like to pray later."

"I shall be in the chapel," he replied, with a warm smile.

"Would you like me to join you, my darling?" Sebastian asked, casually draping his arm over Iris's shoulder.

Iris shuddered at his touch. Arlen glared at Sebastian but somehow managed to remain stony-faced.

"No thank you, I should prefer to pray alone, if you don't mind?" Iris replied, giving Sebastian a sweet smile and believing the situation they found themselves in to be was as difficult for him as it was for her.

"I don't mind at all," he smiled back, placing a gentle kiss to her lips. Iris began to shake uncontrollably.

"Come my darling," Sebastian whispered, wrapping his arm around her. "You must be so tired, let us get you inside as quickly as possible."

Arlen was struggling to contain his outwardly calm composure as he watched the pair enter the house. However, he did now see his chance of speaking with Iris alone later in the chapel. Edwin noticed his brother's sudden change in mood, it worried him greatly.

"Arlen, what the hell is wrong with you today? One minute you are morose, the next even-tempered and now you appear quite tensed. Please tell me what is wrong?" he asked.

"Calm yourself Brother, I am quite well. I have merely accepted the situation, as you say women can be fickle. And Edwin I apologise for what I said about Florence, it was very wrong of me."

"I accept your apology Brother, but promise me Arlen no trouble."

"I promise Brother, no trouble," Arlen replied, promptly following the Howards inside the house.

Edwin exhaled loudly. He didn't believe his brother. He just hoped that whatever he was up to could at least wait until they reached the safety of Mercia.

Dinner was a splendidly grand affair; Lady Howard obviously did not do anything by half. The food was absolutely delicious – chicken stuffed with herbs with an almond sauce, followed by custard tarts. All swilled down with sweet spiced wine. Iris managed to eat a little chicken which pleased everyone sat around the table. Lady Howard and Sebastian were the perfect hosts, entertaining their guests with a certain poise. Under different circumstances Edwin thought the evening would have been quite agreeable. Iris had gained a little colour back in her cheeks and managed a smile, although she was very quiet and only spoke when she was spoken to. Edwin was the first to dismiss himself and thanked Lady Howard for her most gracious hospitality. This time it was not an excuse, he really did need to complete a report for the King. Arlen was pleased as it made his departure very soon after less suspicious. He immediately and discreetly made his way directly to the chapel in order to wait patiently for Iris's arrival.

Iris entered the chapel a while later, as he knew she would, pleased to join Father Peter at the altar.

"How are you my dear?" he enquired, observing her closely. "Have you at least managed to eat something?"

"Yes, thank you Father, a little chicken," she replied, just about to drop to her knees, clutching her mother's journal to her breast.

"Just a moment Iris," the priest said, gripping her arm. "Arlen is here, he wishes to speak with you."

Arlen stepped from the shadows in the far corner of the chapel beside the vestry door. He smiled broadly hoping to aid Iris feel at ease.

"Arlen!" she exclaimed, astonished but so very delighted at the same time.

"Hello Iris, I'm sorry to intrude on your prayers, but I needed to speak with you alone and this seemed to be my only chance."

"I'm so glad you did," Iris smiled, moving closer towards him, struggling to hold back her tears.

"I wanted to apologise for my monstrous behaviour earlier. I had absolutely no right to treat you with such contempt. I know how very much you loved Henry and how much he loved you in return. Iris, he was my greatest friend and his face lit up at the very mention of your name in a way I had never seen before. If there is anything I can do to help you in any way, you merely need only to ask. But know one thing, Henry loves you."

Father Peter threw Arlen a quizzical glance. "Loved," he said, correcting Arlen.

"Yes, I'm sorry Iris, I meant loved. It is still exceedingly difficult for me to believe that Henry has gone."

"Thank you, Arlen. I loved Henry so much too, I always shall. What you have just said to me, it means so much I cannot tell you. Arlen I … thank you," she sniffed, unable to hold back the tears now welling up in her eyes.

Arlen's heart was breaking at the sight of Iris's distress. He turned abruptly, unsure that he could maintain his own bubbling emotions if he did not.

"I shall leave you to your prayers then," he said, hurriedly disappearing back into the shadows.

Father Peter threw his arms up into the air, bewildered, staring after Arlen.

"Please excuse me a moment Iris," he said, rushing off in the direction of the vestry.

Arlen was already charging back towards the house as the priest caught up with him.

"Arlen," he called out. "Please wait … what was that? I thought you were going to convince Iris not to marry Sebastian? Why didn't you tell her you know about the child?" the priest asked, annoyed by Arlen's noncommittal reaction to the situation.

"And add to her already many anxieties? You saw her Priest, she is suffering greatly already, now is not the time. We will aid her, I promise, but at this present time she needs to remain calm for the sake of the child if nothing else."

"But …"

"No buts Priest, please just trust me," Arlen insisted, promptly walking away, leaving the priest opened mouthed and frustrated.

The final leg of their journey back to Trevelyan the following day was thankfully uneventful, with the exception of causing rather a lot of curiosity at the border control even though their arrival had been expected. It was the first time the Howards had set foot on Mercia soil since the civil war, or so everyone believed. Their arrival also caused quite a bit of excitement in Trevelyan as the grand coach, gilded with gold and depicting the Lorimer emblem, appeared from the mouth of the Corridor. Sebastian and Lady Howard waved from the window of the carriage as they passed the inquisitive onlookers. Even Edwin raised his eyebrows dubiously as the pair revelled in all the attention.

"Christ, Sebastian is already acting as if he is the King," Edwin muttered in disbelief.

"Now, now Brother," Arlen laughed. It was a very rare opportunity that he was able to reproach his brother for a flippant remark.

Edwin shook his head frowning. Arlen laughed louder.

Trevelyan House sat unassumingly on a hillside to the west of the town, which afforded breathtaking views of the southern coastline of Mercia. A modern brick house, it was built in symmetry with a mass of windows and a hip roof. The modest gardens were forgivable as a beautiful private isolated beach was accessible via a sloping pathway to the west end of the building. Servants were already in attendance, by order of the King. Provisions of the finest food, wine and brandy had been delivered directly from Kingslea in readiness for their arrival. Sebastian carefully aided his grandmother to alight from the carriage. She placed her foot firmly on the ground, taking in a deep breath. It had been almost twenty years since she had set foot on Mercia soil.

"Are you alright Grandmother?" Sebastian asked, observing her closely before helping Iris from the carriage.

"Yes, my boy," she breathed, turning to face the ocean, the afternoon sun warming her face. "Everything is absolutely perfect."

"Tell me Grandmother why did Drake not accompany us? I would have thought you wanted him by your side?"

"Drake is taking care of our insurance."

"Insurance against what?" Sebastian laughed. "Surely you don't believe anything can possibly go wrong now?"

"What have I taught you Sebastian? Always have a backup plan, it is imperative."

Sebastian scoffed at his grandmother and turned his attention to Iris. She was seemingly lost in thought, looking out over the water; this was the first time she had ever seen the ocean. Henry had described it to her in such magical detail, it was just as she had imagined. She longed for Henry, a lump raised in her throat. She turned away determined not to cry and immediately headed inside the house.

Edwin dismounted and addressed the Crown Knights and soldiers in attendance, issuing orders with impeccable efficiency, including arranging for the immediate despatch of Lady Howard's letter containing the news of Sebastian's betrothal to Iris. He could not help but sigh deeply as he reluctantly handed it over to an enthusiastic messenger.

Arlen remained seated atop his horse. He observed Iris with great sadness as she entered the house, Sebastian once again draped all over her. Scores of servants seemed to appear from nowhere, their numbers excessive, and attended to the horses and all the other paraphernalia brought from the East.

"Brother, Priest," Arlen called out, after it appeared that Edwin had employed every man with a task. "We should make haste."

"Make haste, where?" Edwin exclaimed.

"My rooms in town," Arlen replied. "It is important."

Edwin glared up at Arlen, shaking his head, utterly frustrated by his younger brother. "Very well, but this had better be important," he grumbled reluctantly, remounting his horse. "I cannot be away too long Brother, there is much to do."

"It is Brother, believe me," Arlen replied, pulling on the reins of his horse and swiftly heading back in the direction of town.

The three men quickly stabled their horses at a coach house two streets away from Arlen's rooms. They walked the remaining way in silence, Arlen with a distinct skip in his step. Upon climbing the stairs, he knocked confidently on the boarding house door. Edwin glared at him bewildered. The door slowly creaked open and Kat peered through the small slit. Upon observing Arlen, she madly swung the door wide open and flung herself up at him and showered him with passionate kisses.

"Good God woman, I have to say that is the best welcome I have ever had," Arlen beamed, joyfully spinning her around the landing before releasing her to the floor.

"Father Peter," she smiled, embracing the priest fondly.

"Enough woman," Arlen boomed. "For God's sake, get back inside," he said with an enormous grin on his face, ushering everyone into the modest rooms and closing the door behind them.

Edwin and Father Peter instantly froze to the spot, completely gobsmacked by what they saw.

"Hello Edwin, Father Peter," came a familiar voice from the bedchamber.

Henry Morton stood, very much alive and well, smiling broadly in the doorway.

Chapter 25

Previously at Barlett House.

Kat awoke with a start still lay atop Arlen's bed. She gently nestled her face into the pillow, it smelt of Arlen. It was light outside, but she guessed it must still be early as the city was relatively quiet outside the window. Stretching and yawning loudly she sat up and dangled her legs over the edge of the bed. She was still wearing her soiled dress, stained with Henry's blood. Rubbing her eyes, she jumped up and made her way over to the wash basin on the dresser. As she swilled the cold water over her face, Arlen entered the room.

"Henry?" she muttered, moving towards him. Arlen looked so tired and downcast.

"The fever is fierce, he is barely breathing. Oh, Kat I cannot lose him," he grumbled, embracing her tightly and burying his head into her shoulder.

A bead of water gently dripped from Kat's face onto Arlen's back.

"Arlen," she cried out, forcefully pushing him away. "When folk have a fever in the forest, we lay them out in the cold water of the river, it cools the blood. Many a violent fever has been tamed in this way, perhaps we can do the same for Henry."

"There is no cold river in Kingslea Kat, only the Rame. We cannot carry Henry halfway across the city to immerse him in the water that has already all but killed him," he moaned, shaking his head at the idea.

Kat was not to be put off so easily. "Ask Mrs Brooke, she is a practical woman. Perhaps we can obtain the cold water and bring it here. Surely you have a bathtub, or some such like," Kat enquired, her eyes wide and brimming with determination.

"Yes, we do," Arlen confirmed, "Oh Kat, it must surely be worth a try … Mrs Brooke," he bellowed, rushing towards the doorway, "Mrs Brooke."

The tiny woman appeared almost instantly on the landing as if from nowhere.

"Mrs Brooke," Arlen exclaimed, "fetch the bathtub at once."

"You wish to take a bath, sir?" she asked, rather astonished by the request at such a time.

"No, Mrs Brooke it's not for me, it's for Henry. We need a bath of icy cold water in order to cool his blood," he explained urgently, bouncing up and down on the landing.

"At once," she replied, now completely understanding the request.

She was just about to race back down the stairs when she suddenly stopped and turned. "Master Arlen, would ice perhaps be more suitable?"

"Ice, Mrs Brooke? If you can procure a bathtub full of ice in the depths of summer I should be forever in your debt," he declared, flabbergasted by the woman's abilities.

"It can be done sir," she replied. "The city ice houses will be full this time of year in readiness for the annual balls. It will not be cheap though."

"Whatever it costs Mrs Brooke."

"Very well sir," she replied, her little feet scurrying fast down the stairs.

Arlen and Kat returned directly to Henry's room; he lay stretched out on the bed with a single white sheet covering him, his body dripping in sweat. The laceration to his upper chest had been cleaned and dressed several times, but it still seeped blood through the fresh bandages. The remainder of his upper body and swollen face were covered in numerous gashes and blue-black bruises. He lay moaning and restless in a state of pure delirium, barely breathing.

"Do you think we should change his bandages," Arlen asked, distraught at the sight of his beloved friend.

"Yes, I shall do it," Kat replied, pushing Arlen aside as he continued to stand aimlessly, staring down at Henry.

Kat removed the blood-soaked cloth from Henry's chest, pleased to see that the wound was at least clear of infection so was not aiding his fever. Arlen passed her some clean bandages that had been left on the dresser. Kat worked efficiently, carefully redressing the wound at the same time as attending to the nasty gash above his right eye. In no time at all a bathtub was delivered to the bedchamber and very soon after that, large blocks of ice were being hauled up the stairs. Arlen employed his dagger to break the blocks down, smashing them into smaller pieces. One of the burly young manservants then aided Arlen in lifting Henry's broken body into the bathtub as Kat carefully packed the ice all around him.

"What now?" Arlen asked, turning to Kat his shirt wringing wet, his hands and arms numb and stinging from the freezing ice.

"Now we wait," Kat replied, letting out a deep sigh. "We have to allow the ice to cool his body."

Arlen swiftly changed into a clean shirt and rubbed his hands together in an attempt to get some feeling back into his frozen fingers. Mrs Brooke procured Kat a clean dress that belonged to Lady Barlett. It fitted her well enough, although it was rather too short. Then with nothing else to do but wait, they both sat down beside the bed in order to keep a silent vigil. A short while later Mrs Brooke brought food and hot spiced wine to warm them up, insisting that they drink it so as not to catch a chill from handling all the ice.

The physician returned by late morning. He was sceptical of the idea but agreed that they had nothing to lose. He declared that he would return later in the day to check on progress, interested to see if the experiment aided Henry's recovery. Mrs Brooke continued to provide fresh ice and yet another bathtub so that they could transfer Henry from one to the other. Arlen marvelled at the woman's ingenuity, musing to himself how she would make an excellent quartermaster.

Kian eventually arrived back at Barlett House later in the day. He sauntered into the bedchamber with his face badly swollen and bruised – he had obviously been in some bar brawl. His clothes were stained with blood from numerous sources, no doubt including

Phillip Ainsworth. Arlen dreaded to think what the other man looked like. Kian was a fierce fighter at the best of times, let alone when he was fuelled with such anger. He stood in the doorway of Henry's bedchamber utterly shocked but more than thankful to see the positive activities that had been taking place. He had all but been expecting to hear sorrowful news upon his return.

Hours later, and still packed with ice, Henry's body finally cooled. His restless mumblings ceased and his breathing improved slightly. Kian aided Arlen to lift him from the now icy water and placed him carefully back onto the bed as Kat redressed his wound, which, thankfully, had now ceased to seep blood. Then loosely covering him with a clean sheet, they all sat and waited once again.

"Good evening," the physician said, startling the weary occupants of the bedchamber as he entered the room much later in the day.

"How is he doing?" he asked, curiously observing the patient on the bed. "Mrs Brooke believes he has improved slightly."

"Yes, sir," Kat replied, instantly jumping to her feet. "His body has indeed cooled and his breathing is much steadier. He does thankfully seem to be a lot more settled."

The physician efficiently fussed around Henry. He listened to his breathing, inspected his wounds and hummed and hawed to himself several times, until finally he spoke. "Do you know young lady," he said, directing a respectful gaze in Kat's direction. "I do believe his fever has broken. It is still early days, but, God willing, I think this man may survive. You should be immensely proud of yourself," he declared with a broad smile. "It seems you can teach an old dog new tricks after all."

"I couldn't have done it without Mrs Brooke," Kat replied, blushing modestly.

"Well, between you, you may well have saved this man's life. I shall of course call again tomorrow. I do have certain tonics that may aid his recovery, particularly if he is in a lot of pain if and when he awakes," he added, before bidding the now more than hopeful occupants of the room a good evening.

"Fuck Sis, I do love you," Kian beamed, scooping his sister up into his strong arms and embracing her so tightly that she screamed for him to let her go.

"Thank you," Arlen whispered, placing a gentle kiss to her cheek before sinking into a chair beside the bed and cupping his face in his hands in utter relief.

All three remained in the bedchamber with Henry for another couple of hours. His condition did not worsen, he just appeared to be in a peaceful sleep. Mrs Brooke brought up more food and ale; it was by this time now well into the night. Kat yawned, struggling to keep her eyes open.

"You two best get some sleep," Kian suggested, eyeing his sister. "I shall sit with Henry now; you have both done more than enough for today."

"Thank you, Kian," Arlen replied, holding out his hand to aid Kat to her feet. "Come Kat, you shall be of no help to Henry if you were to fall ill yourself. Kian is right, you need to sleep."

"Very well," she replied, admitting that she was totally exhausted and kissed her brother good night before following Arlen from the room.

Arlen led her directly to his bedchamber. After aiding her to undress, he gently lifted her into the bed before quickly sliding in beside her and wrapping her up lovingly in his arms. The pair fell fast asleep almost as soon as their heads hit the pillow.

Kat was first to awake. It was light outside the window and the city sounded lively. She guessed it must be mid-morning. Arlen still slept soundly next to her. He looked so peaceful. She yearned to kiss him but resisted the urge, quite content to watch him sleep for a while longer. The horrific events of the last two days ran wildly through her mind.

When Arlen did finally open his eyes, Kat smiled sweetly. "Good morning handsome," she whispered, leaning over to place a lingering kiss to his lips.

"Good morning beautiful ... You were wonderful yesterday, Kat," he breathed, placing a gentle hand to her face and gazing into her wild green eyes. "I don't know how I can ever repay you."

"Well, I can think of a few things," she grinned, pushing her body suggestively against him.

Arlen grinned back; he certainly didn't need any more encouragement than that. Still wearing his breeches, he fumbled awkwardly to untie them. Kat giggled as he only managed to loosen them slightly as the laces were all tangled. He resorted to wriggling and kicking them off in haste. Then quickly rolling over, he positioned himself above Kat. He pressed his lips to hers once again and gently guided himself inside her.

"Oh, Arlen," she breathed, wrapping her legs tightly around him and holding him still for just a moment as they kissed. A long, sensuous kiss. Kat then released her hold and allowed Arlen to move inside her. The intense feeling of desire consumed them both as they rocked together, unashamedly hurtling towards release.

Kian's loud voice could be heard bellowing from the landing just before the bedchamber door flung wide open. "Quick, get up, Henry's awake he … what the fuck … are you fucking my sister?" he yelled, staring down at Arlen lying naked between Kat's legs.

"Get out Kian," Arlen shouted, furiously jumping from the bed and madly slamming the door in Kian's face.

Kat sat up, giggling breathlessly.

"It's not funny Kat," Arlen grumbled, immediately reopening the door and striding from the room, calling for Mrs Brooke at the top of his voice.

The housekeeper appeared on the stairs with her usual efficiency and instantly screamed and turned in her tracks at the sight of Arlen stood stark naked glaring down at her.

"Mrs Brooke, will you please arrange for a lock to be fitted to my bedchamber door … At once!" he yelled.

"Yes sir," she shrieked, running back down the stairs much faster than she ascended.

Kat followed Arlen out onto the landing and quickly wrapped a housecoat around him to protect his modesty. "Let's speak with Henry," she smiled, tying the belt tightly around his waist before seductively kissing him on the lips.

"Oh, Kat," Arlen moaned, pulling her close. "Christ woman, will we ever be able to finish what we started?"

Kian shot Arlen an angry look as he entered Henry's room. Arlen ignored him.

"Henry," Kat smiled, rushing to kneel beside his bed. "How are you?"

"I've been better … Kian told me what you did. I owe you my life, Kat," he said, squeezing her hand tightly in appreciation.

"We thought we had lost you Henry," Arlen added, quickly pulling up a chair.

"I thought I was lost," Henry winced, tentatively lifting himself into a sitting position.

"Careful," Kat said, concerned. "You don't want to reopen your wound, it's finally starting to heal nicely."

"Who did this to you Henry?" Arlen asked.

"James Ripley," Henry replied, shaking his head in despair before continuing to relay the full events from Goring End, including the disturbing truth of Sebastian Howard's involvement.

Arlen was just about to do the same in relation to the circumstances regarding their fortunate discovery of Henry in the boathouse, when their attention was diverted by a knock at the door.

"Sir, a letter from your brother," Mrs Brooke said, upon entering. She handed Arlen the letter. "Lord Morton, how wonderful to see you awake. I shall bring some hot broth," she declared, upon seeing Henry sitting up in the bed.

"Thank you, Mrs Brooke, and thank you for all you did for me. I owe you a great deal," Henry replied with an appreciative smile.

"No sir, you owe me nothing I can assure you. However, I cannot say the same for the city ice houses – the bills are rather extortionate I'm afraid … Oh, and Master Arlen, the locksmith is here."

"Thank you, Mrs Brooke," Arlen replied, blushing slightly with embarrassment at his early uncouth outburst.

Kat giggled. Kian grunted. Henry decided he didn't want to ask. Arlen quickly recovered himself and hastily opened the letter and read it aloud.

Arlen

As you can imagine, the King has acted swiftly. Lord Ainsworth and Lord Bentley have been detained along with all other members of their household on the royal progress. Arrest warrants have been issued for all remaining members of their family. I travel to Moorgate tomorrow, from there to Trevelyan, where a request for entry to the East as already been despatched to Lord Lorimer.

The King has entrusted me in bringing the princess, Iris, back to Mercia. I know how difficult a time this must be for you, what with Henry so gravely ill, but I beg you Brother to join me in Trevelyan and aid me in this venture. I am confident it would be Henry's wish also.

Your loving brother
Edwin

"I shall write back at once," Arlen declared, jumping to his feet. "I shall inform Edwin and the King that you are alive and well and we shall ride east together and bring Iris home ourselves."

"No," Henry replied, sharply. "If Sebastian knows I'm still alive, he will also know that we now know the whole truth. He will undoubtedly use Iris against us. No, if Sebastian believes me to be dead, his guard will be down and he will believe he has won. I suspect he will try to use Iris to win favour with the King. He will allow her safe passage back to Mercia I am sure of it, and besides, he still has two Vikrin pearls. We must be clever and lull Sebastian into a false sense of security. Arlen write to Edwin and inform him that I have succumbed to the deadly fever and that I never regained consciousness. Meet him in Trevelyan as he asks. Kian, you should go with him. Ripley must be hiding out there somewhere. He would undoubtedly wish to be close to Sebastian, waiting for his return from the East with Iris. Seek him out and observe from a distance. It's imperative that we know his every move. Their dastardly plans have not gone so well for Ripley, he will almost certainly be extremely vexed. Once Iris is safely back in Mercia then we shall act. Kat and I shall follow in a few days, once I have regained some of my strength. We shall be waiting and ready for when you return from the East."

"I still have my rooms in town, I could secure another month," Arlen suggested, "You will not draw any unwanted attention there as they are used to seeing Crown Knights coming and going."

"Excellent," Henry replied, "Now write to Edwin without delay. It is vital that he receives news of my death before he departs Wenlock. Allow word to spread and it shall strengthen the deceit. Sebastian Howard must have no inkling that I am still alive."

"May I bring Edwin into our confidence once I am in Trevelyan?" Arlen asked, turning back around to face Henry just before he was about to leave the room.

"No, it's better that nobody else knows, not until Iris is safely back in Mercia. Edwin will arrive in the East believing I am dead; it can only strengthen the deception. If Sebastian were to have the slightest doubt, all could be lost. I know I ask a lot of you Arlen, deceiving your brother and you shall also have to lie to Iris. That thought alone vexes me greatly, but it is the only way I know to keep her safe."

"Very well. I shall write to Edwin at once," Arlen declared, promptly leaving the room.

"Iris will be absolutely heartbroken Henry," Kat whispered, busily adjusting his pillows in order to make him more comfortable.

"I know Kat, but what else can I do? It is the only way I know to keep her safe … Kian, will you bring our belongings from the palace. There is a small folded sheet under the paperweight on my desk, would you bring that to me also."

"Yes of course Henry, I shall go at once," Kian replied, already on his feet and heading towards the door. "Oh, and Henry," he said, his tone low and fierce. "If you ever fucking nearly die again, I shall fucking kill you myself." Kian exited the room without another word.

Henry and Kat laughed; Henry winced and tentatively placed his hand to his upper chest.

"Are you in a lot of pain?" Kat asked. "The physician has left some opiates if you care to take them."

"Yes, a little, but I'd rather not take anything if I can help it. I'm sure a few more days of excellent care from you and Mrs Brooke will see me well," he replied, kissing Kat's hand affectionately. "I do think I need to lie back down though Kat." All the talking had tired him desperately.

"Yes, of course Henry, here let me help you." Kat jumped up immediately in order to aid him.

Arlen returned to the bedchamber a while later and woke Henry from a light sleep.

"The letter is sent," he declared, joining Kat beside the bed.

"Good, thank you Arlen," Henry muttered, still a little breathless.

"You need to get some proper rest Henry, we shall leave you now," Kat said, hastily pulling Arlen up from the chair and ushering him from the room.

"Thank you, thank you both for all you have done," Henry sighed, closing his eyes, more than thankful he had such beloved friends.

"Where is Kian?" Arlen asked once they were outside on the landing.

"Henry sent him back to the palace to fetch all our belongings, why?"

"Because the locksmith has just finished fitting a lock to my bedchamber door and if I don't finish what I started earlier Kat, I swear to God, my balls will burst," he grinned, pulling her towards his room.

Kat giggled and closed the door behind them, turning the new shiny brass key firmly in the lock.

Much later Henry awoke. It was dark outside and Barlett House was quiet. He carefully pulled himself into a sitting position, successfully swinging his legs around and placing his feet firmly on the floor. Grabbing onto the table beside the bed, he managed to tentatively pull himself up onto his feet. He felt desperately weak, his head dizzy. He slowly sipped on a glass of water before picking up the folded paper Kian had retrieved from the palace. Very cautiously he moved towards the window, unfolding the sheet and, by the light of the moon seeping through the bedchamber window, he read Iris's poem. Once he had finished reading it several times over, he muttered to himself. "Please forgive me Iris for what I am about to do, but it is the only way I know to keep you from harm my love."

Chapter 26

"Henry!" Edwin exclaimed, glancing first at Henry and then at his brother. "Why did you not tell me?" he asked, feeling rather hurt and betrayed.

"Edwin, please do not blame Arlen, he acted on my strict orders. The deception was all mine. It was imperative no one should know that I was still alive, not until Iris was safely brought back to Mercia."

"But why?" Edwin asked, unable to understand the reason for such deceit.

"Because Sebastian Howard is the blackguard behind the explosion. It was he who arranged my capture and torture in the boathouse at Goring End. He gained immense pleasure in furnishing me with the facts moments before he left me to die. I was concerned that if Sebastian had the slightest suspicion that I was still alive it would put Iris in grave danger. Not to mention the fact that he still possesses two Vikrin pearls. I had to act with extreme caution. Please Edwin you must understand, I forbade Arlen from revealing the truth."

"Very well," Edwin replied with a deep sigh, still feeling slightly perturbed and staring over at his brother.

Arlen however was too busy shifting impatiently on his feet glaring at Henry, clearly with something urgent to say.

Henry noticed at once. "What is it? Tell me Arlen, is it Iris?"

"Iris is well and safely back in Mercia," Arlen assured him at once. "Henry, she is with child," he blurted out.

A gasp echoed around the room as everyone turned to glare at Arlen. Henry stumbled forward, literally caught off balance by Arlen's unexpected words.

"Brother, more secrets," Edwin grumbled, shaking his head upset.

"I'm sorry Edwin, but there seemed no gain in telling you … Henry, Iris has been pressured into marrying Sebastian. Father Peter overheard Lady Howard and Iris speaking in the chapel at Wicken Hall."

"It's true Henry," the priest confirmed. "Lady Howard skilfully manoeuvred Iris, giving her no other option, convincing her that if she did not agree then her child would almost certainly be taken from her. She was desperate Henry; she believed you dead. It was so heart breaking to witness I have to say."

"Oh Christ, what on earth have I done," Henry groaned, gripping onto the back of a chair to steady himself with one hand whilst running his fingers through his thick dark hair with the other. "I must go to her at once," he declared.

"No!" the three men immediately shouted in unison.

"No, Henry," Arlen repeated, although he was more than sympathetic to his friend's dilemma. "You said yourself, we must act with extreme caution. Sebastian will not harm Iris, not whilst he still believes you are dead and he is to marry her. In fact, he is overly attentive of her."

"What do you mean," Henry yelled, suddenly envisaging Sebastian with his hands on Iris.

"Nothing like that," Arlen reassured him at once. "Just fussing around her and making sure she is eating and all that nonsense. It was obviously all for our benefit, but be reassured Henry, Iris is in no immediate danger."

Arlen didn't dare tell Henry how Sebastian continually draped his arm over Iris, even kissing her. He felt quite sure nobody in the room would have the strength to hold him back from running to Iris in an instant if he were aware of that fact, even given his still much weakened state. Traces of the brutal attack was still evident in the form of yellow-brown bruises on his face.

Kat poured out glasses of brandy and quickly distributed them in an attempt to diffuse the air of tension twirling around the room.

"Yes, you are right," Henry agreed finally, swallowing down his brandy in one gulp. "Oh, Christ … a child … I'm going to be a father," he muttered quietly to himself, hardly able to believe it.

The room seemed to settle but the momentary silence was abruptly broken as the door to the modest rooms suddenly flung open. Arlen and Edwin turned, unsheathing their swords with impeccable speed.

"What the fuck," Kian blurted out, hastily jumping backwards from the doorway.

"For God's sake Kian," Arlen yelled at him angrily, whilst lowering his sword.

"Kian," Kat scolded. "You should have knocked you silly fool," she said, grabbing her brother from the landing and pulling him hastily inside the room.

"You're back then?" he grinned, nodding his head at Arlen and Edwin. "Hello Priest," he said, casually plonking himself down into an easy chair.

Everyone ignored him and diverted their attention back to Henry, who had now resorted to pacing up and down the small bedchamber.

"What's going on then?" Kian asked, observing Henry's pensive face. "Please tell me Iris is well?"

"Yes Brother, quite well, in fact she is with child, but it seems she has been coerced into marrying Sebastian Howard," Kat replied quite matter of factly, her eyes still fixed firmly upon Henry.

"Oh fuck," Kian exclaimed, taking a glass of brandy from the table. "Well, I also have news if anyone is interested." He continued anyway not bothering to wait for a reply. "I've been observing Ripley for nigh on two weeks now and he intends fleeing Mercia for Vikrin tomorrow, his ship sets sail at midday. We don't have much time if we are to take the bastard down."

"Henry, what are we to do?" Arlen asked, appealing to his friend to make a decision.

"I must see Iris," Henry replied earnestly, hoping for any kind of agreement from the room.

"But Henry it's not possible, you said so yourself," Arlen replied, although fully understanding his friend's anguish. He would desire the exact same thing if he were in Henry's shoes.

"I know Arlen, but I must see her. She is having my child for God's sake and believes me dead. Oh Christ, what have I done, I can't seem to think straight," he groaned desperately, placing his hands to his face.

"What if I were to go to Trevelyan House, early tomorrow morning?" Kat suggested. "I'm known to the Howards and I am no threat to them. I could perhaps suggest a walk around the gardens. We could arrange a rendezvous, still allowing you time to deal with Ripley."

"No, not the gardens," Arlen added, delighted by Kat's excellent idea. "There is a private isolated beach to the west of the house, there are caves, you could take Iris there."

"How on earth do you know this Brother?" Edwin asked, impressed by Arlen's knowledge.

"You forget Brother, I have been stationed in Trevelyan for three years. The caves are used by smugglers. They are patrolled heavily at night but are quite secluded by day. Henry and I can gain access via the clifftop without having to go anywhere near the house."

"Yes, that sounds perfect," Henry replied, still running his fingers through his hair, causing it to stand on end. "Thank you, Kat. I just hope I have the patience to delay seeing Iris until tomorrow," he said, with the attempt of a smile on his face. Although everyone in the room could clearly see how anxious he really was.

"We are due to quit Trevelyan straight after breakfast tomorrow," Edwin added. "I shall need an excuse for the delay."

"Yes of course, write to the King, Edwin," Henry suggested, the plan aiding him to recover his composure. "Inform him that Iris is unwell and unable to travel. He will depart for Trevelyan at once I am sure of it. Apprise Sebastian of the King's altered plans. He will merely believe that the King is desperate to see his daughter. It will allow us more time to deal with Ripley before descending on Trevelyan House. I suggest we assemble at the clifftop after I have seen Iris and then surprise Ripley at the cottage. Kian has counted four other men hiding out there. Edwin, please arrange a handful of our most able soldiers."

"Yes, of course," Edwin replied, "And I shall write to the King at once, but I must now return to the house Henry if I am to speak with Sebastian tonight."

"Yes, as must I," Father Peter added. "I promised Iris that I would join her in the chapel for evening prayer. Don't worry Henry, I shall not let any harm come to her I promise."

"Thank you," Henry sighed, placing a friendly hand to the priest's shoulder.

With that Arlen and Kat followed Edwin and Father Peter from the modest rooms, leaving Henry and Kian quite alone. They all walked back along the street in the direction of the coaching house in order to retrieve their horses.

"Give me a minute," Arlen whispered in Kat's ear, indicating that he wished to speak with his brother.

Kat nodded and planted a kiss to his cheek before catching up with Father Peter. She cheerfully linked him through the arm as they continued to stride on ahead.

"Brother," Arlen said, grabbing at Edwin's arm and holding him back. "I'm so sorry for deceiving you Edwin, I did want to tell you the truth."

"You could have trusted me, Arlen, you do know that?"

"Yes, of course I do Edwin, but Henry insisted, it was better nobody knew."

The two brothers continued to walk along in silence. Arlen knew Edwin was struggling with something and not just the deceit over Henry's death. He was all too aware how difficult his brother found it to speak of private matters, even to him.

"Edwin, please talk to me," he said, holding onto Edwin's arm, once again forcing him to stop.

Edwin took a deep breath and he glanced upwards; it was a clear night and the sky was full of stars.

"I envy your friendship with Henry; I sometimes think you are more like brothers than we are."

"Edwin, you know I love Henry, like a brother yes. But he is not my brother, you are, and I would do the same for you as I have done for Henry if ever you were to ask me, you must know that?"

"Yes, I do. I'm sorry Arlen … I'm just …"

"Please Edwin, tell me what else troubles you?"

"It's difficult for me Arlen. You so proudly wear your heart on your sleeve. I think perhaps your heart rules your head most of the time. You make everything seem so easy, the way you are with Kat, the affection you have for each other and so openly expressed without any reserve. It is quite the opposite for me. I fear allowing my heart to rule my head and I fear making mistakes Arlen."

"Is this about Florence, Brother?" Arlen asked, placing his hand to Edwin's shoulder. "I know you must have seen her at Moorgate."

"Yes," Edwin nodded, momentarily closing his eyes and taking in a deep breath. "I'm afraid I'm finding it hard to think of much else at the moment; we should have been married by now," he paused, cupping his head to his hands. "I made love to her Arlen, at Moorgate. I knew it was wrong, taking advantage of the dreadful situation she found herself in, but I wanted her, we wanted each other. Then the following morning I so easily allowed her to be taken away as a traitor," he groaned, his shoulders slumping forward.

"What else could you have done Brother? The order came from the King."

"Henry would never have allowed Iris to be taken away so."

"What do you think he would have done, absconded with her and become a fugitive for the rest of his life?"

"Oh, that thought did cross my mind I can tell you." Edwin admitted with a slight smile.

"No, Brother, I shall tell you what Henry would have done. Exactly what you did and then he would relentlessly pursue the truth in order to win her freedom. That is what Henry would have done and that is exactly what you are going to do, and I shall help you Brother and so will Henry and Kian."

"But what if Florence is now with child, just like Iris? I shall truly be powerless to help her."

"Please Brother, why distress yourself with thoughts of things that might not be and even if it was the case, we shall face it together. I am confident that once the truth is revealed all will be well, do you hear me?"

"Yes, thank you Brother. I suppose I just need a little bit of your unfailing optimism don't I."

"Yes, you do indeed," Arlen grinned broadly.

"Why are you grinning at me in that way?" Edwin asked, eyeing his brother sceptically.

"Because big Brother, I believe you have fallen well and truly head over heels in love and I have to admit I never thought it remotely possible."

"No, nor I," Edwin admitted with a laugh and embracing his brother fondly.

Kat and Father Peter had already un-stabled the horses as Arlen and Edwin joined them at the coach house. After bidding each other goodnight they all went their separate ways.

"Is everything alright with your brother?" Kat asked, sat atop Arlen's horse with his arm wrapped tightly around her waist.

"Yes, he's just in love that's all."

"Then why such the long face?"

"Because wench, being in love can be extremely vexing," Arlen replied, gently biting at Kat's ear.

"Ouch," she yelped, pushing back against him. "Anyway, where are we going?"

"The Mermaid," Arlen whispered, kissing her ear better. "Where I'm going to make mad passionate love to you all night."

Kat giggled. "Oh Arlen, I've missed you so much."

*   *   *

Iris sat patiently in the chapel situated on the hillside approximately two hundred yards from Trevelyan House. It was not a private chapel like at Wicken or Rothtir, instead it served the entire parish of West Trevelyan. There were bountiful displays of beautiful summer flowers adorning the walls and ceiling, strung up like ribbons with smaller bouquets tied to the end of each pew. Iris guessed there must have been a wedding there earlier in the day, with the delicate scent and numerous candles left burning at the windows – the space looked quite ethereal.

A Crown soldier had insisted on accompanying Iris to the chapel, but he seemed more than content to wait for her outside which pleased Iris as she wished to be alone. It had been a long tedious day cooped up in a carriage with Sebastian and Lady Howard and she was relishing the silence. Having just finished her prayers, she decided to remain in the chapel for a while longer and wait for Father Peter, who had promised to join her, but who was, curiously, nowhere to be seen. As she waited, Iris tried desperately to occupy her mind with thoughts of her father, the King, her mother, even Sebastian, but no matter how hard she tried thoughts of Henry dominated her head. She found herself reliving every precious moment they had spent together over and over again, still unable to truly believe he had gone. Determined not to cry again, it seemed it was all she had done for the past week, she pulled herself upright on the pew, straightening her skirts. She clutched her hands to her stomach. *You are all that matters now, for you I can endure anything,* she mused to herself.

Iris suddenly shot from her seat as the door to the chapel swung open. Believing it to be Father Peter she turned with a broad smile; however, it was Sebastian standing in the doorway. Iris felt slightly disappointed although she was careful not to show it.

"There you are," he beamed back, casually striding towards her. "I have been looking for you."

Sebastian had grown bored of all the pretence between the pair of them. With a letter already on its way to the King announcing their engagement he felt there no more need to feign concern for Iris or her feelings. It was time she understood exactly what she had agreed to. As far as Sebastian was concerned, Iris had made her bed and he intended to lie in it.

"You have been looking for me, why is there something wrong?" she asked, concern in her voice.

"No, nothing wrong, I just wanted to spend some time alone with you," he replied, wrapping his arms around her waist and pulling her towards him.

Iris tried to pull away, but he tightened his grip. "Sebastian, please, what are you doing?"

"Oh, come on Iris, you know perfectly well what I want," he smirked, pressing himself purposefully against her.

"But I thought …"

"Thought what? That I would agree to marry you, take on Henry Morton's bastard as my own and not expect anything in return?" he replied with a cruel laugh, his face pressed firmly against hers.

Iris could smell the brandy on his breath. The coarse stubble on his chin brushed against her face. "Oh no Iris, if we are to be married I shall expect you to fulfil all your duties as my most obedient wife, especially in the bedchamber."

"But we are not yet married Sebastian," Iris replied defiantly, trying desperately to remain calm.

Sebastian laughed even louder, tossing his head backwards. "There is no need to wait, our engagement is announced. We are as good as married and besides, it's not as if you are a virgin is it, Iris? No, I see no need to wait," he grinned, roughly forcing his mouth to hers.

Iris could feel he was already aroused as he rubbed his body suggestively against her. She let out a distressing cry.

"You're hurting me," she screamed, finally managing to release his hold on her and pushing him backwards.

"Oh, come now Iris, I know you like it rough," he grinned, cupping his hand around the back of her head and forcing her face back to his. "I observed you and Morton at Rothtir."

"Please Sebastian, no," she cried out, a tremor in her voice.

Sebastian suddenly released his hold on her and Iris hastily stepped backwards trying to catch her breath, shaking uncontrollably.

"I will not be denied Iris," he hissed, his spittle covering her face as he grabbed at the shoulders of her dress, yanking the material down with such force that Iris's knees almost buckled under the pressure.

"No," she objected vehemently, bringing her arms up in a desperate attempt to cover herself.

Sebastian howled with the most wicked of laughs. He grabbed her wrists and pinned her arms down to her side, all the time pushing her backwards until she was forced up against the wall. Then, releasing his hold, he gripped the fabric at the front of her dress and ripped it in two as if it were merely fine parchment.

"Now, that's better," he mocked, roughly fondling her now naked breasts and forcing his lips to hers once again.

Iris froze in sheer terror, unable to struggle against him anymore. Inside she was screaming to break free, but her limbs would not move. She could feel his brutish hands touching her body, his mouth against hers, then at her neck, then her breasts. Iris opened her mouth to scream but no sound came out. She was paralysed in the clutches of a monster. Tears began to roll freely down her cheeks as Sebastian released his hold on her momentarily, stepping backwards in order to untie his breeches, all the time grinning menacingly without mercy. He gripped the hem of her dress and swiftly ruched up her skirts and forcibly parted her legs with his knee.

"No," she screamed, finally finding her voice and lashing out at him furiously kicking and scrambling to break free from his iron grasp.

Sebastian immediately struck her hard across the face with the back of his hand causing her to fall back against the wall stunned, blood pouring from her nose. He angrily grabbed a handful of her hair and literally dragged her along the floor towards the altar. All the time Iris continued to scream, kicking and fighting against him. He struck her again hard before lifting her up and throwing her forward over the altar. He forcibly pressed the side of her face down onto the cold stone, blood pouring from her nose as he gripped hold of her skirts and pulled them up until she lay bent over, utterly exposed at his mercy.

"I'm going to enjoy this," he laughed cruelly, his hand fondling her roughly between her legs and fiercely kicking them apart with his foot.

Iris closed her eyes, her tears dripping onto the cold stone. Sebastian's naked flesh pressed against hers powerless to prevent him from brutally violating her.

The door to the chapel suddenly swung wide open. Father Peter stood in the doorway, glaring angrily over in the direction of the altar.

"Get out Priest," Sebastian roared. "Your prayers are not wanted here."

Father Peter gripped hold of the pew in front of him, poised to vault over and strangle the pathetic excuse of a man where he stood, just as the Crown Knight who had been waiting outside appeared in the doorway behind him.

"Lord Howard, you are needed at the house, it is urgent," he said, also alarmed by what he saw.

Father Peter was seething, his fists clenched tight. It took all his strength to restrain himself from attacking Sebastian. Thankfully, Sebastian stepped back from Iris and lowered her skirts.

"We shall continue this another time," he said leaning down and whispering in her ear, whilst adjusting his breeches. "This had better be important," he shouted over at the Crown Knight, striding confidently past the priest and exiting the chapel.

Iris had already crumbled to the floor, desperately clutching at her torn dress. Father Peter sped over to her removing his cloak and gently placing it over her shoulders. Iris remained on the floor and pulled the cloak tightly around her, wiping the blood from her face.

"I'm alright Father," she insisted, recoiling from the priest as he tried to aid her to rise.

"Iris please, allow me to help you."

"Nobody can help me," she muttered, finally scrambling to her feet. She stumbled forward, visibly trembling.

"Iris, please," Father Peter implored, following closely behind her as she made her way towards the door.

She suddenly stopped and turned to face him. "Very well," she said, her tone deadly serious. "If you want to help me, give me your dagger."

"My dagger."

"Yes, I know you carry one. I need a dagger so that monstrous man will never touch me again."

"Oh, Iris please don't do anything reckless," he begged, clasping his hands together. "Kat is here in Trevelyan, I have already seen her. She said that she will attend you tomorrow," he blurted out, desperate to diffuse the situation.

"Kat is in Trevelyan?" Iris gasped, a modicum of relief in her voice. "But why?"

"She travelled here with Arlen; she has been waiting for his return. Kian, he is here also. Please Iris, speak with Kat tomorrow, I'm sure things will seem much better in the morning."

Iris, still with her hand held out for the priest's dagger, hesitated to reply.

"Yes," she replied finally. "Yes, perhaps Kat can help me, you are right … but I still need your dagger," she insisted, shaking her hand out in front of her furiously.

"Very well," the priest sighed, reluctantly handing his dagger over. "But promise me that you will be careful?" he implored.

But Iris had already quit the chapel and was hurriedly heading down the hill, back towards Trevelyan House.

* * *

It was very late when Sebastian Howard knocked on the old fisherman's cottage door, not quite sure he could be heard over the raucous merriment that was taking place inside. He knocked again, this time banging his fist so hard against the weathered wood that the cracked glass rattled in the windowpanes. The room suddenly fell silent. Sebastian heard muted whispers and a lot of shuffling feet just before the battered old door slowly creaked open. Sir James Ripley peered from the gap, dagger firmly in one hand, and candle in the other. Upon eyeing his nephew, he flung the door wide open much to the relief of the four swords for hire and the other numerous female and male guests present.

"About time," Ripley snarled, moving aside to allow Sebastian to enter.

The room was relatively well lit and jugs of ale covered every surface. It smelt of roasting meat, ale and hot sweaty bodies; Sebastian observed a piglet roasting above the fire and a woman straddled across one of the swords for hire wearing nothing more than her stockings, happily riding him enthusiastically. Sebastian relished the smell of debauchery, it reminded him of his favourite brothel. One of the other naked young women casually floated over to him and loosely draped her arm around his neck. Sebastian aggressively pushed her aside, almost knocking her to the floor.

"Hey," she squealed, throwing him an angry look.

One of the other swords for hire quickly came to her aid, roughly fondling her breasts before dragging her into the back room.

"Where have you been?" Ripley snapped, pulling Sebastian aside and dismissing the woman who had been pleasuring him. "My ship to Vikrin sets sail tomorrow."

"I got here as soon as I could Uncle," Sebastian assured him, handing Ripley a large purse containing a sizable amount of gold.

"Good," Ripley replied, weighing the bag up and down in his large hand. "It had better not be light," he said in a warning tone.

"It's not Uncle, I can assure you, in fact there is more than we agreed … here," he said, throwing Ripley another much smaller purse, "for the men."

"What have you done with the Westonhall girl?" Ripley asked, tossing the smaller purse at one of the swords for hire.

The naked women immediately flocked around him like vultures.

"I take it you mean Iris, my future wife and queen," Sebastian grinned, pouring himself a cup of ale.

"You shrewd bastard, how on earth did you manage that?"

"I didn't, she did. She is carrying Morton's child; Grandmother just conveniently relayed some home truths. You know what I mean, princess, bastard, not possible, and all that."

Ripley grinned, Lady Howard certainly never failed to surprise. She always seemed to have a canny way of turning around an impossible situation.

"Every cloud has a silver lining then," Ripley laughed. "So, when do you depart for Kingslea?"

"We were due to leave tomorrow morning, but it seems the King has other ideas. Apparently, he is now to join us here in Trevelyan, desperate to see his daughter no doubt. But no matter, the outcome remains. Uncle, as soon as we reach Kingslea I shall send for you, Grandmother agrees. There is no solid evidence against you, we shall merely say you were deceived by the Ainsworth's. By this time I should have the King and Iris eating out of my hand, I promise you Uncle, our victory is in sight."

"Good," Ripley scoffed, placing his hand to Sebastian's shoulder. "We do still have one problem," he said. "Beatrice. She didn't return the day you left for the East. If she is apprehended, things may become very awkward, particularly if she were to talk."

"Don't worry about Beatrice, Uncle. I shall make sure a kill-on-sight order is issued for her, right after I start spreading the rumours that she has the remaining Vikrin pearls," Sebastian laughed cruelly, eyeing a scantily dressed young man slouching in an easy chair in the far corner of the room.

"No time like the present," he grinned, casually sauntering over towards him.

He may have been denied earlier in the chapel, but he was certainly not going to be denied a second time. Holding out his hand to the young man, they proceeded into the back room.

Chapter 27

Henry was wide awake, having been unable to sleep all night. It was barely sunrise outside as he paced the boarding house room impatiently waiting for Arlen and Kat to return, peering from the window every few minutes in the hope of catching sight of them. Kian was fast asleep, loudly snoring in the corner stretched out on a chair. Henry angrily kicked the leg.

"Wake up," he grumbled, returning to stare from the window.

"Fucking hell," Kian hissed, really annoyed. He'd hardly had more than two hours sleep himself. "You need to pull yourself to-fucking-gether Henry, I've never seen you so fucking agitated."

"I'm sorry Kian," Henry moaned, slumping himself down into a chair just below the window. "I just can't seem to settle … Did you go back to the cottage last night?"

"Yes," Kian replied, standing up and stretching and yawning loudly. He poured himself a glass of brandy. "There were whores there last night. Ripley was obviously intent on enjoying his final night in Trevelyan and you will never guess who else turned up?" Kian smirked, promptly returning to his chair.

"Who?" Henry grumbled, not in any kind of mood for Kian's silly games.

"Only fucking Howard." Kian replied, emptying the contents of his glass.

"I imagine he was informing Ripley of the King's change of plans," Henry mused.

"Possibly or to bid him farewell … Either way Henry, we should not allow any delay in dealing with Ripley," Kian urged, desperately wanting to finally get the job done. He had been doing nothing more than observing Ripley, for far too long in his opinion. His patience was beginning to wear very thin.

Henry let out a deep sigh. "Yes, I know, you are right Kian. My judgement last night was clouded, we should deal with Ripley at once. It was just … well when I heard Iris was with child, I …"

"I know Henry," Kian replied, with a very rare fond smile. "Jesus Christ, what the fuck is happening to us?"

"What do you mean?"

"Well, with you about to become a father, and now Arlen it seems is in love with my sister. Do you know I actually walked in on them in bed back at Barlett House, actually fucking? I could hardly believe my eyes," Kian grumbled, screwing up his face as if in disgust.

"You never did," Henry laughed.

"Yes, and they were probably at it like rabbits last night. You did notice, I presume, that Kat didn't bloody well come back here after they all left … I suppose she could do a lot worse."

The two men glanced over at each other before bursting into fits of laughter, lightening the mood if only for a brief moment.

Their amusement however came to an abrupt halt at the sound of a soft tapping at the door. Kian shot from his chair, his dagger already firmly in his hand.

"Who is it?" he hissed.

"Father Peter," came a hushed reply.

Kian hastily unlocked the door to find Father Peter stood on the landing, looking extremely anxious.

"What the fuck is wrong with you?" Kian grumbled, stepping aside to allow the priest to enter.

"I know it's incredibly early; I'm sorry but I had to come. I have hardly slept a wink all night," he blurted out, glaring at Henry. "Iris, she …"

"Iris, what?" Henry screamed, not allowing the priest to finish. He already had him by the throat and pinned up against the back of the door. "What about Iris?" he hissed; his face pushed up flat against the priest's.

"She's alright, Henry please," Father Peter insisted, struggling to breathe as Henry tightened his grip around his throat. "I arrived at the chapel just in time. Sebastian, he was forcing himself on …"

Father Peter didn't have chance to finish his next sentence either. Henry planted a punishing blow to the side of his jaw before releasing his iron grip. Father Peter slid to the floor.

"You were supposed to be looking after her," Henry roared, grabbing the priest by the shoulders and pulling him back to his feet, his fist clenched ready for a second round.

Kian quickly intervened, pulling Henry backwards, "Enough Henry, let him fucking speak … Priest is Iris alright?"

"Yes," Father Peter winced, rubbing at his bruised jaw. "I'm more worried about what she might do next. Everything seems quiet at the house at the moment, but I needed to know you were still going to her this morning. She insisted on having my dagger."

"And you gave it to her?" Henry yelled, furiously lurching at the priest once again.

"Enough," Kian shouted, roughly forcing Henry into a chair. "Calm the fuck down. Henry, you shall rendezvous with Iris as planned. Priest get back to the house and try to keep a fucking eye on Iris until Kat arrives … Iris is not stupid Henry."

"No, but she is reckless Kian, and you know it," Henry moaned, cupping his head into his hands.

"Maybe, but she now has her child to consider. I'm sure that fact alone shall at least temper her mood," Kian replied, hoping to God he was right.

"Yes," the priest sniffed, "I informed her last night that Kat was to visit this morning. She mumbled something about Kat helping her. I'm not sure what she meant but let's hope you are right Kian and she will not act recklessly on impulse."

"We had better be right," Henry growled. "If anything were to happen to her Priest, I shall kill you."

"Go," Kian shouted at the priest and hastily ushering him from the room before he turned his attention back to Henry.

"I have to go to her Kian," Henry moaned, running his fingers through his hair.

"I know you do," Kian nodded in agreement, placing his hand to Henry's shoulder. "I know you do, now where the fuck is Arlen and Kat?" he grumbled, gulping down another large glass of brandy.

* * *

Iris had locked herself in her bedchamber after the brutal assault at the chapel, lodging a chair under the door handle for added security. She had tucked Father Peter's dagger safely under her pillow and finally managed to get a couple of hours sleep before she was abruptly awoken by Lady Howard knocking loudly at the door.

"Are you alright my dear?" she bellowed from the landing. "Why is the door locked?"

"I'm sorry," Iris called out, jumping from the bed, hastily removing the chair and placing it back against the wall. "I must have locked it without thinking," Iris lied, allowing Lady Howard entry.

"Oh my dear, what on earth have you done to your face?" she declared, alarmed at the injuries to Iris's face, knowing only too well what had occurred in the chapel the previous evening. The Crown soldier had relayed the facts at Lady Howard's insistence. Iris was still far too fragile – this would not do at all. She would have to speak with Sebastian at once. She could not have him jeopardise their situation, not now, not as they were so close to finally realising their goal.

Iris crossed the room to peer into the mirror. Her left cheek was badly bruised, along with a gash across the bridge of her nose. She tentatively touched her face, the horror of the night before flashing through her mind.

"I … I fell in the night," she muttered. "Rather stupid really, I forgot where I was for a moment."

"Oh my dear, what on earth will your father think when he sees you all battered and bruised? Come now, you still look extremely pale. Get back into bed my dear and I shall have breakfast sent up, as long as you promise to eat something."

Lady Howard aided Iris back to the bed. "All will be well my dear, you mark my words," she whispered, gently stroking her hair. Despite everything, she had grown quite fond of Iris.

"But I thought we were to travel to Kingslea this morning?" Iris asked curiously, climbing back into bed.

"Your father has altered his plans my dear, we are to remain in Trevelyan. He travels here this very moment. If he does not arrive before dark, I shall be most surprised."

"Oh, I see, thank you," Iris replied.

How convenient, she thought, *what with Father Peter informing her Kat was to call this morning. Perhaps Arlen and his brother had engineered it this way.* Whatever the reason Iris now saw a golden opportunity to amend her present untenable situation.

A short while later a maid brought up a breakfast tray laden with bread, jams, porridge and a large glass of milk. Iris tucked into the feast enthusiastically, her nausea seemed to have passed and she was very hungry. She also had a renewed sense of optimism for her future and Kat was just the person to aid her. After almost finishing the whole tray of food, the maid helped her dress. Iris chose a plain blue woollen dress along with her most comfortable shoes and requested that her hair be plaited tightly and pinned up out of the way.

"You do know you are not to travel today miss?" the maid said, curious at Iris's choice of attire, which was more suited to traveling.

"Yes, thank you," Iris replied, "I just wanted to wear something comfortable."

"Very well miss," the maid said, scooping up the tray from the table before leaving the room.

She returned almost instantly. "Miss, you have a visitor."

"Thank you," Iris nodded, smiling broadly and hurriedly following the maid along the landing and down the stairs.

Kat was sat patiently with Lady Howard and Sebastian in the expensive simplicity of the drawing room at Trevelyan House. The walls were pale in colour and the room was sparsely furnished, which seemed fitting as the enormous window filled the room with sunlight as well as allowing an excellent view of the coastline.

"What a beautiful room," Kat remarked, suddenly standing and moving towards the window. "And what a wonderful view."

"Yes indeed," Lady Howard agreed, slightly perturbed by Kat's presence. "Tell me my dear, are you in Trevelyan with your brother?"

"Yes milady, I am. We travelled here with Sir Arlen Barlett after the death of Lord Henry Morton. Arlen and his brother believe Sir James Ripley to be hiding out here. Do you know he still has two Vikrin pearls?" Kat declared, turning and observing the pair very closely for any reaction.

"The Vikrin pearls?" Lady Howard replied, feigning astonishment. "Oh dear, then let us hope he is apprehended without delay," she added, clutching at a small velvet pochette hanging from the waist of her skirts.

"Yes, indeed," Kat nodded, curling her lips in a slight smile. "Then we can all breathe a little easier," she said, turning to gaze at the view once more.

Iris literally burst into the room and startled the occupants. She wildly flung her arms around Kat, almost knocking her off her feet.

"Oh, Kat how wonderful to see you," she exclaimed, embracing her tightly.

"Wow Iris, it's so wonderful to see you too," Kat replied, holding her friend at arm's length. "Oh, how pale you are," she remarked. "And your face, what on earth happened?"

"Oh, nothing," Iris replied, dismissing Kat's concern with a wave of her hand. "Oh Kat, it has been such an awful time," she continued, clutching onto her friend's hands tightly.

"I know Iris, I'm so sorry, I can only imagine your anguish," Kat replied, kissing Iris lovingly on the cheek. "But I hear Sebastian has taken very good care of you, congratulations are in order I believe?"

"Oh, yes thank you Kat," Iris replied, a lump rising in her throat as she spoke. She was desperate to reveal the truth.

"How are you feeling this morning, my dear?" Sebastian asked, feigning concern.

"Grandmother and I have been so worried about you."

"A little better, thank you," Iris replied, in as much of a sweet manner as she could muster, not daring to have eye contact with Sebastian. She was already beginning to tremble and doubted she could maintain her calm demeanour if she did.

"Sitting in that damp old chapel for hours on end is no good for you. You shall pray in your room from now on," Sebastian declared, leaving Iris in no doubt that it was not a request but an order.

He casually draped his arm over her shoulder. Iris tried to pull away from him, but he was too quick and he pulled her closer, kissing her gently on her bruised cheek.

"Ah, that will make it better," he smirked, still gripping her tightly.

Iris wrestled to maintain her composure, breathing slowly, her whole body tensed at his touch. Kat could clearly see Iris was hopelessly struggling. She needed to get her away from Sebastian as quickly as possible.

"I know what might put some colour back into your cheeks," she declared rather boldly. "A walk along the beach. It is wonderful Iris. The ocean breeze is so uplifting. I can see you have a beautiful private beach here, have you been down there yet?" she asked, turning to gaze at the view once again, praying that Sebastian would agree to the idea.

"No," Iris replied, desperate herself to quit the room and speak with Kat alone. "That sounds wonderful, may I Sebastian?" she asked, rallying all her courage to face him.

Sebastian hesitated. He stared at Iris, his menacing blue eyes undressing her. She thought she would truly faint if he did not answer soon.

"Very well," he replied, finally. "I don't see why not, considering we are not to leave Trevelyan today as planned … but don't be too long Iris, I wish to speak with you … alone." he grinned, removing his arm from her shoulder.

Kat instantly grabbed Iris's hand. "Come on then, we should make haste," she said cheerfully, pulling Iris from the room as quickly as possible before Sebastian had any chance to change his mind.

Sebastian followed the women from the drawing room and watched from the entrance as they headed down the pathway towards the private beach.

"Are you sure you should have allowed her to go?" Lady Howard asked. "She is still very fragile. That episode in the chapel last night won't help, Sebastian you should take heed."

"Don't worry Grandmother, anyway what choice does she have? That wild redhead can't do anything to help her even if she does confide in her."

Sebastian turned to the Crown soldier in the doorway. "Upon their return ensure that the Munro woman is denied entry to the house and make sure she leaves at once."

"Yes milord," he replied, without hesitation.

Kat and Iris hurried along down the sloping path, reaching the beach in no time at all.

"Oh Kat, it is so wonderful to see you," Iris declared, as soon as they were far enough from the house so as not to be overheard.

"It's wonderful to see you too Iris. How are you really?"

"Wretched Kat, absolutely wretched. Please Kat, I need you to take me back to Corstir, I cannot stay here a moment longer … Sebastian he …"

"He hurt you, didn't he?"

"Yes, he did,"

"Did he do that to your face?"

"Yes. He is not the man I thought he was."

"Well, you are right about that, come on," Kat urged, pulling Iris along the beach at quite a pace. "Don't worry Iris, I can assure you that he will never hurt you again I promise."

"That's why I need you to take me back to Corstir … Kat, I'm with child."

Kat didn't reply, she just continued to drag Iris along the beach.

"Kat, please did you hear me? … I'm with child … Please Kat, stop."

Iris refused to go on, stopping dead in her tracks, her eyes filled with tears. Kat turned to face her and smiled sympathetically.

"Oh, my darling Iris, if you really want me to take you back to Corstir of course I will, without hesitation, but first you need to go there," Kat replied, pointing towards an opening in the cliffside.

"Kat," Iris whispered, at a loss to understand her meaning and staring first at her friend, then at the entrance to the cave. "What's going on?" she asked nervously.

"Go," Kat urged, pushing Iris gently towards the opening.

Iris tentatively moved forward, looking back over her shoulder at Kat once or twice. Kat maintained her position smiling and gesturing for Iris to move closer towards the cave. As Iris turned again to face the opening in the cliffside, Henry very slowly stepped from the shadows. Iris instantly crumbled; Henry rushed forward and scooped her up his arms.

They stood together for a while quite still, embracing each other. Iris gently wept as Henry held her tightly, finally cradling her in his arms once again.

"Oh, Henry is it truly you?" she whimpered, afraid to even open her eyes in case it was all just a dream.

"Yes my darling, it's truly me," he replied, lifting her face to kiss her gently on the lips. "I'm so sorry my love, putting you through such heartache. I should never have left you in the East." Henry groaned, gently stroking her bruised face. "Sebastian Howard shall pay for this Iris, I promise you,"

"Oh, Henry," she breathed, all the emotional tension draining from her body in an instant now that she was safe once again in Henry's strong arms.

"Iris, listen to me; we don't have much time. Sebastian was behind the explosion in the Corridor – he deceived us all. He revealed himself to me only moments before he left me to die. If he knew that I had survived I feared what he would have done to you. I had to ensure your safe return to Mercia before I could act, please forgive me my darling."

"Oh Henry, I do forgive you, I love you … Henry, I'm with child."

"I know, my love, Father Peter overheard you at Wicken Hall," he whispered, placing his hand to her stomach and kissing her lips. "I love you my darling."

Arlen and Kat joined them at the entrance to the cave. "Henry it's time, we must go," Arlen said, his tone urgent.

"Go where," Iris asked, gripping hold of Henry's hand tightly, not daring to let go.

"We have located Ripley, Sebastian's accomplice. We need to deal with him right away, he is about to quit Mercia. Then we shall come for Sebastian. Kat, please take Iris back to our rooms in town. You shall be safe there my love."

"Lady Howard has the pearls," Kat blurted out excitedly. "I mentioned them at the house whilst I was waiting for Iris and she grabbed at a small pochette around her waist. She has them, I'm sure of it."

"Lady Howard!" Iris gasped with a real sad sense of betrayal. "I cannot believe it, and she has been so kind to me, can we really trust no one?"

"I'm afraid not my darling," Henry replied, wrapping her up in his arms once more.

Iris pulled away from him, her fervent spirit returning. "Henry, if I don't go back to the house, Sebastian will surely know something is wrong. I must return. It will allow you time to deal with this Ripley person. Kat and I can perhaps retrieve the pearls," she suggested, her courage rising fast along with a wilful desire for revenge.

"No," Henry replied, adamant. "It is far too dangerous."

"I shall remain with Iris at all times," Kat promised, liking the sound of Iris's plan. "We must take advantage whilst Sebastian's guard is down. Please allow us to try Henry, I promise we shall not take any undue risk."

Iris nodded enthusiastically; the women felt quite empowered. Henry ran his fingers through his hair, staring at Arlen for support.

Arlen nodded, "It would allow us more time."

"Don't do anything foolish. I mean it, both of you," Henry commanded, staring intensely at the two women, leaving them under no doubt that he was putting a lot of trust in them to act responsibly. "Father Peter is at the chapel if you have any kind of inkling that you have been discovered or are in danger, you must go to him at once. Do you hear me? We shall come for you as soon as we have dealt with Ripley."

"Don't worry Henry, I have Father Peter's dagger," Iris replied, happily revealing the dagger beneath her skirts.

"Oh Christ. No, this is a bad idea," Henry sighed, running his fingers through his hair once again.

"No, it's far too risky. Kat take Iris back to our rooms at once," he announced, furiously shaking his head at the two women.

"Henry please, it's just a precaution. I shall not take any undue risks, I promise you," Iris insisted, grabbing Henry's hand and placing it to her stomach. "I promise Henry, I would never put our child in any risk."

"Oh Christ Iris, what are you doing to me woman, why can't I refuse you? ... very well," he sighed, finally relenting and scooping Iris up in his arms. "I love you."

Arlen embraced Kat and made her swear to take care, and with that the two women swiftly headed back along the beach towards Trevelyan House.

"I hope to God we have done the right thing," Henry groaned as he and Arlen climbed the cliff path to join Edwin and four Crown soldiers who had assembled at the top waiting patiently for their return.

"Henry," Edwin called out, as the two men appeared at the top of the cliff.

Henry hastily mounted his horse and rode over to Edwin's position.

"What is it?" he asked, anxious to get moving.

"I have just received word that the King has departed Kingslea. He rides hard towards Trevelyan."

"Good, we must make haste, it is imperative that we get back to Trevelyan House before the King arrives."

"Henry there is more," Edwin sighed. "Phillip Ainsworth has escaped the tower. It seems that the guard on duty can remember nothing more other than a beautiful woman with black hair."

"Beatrice," Henry hissed. "When was this?"

"Two nights ago. Ainsworth is still very weak, I'm sure he is not a threat to us, even if he has managed to travel back to Trevelyan," Edwin added.

"No quite right, in fact it is a wonder he is still alive," Henry replied, dismissing Ainsworth as any kind of threat at this present time.

"Where is Kian?" Edwin asked, quickly glancing round for him.

"Watching the fisherman's cottage. Come, we must make haste. We shall consider Ainsworth and his sister later," Henry declared, pulling on the reins of his horse.

The men then rode hard, heading back in the direction of town.

Chapter 28

Kat and Iris hurried back along the beach; Kat gripped onto Iris's arm as the house came into view.

"Slow down Iris, we don't want to draw any attention to ourselves. They may conclude that something is wrong," she said, raising her beautiful green eyes up towards the house.

"No, quite right," Iris agreed, slowing her pace right down to a casual amble.

"Iris are you alright?" Kat asked, turning to face her friend. "It must have been quite a shock seeing Henry after believing him dead and what with the baby. Are you sure you want to do this? We could still go back and wait it out, it's not too late?"

"Yes, it was a shock Kat, but oh so very joyous. To be honest I can still hardly believe it," Iris replied, staring intensely at her friend; Kat's curly red hair swirling wildly in the warm breeze.

"When I first realised I was with child, I was so utterly shocked and amazed but so very happy. I longed for nothing more than Henry to join me at Wicken Hall to tell him my news. Then when I was told he was dead, I have never felt so alone and so frightened in my whole life. Lady Howard convinced me that I had to marry and quickly, I was terrified of losing my baby Kat, it was all I had left of Henry. That's the only reason why I agreed to marry Sebastian, you do understand don't you?"

"Yes of course I do Iris, of course I do. Please don't trouble yourself, I would have done the exact same thing if I thought for one minute that Little Kian could be taken from me."

"They have used me abominably Kat, used my grief, my vulnerability to convince me that my child would be taken from me. Yes Kat, I want to do this. I want to see them both held accountable for what they have done to me and for everyone else whose lives have been so cruelly ruined or even worse lost."

"Good," Kat replied with a huge smile. "Because I have a plan," she said. "Come, follow me."

Kat led Iris to the bottom of the pathway where the garden met the beach. Kneeling down, she pointed to a cluster of small pretty white flowers growing at the very edge.

"Devil's Angel," she declared, ripping a strip of linen from the hem of her chemise and carefully wrapping the cloth around her hand. She pulled at the base of the small white flowers, revealing the root.

"Devil's Angel?" Iris muttered, raising her eyebrows quizzically. "I have never heard of it."

"Yes, well that's what we call it in Corstir. I noticed them earlier; they like to grow near water. The pretty white flowers resemble tiny angels but don't let that deceive you, they are quite poisonous, especially the root."

"You mean to poison them?" Iris gasped, stepping back, a little startled.

"No, silly," Kat laughed. "They would need to eat the root for that. I just mean to make them sleepy. We shall crush the flowers and add them to the wine."

"Let me see," Iris said, moving closer in order to touch the tiny white flowers.

"Careful," Kat exclaimed, hastily pulling away. "Don't touch them with your bare hands, hold them in the cloth. They can cause a nasty rash and if you were to touch your eyes or face, why they might even render you blind."

"Oh, Kat you are so clever," Iris declared, mesmerised by the Devil's Angels.

Kat then swiftly pocketed the linen cloth bundle into her pocket as the two women climbed the path back up towards the house. Just as they reached the entrance a Crown soldier stepped from the doorway, blocking their entry.

"Lord Howard's orders, you are not permitted to enter," he snarled at Kat, holding his hand out directly in front of her.

"What, why ever not?" Iris exclaimed, most put out by the soldier's rudeness. She wanted to ask him if he knew who he was talking to but refrained, knowing only too well that Sebastian would overrule her anyway.

"Orders come from his Lordship, and she needs to leave now," the man added, clearly not appreciating having to explain himself.

Kat thought quickly, pulling Iris aside so as to be out of earshot of the soldier. "We best go to the chapel to Father Peter and wait for Henry and Arlen there. I cannot allow you to go back inside the house alone," Kat whispered, with one eye on Iris and the other on the miserable Crown soldier.

"No, give me the flowers. I can do this Kat," Iris replied, calming her fears. "If I can get them to drink the wine before Henry and Arlen's return, it shall make their arrest so much easier and we shall have no trouble retrieving the pearls from Lady Howard's skirts."

"No, it's far too dangerous Iris; Henry would never forgive me if anything were to happen to you."

"I shall be alright Kat; don't forget Sebastian is expecting the King to arrive at any moment. He still believes he has won; he would not dare do anything to jeopardise that, not now. Please, let me do this Kat. I need to, and I do promise to be very careful."

"Very well," Kat sighed, eventually handing over the small linen packet. "I shall go to the chapel and wait with Father Peter; you must come to us at once if you believe you are in any kind of danger. Promise me?"

"Yes, I promise, please don't worry," Iris whispered, just as the Crown soldier appeared annoyingly at her side.

"You need to go," he snarled, glaring at Kat. "Now."

"Yes, yes, I'm going," she replied, but not before throwing the soldier a disdainful look. She quickly embraced Iris lovingly before rushing off in the direction of the chapel.

Iris waited and watched until Kat had disappeared out of sight. She was just about to enter the house when Sebastian appeared in the doorway, grinning. Iris quickly tucked the small linen packet into her pocket and silently followed him back inside the house.

"I need to change my shoes and stockings," she declared, stopping at the foot of the stairs. "They are filled with sand."

Sebastian turned, still grinning he looked Iris up and down as if undressing her with his eyes. Iris shuddered, not daring to make eye contact with him.

"Very well," he replied. "But don't take too long. Oh, and Iris, change into something more becoming, I don't like you in that plain woollen dress. You are a princess and it's about time you started acting like one."

He then turned from the stairs and was about to enter the drawing room when he suddenly stopped in his tracks, his back still to Iris.

"Oh, and Iris one more thing, you will never see that Munro woman or her brother ever again, do you hear me?"

"Yes, Sebastian," Iris replied, hastily running up the stairs.

Upon entering her bedchamber, she observed that a pink satin dress trimmed with delicate lace and adorned with precious pearls had already been laid out on the bed.

It seems Sebastian wishes to control all areas of my life, she mused sardonically to herself.

A young maid suddenly appeared behind her in order to aid her to dress. Iris smiled broadly. After she had changed, Iris thanked the maid and asked to be left alone. Once she was confident the girl had left, she very carefully placed the Devil's Angel flowers on to a small glass tray on her dresser. Then using the back of her hairbrush, she gently crushed them into a pulp before transferring them into a small glass vial. Quickly disposing of the torn linen, hairbrush, and glass dish at the back of the fireplace, she wrapped the glass vial in a clean handkerchief and carefully concealed it in her pocket before descending back down the stairs.

Iris could hear Sebastian and Lady Howard talking and laughing loudly in the drawing room. Seeing her chance, she headed straight for the dining room, careful not to be observed. A decanter of red wine was sat atop a side table where it had been left the previous evening. Hastily retrieving the vial from her pocket, she carefully emptied the crushed flowers into the decanter and, picking it up, she gently swirled it around in order to distribute the pulp. Just as she replaced it on the side table and returned the vial to her pocket, Sebastian appeared in the doorway.

"What are you doing?" he asked sharply, glaring at Iris suspiciously.

"I ... I ... I was looking for some fresh water, the sea air seems to have dried my throat," she replied nervously, rubbing her sweaty palms down the front of her skirt.

"Here, why don't you have some wine," he said, heading directly for the decanter.

"No, no thank you, I think I shall fetch some water," she replied, attempting to shuffle past him.

"Not so fast," he insisted, tightly grabbing hold of her arm and roughly pulling her towards him. "I'm sorry we were so rudely interrupted in the chapel last night Iris; I shall come to you tonight and finish what we started," he smirked, placing his hand to the back of her head and forcibly pulling her face towards his and kissing her hard on the lips. Iris desperately struggled to pull away.

"That is the last time you pull away from me Iris, do you hear me?" he hissed, placing a cruel hand to her throat and squeezing very gently. "The very last time, you will crave the touch of my skin if it's the last thing you do."

He then proceeded to pick up the wine decanter from the side table and, grabbing Iris's arm, escorted her back to the drawing room. This time Iris didn't resist him.

* * *

Beatrice Ainsworth precariously navigated her horse and cart through the town gates of Trevelyan. She had been travelling for two days solid. Her brother Phillip was lying down in the cart and had hardly moved for the entire journey from Kingslea. He was lethargic and drifting in and out of sleep. He was barely alive. His face was so badly swollen from the torturous beating and subsequent ferocious assault that he was unable to speak. He could only manage to suck on a water-soaked cloth for sustenance – blood and saliva continually dripped from his broken deformed jaw. Fearing for his very life, Beatrice hoped their uncle would be able to provide some sort of refuge until such time that they could travel to possible exile in Vikrin. The situation they found themselves in was not at all how Phillip had envisaged their involvement with the Howards. Phillip and her uncle had coerced Beatrice into supporting their cause with a promise of advancing their whole family; even her marriage to Lord Bentley had been part of the plan as his lack of intelligence and extensive wealth was a desirable asset. Sebastian had promised that once he was officially named heir he would markedly diminish the control of the other Lords and make their family the most powerful in Mercia. Beatrice had been opposed to the idea right from the start, but Phillip always had a way of persuading his sister to yield to his will – most recently, and after her defiant attitude regarding Henry Morton, it involved a cat-o-nine tails. Rescuing Phillip from the clutches of the Crown may have seemed absurd considering his brutal treatment of her, but Beatrice had nowhere else to turn as her whole family were now detained in the tower because of their actions. She was desperate and no matter how badly Phillip had treated her, at this present moment in time he was all she had.

Skilfully manoeuvring the cart through the narrow streets, she headed in the direction of the fisherman's cottage on the west side of the town. It was mid-morning and the streets were already beginning to fill, delaying her progress, much to her annoyance. She had however fortunately gained an excellent knowledge of Trevelyan whilst hiding out at the cottage, enabling her to make strategic diversions in order to reach her destination as quickly as possible.

As she approached the waterside, she immediately realised that something was terribly wrong. Two Crown soldiers were blocking the road and local residents were being hastily ushered into their homes and off the streets. Three Crown Knights were mounted on their horses further down the quayside, facing the direction of the fisherman's cottage.

"Ripley has been discovered," she muttered, barely above a whisper; Phillip stirred, suddenly becoming restless in the back of the cart as though he had overheard her. He moaned loudly.

With no possible way of warning Ripley of the impending danger, Beatrice frantically considered her next move, at the same time she pulled on the reins in order to quickly turn the cart around. She glanced back down the street and observed Henry Morton dismounting from his horse.

"Henry is alive!" she gasped, now pulling hard on the reins to swiftly manoeuvre the cart back along the street before she was observed.

Having already heard the news at an Inn on her way into Trevelyan that the Howards had arrived in Mercia, Beatrice thought quickly. If she could somehow get to Trevelyan House, perhaps they may be able to aid her in some way, after all it was the least they could do. Knowing full well the house would be heavily guarded or worse, they had also been discovered and were under house arrest, she suddenly remembered the old priest hole; the one Phillip had locked her in years previous. If she could reach the chapel, there may be a way of contacting the Howards unobserved. Momentarily glancing over her shoulder, she eyed Henry Morton now staring right in her direction. She swiftly pulled the hood of her cloak over her face as the cart clattered quickly along the cobbled street leaving the waterside at a hasty pace.

"What's wrong?" Arlen asked, seeing Henry staring studiously back down the street.

"Nothing," Henry replied, squinting into the morning sunlight. "It's just I thought I saw … never mind, let's finish this," he said authoritatively, turning towards the fisherman's cottage and gesturing for the other men to follow him.

"Ripley is mine," he commanded, clasping the cruciform hilt of his double-edged sword tightly in his hand.

The fisherman's cottage was situated at the end of the quay, set back from the other dwellings. It was an old building, one of only a handful of homes remaining that had been built when Trevelyan was all but a small fishing village. The neighbourhood was relatively quiet. It was a mainly residential area with small fishing boats neatly lined up along the water's edge and fishing nets and pots hung up on lines, left out in the sun to dry. The men slowly descended upon the cottage.

Ripley kicked at the chair of one of his swords for hire who sat near the fireplace; he snorted loudly throwing Ripley a disdainful glare.

"Get up," Ripley snarled as he leisurely sauntered over towards the window. "It is time."

The disgruntled man got up from his chair in order to rouse the other men languishing in the back room.

"There is something wrong," Ripley muttered, glancing out of the grubby small cracked window at the front of the cottage.

The street outside was empty and the street was never empty. The man who had been sat near the fireplace hastily woke two other men who were asleep, raising a finger to his lips to quieten them before they had time to object. They reacted quickly, retrieving their swords. A fourth man quietly descended the ladder in the centre of the back room.

"Crown Knights and soldiers," he muttered. "I have counted at least seven."

Ripley was seething. He let out a disgruntled roar, shaking his head furiously. He knew it was only a matter of time before he was discovered, he had waited around for far too long.

"Are you ready?" he asked the men, his eyes wide and his lips narrowing as he moved towards the doorway of the cottage.

The four men all nodded with what could only be described as excitement. They were hardened fighters who were not accustomed to sitting around, no matter how much they were being paid. They relished the battle; young Crown soldiers were no match for them, however brutal their training was reputed to be, this was a street fight and this was what they did best.

Ripley then confidently stepped from the fisherman's cottage into the morning sunlight, the four swords for hire right behind him. The furious expression on his face suddenly changed.

"Well, well," he smirked, upon eyeing Henry. "Lord Henry Morton alive and well … good … he's mine," he hissed, pointing the tip of his arming sword menacingly in Henry's direction.

"Good," Henry replied in return. "Now you shall finally fight me like a man."

With that, the sword fighting began. The clashing of steel was deafening as the men lurched at each other repeatedly. Henry wielded his sword skilfully, pushing Ripley backwards towards the cottage and swinging and thrusting his weapon relentlessly. Ripley made little effort to fight back, he only defended the continuous attack being rained down upon him. Ripley was toying with Henry; he knew he must be weakened after Goring End so he was doing just enough to ward him off; successfully tiring Henry in the process. When finally and without warning he suddenly began to fight back with as much skill and determination this time, Henry had to step backwards. Each powerful blow met with another and another; Ripley showed no signs of weakening as the battle continued. Henry's stamina however was beginning to wane. Ripley sensed his fatigue and grinned as he pushed forward with evermore vigour, bringing his sword down hard upon Henry again and again. Henry was now only able to defend the constant onslaught. Ripley drove him closer to the water's edge with every blow.

The four swords for hire fought viciously, relishing in the fight. One fatally injured a Crown soldier and one wounded another.

"Four against five," one of the thugs jeered, standing above the dead soldier gleefully wiping his bloody sword on the sleeve of his shirt.

Edwin lurched at him furiously and the two men proceeded into battle with unrelenting fury.

Henry was managing only to defend himself from the continual onslaught raining down upon him by Ripley. He was desperately struggling to gain the upper hand as one of the thrusts sliced through the top of his left arm. He staggered backwards, further towards the water's edge. Kian, who had been keeping an awfully close eye on Henry, was also conscious of the fact that he was weakened after the assault at Goring End. Immediately realising he was in peril, he quickly diverted his attention from his current opponent.

"No," Henry roared, observing Kian getting ready to strike at Ripley. "He's mine."

Ripley's attention was momentarily diverted as he swung around to counterattack Kian just as Kian's sword bore down on him, which fortunately gave Henry enough time to steady himself and move from his precarious position at the water's edge. Kian then, giving way to Henry's plea, raised his sword in the air and backed up. Ripley spun back around to face Henry and, upon observing the blood seeping from his left arm, he grinned.

"It's true what they say about you," he laughed callously. "Proud and arrogant, now breathe your last breath Henry Morton," he growled, lunging at Henry once more with brutal ferocity.

This time however, Henry was able to counterattack and, at the same time, threw a handful of grit up into Ripley's face, knocking him off balance. Ripley staggered backwards just as Henry thrust his sword forward and pierced Ripley's left shoulder. Ripley winced, blinking furiously to clear his eyes and spitting debris from his mouth. Henry withdrew his sword, immediately thrusting forward again. This time Ripley was ready and he blocked Henry, forcing his sword upwards. Ripley hastily released his hold and thrusted his own sword forward but Henry was too quick. He stepped back, bringing his sword down and sliced into Ripley's arm, causing him to drop his weapon.

"Pick it up," Henry screamed. He would never fight an unarmed man.

Ripley hastily retrieved his sword from the ground and moved backwards, gripping his wounded arm. He observed that two of his thugs now lay dead on the ground. Kian and Arlen were still fighting the other two as Edwin dealt with his wounded soldier. The other two Crown soldiers stood back watching in awe as Kian and Arlen powered forward, completely overpowering their miserable opponents. The thugs knew the battle was lost and were both frantically looking for a way out. Kian gestured for the Crown soldiers to join in the fight and finish these men off once and for all. He had absolutely no intention of letting them get away.

Henry and Ripley reconvened their assault upon each other. Ripley was weakening. His left shoulder gushed blood and his right fighting arm was gravely wounded. However, the determination of the two men was unrelenting, neither were willing to succumb to the growing sense of utter exhaustion that was consuming them both as they fought on, blow after blow.

Ripley's men now all lay dead on the ground. Kian roughly pulled Arlen back as he advanced to aid Henry.

"No," he yelled. "He needs to finish this himself."

"But he's going to collapse," Arlen cried, observing Henry desperately struggling to maintain his stance.

"Let him do this," Kian urged, holding tightly on to Arlen's arm.

Henry suddenly steadied himself, lurching forward in one final desperate attempt. Rallying all of his remaining strength he pushed Ripley backwards and drove his own sword forward until it finally found its target deep in Ripley's chest. Ripley froze. He looked down at the weapon piercing his body before looking up at Henry, his eyes wide and cold, registering the defeat. Henry sharply twisted his sword that was still embedded in Ripley's chest and allowed the warm blood to run down the fuller before swiftly and mercilessly withdrawing it. Ripley fell to his knees before falling forward, dead at Henry's feet – no longer his arch nemesis. Henry immediately collapsed to his own knees, utterly and totally exhausted. Cupping his face in his bloody hands he was barely able to hold himself up right.

Arlen sped over to his position, holding out his hand in order to aid him back to his feet.

"Give me a minute," Henry moaned, falling back onto his ankles, depleted of all energy.

"You are wounded," Arlen exclaimed, removing his surcoat and hastily tearing at the sleeve of his shirt to use as a makeshift bandage.

Henry tentatively removed his own surcoat and doublet and allowed Arlen to tightly tie the cloth around his left arm in order to stem the flow of blood.

"Are you alright Henry?" Arlen asked, gravely concerned that Henry's body was unable to take much more of this punishing abuse.

"I will be," Henry breathed, holding on to Arlen's arm for support. "I will be … We need to get back to Trevelyan House."

"Yes," Arlen confirmed anxiously. "I'm concerned for the women."

Edwin and the Crown soldiers were busy holding back the growing crowds on the quayside. Edwin shouted over to Arlen.

"You should make haste, word travels fast here in Trevelyan. I shall deal with the dead bodies."

Kian as efficient as ever had already retrieved the horses and was mounted ready to go.

"Yes, thank you Edwin," Arlen replied, carefully aiding Henry to his feet.

Henry's whole body ached terribly, he was utterly exhausted. The slash across his upper body was still raw and it stung dreadfully as he mounted his horse. He winced, laying his hand to his chest in pain.

"Are you sure you are alright Henry?"

"I have to be Arlen, I have to be," Henry replied. "Let's finish this once and for all," he said, strenuously pulling on the reins of his horse and heading back in the direction of Trevelyan House.

Chapter 29

Kat paced impatiently up and down the chapel in West Trevelyan, the hem of her dark blue linen dress brushed against the edges of the pews as she swept along the aisle. It had been over an hour since she had left Iris to go back into the house alone. She was becoming increasingly anxious for any word. Father Peter remained on his knees, praying in silence at the altar.

"Something is wrong," she grumbled, coming to an abrupt stop beside the priest. "Iris should have come to us by now, Devil's Angel is swift."

"Calm yourself Kat, they may not have taken any wine, it is still early," the priest reassured her, slowly rising to his feet and rubbing at his sore knees.

"I should go to her, I'm sure I could evade the soldier," Kat suggested, dismissing the priest's words with a casual wave of her hand.

She stared intensely at Father Peter as if pleading for any kind of sanction.

"For what purpose?" he replied, shaking his head. "No, you would only provoke suspicion and probably get yourself into a lot of trouble at the same time. Kat, please give Iris time, besides Henry and Arlen will be returning soon and it will all be over."

"Yes, as long as nothing as gone wrong at the quayside," she moaned, beginning to impatiently pace the aisle once more. "Oh Father, I'm getting awfully worried, we can't just sit around doing nothing."

"Please Kat, you are not helping," the priest replied. He too was becoming increasingly anxious, although he was trying desperately hard not to show it as he was fearful as to what action Kat might decide to take.

All of a sudden their attention was diverted to what sounded like a horse and cart drawing up to the front of the chapel.

"Quick Kat to the vestry, it is better if we are not seen," the priest urged, hastily ushering Kat towards the small room at the back of the chapel.

Leaving the door slightly ajar, Father Peter peered from the crack, waiting apprehensively for someone to enter.

Beatrice Ainsworth burst through the front doors of the chapel. She looked flushed and frightened and was shaking nervously as she quickly glanced around the space, breathing a sigh of relief upon believing the chapel to be empty. She immediately made her way over to the wall at the back of the altar, frantically pressing it with the palm of her hands. Up and down and from one side to the other. Father Peter watched her curiously.

"What in God's name is she doing?" he muttered quietly to himself.

Beatrice repeated the action again, this time moving more slowly and carefully feeling the wall as she went. Suddenly, a faint clicking sound was heard as a small hidden panel in the far-left corner of the wall sprung open.

"Thank God," she breathed, opening the panel wider and peering into the empty damp darkness.

Hastily retrieving a candle from the alcove above, she crouched down and immediately disappeared inside the wall.

Father Peter stepped from the vestry. Kat was right behind him.

"Well, what do you know," he mused, rubbing at his chin. "A priest hole, it must lead directly to Trevelyan House."

"That was the woman at the Kilve Palace, the one that took Henry. I'm sure of it," Kat declared, peering curiously into the hole in the wall. "What on earth is she doing here?"

"Beatrice Ainsworth," the priest added, feeling slightly perturbed. "I have absolutely no idea, but it can't be good news. Something must have gone wrong at the Fisherman's cottage. Quick Kat a candle, we must pursue her at once."

Kat didn't hesitate in grabbing a candle from the alcove on the opposite side of the wall and swiftly handed it to Father Peter. Her thoughts suddenly turned to Arlen, praying to God he was not hurt as she followed the priest into the dark narrow tunnel.

Iris sat slightly nervously on a chair opposite Lady Howard in the drawing room of Trevelyan House. She had not spoken or moved since Sebastian had insisted that she join them. Frustratingly staring down at an open book on her lap, of which she had not read a single word, she glanced up at the untouched decanter of wine on the side table beneath the window.

"Would you like a glass?" Lady Howard asked, observing Iris staring at the wine. "It is almost lunch time," she said, placing her needlework beside her on the chair and rubbing her tired eyes.

"No thank you," Iris replied, returning to stare aimlessly at the book.

"Well, I think I shall have one," Sebastian declared, confidently striding back into the room.

He had been drifting in and out all morning anxiously hovering at the entrance to the house; impatiently waiting for the arrival of the King.

"Grandmother?" he asked, lifting the decanter in the air.

"No thank you, my dear," she replied, leisurely leaning back in her chair. "Sebastian, please come and sit, the King shall arrive in due course I am sure of it. Pacing up and down will not make it happen any sooner my boy."

Sebastian let out a disgruntled groan before filling his glass almost to the brim and swallowing the contents down in one. He then refilled his glass before sitting uncomfortably close to Iris and placing his hand to her knee. Iris resisted the urge to pull away, fearful it would make him angry; what she wanted now was for him to relax and drink the wine. Tossing down the second glass, he casually draped his arm around her shoulder. No matter how hard Iris tried, she was unable to prevent herself from tensing at his unwanted touch. Sebastian cruelly dug his fingers into the top of her arm as a warning.

"I shall leave you alone for a while," Lady Howard declared cheerfully, slowly rising from her chair. "Allow you to get to know one another a little better," she smiled.

"No, please don't go," Iris blurted out nervously, attempting to rise herself.

Things were not going quite as she had envisaged. She suddenly wished she had accompanied Kat to the chapel. Sebastian forced her back down, pressing his fingers punishingly harder into her arm. Iris winced.

"It's alright my dear, you must allow Sebastian to love you," Lady Howard smiled, patting her grandson affectionately on the shoulder. "After all he is to be your husband my dear."

Just as Lady Howard neared the door to leave, she turned to a faint knocking noise which appeared to be coming from inside the wall.

"What on earth is that?" she asked, instantly turning on her heels and glancing over at Sebastian.

Sebastian jumped to his feet, pressing his ear to the wall.

"It sounds like Beatrice," he exclaimed, raising his hand in order to silence Lady Howard.

He replaced his ear to the wall once again, straining to hear what Beatrice was saying.

"She says there is a lever … the fireplace … under the mantle."

Lady Howard proceeded to the fireplace, feeling under the mantelpiece. Much to her surprise she discovered a tiny lever protruding from the wall and, catching her finger above it, she gently pressed it down. A faint clicking sound was heard before Beatrice literally fell through a small panel in the wall. Lady Howard gasped. Sebastian held out his hand to aid Beatrice to her feet. Iris stared in horror. *This cannot be good news*, she thought to herself, jumping to her feet and feeling for the dagger beneath her skirts.

"Beatrice, what in God's name are you doing here?" Sebastian exclaimed, suddenly stumbling backwards and gripping onto the mantelpiece in order to steady himself.

He suddenly felt extraordinary dizzy.

Iris guessed that the Devil's Angel was starting to take effect, or at least she hoped it was.

"Ripley has been discovered," Beatrice blurted out breathless, her coarse woollen russet dress completely covered in cobwebs. "I returned from Kingslea this morning with Phillip; he is at the chapel. We reached the fisherman's cottage and I observed Crown soldiers clearing the streets. There were Crown Knights too, it was Henry Morton … he is still alive."

Iris pulled the dagger from her skirts and, gripping the hilt tightly, she swiftly backed up towards the door. The room fell into an eerie silence as the occupants all turned to glare in her direction.

"You knew, didn't you? You scheming bitch," Sebastian snarled angrily through clenched teeth, his nostrils flared.

His head felt heavy and he was having trouble focusing. He shook his head furiously.

Lady Howard came to his aid. "What's wrong my dear?" she asked, frantically gripping onto Sebastian's arm.

"I suddenly feel quite faint," he murmured, glancing over at the decanter of wine on the side table. "What have you done to me?" he hissed, staring angrily over at Iris.

"Poisoned you," Iris screamed back, backing herself further against the door and desperately feeling for the door handle in order to make her escape.

She raised the dagger up in front of her, wildly waving it at Sebastian. "You are a monster Sebastian Howard, and I shall never marry you," she cried out, her hand trembling.

Sebastian lurched towards Iris, his arms raised as if about to strangle her. Iris thrust the dagger forward, pressing it as hard as she could into his shoulder.

"No!" Lady Howard screamed, frantically pushing Iris back against the door.

Beatrice swiftly stepped out of the way as Sebastian staggered backwards, almost falling to the floor, with the dagger still protruding from his shoulder. Lady Howard successfully steadied him; observing that the dagger had fortunately only grazed him as she pulled it from his flesh. Sebastian furiously shook his head again in a desperate attempt to clear it. The Devil's Angel was beginning to dampen his senses.

"And you shall never marry Henry Morton," he growled hatefully, retrieving the dagger from his grandmother. Precariously raising his arm and using all of his remaining strength, he lunged forward again towards Iris. Iris froze, backing herself up against the door. She closed her eyes as Sebastian mercilessly brought the dagger down upon her.

Kat and Father Peter emerged from the tunnel in the nick of time. Father Peter literally flung himself between Iris and Sebastian as the sharp blade of the dagger bore down and pierced the priest's chest. Sebastian fell against the priest, his body weight driving the dagger deeper as the two men fell back against Iris causing her to be crushed against the door before all three bodies fell tangled together on the floor.

Sebastian still had his hand firmly on the hilt of the dagger. He slowly managed to pull it from the priest's chest and raised his arm one final time, determined not to miss his target again. Iris screamed. Kat however was far too quick-witted. She had already retrieved the poker from the fireplace and, wildly swinging it around, she hit Sebastian so hard that she knocked him triumphantly to the floor, out cold.

Beatrice watched in horror as the surreal drama played out in the room. It was now more than evident that she and her brother were not going to find salvation here at Trevelyan House.

"We must go," she uttered, barely above a whisper and pulling at the sleeve of Lady Howard's dress, whilst edging herself towards the panel in the wall. "Henry Morton will be here soon, all is lost Margaret, we must go."

Lady Howard stared down at her grandson, paralysed as if she were in some dreadful nightmare. Everything they had worked towards over the last few months and their new lives in Mercia, now lay ruined on the floor. Beatrice frantically pulled at her dress once again. Lady Howard finally turned, knowing it was all lost and, without looking back, hurriedly followed Beatrice into the priest hole. Thankful at least that she had employed Drake in procuring some insurance. Her mantra 'never leave anything to chance' nevermore apt.

Unfortunately, Iris and Kat were too distracted, attending to the priest to notice the two women crawling back into the panel in the wall.

"Lady Howard," Iris groaned moments later as she cradled the dying priest in her arms.

Kat quickly spun around. The room ... it was empty. "She's gone," Kat declared, already halfway through the opening in the wall. "I must go after her Iris; she has the pearls."

"No, Kat it's too dangerous, let her go." Iris cried after her.

But it was too late, Kat had already disappeared out of sight.

Kat scurried along the damp narrow passage. She could just about make out the faint light of a candle flickering and bouncing off the walls only yards ahead of her. Lady Howard moved slowly as the journey back to the chapel was uphill. Kat was young and nimble and very quickly shortened the gap between herself and the two women. Beatrice emerged first from the tunnel and, just as she turned to aid Lady Howard, Kat grabbed onto the old woman's skirts and pulled her backwards. Lady Howard let out a high-pitched scream as Kat roughly grappled with her in the tunnel. Lady Howard feebly kicked and scrambled to break free, but Kat was far too strong and gripped tightly, pulling her further backwards.

"Margaret," Beatrice screamed frantically. "Here, grab my hand."

Lady Howard eventually managed to reach out and grab at Beatrice's hand as the two women finally fell through the panel together. Kat was just about to jump back onto her feet when a heavy thud to the back of her head caused her to collapse forward and fall heavily to the floor. Beatrice stood above her clutching a large silver chalice in her hands.

"Quickly Margaret, we must go," Beatrice urged, throwing the chalice aside and pulling Lady Howard to her feet. The old lady was clearly very shaken. They both fled the chapel at once, leaving Kat motionless on the ground and blood seeping from a wound to the back of her head.

Henry burst into the drawing room of Trevelyan House moments later followed by two Crown soldiers who were completely oblivious to what had been going on behind the closed doors. Iris was still cradling the priest in her arms and Sebastian Howard lay lifeless in a puddle of his own blood next to her on the floor. Henry instantly fell to his knees beside Iris.

"Iris, my love, please tell me you are not hurt?" he implored, observing her blood-soaked dress.

"I'm not hurt my love, Father Peter, he saved my life," she sniffed, pulling the priest to her breast. "Please don't die Father Peter, I need you," she whimpered, tears flowing freely down her face.

"I fear there is nothing to prevent it my child," he breathed feebly, clutching his hand to hers. "God, it seems, has allowed me to finally atone for my sins. I am happy to die Iris, please don't mourn for me. I had a heavy debt to repay and now it has been done. I leave this world a happy man."

"No, please," Iris pleaded, now sobbing uncontrollably as the priest slipped gently away in her arms.

Henry lovingly embraced Iris, he too was surprisingly moved by the priest's passing.

Arlen and Kian sped into the drawing room moments later having scoured the rest of the house.

"Where's Kat?" Arlen asked, frantically glancing around the room.

Iris pointed to the open panel in the wall. "She went after Lady Howard and a woman called Beatrice … Lady Howard still has the pearls," Iris replied, gently laying the priest's head carefully on the floor as Henry aided her to her feet.

"Beatrice was here?" Henry growled, "I knew I had seen her on the quayside. They will be heading for the port, Ripley's ship."

"Quick," he shouted over to the Crown soldiers. "Get after them at once. They cannot be allowed to board that ship."

"Yes milord," the Crown soldiers replied simultaneously, hastily turning on their heels and heading for the door.

Arlen had not waited around to hear any explanations, he had already disappeared deep into the tunnel in pursuit of Kat.

"Fucking hell, he's still alive," Kian remarked, examining Sebastian Howard sprawled out on the floor.

"Who did this Iris?" he asked, inspecting the head wound.

"Kat, she was absolutely amazing," Iris replied. "He would have stabbed me if she hadn't reacted like lightening."

Kian grinned with a certain pride at the heroics of his sister, not before deliberately dropping Sebastian's head back onto the floor, hard.

"Good, I'm glad he's still alive," Henry added, "I don't want him to have such an easy death. He shall be executed in Kingslea as the traitorous bastard that he is and the whole of Mercia shall know of it."

Arlen was racing through the narrow tunnel. It was pitch black as he felt along the damp slimy walls on either side to guide him as he rushed along before finally emerging into the chapel at the other end. Upon adjusting his eyes to the light, he immediately observed Kat lying motionless on the floor with blood matted in her hair from a gash to the back of her head.

"No," he screamed, desperately falling to his knees beside her. "No, please God, not Kat."

Arlen carefully turned her over and cradled her gently in his arms, pulling her head up onto his lap. She was extremely pale and cold to the touch; he kissed her lips, softly whispering her name.

"Please Kat, I cannot lose you," he implored, tears welling up in his eyes as he sat lightly rocking her backwards and forwards muttering her name over and over again.

Very slowly Kat began to open her eyes. "Arlen … Oh Arlen, is that you?"

Arlen almost dropped her back to the floor, furiously jumping to his feet and quickly wiping away the tears from his eyes.

"You bloody foolish, reckless woman," he bellowed, angrily as she lay on the floor. "You could have been killed. Which part of 'do not do anything foolish' did you not understand … Well?"

"Arlen," Kat muttered, taken aback by his sudden angry outburst. Her senses were still dulled from the blow to her head.

"Don't you dare Arlen me; I'm so bloody annoyed with you Katherine. What if you had been killed, what then? Don't you know I'm in love with you woman?"

"I'm sorry Arlen; I didn't think," she said, pulling herself into a sitting position.

"No, you're damn right about that, you didn't think. I have a bloody good mind to take my belt to you," he shouted, pacing the chapel all red faced and with no purpose.

"Please Arlen, I promise never to do anything so reckless ever again."

"No, you damn well will not," he snapped. "Now get up."

With that Arlen charged from the chapel, slamming the door madly behind him before returning almost instantly. Kat smiled up at him sweetly.

"Smile all you like young lady, I'm still really annoyed with you," he grumbled, as he carefully aided her to her feet.

"Well, perhaps you can punish me later," she grinned suggestively.

Arlen glared at her crossly and grunted loudly before effortlessly scooping her up in his arms.

Kat giggled. "You have no need to carry me Arlen, I'm quite capable of walking."

"I know you are, I just want to that's all," he sniffed, shaking his head in disapproval before leaning down and planting a kiss to her lips. "Jesus Christ. I love you, Katherine Munro; don't you ever do anything like that to me again. Do you hear me?"

"Yes, Arlen, I promise. I love you too," she smiled, wrapping her arms around his neck and snuggling her head against his broad chest.

Arlen carried Kat down the hill from the chapel to the house, forcefully pushing past the Crown soldier at the entrance who muttered something about Kat not being permitted entry.

They made their way directly to the drawing room.

"Oh Kat," Iris cried, as they entered. "Are you alright?"

"I'll mend," she winced, tentatively rubbing the back of her head.

Arlen shot her a disapproving look, before releasing her to the ground. She stumbled slightly, still feeling a little dizzy. Arlen quickly pulled up a chair for her to sit.

"Fuck sake Sis," Kian grumbled, observing the blood on the back of her head.

"Oh, it's nothing Kian, please don't fuss," she laughed, dismissing him with a shake of her hand.

"It's not funny Kat, you could have been killed," Arlen complained, pouring himself a brandy.

"As much as it vexes me to agree with Arlen, he is absolutely right Sis, next time take heed."

"I can assure you Kian, there will not be a next time," Arlen added, leaning down and giving Kat a warning kiss to her lips.

"Oh, I do love you," she giggled, planting another to Arlen's lips in an attempt to finally quieten him.

The Crown soldier from the entrance suddenly appeared in the doorway, diverting everyone's attention, much to Kat's relief.

"The King milord," he said, addressing Henry with a deep bow.

"Thank you," Henry replied, quickly ushering everyone from the room and outside to the front of the house.

Kian grabbed hold of Sebastian's collar, unceremoniously dragging him along the floor and literally throwing him out on to the ground in front of them all at the entrance.

The King and his entourage were already fast approaching the house. Lord Douglas Barlett rode beside the King. He smiled broadly upon observing the welcome party looking dishevelled and bloody but thankfully all well. He was also rather shocked, but not completely surprised, to see Henry Morton alive and well. The King however had his eyes fixed firmly upon Iris, as the riders all came to a halt. Sebastian groaned on the floor. Raising his head slightly, he was still dazed but fully aware of the position he now found himself in. Scrabbling to his knees he began to pitifully beg for mercy. Kian happily kicked him hard in the back to shut him up, causing him to fall forward face down in the dirt.

"Stay down you fucking traitor," he hissed, placing a firm foot to his back.

Henry moved forward, grabbing a handful of Sebastian's hair and yanking his head up from the ground in order to face the King.

"Your Majesty," he said with a deep bow. "The traitor behind the explosion in the Corridor." He then roughly released him back down into the dirt.

"And your Majesty … may I present your daughter, Iris," he continued, stretching out his hand for Iris to step forward.

"Henry," Kat whispered, holding out her hand and revealing a small velvet pochette. "The Vikrin pearls," she smiled. "I managed to pull them from Lady Howard's skirts before Beatrice knocked me out."

"Christ woman, you're bloody wonderful," Arlen exclaimed, scooping Kat up in his arms, swinging her wildly around and kissing her passionately as if no one were looking.

"Am I forgiven now?" she grinned, tightly wrapping her legs around his waist.

"Maybe," Arlen sighed, kissing her again.

Lord Barlett squirmed in his saddle and went a trifle hot under the collar. He raised a disapproving eyebrow at the sight of his son embracing and kissing a woman in public and in such an inappropriate manner, particularly in the presence of the King. The King however was completely oblivious to anything that was going on around him. He had not taken his eyes from Iris from the moment he first saw her. She was indeed the very image of her mother. Hastily dismounting his horse, he moved tentatively towards her.

"Iris," he whispered, tears filling his eyes. "Is it truly you, my darling?"

"Yes Father," she replied, tears filling her own eyes as she flung herself up at him.

The King wrapped his arms tightly around her. Everyone stared, lost in utter admiration for the King and his beautiful daughter, finally united.

Chapter 30

It was early morning when Henry and Arlen stood at the tower prison in Kingslea, a bitter cold wind whirling around the grey stone courtyard. Carpenters had been busy at work all week erecting a scaffold, the smell of freshly sawn timber filled the air. It had been just over a month since the capture of Sebastian Howard, but the King had insisted on delaying his trial even though it was a forgone conclusion. He had felt a prolonged stay in the tower could only add to Sebastian's current agonies and he certainly did not want any unpleasantness to detract from the opening of the annual balls and the introduction to the whole of Mercia of his daughter Iris.

Henry and Iris had been married in a private ceremony at the chapel within the Kilve Palace and the King bestowed them the title of Duke and Duchess of Trevelyan. The Privy Council were unanimous in declaring Henry Morton, Duke of Trevelyan and Master of the Crown Knights, successor to the throne of Mercia to rule as Lord Regent with Iris as his Queen until such time as they produced an heir, and said heir came of age. The King had initially favoured Henry and Iris to rule as King and Queen until death, but Henry had been quite insistent. Henry was also elevated to King's advisor to serve on the Privy Council. Lord Douglas Barlett maintained his position as Lord President of the Council and Lord Gilmore was elected Lord Keeper of the Privy Seal. Lord Gilmore however had yet to return to court due to his ill health, although it was thankfully improving daily. Gilmore had been awarded all properties and lands owed by Lord Edward Bentley, compensation for his wrongful imprisonment. Lord Ainsworth had been stripped of his title, Moorgate Hall and all its lands. He had however been granted permission to keep his wood mill in Cambrian with his family being released on licence. Rothtir Hall, Trevelyan House and Moorgate Hall were now all under the ownership of the Crown.

It was unusually chilly for the time of year; Henry tugged his cloak tightly around his shoulders. The courtyard was empty, the chief yeoman warder not yet having opened the doors to the viewing public. The impending executions were creating quite a crowd with many attendees travelling from Trevelyan to witness the end of the traitor who had so ruthlessly devastated their town.

"Where is Edwin?" Henry asked, watching as the execution party exited the tower and began to assemble on the scaffold.

"He has taken a post in Cambrian," Arlen replied, blowing into his hands to keep warm. "You know he is to marry Florence?"

"I do," Henry grinned, "I advised the King to allow it."

"You did?" Arlen replied, throwing his friend a broad smile.

"Well, it was the least I could do. Edwin played a large part in bringing Howard to justice, and besides, he did rather get you out of a sticky situation," Henry added with a laugh.

"Yes, he did indeed," Arlen replied, relief in his voice. "Henry, I have asked Kat to marry me."

"You have? That's wonderful news Arlen … Well what did she say?"

"She said yes of course, but she wants me to meet her son first. We are travelling with Kian to Corstir. We shall be married there with all her family, although I'm uncertain of the legality so we shall have another ceremony once we return to Wenlock. You will attend, won't you?"

"Yes, of course, besides I already have the best man speech written out, although it may need some slight alterations."

"Yes, quite." Arlen replied with a brief smile.

"And when do you return from Corstir?" Henry asked.

"Kat and I shall return before winter; I'm unsure of Kian's plans. I do believe he wishes to stay a little longer; it is his home after all."

"Yes, indeed it is. I shall miss the miserable bastard," Henry mused, more than he cared to say in fact.

407

"And what about you Henry?"

"Iris and I travel to Elmbridge tomorrow; Iris has not yet seen my family home. I commissioned the whole of the east wing to be refurbished in readiness for her arrival."

"The east wing? Were they not your mother's rooms?"

"Yes, indeed they were. My father shut them off after her death. They are quite the most spacious at Elmbridge and are positioned perfectly to provide an excellent view of the morning sunrise. They are my gift to Iris."

Their conversation came to an abrupt halt at the arrival of Guy and Gregory Bentley, Lord Bentley's two sons from his first marriage. It had been altogether clear that Lord Bentley had been oblivious to his wife's involvement with the Howards, but under Mercia law a husband's authority over his wife was a fundamental principle – married couples were legally one person. Lord Bentley's eldest son Guy had relentlessly petitioned the King for clemency, only to have it denied time and time again. The King refused to even hear their case.

"Your Grace," the two men said and addressed Henry with a deep bow.

Both men were of average height and build. Guy appeared much older than his years with thinning grey hair and deep brow lines. Henry concluded it was perhaps due to hours of study as he also appeared to be always squinting – a result of poor eyesight. Gregory was by far the more handsome of the two men, even considering the fact that he wore a patch over his left eye due to a childhood quarrel. Guy had never been able to forgive himself for injuring his brother and blindly devoted himself to Gregory, who, much like his father, lacked any intelligence or common sense. Guy on the other hand was exceedingly intelligent, having studied the law and not only Mercia law but also Norland and Vikrin law. He acted as chief advisor to his uncle, Robert Quinn, Duke of Glen Ivor, who had married his aunt, Lady Eleanor Bentley, sister to his father.

Quinn owned extensive lands in the north of Mercia as well as the Northern Isles and had a reputation for being an unscrupulous and ruthless man. Not often seen at court, regardless of the fact that he held a seat on the Privy Council, he tended to ignore most matters that did not have a direct effect on him. The loss of Bentley's estate and land however affected him greatly. He had, in all but name, lorded over the lands which bordered his own, whilst Edward Bentley resided at court. Henry was under no illusion that Guy and Gregory were not here to save their father but their family estate. He knew they hoped desperately to reverse the King's decision in awarding their lands to Lord Thomas Gilmore.

"Gentlemen," Henry replied, with a nod his head.

"Your Grace, do you bring us any news?" Guy asked urgently, clutching at an enormous pile of papers and journals.

"News?" Henry replied, feigning confusion.

"Yes, your Grace. I have again petitioned the King for a stay of execution. As I wrote, the law states that where in the case of a wife committing a crime the husband can only be sentenced once his wife has been found guilty, as you are well aware your Grace, Beatrice has not yet been apprehended therefore a sentence cannot be determined."

"Do you doubt her guilt, Guy?" Henry asked, deliberately evading the question.

"It is not for me to say your Grace, but the fact remains that until…"

Henry raised his hand, cutting Guy off mid flow.

"Guy, I'm sorry I bring no news. The King signed the order of execution for your father and the confiscation of his lands weeks ago. I know not of any other petition or that the King has agreed any stay of execution. I'm sorry Guy there is absolutely nothing I can do."

"You will be sorry," Gregory snarled. "You just wait until Quinn hears of this travesty."

"Do you threaten me sir?" Henry asked glaring at Gregory, his tone sharp.

"No, your Grace, please forgive my brother," Guy pleaded, hastily pulling Gregory aside and throwing him a warning look. "He knows not what he says, please forgive us," he repeated, bowing his head and swiftly moving away from Henry and Arlen to the opposite end of the courtyard. Gregory however was still staring wildly at Henry.

"Christ, that Gregory Bentley is as mad as a box of frogs," Arlen declared, watching as the brothers walked away across the grey cobbles.

"Gregory may well be," Henry confirmed, "but Guy is most certainly not. He is absolutely right in what he says, I read his petition."

"Christ Henry, then why …?"

"The King would not be moved; he became quite animated on the subject in fact. Quinn was the Master of the Crown Knights stationed in Glen Ivor when Osbert and Caroline fled there. It was Quinn who discovered the King and personally accompanied him back to Kingslea and revealed Caroline's whereabouts. Osbert has always had a hatred for Quinn, even more so now he knows the awful truth."

"Even so Henry, Bentley's execution is unlawful," Arlen muttered under his breath.

"Yes, indeed," Henry replied, exhaling loudly. "And without the law there is only tyranny. Your father and I both believe the King has made a poor judgement here. It has certainly vexed the Privy Council greatly. But let us say no more on the matter, at least for the time being," Henry insisted, as the large wooden doors to the courtyard finally swung open.

The sizeable crowd were surprisingly sombre and filed in, in an orderly manner. Henry doubted that there were many among them that were attending just out of morbid curiosity. There was a real sense of sadness and grief within the high stone walls of the tower courtyard, old and young alike. Finally, the large doors were closed shut as the sombre space very quickly reached its capacity. The crowd, all standing in relative silence, waited patiently for the proceedings to commence. The whistling of the bitter cold wind swirling around the yard added to the sorrowful atmosphere.

Edward Bentley was the first to be brought out. The old man looked dreadfully ill. His white hair was hidden under a cloth cap and his long linen smock was stained with all manner of bodily fluids. He just about managed to hold his head high and walk unaided, which in itself appeared to be a miracle judging by his frail appearance. His stance only faltered at the sight of his two sons.

"Poor old Bastard," Arlen whispered, shaking his head in sympathy. Beatrice, it seemed, had indeed beguiled the foolish old man.

Bentley slowly climbed the steps of the scaffold, stumbling on the final step. The Bishop of Kingslea gripped hold of his arm to steady him. The old man smiled with appreciation and thanked the bishop for his assistance.

"Do you wish to speak?" the bishop asked with pity in his voice.

The old man nodded and turned tentatively to face the melancholy crowd, all of whom remained silent.

"Good people of Mercia, I come hither to die. I know not of any crime against you committed by my hand, I am and always have been your most loyal servant. However, I have been judged guilty and sentenced to die, so shall speak no more against it. I pray for the King, the most gracious of all sovereigns, I pray for Mercia, our glorious land and I ask you all to pray for me, the most wretched of men. O Lord have mercy on my soul."

Bentley then turned and paid the executioner, forgiving him for what he was about to do, before courageously kneeling in silent prayer and accepting his fate with good grace. Upon finishing his prayers, he gently lay his head down on the block with his arms outstretched. The bishop continued to pray aloud as the executioner efficiently raised his axe and skilfully brought it down, slicing off the pitiful old man's head with one almighty blow.

A loud gasp resonated around the courtyard as the severed head rolled to the floor. The crowd, finally finding their voices, jeered loudly as Lord Edward Bentley's body was placed in a plain wooden coffin.

Henry had not taken his eyes from Bentley's sons as they stared in horror at their father's execution, crossing themselves before turning to leave the dismal courtyard. Gregory shot Henry a menacing look through the crowd as he furiously exited behind his brother.

"My God, that was all over very quickly," Arlen remarked, also crossing himself. "No going back now." he sighed.

Henry remained silent.

There was a sudden burst of activity on the scaffold as Bentley's coffin was swiftly carried away. Fresh sawdust and straw were being hastily scattered over the floor to give the pretence that nothing had occurred, even though Bentley's fresh blood was already seeping through the wooden boards and dripping onto the grey stone cobbles beneath.

Moments later Sebastian Howard appeared at the door of the tower; his appearance showed signs of brutal torture. He was struggling to walk.

The crowd suddenly erupted, taunting and heckling the monstrous traitor. Their desire for bloodthirsty revenge was now more than evident.

"Jesus Christ Henry, what on earth have they done to him?" Arlen asked, visibly shocked by Sebastian's appalling state.

"I have no idea, but I imagine whatever they have done was on the King's orders," Henry replied. Unconcerned for Howard himself, he was alarmed at the ease of which Mercia resorted back to brutal torture as an acceptable form of punishment. "The King's need for retribution is unrelenting it seems," he added gravely.

Sebastian was barely able to scramble up the steps of the scaffold. The raucous call of the crowd was deafening; jeering and baiting him as he fell up onto the freshly sawn boards. The bishop raised his arms, appealing for quiet and calm as a muted hush rippled amongst the spectators.

"Do you wish to speak?" he muttered at Sebastian on his knees, indifferent to his suffering.

"Yes," Sebastian croaked, defiant to the end and mustering all of his strength to pull himself upright.

"I see you have all come to witness my end. Well let me reassure you Mercia, this is not the end, vengeance shall be ..."

The crowd didn't allow him to finish; they erupted like an angry mob, pushing themselves forward towards the scaffold, all desperate to reap their own revenge upon Lord Sebastian Howard.

"Death to the traitor," rang out around the grey stone courtyard.

The Crown soldiers circling the perimeter hastily raised their swords as a stark warning to stay back. The crowd hastily retreated in panic.

Sebastian's momentary bravado seemed to suddenly desert him as his dazzling blue eyes darted around the courtyard like a terrified animal caught in a trap. He tried to retreat from the scaffold. Two tower guards grabbed at his arms and pushed him back down onto his knees. The bishop began to pray frantically, terrified for his own life as the angry crowd showed no sign of abating. The proceedings were very quickly spiralling out of control; the crowd were becoming evermore animated. Sebastian's purse, full of coin, dropped onto the scaffold. One of the tower guards hurriedly picked it up and threw it at the executioner in an attempt to hasten the fiasco playing out in front of him. Sebastian screamed and refused to lower his head to the block. The bishop continued praying and reassured the executioner that he was forgiven for what he was about to do; he urged the man to get on with it. The guards vigorously pinned Sebastian down, forcing his miserable head to the block and pulling and stretching out his arms. All the time Sebastian resisted, screaming louder. The executioner panicked and hastily brought down his axe hard in an attempt to end the travesty. The first blow missed Sebastian's neck and sliced through his shoulder. He let out a blood-curdling scream as he continued to struggle against the guards who were now showered in his blood. The crowd bellowed with excitement as the axe came down again, thankfully finding its target this time. The head of Sebastian Howard rolled unceremoniously onto the scaffold floor to the thunderous cheer of the watching crowd.

"Jesus Christ," Arlen moaned, disturbed by the harrowing scene and holding a handkerchief to his mouth.

Henry remained silent and expressionless, staring at the severed head on the scaffold and contemplating Sebastian's final words.

* * *

Mrs Brooke outdid herself for the farewell dinner at Barlett House. Everyone agreed it was utterly delicious. The meal consisted of crayfish followed by duck, then cheese and wafers, pomegranates and figs. Lord Barlett opened a bottle or two of his finest Mercia wine and one of his treasured bottles of vintage Vikrin brandy. Kat rivalled her brother in entertaining the table with a certain aplomb, causing much laughter and occasional blushing from Iris and Lady Barlett particularly, as she was not so accustomed to Kat's frank assessment of the world. Arlen watched Kat with immense pride, overjoyed that his father and mother had not only accepted his unconventional choice of wife but genuinely rejoiced at the news. Kian, not one to be outdone, concluded the evening with one of his many stories from the time before he was condemned to a life of servitude at Chesterford. Henry strongly objected to the term servitude and insisted it was quite the opposite, but the ladies all sided with Kian. Henry finally relented to more roars of laughter and merriment.

The ladies retired soon after, followed by Lord Barlett, leaving Henry, Arlen, and Kian alone in the drawing room to finish of the last of the excellent brandy.

"Father tells me that the King has commissioned the royal barge so you may travel to Elmbridge by river," Arlen said, sinking down into an easy chair with a glass of brandy.

"Yes indeed," Henry confirmed. "The house is best viewed from the river; I do hope Iris will like her new home."

"What's not to like?" Kian huffed, busily munching on a fig. "It's probably the finest house in Mercia, and we have visited quite a few in the last few months, one way and another."

"Yes, we have indeed," Henry replied sounding amused. "Far too many in fact … Do you know when you might return from Corstir Kian?"

"I'm not sure, probably not until I become desperate for a decent jug of ale. Why Henry, will you miss me? … I know you will, Arlen has already told me so." Kian laughed loudly.

Arlen furiously shook his head in denial, throwing Kian a disapproving look. "I promise you Henry I have not said one single word."

Kian laughed even louder and jumped up from his seat in order to refill his glass with more brandy.

"Yes, I shall miss you, you grumpy bastard," Henry confirmed. "Particularly once I am back at court and need to know who is plotting and scheming."

"Oh, that's fucking great, it seems I'm only good for the whispers and rumours," he huffed, settling back down into his chair.

"You know full well I shall miss you both very much. You are my dearest friends … no, not just friends, brothers, and never more so than in recent weeks. I could not have done any of it without you … I owe you both my life," Henry replied, the sincerity in his tone was unquestionable.

"We have had some fucking good times, haven't we?" Kian mused, placing a loving hand to Henry's arm. "And some pretty scary ones too," he concluded with a shrug of his shoulders and a small smile.

"Yes indeed," Henry agreed, placing his hand to Kian's.

"Henry, do you believe all shall be well in Mercia now?" Arlen asked, contemplating the future for a moment. "We still have no idea of the whereabouts of Lady Howard and the Ainsworth's since they fled the chapel. They must still be in Mercia somewhere; we know they didn't board Ripley's ship. Then there is this business with Bentley and his estate."

"I have absolutely no idea Arlen, but let us hope so, let us very much hope so," Henry said, raising his glass.

The three men raised their glasses to each other before finishing off the remains of the excellent vintage Vikrin brandy.

Chapter 31

Seven months later.

A scrawny young boy, no more than nine or ten years old with a mop of curly dark hair, ran up and down the freezing cold waterfront at Salford Priory, a small fishing village on the southwest coast of Mercia. His elderly grandfather sat on the quayside repairing his old fishing nets and pulling his moth-eaten cloak tightly around his shoulders to keep out the biting cold wind coming off the ocean.

"Is it time for breakfast yet Grandfather? I'm hungry," the young boy grumbled, aimlessly breaking the ice off the top of a water barrel with a piece of driftwood that he had retrieved from the beach.

"You are always hungry boy, you shall eat your poor mother out of house and home," his grandfather laughed, ruffling the boy's hair with affection as he came to a stop beside the old man.

The young boy lowered his head and kicked at the sand with his battered boots that had long since lost their laces. His stomach grumbled loudly.

"Come here boy," the old man said, producing a small parcel from his pocket. "Here have this, but don't tell your mother."

The young boy felt a pang of guilt. His grandfather was always giving him his own food and going without, but the young boy was so hungry he couldn't resist the temptation and accepted the parcel in an instant, giving his grandfather a huge smile in thanks.

"Thank you, Grandfather," he muttered, already devouring the meagre slice of bread and lump of mouldy cheese contained within.

"It be March tomorrow boy," the old man mused, neatly tying up his fishing nets.

"Springtime," the young boy declared.

"Yes," his grandfather replied. "Let's hope we have ... well I'll be damned," he exclaimed, staring out to sea.

"What is it Grandfather?" the young boy asked, following the old man's gaze out over the water.

"Another Vikrin ship," the old man declared, rubbing his tired eyes as if to ensure he was not dreaming.

"Another," the boy enquired. "Why, when did you see the first?"

"Only two days since … never in my long years have I ever seen such a ship in Salford Priory, now would you believe it, two in as many days."

"How do you know it is a Vikrin Ship Grandfather?"

"Look boy," the old man replied, pointing towards the enormous craft. "The long prominent beak and the decoration beneath, it is of a phoenix."

"A phoenix?" the boy replied, shrugging his shoulders.

"Yes boy, a phoenix. An immortal mythical bird said to have risen from the flames of the Vikrin mountains over a thousand years ago."

The pair remained silent for a while, transfixed upon the colossal vessel sat proudly above the water.

"There be someone coming ashore, Grandfather," the young boy muttered, watching as a small rowing boat pulled away from the port side of the ship.

The old man and his grandson continued to watch curiously as the rowing boat was skilfully manoeuvred over the choppy waters towards the shoreline.

An elegant tall figure wearing a black cloak trimmed with fur, their face hidden under the hood, stepped from the boat onto the beach. They spoke briefly with the oarsman before he heaved his little boat back out onto the water. The person remained motionless, facing the ocean, watching as the rowing boat left the shoreline. Finally, picking up their bag they turned to face the small fishing village of Salford Priory.

"It's a lady Grandfather and she be coming this way," the small boy whispered nervously, positioning himself behind his grandfather.

The old man remained seated, still with all his fishing nets spread about him. He watched the woman intriguingly; the hood of her cloak fell from her head as a heavy gust of wind swirled around the deserted beach. She was beautiful in appearance – tall of stature with dark skin and dark oval shaped eyes; her raven black hair, long and sleek, was adorned with precious jewels. The black velvet cloak swished open as she walked, revealing a gown of sumptuous black brocade worn tightly to her womanly figure.

The young boy's mouth fell open as she effortlessly glided towards him and his grandfather as if she were merely floating on air.

"Are you a princess?" the young boy blurted out, mesmerised by the lady's exotic appearance.

"No," she smiled sweetly, observing the pair very closely. "But I'm very honoured that you should think so. My name is Pirjo de Castella and I am from Vikrin. I wonder if you might be able to help me with something?" she asked, her Vikrin accent, rich and melodious.

"Perhaps," the old man muttered, twisting one of his fishing nets around his fingers and attempting to appear aloof.

Pirjo grinned. "I can pay," she said, sounding amused. "Handsomely."

"How can we help then miss?" the old man replied after a noticeably short pause.

He shuffled nervously on his seat. His grandson still stood behind him clutching the old man's shoulders.

"I wondered if you have happened to observe another Vikrin ship laying anchor here in the last couple of days?"

"Aye, I have."

"And did anyone disembark?"

"Aye, three of um, one man and two women. One of the women had a babe in arms."

"Can you tell me, how did they quit this place?"

"A fine carriage come for 'em, not long after they arrived. A strange looking little man was there, he knew um alright."

"Do you know where I might be able to purchase a horse?" Pirjo asked, looking pleased with the old man's answers so far.

"A horse?" the old man laughed. "You won't get no horse around here miss."

"So how far to the nearest town where I might purchase a horse?"

"Well," the old man mused, rubbing his fingers over the white stubble on his chin. "You could go to Craymouth I suppose, you might get yourself an old nag from there."

"And how do I get to Craymouth?" she asked, beginning to lose a little patience with the old man.

"About ten mile in that direction," he sniffed, pointing east.

"She could catch the post train Grandfather," the young boy added nervously, lowering his head as soon as Pirjo made eye contact with him.

"Please tell me about the post train?" she asked, giving the boy a friendly smile.

The young boy clammed up and shuffled further behind his grandfather.

"Please," Pirjo continued, "I would be extremely grateful," she said, producing a black velvet pochette from beneath her cloak that was clearly filled with an abundance of coin.

"Go on then boy," his grandfather urged, his eyes wide staring at the purse. "Tell the lady."

"It's the carriage miss, that carries the post from Craymouth to Oystermouth. Folk use it if they wish to travel about," the young boy replied, pointing to a rounded hill rising up from the small village. "There miss, see the tor up on the moor, it passes by twice a day."

"And at what time does it travel back to Craymouth," Pirjo asked, tossing the purse from one hand to the other, teasing the old man cruelly.

"Midday," the old man replied instantly. "You best not delay though; the walk be a lot further than it looks."

"Thank you. Perhaps the young man could show me?" Pirjo asked, producing a gold Vikrin doubloon from the pochette.

The old man almost fell from his chair and the young boy's eyes grew wide as the pair stared, captivated by the shiny gold coin in Pirjo's hand.

"Oh, just one more thing," she said, baiting the pair with the coin. "Does the name Iris Westonhall mean anything to you?"

The old man laughed aloud. "Why, everyone in Mercia knows that name, it be the King's daughter. But it be DeBowscale now, Iris DeBowscale … or is it Duchess?" the old man mused for a moment, tilting his head upwards.

"The King's daughter!" Pirjo exclaimed, puzzled.

"Yes, that's right, his long-lost daughter. There been talk of nothing else these past few months."

Pirjo paused for a moment pondering the old man's words. She turned to look out over the water; the ship was now barely visible on the horizon. The old man had his eyes fixed firmly on the coin. One gold coin like that could feed his entire family for a whole year.

"Thank you," Pirjo replied, eventually tossing the doubloon at the old fisherman. "Will you take me to the tor young man?" she asked, smiling at the young boy.

He nervously shuffled further back behind his grandfather.

"Go on then lad, the lady won't bite," the old man laughed, roughly pulling his grandson from behind him in order to face Pirjo.

Then without another word, the young boy hastily picked up Pirjo's bag and swiftly scurried off in the direction of the moor. Pirjo pulled her black velvet cloak tightly around her shoulders before following on close behind him.

Chapter 32

Arlen gently tugged the bedcovers tightly over his shoulder having awoken and feeling cold. He stretched his arm out in order to embrace Kat only to discover that the bed was empty.

"Kat," he whispered into the darkness, slowly opening his eyes and adjusting them to the low light coming from the window.

Kat stood beside the window, staring out over the city in deep contemplation.

There were still many people milling around on the street below; Kingslea never really slept.

Arlen observed Kat stood in only her nightgown. "What's wrong my love?" he asked, rising from the bed and standing behind her, embracing her in his strong arms. She was shivering from the cold.

"My God Kat, you are so cold, what on earth is wrong?" he asked with concern in his voice.

Kat remained silent.

Arlen pulled her closer. "Is it because you are with child?" he asked tentatively, gently kissing her on the neck.

"How did you know?" Kat replied softly, resting her head back against his shoulder, thankful for the warmth of his body.

"We share a bed Kat; I know you have not bled since we returned from Corstir and your breasts are swollen," he replied, gently cupping her breasts in his hands. "Why have you not said? ... Don't you want this child?"

"Oh yes, Arlen I do with all my heart ... I'm just afraid."

"Afraid! Why on earth are you afraid? Did something happen when you gave birth to Little Kian?"

"No, nothing like that, it was an easy birth."

"Then what?"

Kat didn't answer.

"Kat please," Arlen urged, becoming increasingly worried by her continued silence on the matter.

"Oh Arlen, when I told Little Kian's father that I was with child he no longer desired me. I could not bear it if you did not desire me Arlen, I love you so very much," she sniffed, fighting back her tears.

Arlen heaved a deep sigh of relief and promptly turned his wife around to face him. He stared deep into her beautiful green eyes.

"Katherine Barlett, I love you so very much. There is not a man alive that could love a woman more, not a day goes by that I don't desire you. Knowing you are carrying my child has made me the happiest man in Mercia, I could never stop desiring you, loving you. Do you hear me."

"Do you really mean it Arlen?" Kat whispered, wiping her tears on the back of her hand and feeling a little foolish.

Arlen kissed her gently on each eye, then, scooping her up in his arms, he passionately kissed her on the lips. "Good God woman, of course I mean it and don't you ever doubt it. I have been waiting for you to confirm what I have suspected for weeks and weeks now." He placed his hands to her stomach, where there was already quite a bump. "Christ Kat, how long?"

"You were right Arlen; it was when we were in Corstir. I'm sorry I've been really rather silly, haven't I?" she smiled up at him coyly.

"Yes, you have. But no matter as long as all is well?"

"Yes, everything is perfect Arlen," Kat replied, pressing herself against him and planting a lingering kiss to his lips.

"I love you Katherine Barlett," Arlen breathed. "And besides I can prove that I still desire you," he grinned, pressing his erection firmly against her.

Kat let out a pleasing giggle. "Oh, I do love you too Arlen."

"Kat, we can still …"

"Yes of course."

"Well in that case wench, get back into bed because I'm going to show you just how much I desire you," he said, scooping her up in his arms and carrying her towards the bed.

Later that day Kat was sat in the kitchens at Barlett House with Mrs Brooke and other members of the household staff. In fact, Kat could be found most days in the kitchens when Arlen was at the palace. He frowned upon her spending too much time below stairs, but Kat was not used to sitting around with nothing practical to do and besides, she enjoyed the company.

After lots of congratulations at Kat's joyful news, then an awkward silence and then even more laughter, it seemed that everyone at Barlett House had suspected Kat to be with child for weeks but where waiting patiently for her to finally confirm it.

Mrs Brooke gave her an affectionate peck on the cheek. "Well done my dear, I'm so pleased for you and Master Arlen," she said with an exceedingly rare broad smile.

The kitchens then quickly settled back down into the routine of the day. The cook and the scullery maid were busy preparing vegetables for dinner, Kat sat sewing one of Arlen's shirts at the large table in the centre of the room and Mrs Brooke was busy going through the household accounts. They all jumped with a start as Arlen burst through the door looking extremely serious. The servants all instantly rose to their feet and Kat, without thinking, followed suit. Arlen glared at her with an exasperated expression on his face.

"I only briefly came down to speak with Mrs Brooke," she blurted out, holding Arlen's shirt behind her back.

"What?" Arlen exclaimed, not really listening to her phoney explanation.

"I promise Arlen I have only just come down," she repeated, convinced he was angry with her for being in the kitchens again.

Arlen continued to ignore her protestations. "Come up stairs Kat, I have something very important of which I need to speak to you about," he said sternly, darting his eyes over the other occupants of the kitchen.

Kat grimaced, glancing over at Mrs Brooke who tilted her head knowingly. Then, leaving the shirt on the kitchen table, she hastily followed Arlen up the stairs.

"I'm sorry Arlen," she continued as soon as they reached the drawing room, not allowing him time to speak and believing that he was about to scold her. "I know you don't like me going down in to the …"

Arlen cut her off with a shake of his hand. "Never mind all that now," he said, throwing her a disapproving look. "Kat, there has been a case of the sweats at court."

"The sweats?" Kat asked raising her shoulders. She had never heard of the sweats.

"Yes, it's a deadly fever and now you are with child I'm not going to take any chances. Ask Mrs Brooke to help you pack, we shall quit town first thing in the morning. I have already written to my father advising him not to return to court. The King is to resume residence at his house in the country until such time as it has receded. We shall stay at Wenlock. I have also written to Henry to ask if we can break our journey at Elmbridge."

"Oh, you have, that's wonderful," Kat replied, overjoyed at the prospect of seeing Iris.

"Yes, I thought that might please you. We can also share our good news at the same time," Arlen smiled broadly.

"And what with Iris so close to her time, you never know Arlen we may even get to meet the newest member of the Morton family," Kat mused, happily.

"Yes indeed, but now I must return to the palace to tie up some loose ends, but I shall return shortly."

Arlen kissed his wife lovingly on the cheek before turning to leave the room. "Oh, and Kat let Mrs Brooke deal with your packing, no lifting … do you hear me?"

"Yes Arlen, I promise," she replied, coyly.

Arlen suddenly turned back around; he moved towards Kat, this time planting a kiss to her lips. "I love you Katherine Barlett," he breathed.

"And I love you too Arlen Barlett," she replied with a huge beaming smile.

"Then stay out of the bloody kitchens," he scolded, and with that he was gone.

Kat twirled on the spot, giggling to herself.

* * *

Henry Morton sat at his desk in the spacious study at Elmbridge Hall surrounded by piles and piles of papers, all for his perusal. His recent decision to remain at Elmbridge in order to be close to Iris as her time drew closer seemed quite fortuitous having just read the first of the many letters that arrived daily from court. There had been an outbreak of the sweats. He fastidiously waded through the other correspondence and filed it in order of importance, until he read Arlen's letter, when he eagerly jumped up from his chair.

"Iris," he bellowed loudly from the study. "Arlen and Kat shall be arriving here tomorrow. Arlen writes that they have some exciting news … Iris, where are you?"

Iris was busy pacing up and down the magnificent grand hall. No matter what she did she could not get comfortable. If she sat her back ached, if she stood her back ached; walking seemed to give her at least a modicum of relief. The midwife had been on standby for days now, but the baby had showed no signs of making any kind of appearance.

The grand hall was higher than it was wide with an oak carved vaulted ceiling. Entered via the private rooms at the one end and with a screen passage at the other, it led to the kitchens with a minstrel's gallery above. The room contained an enormous fireplace, large enough for four strong men to stand in upright. The floor of polished Vikrin marble resembled a glistening frozen lake. Two large bay windows either side of the fireplace were framed by richly carved oak mouldings, whilst the remainder of the room was encased in dark oak panelling.

"I'm in here," Iris called out, upon hearing Henry shouting her name.

She shivered and suddenly realised how cold it was in the grand hall; a misty cloud appeared as she spoke.

Henry hurried into the hall; he could not help but smile at Iris's comical appearance as she slowly waddled towards him.

"Don't you dare laugh at me Henry Morton," she hissed. "Your child is causing me much vexation today."

"Oh, it's only my child now, is it?" Henry smiled, embracing her lovingly and planting a lingering kiss to her lips.

"Iris you are so cold," he exclaimed. "Come, let us get you into the warm at once."

"What was that about Arlen and Kat?" Iris asked, gripping tightly onto Henry's arm as he aided her from the room.

"They shall be arriving here tomorrow. There is a case of the sweats in Kingslea, your father has already quit the palace. Arlen writes that they have exciting news."

"Kat must be with child, oh, how wonderful."

"How do you know that?"

"What other exciting news could it be Henry?" Iris snapped back at him.

Henry shrugged his shoulders. He was certainly not going to question his wife's assumptions, not in her current irritated mood anyway.

"Would you like me to rub your back?" he whispered softly, gently nipping her ear with his teeth.

"Oh, yes please," Iris sighed, "I'm sorry Henry, I don't mean to be so disagreeable."

"I know you don't, but you can be as disagreeable as you like … come, I shall ask Mrs Burns to prepare a mulled wine."

Before they had time to quit the hall, Iris let out a loud gasp at a sudden gush of fluid from between her legs.

"What is it?" Henry cried out, holding tightly on to his wife.

Iris looked down at the floor. "I think the baby is coming Henry," she smiled up at him calmly.

Henry's usual calm composure however suddenly deserted him as he dashed for the door shouting for Mrs Burns, the Elmbridge Hall housekeeper, at the top of his voice. This time it was Iris's turn to smile as she watched him frantically pacing backwards and forwards, running his fingers through his thick dark hair.

"Henry, my love, please calm down, all is well."

Henry promptly returned to Iris's side, holding on to her hands. "What should I do?" he asked, brimming with a mix of excitement and apprehension.

"Just try to remain calm," Iris replied with a broad smile.

Mrs Burns flew into the hall followed closely by Kate. Iris had insisted her maid Kate join her at Elmbridge from Baines Abbey. Mrs Burns immediately understood the reason for her raucous recall.

"Kate," she bellowed, turning abruptly to the young woman and almost knocking her off her feet.

"Fetch the midwife at once and ask Lucy to bring clean water and cloth up to the mistress's room. Oh, and Kate ask someone to come at once and clean this floor."

Kate wildly nodded her head, looking totally overwhelmed by the flurry of demands.

"Now," Mrs Burns barked, causing Kate to run nervously from the room.

Mrs Burns then turned to address Iris. "Your Grace, we should get you to your bedchamber," she said, her tone now decidedly softened.

"Henry," Iris whispered, still holding tightly to his hands. "Will you help me?"

"Yes, of course my darling," he replied, gripping hold of her arm and accompanying her from the room.

Upon reaching the bedchamber Mrs Burns efficiently took charge of the situation, taking Iris's arm from Henry and leading her inside the bedchamber.

"Your Grace," she said, turning with a small curtsey before literally shutting the door in his face.

Henry was clearly not needed at this moment in time. However, he remained on the landing, pacing up and down and continually running his fingers through his hair causing it to stand up on end. The midwife arrived about ten minutes later closely followed by Kate. Numerous other female servants came and went carrying bowls of water and clean cloth. Mrs Burns emerged from the bedchamber a short while later.

"Your Grace, all is well. The midwife is very happy … but it is likely to be quite some time yet."

Henry got the distinct impression he was being told in no uncertain terms to stop pacing the landing. He had absolutely no knowledge of the intricacies of childbirth and was quite sure he didn't want to. He was however under no illusion as to it being an extremely dangerous time for a woman and if Iris was vexed with him pacing up and down, he was more than happy to quit at once.

"Thank you, Mrs Burns, I shall be in my study," he replied, heading directly for the stairs.

Afternoon turned to evening and evening turned to night. The house remained quiet and calm. Henry ate his dinner in his study and at some point after that fell asleep slumped over his desk. It was well after midnight when he was awoken by a loud moaning sound coming from the east wing. He instantly jumped up from his chair, knocking all his neatly piled papers from the desk onto the floor. Rushing towards the door he bolted up the stairs, three steps at a time as the loud moaning sound was proceeded by short, panty breaths. Henry assumed his previous position on the landing pacing up and down. Nobody could compel him to desert his post this time. The moaning and panting seemed to go on for hours. Henry resorted to sitting on the top stair, where the young hall boy found him as he was about to start the first of his daily chores, cleaning the stairs. Henry reemployed the lad and asked him to fetch a glass and a decanter of brandy.

Iris's moaning then turned to grunting. Henry continued to wait patiently on the stairs for what felt like an eternity, until all of a sudden, the room fell silent. Iris had ceased her grunting and panting; the other women inside the room were not talking. Henry jumped up from his position and headed directly for the bedchamber door, convinced that something was wrong. Suddenly, the loud joyous cry of a newborn baby filled the whole house. Henry stepped backwards from the door, taking in a deep breath before letting it out and cupping his face in his hands, ecstatic.

"Thank God," he muttered to himself.

Finally, the door to the bedchamber opened and an extremely excited Kate exited first, closely followed by the midwife and Mrs Burns.

"Your Grace," Mrs Burns said, curtsying with a huge smile on her face. "Her Grace is ready for you now."

"Thank you," Henry replied, darting past the women, desperate to get inside the room.

He froze in the doorway and observed Iris lying in the bed. She looked radiant. Her auburn hair framed her flushed face and her blue eyes were wide and sparkling in the candlelight. Their newborn child cradled in her arms.

"Henry," she smiled, holding out her hand for him to come closer.

Henry sped to the side of the bed, kneeling and taking Iris's hand and kissing it lovingly. The whole room smelt of clean linen and lavender.

"Say hello to your son Henry," Iris whispered, staring down at the beautiful baby boy in her arms.

"A son," Henry exclaimed, "Oh Iris, how wonderful. I do love you."

"I love you too Henry," she breathed, allowing him to join her on the bed. "I should like to name him George after your father, and Bennett after my father … well my stepfather anyway." She smiled up at Henry.

"George Bennett Morton," Henry mused. "Yes, I approve," he nodded, wrapping his arm lovingly around his wife.

Mrs Burns returned a while later to take George to his wet nurse, who was already in residence in the nursery in the west wing of the house. Ruth was from the local village. She was seventeen years old and had recently given birth to an illegitimate son. The child's father was from a wealthy family in Kingslea, but unfortunately had died of consumption before they were able to wed. His family had agreed to take the boy. Mrs Burns had arranged for Iris to interview several potential women for the post, but Iris had warmed to Ruth almost instantly.

Henry remained with Iris as they watched the sunrise together in each other's arms.

"This is truly the most perfect day," Henry mused, embracing his beautiful wife as she quietly drifted off to sleep. He had never been so happy.

A short while later Mrs Burns returned with George.

"Her Grace is sleeping," Henry whispered, holding out his hands for his son. "I shall take George for a while."

"Yes, of course your Grace," Mrs Burns replied, carefully passing the tiny baby to his proud father.

"Mrs Burns, would you kindly deal with the fire before her Grace awakes? I don't want her to catch a chill." Henry asked, before leaving the room.

"Yes, your Grace, at once," the housekeeper replied, giving a curtsey before following Henry from the room.

"Lucy ... Lucy," Mrs Burns boomed, whirling around the extensive kitchens at Elmbridge Hall.

"Where the hell is that girl," she muttered to herself, observing several strangers congregating around the fire in the servant's hall.

"Good God, the baby's hardly an hour old!" she groaned aloud, directing her gaze at a young woman sat near the fireplace and wrapped up in a vibrant red woollen blanket. She appeared to have strange markings on her face. She sat beside a young man whose face appeared disfigured.

Henry had agreed to open Elmbridge Hall to the entire estate, providing food and refreshment for all his tenants, on the birth of his child. Kate sped into the room suddenly diverting Mrs Burns' attention.

"Kate, where the hell is Lucy, the fire in her Grace's room needs attention."

"I don't know Mrs Burns, but don't worry I shall attend to it at once."

"Oh thank you my dear, you are so good," Mrs Burns replied, dabbing her brow with her apron.

She then turned from the room in desperate need of a large brandy, only to bump into Lucy running in the opposite direction down the corridor.

"There you are girl, where have you been?"

"Sorry madam, I've been in the …"

Mrs Burns cut her off with a shake of her hand. "Never mind all that now. Kate has already gone up to the mistress's room to attend to the fire. Come and aid me with all these people. It seems the good news has travelled fast, we shall be feeding the five thousand at this rate," she grumbled, pulling the young maid along with her.

Mrs Burns and Lucy swiftly returned to the servants' hall. The young woman wrapped in the red blanket and the man who had been sat beside her seemed to have disappeared. Mrs Burns merely shrugged her shoulders and promptly got on with the job in hand.

Henry slowly walked across the formal gardens to the front of Elmbridge Hall, the only sound being the soft crush of his footsteps on the frozen lawn. He smiled down in awe at his beautiful baby son wrapped tightly in his arms, peacefully sleeping. He was heading towards the Morton family private chapel situated to the right of the formal gardens within a small coppice. He didn't enter the chapel but instead made his way to the family cemetery. He stood proudly in front of his father's and mother's headstone and lifted up his newborn son.

"Father, Mother," he whispered, "Say hello to your grandson." With that he lowered his head and, very rarely for Henry, stood in silent prayer. Unashamedly overjoyed.

Several minutes passed when a chilly wind whistled around the trees, causing Henry to break his silent vigil. He gently adjusted the shawl around his young son before crossing himself and turning to head back towards the house.

Henry had barely stepped back onto the frozen grass when an almighty deafening boom echoed all around him, the very ground beneath his feet vibrating. He immediately ran out into the centre of the frozen lawn and stared in absolute horror before desperately collapsing to his knees in devastating anguish and clutching his newborn son tightly to his breast.

Pirjo de Castella pulled her horse to an abrupt halt on the brow of the hill adjacent to Elmbridge Hall. She watched in utter dismay as the whole east wing of the grand house crumbled and was entirely consumed by the flames of **Vikrin Fire**.

To be continued …